## ALSO BY TERRI PERSONS

Blind Rage

Blind Spot

# BLIND SIGHT

## A Novel

## TERRI PERSONS

*DOUBLEDAY*

New York   London   Toronto   Sydney   Auckland

**DD**

DOUBLEDAY

Published in the United States by Doubleday, a division of Random House, Inc., New York.
www.doubleday.com

Library of Congress Cataloging-in-Publication Data
Persons, Terri, 1958–
   Blind sight / by Terri Persons. — 1st ed.
     p. cm.
   1. Saint Clare, Bernadette (Fictitious character)—Fiction. 2. United States.
Federal Bureau of Investigation—Officials and employees—Fiction.
3. Precognition—Fiction. 4. Minnesota—Fiction. I. Title.
   PS3616.E797B55 2009
   813'.6—dc22
   2008041781

ISBN 978-0-385-52653-1

PRINTED IN THE UNITED STATES OF AMERICA

10 9 8 7 6 5 4 3 2 1

First Edition

This book is dedicated to Keith, Kay, Britni, and Angie—dear family friends who have made their cabin our cabin.

# ACKNOWLEDGMENTS

As always, I must first thank my amazing husband, David, and our wonderful sons, Ryan and Patrick. I couldn't function without the constant encouragement and practical assistance from my guys. Ryan, a budding author, is my writing critic and firearms expert. Patrick is the computer guru. David gives me everything from moral support to help with a jammed printer.

For medical expertise, I relied on dear family friend Jacalyn DiCello, MD, who patiently answered questions related to childbirth. I hope I didn't embarrass you, Jackie.

Once again, I turned to my sister-in-law, nurse Rita Monsour, for all sorts of medical information. I trust I didn't embarrass you too badly either, Reetz.

Carrie Wallin, who works in marketing and communications for hospitals and clinics, provided valuable background on small medical centers.

I have the best team in the publishing world in my agent, Esther Newberg, and my editor, Phyllis Grann. Thank you both for your faith in my writing.

Finally, thanks to my friend John Camp for help and advice.

# CHAPTER ONE

The last day of December, and the sky was going dark fast. Landon Guthrie ran his tongue around his teeth, tasting stale peanuts and bitter chocolate, the remnants of the energy bar. Pushing up the cuff of his glove, he checked his watch. The puff of breath that followed was a silent curse. In less than an hour, the season would be over and he had yet to get his buck.

His compound bow lay across his lap with the arrow nocked. He sat fifteen feet off the ground in his deer stand, looking down at a clearing. No fewer than three deer trails spilled into the circle of dead grass and fallen leaves. Less than half a mile behind him was a slushy stream, the animals' drive-thru window for drinks.

The temperature had been dropping all day, but Guthrie was dressed for it—a walking testament to the power of synthetics: Polar fleece. Thinsulate. Polypropylene. Nylon. Acrylic. Vinyl. He was windproof, water-repellent, slip-resistant, and warm.

Everything had been doused with scent blocker and all the outer layers were in a Mossy Oak fall camo of branches and brown leaves. He didn't need the winter camo, which had branches against a white background, because the snow had yet to fly in northern Minnesota.

Glancing up at the sky, Guthrie wondered if they'd finally get snow that night. If not a white Christmas, they could at least enjoy a white New Year's Day. A hawk glided overhead in search of something to eat, and he wished the bird better luck than he'd had. Time to start packing it in. He stood up on the platform and stretched, the bow still in his hand.

A rustling across the clearing froze him. A buck stepped out from between the trees. As the metallic taste of adrenaline bit the back of his throat, Guthrie willed himself to stay calm. He told himself not to look at the rack; it would only make him more nervous. Ignoring his own directive, he counted. Ten points. Good enough.

Fifty yards from the stand, the buck paused, surveying the clearing. Ran on. Thirty yards. Twenty. It stalled again; something had spooked it. The buck took a ninety-degree turn to the right. Guthrie released the arrow, and the broadhead went in just behind the rib cage.

The buck sprinted from the clearing, seeking refuge amid the trees. Guthrie got out of his safety harness and took his time climbing down from the stand. Chasing the wounded deer immediately would make the animal run too hard, and increase the possibility of losing it. Better to give it a chance to lie down.

After strapping a headlamp on over his cap, Guthrie hiked into the thick woods behind the stand to track his prize. His breath hung in the air as he threaded between the trees. He was halfway between the clearing and the stream when he lost the blood trail in the growing darkness. The ground beneath his feet was as hard as concrete, and dry as dust. He wished there had been snow on the ground; it would have made the tracking easier. He stayed on a straight path, heading for the stream. Instinct told him that was where he needed to go.

At the edge of the water, Guthrie found her. "Jesus!"

Guthrie stumbled backward, pulled his right glove off with his teeth, and fumbled around his clothing. Damn jacket had too many pockets. His fingertips finally touched the square edges of the cell and he pulled it out. He knew from experience that he couldn't get a signal where he was standing, but he tried anyway. Hands shaking, he pressed the green button and eyed the screen, praying for bars. Nothing.

Phone still in his hand, he took a step forward. His headlamp illuminated the body and the area around it with a round, soft glow. Snow drifted down from the night sky, sparkling in the lamp's beam like shards of glass. Flakes disappeared against her nightgown and melted into the red staining the fabric. He looked down at the phone and repeatedly pressed the green button, hoping for a miracle. Still no bars. He shoved the cell in his pocket.

He turned his back to the body, leaned a hand against a tree, and vomited peanuts and chocolate. As he wiped his mouth with the back of his hand, he eyed the forest with fresh fear. Since he was a child, the woods had been his second home. He knew every ridge and ravine, every clearing, every hollow. Every marsh and slough. He was familiar with where the deer liked to hang out during deep snows and where they went during droughts. He could correctly identify the different hardwoods and pines. He could pick out the chatter of a gray squirrel and describe how it was different from the racket made by a red squirrel.

Now a monster had invaded his home.

He ran away from the stream, diving back into the trees. He aimed for his stand. North of that would be the road, and his truck. As he pumped his legs, his heart pounded hard in his chest and the cold night air burned his throat.

*All that blood. That thing on her face. Who'd done that? What did it mean?*

*No,* he told himself. *North.* Worry about heading north and stop thinking about what was by the water.

What he'd seen by the stream was a girl sprawled on her back in a blood-soaked nightgown.

On her forehead, a five-pointed star drawn in red.

## CHAPTER TWO

Who'd be calling first thing in the morning on New Year's Day? Instead of reaching for the phone, Bernadette Saint Clare pulled a pillow down over the back of her head.

"Is that your work cell, Bern?"

With both hands, she pressed the pillow tighter and wished her guest and the ringing would go away.

"I think that's the bureau calling, Bern."

The ringing stopped. One wish granted.

She could hear him stomping around the bedroom and fumbling with her phone. "Garcia. Shit. He'll call back if it was important, right? Want me to make you something? Got eggs?"

"No," she said into the mattress.

She'd had a little too much to drink at an unofficial bureau bash and had asked one of the tech guys to drive her home. He'd spent the night on the couch.

A tech guy!

She heard more stomping around the bedroom. This guy was enormous.

"I left some Tylenol and water by the bed, Bern."

She sat up, hugging the pillow to her front. To make matters worse, it was B.K., the most junior guy on TSS, the Technical Support Squad. They'd been nicknamed the Tough Shit Squad because that's what they said when turning down the other agents' many requests for their help. Admittedly, he'd helped her out last night. "Thank you for the ride," she said, running a hand through her short blond hair. Her forehead felt ready to explode, and her mouth tasted like the inside of an old tennis shoe.

He sat down on the edge of the bed and folded his long arms in front of him. In his white T-shirt and jeans, he looked like a super-sized toddler. "Breakfast?"

She curled her legs up to her chest and struggled to remember his real name. Everyone called him B.K., which stood for Big Kid. She scooped up the Tylenol and downed it with a hit of water. "This is all I want this morning, B.K."

He got up off the mattress. "Everybody at the soirée sure had a good time."

The *soirée*. A kegger held in somebody's basement rec room. She hardly knew most of the other partiers, agents stationed in downtown Minneapolis. She worked solo out of downtown St. Paul. Assistant Special Agent in Charge Anthony Garcia was her only regular visitor and an occasional partner. He'd been at the party but had kept his distance. That had ticked her off, and caused her to down a few too many. She looked up at the kid and wished like hell she could ask: *Did Garcia see us leave together?* Instead, she smiled weakly and said nothing, waiting for him to leave.

He shifted his weight from one foot to the other. "So . . ."

"So . . ."

He rocked back and forth on the balls of his feet. "I guess I could go home and feed my cats."

"I guess you could," she said, wondering why he was stalling.

Did he expect a more elaborate expression of gratitude? He wasn't going to get it.

"Uh . . . you have to give me a ride to my car. I drove your truck, remember?"

She felt her face heat up. "Be down in a sec."

"I'll get some coffee going."

"Good idea." As she watched B.K. heading for the stairs, she felt guilty that she'd harbored nasty thoughts about him. She should make *him* breakfast.

Her cell rang again, and she picked up. "Yeah."

Garcia: "You sound like shit."

As if he could see her through the phone, she hugged the pillow tighter to her chest. "I'm fine. Sleepy."

"Wake up fast, because I've got a bad one, Cat," said her boss, calling her by her nickname. "Really need you on it. It's all . . . political and messy."

She leaned back against the headboard. "Tell me."

"A teenage runaway was found dead in Paul Bunyan State Forest last night. Bow hunter came across the body while tracking a deer. She was . . . sliced up."

"Stabbed to death?"

"Back of the head bashed in." Garcia cleared his throat. "Let me back up. This girl was pregnant and the baby was . . . removed after the mother died."

"That's sick. That is just fucking sick. So they found the dead fetus near the—"

"The fetus is missing."

Bernadette sat upright in bed. "Someone killed her, cut her open, and stole her baby?"

"Yeah."

"Did it survive? Did the baby survive?"

"A big question mark," said Garcia.

"They took it, so it has to be alive," she said. "Otherwise, why bother?"

"Maybe they started out wanting a live baby, but who knows what they ended up with? This was a very brutal, slipshod job. Vertical slice right through the navel."

She switched the phone to her other ear. "There've been other stolen-fetus cases."

"There's more. There was a five-pointed star—"

"A pentagram?"

"Yeah. There was a pentagram drawn on her forehead, apparently in her own blood."

Bernadette had worked on some ritualistic slaying cases for the bureau. "A cult thing?"

"I don't know what we're thinking," Garcia said.

"How's this a bureau case?"

"It's because of the victim's father," said Garcia. "That's where politics come into play."

"I'm listening."

"Dead kid was Mag Dunton's daughter."

"Crap," she said.

United States Senator Magnus Dunton, an independent from Minnesota, was not a friend of the FBI. While a chorus had accused the bureau of abusing civil liberties via the Patriot Act, Dunton's voice had been the loudest. Not content to call for tougher limits on antiterrorism laws, the senator had come up with a scheme to dismantle the FBI and divide its duties among other agencies. Though his outrageous plan wasn't being taken seriously on Capitol Hill, he'd opened up a discussion regarding the bureau's functions and its budget. Suddenly there were proposals being floated to close several FBI field offices.

"I suppose Dunton doesn't want us anywhere near the case," she said.

"His people won't return my messages, but I think that's a safe assumption."

"Why not let the BCA take care of it?" she asked, referring to the Minnesota Bureau of Criminal Apprehension, a state criminal-investigation agency.

"The BCA thought it was taking care of it, partnering with the locals. The sheriff up there, Seth Wharten, he's a fishing buddy of mine. His people are the best. But it's not my call. Headquarters handed me my marching orders this morning. Minneapolis Division is to take point on this thing. We're treating it as a kidnapping."

"Did they ask for *me* specifically?"

Garcia sighed. "What do you want me to say, Cat? They asked for you without asking for you."

"I know how it works." Bernadette rubbed the sleep from her eyes. "Pentagram, huh? This could be interesting."

"Loads of fun."

"I'm sorry the man lost his daughter," she said quickly. "What was her name?"

"Lydia."

"What was she doing way in the hell up north?"

"Good question."

"I've got about one million others."

"We can talk on the road," he said. "Pack enough clothes to last awhile, including some serious outdoor gear. My cousin's got a cabin on the Crow Wing chain of lakes and he said we could crash there."

*We.* Quite a change from the night before. A couple of months earlier, they'd come close to hopping in the sack together. They avoided talking about it now, acting as if it had never happened. Maybe that was why he was behaving inconsistently. Still, she wasn't going to be the one to break the code of silence on the subject. Bernadette smelled coffee and heard her guest clomping around downstairs. Getting B.K. to his car was going to take time. "I have to pull myself together," she said.

"I'll pick you up in an hour. We're going to have to drive. Nothing can fly in this stuff."

She looked out a window across from the bed. The snow was coming down thick. "I'll be ready to rumble," she said, kicking off the covers.

"Let's hope like hell your hands and eyes feel the same way."

When Bernadette's bare hands touched an object once held by a killer, she could see through the murderer's eyes. Her sight didn't come with any guarantees, however, and Garcia knew that. *Let's hope like hell* summarized its reliability.

In even the most ideal settings of calm and quiet—she'd used everything from empty churches to dark cellars—she could fail to lock on to the killer. At other times the sight could surprise her, coming on suddenly as her fingers casually brushed an object.

Even when her sight was cooperating, she couldn't count on viewing a worthwhile show. Another slaying could unfold before her eyes, or she might watch the murderer assemble a sandwich. Her special sight was filmy and out of focus, as if she'd popped in someone else's contacts. She couldn't always tell if she was observing something as it was happening or if it was from recent history.

Each time she harnessed her ability, it exhausted her. It could even put her in the same emotional state as the murderer she was pursuing, causing her to become violent or paranoid or sexually aroused. During a case she and Garcia had worked in the fall, she'd stepped even deeper into the killer's body. She carried a faint scar on her cheek from the cut that materialized on her face while the murderer was shaving.

• • •

Garcia pulled up in front of her condo in a big gray Nissan Titan. Bernadette went around to the rear of the pickup with her bag, threw her duffel onto the bed, and slammed the gate. She went around to the front passenger door, scaled up the side of the Titan to reach her seat, and muscled the door closed. "Where'd you get this monster from?"

"It's a company car," he said.

"No way."

He checked his rearview mirror and steered away from the curb. "We needed something that could get through the snow."

"Shut up."

He handed her a file folder. "Picked this up from the St. Paul cop shop on my way in."

Bernadette flipped it open and read. Lydia Dunton attended a public arts high school in St. Paul. Her folks had been having trouble with her over the previous year. Violated their curfew. Skipped classes. Caught drinking at a school dance. Grades started to tank. Put on academic probation. Her parents left for the long Thanksgiving weekend—the daughter had begged off, supposedly to work on a school film project—and when they got back she was missing. Took some clothes with her, cleaned out all the cash in the house, made off with some jewelry. Her mother called it in. Cops interviewed the girl's friends. They claimed ignorance.

She held up a five-by-seven studio portrait of a girl with long red hair and green eyes. Lydia was dressed in a fuzzy white sweater with red heart buttons running up the front. Her head was tilted to one side. Her nose was turned up at the end. Not enough to make it a pug nose but enough to make it endearing. Her hair was pulled back from her face and her ears were visible. They stuck out a little too much. Again, endearing in an odd sort of way. Minimal makeup—just a bead of peachy gloss on her lips—and no smile. Heart buttons aside, it was a sober picture for such a young girl. "Was the pentagram pointing up or down?"

"Check the photos. I printed out some stuff from the coroner up there. Stuck it in the folder. Should be in there."

She went to the back of the file and pulled out a stapled packet. Flipped through it. The star was inverted, making it a satanic symbol. She read the coroner's report. From the size of the placenta, he thought the baby was full term. "Tony, I think—"

"Not now." Garcia was preoccupied with navigating. Traffic downtown was a mess. It was the first storm of the season, and after eight months of being spoiled by clear roads drivers had to learn how to maneuver in the snow again. It didn't get any better once Garcia steered onto Interstate 94 heading west. When they came to a dead stop behind a semitruck, Garcia glanced at his passenger. "Go ahead."

"She would have been pretty far along when she took off, but there's nothing about her pregnancy in the stuff from the St. Paul cops. Didn't her parents know?"

The semi rolled forward a few car lengths and Garcia followed. "She could have kept it from them. Bulky sweaters and such."

"Runaways go to big cities. Plus, she was an artsy-fartsy film student. Wouldn't she head for someplace more bohemian than northern Minnesota?"

"Boyfriend from up there?"

"No mention of one in the report."

"*Some*body got her pregnant," said Garcia.

"Where's the body right now?"

Garcia told her the girl's remains were at the local hospital. They'd have time for a look before the Ramsey County ME's wagon arrived for transport to the Twin Cities. The crime scene itself was buried, because the hunter was so rattled he'd had trouble leading the law to the body. By the time they got to the remains, they were under a drift. No footprints, because the ground had been frozen. Nothing *in* the snow, because the stuff had just started to fall when the hunter made his grisly discovery.

Beyond downtown Minneapolis, traffic thinned. They listened intently to a radio report on the killing.

*"The body of a sixteen-year-old girl was discovered by a bow hunter in Paul Bunyan State Forest last night. Authorities are not commenting on a possible cause of death, or speculating on how long the body had been in the woods. The Ramsey County Medical Examiner is conducting the autopsy. The young woman's name is being withheld until relatives can be notified. In other news . . ."*

"No missing fetus, no pentagram, no senator father," observed Garcia.

"Details will come out," Bernadette said. "Media's tied up with the storm and the fender-bender count right now."

"Speaking of benders, how'd you get home last night?"

She didn't want to talk about it, and the radio gave her an out. "The weather," she said, turning up the volume.

*". . . and parts of the Twin Cities could see fifteen to eighteen inches. Northern Minnesota may get slammed with up to two feet by the time this storm system pushes its way across the Midwest. The Minnesota Department of Transportation is asking drivers to give their plows plenty of . . ."*

"I've never dealt with a crime scene in the middle of a blizzard," she said.

"Me neither."

They came up on a roadside yard littered with miniature windmills and a homemade billboard: WINDMILLS AND WINDMILL PARTS WANTED. "It's almost like someone timed it with the weather," she said as she looked out at the windmills' blades, frantic arms reaching up from the drifts. "The body, possible evidence, all of it harder to get to because of the storm."

"More likely, they lucked out."

"Question: What's worse, a lucky homicidal maniac or a smart one?"

"I'd rather come up against a smart maniac," he said. "Good luck can be harder to beat than brains. You can't outthink good luck."

"But sooner or later luck always runs out."

In the tiny town of Motley, Garcia turned in to a gas station to feed the beast. "Here's your chance to stock up on munchies," he said, hopping out of the truck.

"Grab me some candy."

Garcia went inside to pay and came out with a fistful of bars. "Emergency provisions," he said, handing her one and dropping the rest into the storage compartment between them.

As Bernadette unwrapped her chocolate dinner, she glanced across the street at a small grocery store. "Shouldn't we buy some real food?"

"Ed's got stuff in the freezer," he said, getting back on the road.

"I feel funny about sponging off him." Garcia's cousin was a homicide detective with the St. Paul Police Department, and although Bernadette didn't know him well, she was certain that he disapproved of her and her unique talent. Most cops wrote her off as a freak.

"Don't worry about it, Cat," said Garcia. "I do plenty of work around his cabin. He owes me big-time."

Garcia hung a right onto Minnesota 210 and steered the truck over the Crow Wing River. A block later, he hung a left onto Minnesota 64 heading north. They plowed past a logging company, its lot loaded with trucks carrying logs. This was a big lumber area.

The snow was coming faster and thicker, and even the beams of the monster truck couldn't completely punch through the curtain. There were no other cars behind or ahead of them. The forest came up on both sides of the highway. "I didn't realize Paul Bunyan was so big," she said.

"More than seventy thousand acres. There's a north section and a south section. Highway 200 cuts between them horizontally. North is kind of flat and has more pine trees. South—where the Dunton girl was found—is hilly. Aspen trees. Ponds."

He slowed and took a right down a rough, narrow road. Trees scraped against the sides of the truck. Garcia activated the truck's high beams. They came to a T in the road, and Garcia hung a left. He drove with confidence until they came to a fork. The truck lurched to a halt. "Hmm."

"Anthony?"

"Let's take a chance," he said, and steered the truck to the right.

# CHAPTER THREE

The Titan came up over a hill and Bernadette saw deputies milling on the road ahead of them. "Hallelujah," she said.

"It wasn't that scary." Garcia pulled the truck to the right and put it in park. "I knew where I was going the whole time."

"Sure you did." Her side of the truck was buried in the brush. To extricate herself, she had to force the door open and drop onto some bushes.

A trio of deputies stepped into the middle of the road as Garcia and Bernadette approached. The middle guy examined the agents' ID wallets, handed them back, and thumbed over his shoulder.

"You'll come to a large clearing with a metal stand mounted to a tree. Behind that is a deer path. Follow it. You'll come to a smaller clearing and then . . . well . . . You'll know you're in the right place. At the edge of the water there's a big canopy thing."

Bernadette didn't think a north-woods sheriff's office would have its own tent. "Did the BCA boys leave it behind?"

The deputy dragged a gloved hand across his dripping nose.

"We borrowed it from one of the bars. They use it for wedding receptions."

"I take it our other folks haven't arrived," said Garcia. They were going to be joined up north by the Evidence Response Team, experts in crime-scene processing, and some agents from the Minneapolis office.

"Not yet," said the deputy, wiping his nose again.

As she and Garcia hiked, Bernadette looked up into the sky and blinked through the snow. The sun would be down soon, and a difficult crime scene would become next to impossible.


They heard the tent before they saw it. Its sides and roof were vibrating furiously in the wind, and the whole thing looked ready to launch into the sky with the next gust. The white walls were lined with arched clear plastic windows. In a noble attempt to establish a secure perimeter, police tape had been tied to the half circle of trees surrounding the shelter. The yellow ribbons whipped around and flapped like kite tails. A deputy was trying to tie an errant end to a tree when the other end came undone. Three other deputies were standing at a corner of the tent, talking and moving their feet around, undoubtedly trying to keep from losing feeling in their lower extremities.

Garcia and Bernadette stood along one side of a stretch of yellow with their identification wallets open. The police-tape deputy came up to them and reached over to untie the ribbon. The thing came undone by itself and flapped in the wind. "God bless it," sputtered the frustrated deputy, a young guy with red ears and cheeks. He chased the wild end.

An older deputy—a heavyset man with gray hair poking out from his hat and a frosty gray mustache—came up behind the young man and put his hand on the guy's shoulder. "Give it up, Billy. No one's in the woods tonight except for us idiots."

"Is the sheriff around?" asked Garcia, extending his hand.

"You must be Antonia," said the guy, shaking Garcia's hand and grinning broadly through the frozen facial hair. "Everyone speaks highly of your angling skills. I'm Marty Martin."

*Antonia.* Bernadette liked that, and suppressed a chuckle.

"Where is Seth?" asked Garcia.

"He was here a minute ago. Probably left to take a—" Martin stopped himself as he noticed Bernadette. "To use the facilities."

Bernadette extended her hand and Martin took it. "Bernadette Saint Clare."

"Oh," he said flatly. "Heard about you, too."

Bernadette didn't want to know what he'd heard. She looked past him at the tent. "Can we get a gander before it goes dark?"

Martin moved to one side. "It's your show."

The two agents stepped up to the shaking walls. Since the frozen ground didn't allow staking the shelter, it had been anchored with a series of weights. Bernadette used the tip of her boot to kick the snow off one of the lumps. Ice-cream bucket filled with concrete. "This seems—I don't know—extreme."

"Desperate might be a better word," said Garcia.

They each took a window. The interior was well lit, but there wasn't much to see since the body had been removed. Evidence-eradication gremlins—the nickname fondly given to first responders—had done their job. There were boot prints everywhere, the indentations muffled by a layer of snow before the tent could be erected. Garcia had said there had never been any perpetrator footprints. Still, the crime-scene guys were going to get their DNA shorts in a bundle. As it was, they weren't going to like dropping into a case after the BCA. She saw a concave area, where the body must have rested before it was lifted out of the snow. Splotches of red against the white. She'd expected more blood, but maybe the bulk of it had been buried by the time the shelter was put up.

Bernadette could often tell at first glance if a crime scene would surrender anything useful, and her gut told her this snowy mess was going to produce little. In fact, the entire spectacle—the tent and the police tape and the shivering deputies planted in the middle of a blizzard in the middle of a forest called Paul Bunyan—seemed absurd. Ludicrous.

She stepped away from the window, and Garcia did the same. He apparently shared her thoughts but expressed them more succinctly than she could have. "Not feeling it."

"Neither am I," she said.

"Let's go to the hospital."

"You don't want to wait and meet our CSI stars?"

"They're big boys," said Garcia. "They don't need me watching them play in the snow."

## CHAPTER FOUR

Crow Wing Lakes Memorial, a one-story, U-shaped brick build-ing, was halfway between the tiny towns of Nevis and Akeley. Garcia turned in to the hospital parking lot, which was already plowed and sanded. There were a handful of other vehicles. Before jumping out, Bernadette took Lydia's photo from the file and tucked it inside her jacket.

A gust of wind slammed their backs. Hunching their shoulders, they hurried to the double glass doors of the front entrance. As soon as they stepped through, a thirty-something man greeted them with a stethoscope draped around his neck. He had short sandy hair and blue eyes framed by wire-rimmed glasses. Tall and thin, he wore a lab coat that was too short at the sleeves and too roomy in the shoulders. When he spoke, he folded his hands in front of him, giving the appearance of a giant praying mantis. "Dr. Sven Hessler," he said with a nod.

"Assistant Special Agent in Charge Anthony Garcia." He ex-tended his hand and Hessler accepted it. "This is Agent Bernadette Saint Clare."

Bernadette shook the doctor's hand.

"Cold out there," Hessler said.

"Sure is." Bernadette pulled her gloves tighter over her fingers. She kept them on to avoid surprise sights while on the job.

"I could have someone make a fresh pot of coffee," Hessler offered. "We've got some cake back in ER. One of the nurses had a birthday."

"Not this time of night," said Garcia. "Thanks anyway."

"Let's use the stairs," Hessler said, leading them down a hall past the elevators, his lab coat billowing behind him.

"Thank you for taking the time," Garcia said.

"You expect this stuff in the cities," said Hessler, using the term rural Minnesotans used for the Twin Cities area. "I never thought I'd see anything like this up here."

"You from this neck of the woods?" Garcia asked.

"You betcha. Happy to come back and serve my people."

The trio jogged down a flight of stairs, and the doctor pushed open the door to the hospital's lower level. Hessler led the way past a dark laundry room and a couple of janitorial closets. The hallway was long, narrow, and poorly lit. It smelled of mildew and pine-scented floor cleaner. The floor was covered in gray linoleum and nothing decorated the white walls, but hanging from the ceiling tiles were paper snowflakes suspended by nearly invisible string. As they fluttered from some random draft, they resembled little ghosts dancing in the dimness.

"We've got pretty much everything," said the physician, sounding like a salesman. "State-of-the-art diagnostics, including an eight-slice CT scan, MRI, and mammography. Top-notch surgical suite. Besides the usual bowel resection and hernia repair, we can do cancer surgery and ortho surgery. C-sections and hysterectomies. Our radiology department—"

"You have obstetrics services?" interrupted Bernadette.

He stopped in front of a door. "Certainly."

"Did one of your doctors have this girl as a patient?" she asked.

"I'm not . . . I don't know. There are a couple of women's clinics in the area, and their physicians have privileges here. Whether any of them saw this young woman . . ." His voice trailed off, and he buried his hands in his lab coat. "I don't think I should be talking with you about it. We have a legal department."

"You *do* have everything," Garcia said dryly.

"I'm not trying to be evasive." Hessler dug into his coat pockets and produced a key attached to a yellow rabbit's foot. "I don't know anything. I wouldn't have even brought you down here, except Sheriff Wharten called and told me to."

"Appreciate the cooperation," Bernadette said.

"Not much of a morgue," Hessler warned, as he shoved the key into the door's lock and turned the knob. "Two drawers. Don't use it much. Usually the funeral home comes by and takes the remains. These circumstances were highly unusual. Unfortunate."

Hessler pushed the door open and flicked on a light. "Watch your step."

"What's with the boxes?" Garcia asked. Cardboard cubes were stacked along the walls to the right and left of the door. Most of the cases contained cafeteria supplies: Styrofoam cups, paper napkins, drinking straws. There were also giant cans of food: peas, pudding, beans.

"Space is at a premium," Hessler explained. "We usually use this room for storage."

Bernadette frowned. "Can anyone stroll down here and let themselves in?"

"No," Hessler said quickly. "When the room is in use as a morgue, the door is locked and the key is kept by the nursing supervisor."

"Let's get comfortable," said Garcia, pulling off his jacket and tossing it over a case of toilet paper.

"Good idea," said Bernadette, throwing her jacket over Garcia's. She yanked off her leather gloves and snapped on the latex.

"Which drawer?" asked Garcia as he slipped on a pair of work gloves.

"Uh . . . I don't know," Hessler said sheepishly. "I haven't actually seen the body."

The two agents walked up to the pair of waist-high metal squares planted in the middle of the wall opposite the door. The drawers had handles, and sat side by side. They could have been a set of built-in file cabinets. Bernadette opened the hinged door on her side, to their right. She grabbed the edge of the slab inside and pulled it out partway. Empty. "Try door number two," she said, sliding the slab back inside and snapping the door closed.

Garcia opened the hatch on the left, hooked his hand under the slab, and pulled it out. The tray contained a black body bag. The bump at the top of the sack indicated that the corpse had been placed feetfirst. "You want to leave the room, Dr. Hessler, or are you okay with this?" Garcia asked.

"I'm a medical professional," Hessler said indignantly. Still, he stayed behind Garcia and Bernadette.

Reaching down, Bernadette started unzipping. The bag fell open just past the girl's chin. Bernadette inhaled sharply and withdrew her hand. "It's gone."

"What's wrong?" asked Hessler, looking over their shoulders. "What's gone?"

Bernadette shook her head slowly. "So that means—"

"Let me make sure," said Garcia, gently picking strands of hair off the young woman's forehead, to get a clear view of her flesh.

"What happened to it?" asked Bernadette.

Garcia leaned close to the girl's forehead and sniffed. "Antiseptic or disinfectant. That's what they used to take it off."

"What are you talking about?" asked Hessler, coming up next to the slab and standing alongside it with a quizzical look. "Take *what* off?"

"A pentagram," said Bernadette. "She had a pentagram on her forehead."

Hessler took a step back and folded his arms in front of him. "I didn't know that. I didn't hear anything about a pentagram."

"We were trying to keep it quiet," said Garcia.

Bernadette stared at the corpse's clean white forehead, almost luminescent under the fluorescent lights of the storage room/morgue. "Someone found out and took it off."

"Why?" asked Garcia.

"Maybe it wasn't drawn in *her* blood," suggested Bernadette.

"The killer's blood?" asked Garcia. "That'd be stupid—or brazen."

"Or maybe he was worried that the *way* he drew it was telling. Regardless, he had second thoughts about his artwork and decided to erase it."

"Morgue isn't exactly on Main Street," said Garcia. "He'd have to know the body was down here."

Bernadette looked at the doctor. "Who knew about this room? Who had access?"

Hessler: "I told you, the door was kept locked."

Bernadette: "Dr. Hessler, no one enters or leaves this hospital tonight."

The doctor flew out the door, leaving the two agents alone with the corpse.

Garcia took out his cell and started calling. "We'll need Seth's men to help us do this."

"We need someone outside this room."

"Can't get through. Probably have to wait until they get out of the woods." Garcia started punching in another number. "Our Minneapolis guys. They've gotta be up here by now."

"Where'd you tell them to meet us?"

Garcia held up his hand. He had someone on the line. "What's the story? Where are you?"

While Garcia talked on the phone, Bernadette went to the door and scanned the hallway. Hessler wasn't coming back for a while. She closed the door and returned to the slab. She had to do this quickly, before the army descended. As she pulled her gloves tighter over her fingers, she looked down at the dead teen.

The girl's face was covered in acne and freckles, both of which had apparently been airbrushed from the studio photo. Upturned a bit at the end, the nose was the same as in the portrait. Like the portrait, her ears stuck out a bit too much. The lobes were dotted with gold earrings shaped like hearts, and a plastic heart barrette was caught in her straight, shoulder-length red hair. The blood-drenched nightgown was a long-sleeved flannel sprinkled with more hearts. This girl had been too young for motherhood, and too innocent to be a murder victim. She should be home with her parents—and where were *they*?

Garcia closed his phone. "Our Minneapolis crew is gassing up at a station in Akeley. I gave them directions to the hospital. They should be here pretty quick."

"Where are her folks?" Bernadette asked.

"Trying to get out of Dulles." He saw what she was getting ready to do. "You want me to do anything?"

"I can handle it." She reached down and walked the zipper to the bottom of the bag.

"Need a tool?"

"Got one," she said, dipping her hands into her jacket pocket and producing her keys. On the keychain was a small pocketknife.

"Be discreet."

"I've done this a few times before," she said as she opened the knife.

"I know," he said.

Indeed, he did. Unlike her previous supervisors and their ignorance-is-bliss approach, Garcia insisted on watching her use her sight.

She ran her eyes around the corpse. The butcher must have laid hands on the nightgown to cut out the fetus. If he wore surgical gloves, however, they could be screwed. No reading.

"Why would someone do this to a kid?" Garcia asked.

"A pregnant kid, no less." She sighed, and reached for the flannel sleeve closest to her. It was free of blood. She turned up the cuff. "This should be safe."

"Good spot," said Garcia.

It had been a sloppy factory sew job, and a wide flap of fabric was hanging where the sleeve was attached to the cuff. Bernadette held the fabric away from the body with one hand and sawed off a patch of flannel with the other. "Not much to work with," she said, holding the sliver between her thumb and index finger. She passed the fabric to him.

He cupped it in his palm and watched her take off her gloves. "A quickie?"

Garcia's question was more skeptical than hopeful. He knew quickies rarely worked for her, but she had to try. If she determined that the killer was still in the hospital, it would make quick work of the case. She sat down on a box of computer paper that was pushed against the wall and propped her back against the concrete block. Rolled her head to the right and left. "Lights."

Garcia flipped the switch and the room went black, save for a white band at the door's threshold. She closed her eyes. Through the heating vents, she could hear the rumble of the hospital's heating system struggling to keep up with winter. Then she heard her boss bump into a box as he made his way back to her. "Fuck."

"Careful."

"Thanks."

She inhaled deeply and exhaled slowly. Thought about the girl a few feet away from her, on a slab. Wondered about the missing baby. The missing pentagram. She held out her right hand. "Let's go."

"Here it is." Garcia set the sliver in her palm.

As she made a fist around the fabric, she said the short prayer she always offered: "Lord, help me see clearly."

She closed her lids tighter, waited a few seconds, and slowly opened her eyes.

All she saw was the dark profile of her boss standing in front of her.

"Shit," she said.

"Nothing?"

"Yup."

"Ah, that's what I figured. It'll work later."

"Later," she repeated, and stood up.

Garcia flipped the lights on, went to his jacket, and foraged around its pockets until he found an evidence bag. He opened it and held it out to Bernadette. She dropped the fabric inside and he sealed it. She tucked the bag into the front pocket of her jeans and pulled her gloves back on.

Bernadette went over to the corpse's feet, grabbed the zipper, and walked it back to the head of the bag, pausing to take one last look at Lydia's face. Her brows came together. She went to her jacket and took out the girl's photo. She held it up while tipping the corpse's head to one side. "Thought this was a pimple at first, but—"

"My flashlight's in the truck," he said.

He left the room for a couple of minutes. Bernadette continued studying the right side of the girl's face, focusing on the area just below the outside of her eye, along the cheekbone. She looked back at the photo. "Really liked your hearts, didn't you, kid?"

Garcia came back in with a desk lamp and plugged it into a wall outlet close to the slab. He took off the shade and held the bare bulb over the corpse. "A tatt. Tiny, tiny heart tatt."

"Didn't have a tattoo in her school photo," said Bernadette, holding the portrait up for Garcia to see.

"Got it while she was on the road?"

"Maybe."

"There's a shop in Walker."

"We'll check it out," she said as she zipped the sack all the way to the top. "People empty their guts while sitting for a tatt. Sort of like going to the hairdresser."

Garcia pushed the slab back into the cooler and snapped the compartment door closed. "Let's get out of here before we get spanked by the CSI guys. We've compromised fibers and microbes and shit just by being in here."

The two agents grabbed their jackets and stepped out into the hallway, closing the door after them. "Where do you want to start?" she asked.

"Maybe one of the nurses knows something, saw someone skulking around the main floor or heading down here."

Garcia's late wife had been a nurse, and Bernadette suspected that he still had a thing for them. "You know, one of them could be the—"

"I know," he said quickly. "I'm not dismissing the possibility."

"Go upstairs and start questioning them. I can babysit the body."

"You sure?"

"When the rest of our guys show, send one of them down."

●　●　●

Twenty minutes after Garcia left, one of the Minneapolis agents appeared in the hallway. "Hey, Bern."

She blinked twice. What was *he* doing here? "Hey, B.K." He was dressed in a work suit but had a puffy down coat in his arms and clunky, fat boots on his feet. "You're a tech guy. I didn't know Garcia needed—"

"I volunteered," he said cheerfully, and then added, "I don't work exclusively with technology, you know. I *do* do other things."

Garcia came down the hallway. "You're with me now, Saint Clare. Cahill is going to relieve you."

*Carson Cahill.* That was Big Kid's real name. Bernadette stepped around the big blond boy. "Thanks, Carson."

"Wait," Cahill said after her. "Where's the body, exactly?"

Garcia opened the door to the room. "Against the far wall."

Cahill looked at a stack of cardboard boxes sitting against the wall. "No way."

Bernadette stepped next to Garcia and pointed to the closed door of the compartment. "In there. That's a cooler."

Cahill nodded. "Oh, yeah. Right."

Bernadette closed the door to the room. "No one enters. The crime-scene guys have to do their thing."

"I'm on it," said Cahill, pulling back his blazer to reveal a gun tucked into a shoulder holster.


"I don't know about leaving him alone," said Bernadette as she and Garcia climbed the stairs to the first floor.

"What do you mean?"

"Thought he worked with computers and phones and cameras. Surveillance equipment. Junk like that."

"He's young, but he can handle himself." Garcia opened the door to the first floor and motioned toward the ER, which occupied one of the tips of the U-shaped hospital. "Reinforcements have landed and the place is on lockdown."

"Great."

"I told the nurses that something had been drawn on the girl's body and then removed while she was here," said Garcia. "I didn't describe the symbol, but one of the gals immediately asked if it was a devil or witch sign."

"I'm going to want to talk to that nurse."

"She said there're things going on we should know about," said Garcia.

"Like the sound of that," said Bernadette.

"Figured you would."

# CHAPTER FIVE

The ER break room reeked of burned microwave popcorn, scorched coffee, and chocolate cake. Paper cutouts of mittens and snowmen were taped to the walls, each ornament labeled with a name drawn in glitter. Bernadette assumed they were all ER staff members, as one of the mittens was labeled "Sven." Bernadette sat across a sticky Formica table from one of the nurses while Garcia talked with a soggy hospital administrator out in the hallway. The man's wife had dragged him out of the shower to take Dr. Hessler's frantic call. He'd driven over to Crow Wing Lakes Memorial immediately, pulling a stocking cap on over his wet head. He'd repeatedly asked Bernadette to excuse him for not removing the hat.

"Officer Garcia, I am so sorry this . . ."

Bernadette got up and closed the door. She'd heard the apology multiple times, and with each mea culpa the fellow had used a different rank or title for her boss. Sergeant. Captain. Detective. He had yet to get it right. At least she knew the poor guy was taking the corpse-tampering seriously. So were the nurses, and one in particular had some ideas on who had been involved.

Bernadette went back to the table, sat down, and flipped her notebook to a clean page. "I missed that last part, Delores."

Delores Martini—a husky woman with black hair tied in a severe bun behind her head—took a sip from her ER TAKES THE PRESSURE coffee mug and smiled grimly, revealing a gap between her top front teeth. "I knew something like this was going to happen. Predicted it."

Bernadette frowned. "By that you mean—"

"Break-in, not the murder. The murder threw me for a loop. Who knew that crap could happen around here? Security screwup—that's what I'm talking about. I told them they needed cameras. Needed to staff the front desk around the clock. Nobody listens." Nurse Martini took another sip of coffee. "Always trying to do it on the cheap. Now they've got a witch running around the place, messing with bodies and whatnot. Serves them right, I say."

Bernadette put her pen to her pad. "Yeah. Let's go over that again. This Jordan Ashe is—"

"An authentic, certified, bona fide, licensed, bonded, and insured witch. Probably has framed witch diplomas hanging from her black walls."

"How do you know?"

"She told me. Calls herself a *Wiccan*. Know what I say? A witch by any other name—"

"Are there other practitioners around town?"

"Hell, no. She's the only oddball. Everyone else is Lutheran or Methodist or some other proper Christian religion." She pointed at Bernadette's notebook. "I'm a Catholic. Put that down for the record. Born and raised Roman Catholic."

"But no one reported seeing her in or around the hospital?"

"Too smart to get caught. Too sneaky. Besides, the way this place is run these days Charles Manson could waltz in here with a machete, sign the visitor log, and pin on a badge. No one would stop him."

Bernadette slapped the photo of Lydia on the table and slid it across to Martini. "Take a good look. Ever see Ashe with this girl?"

"What was her name?" Martini asked.

"If you could just look," said Bernadette.

Martini picked up the picture, studied it hard, and shook her head. "Never laid eyes on that kid before. Don't know nothing about her."

"You think Ashe drew the pentagram in the first place?"

"She's a witch," said Martini, sliding the photo back to Bernadette. "That's what they do, isn't it? That's their deal. Pentagrams. Monograms. Other Devil symbols and signs."

"Ever see her display a temper or heard her threaten anyone?"

"Not really."

"Is Jordan Ashe capable of murder?"

A shrug. "As far as murder goes, I don't know. She's capable of being a witch. That alone should get her locked up, I say. Good-for-nothing witch."

"You really don't like this woman," said Bernadette.

"She came in here a while back and wanted to peddle that healing-touch bullshit to our patients. Idiot administrators were ready to give her the green light until some of the docs pulled their heads out of their asses. Opened up their mouths and said they didn't want that healing-touch mumbo jumbo around here."

"Healing touch?"

"You put your hands over the patient, kind of wave them over the body without actually touching it." She took a deep drink and set down her mug. "Your good energy or electricity flows into the patient and helps them get better."

"So it's an alternative therapy."

"A load of malarkey."

"Is that how Ashe makes her living? Healing touch?"

"Hear she does it out of her home for fifty dollars a session. Plus she makes these pots and figurines, sells them out of witch headquarters. On top of all that silliness, she does psychic readings. A real medical professional, this chick. And the hospital was ready to give the flake her own flipping office."

"Where does she live?"

"In the woods with her fat hippie boyfriend, Karl Vizner."

"What does he do?"

"Drives a snowplow." Martini took a sip of coffee. "A real loser."

"Can you give me directions to their house?"

"I can draw you a map."

"A map would be good." Bernadette tore a page out of her notebook and handed it to the nurse.

Martini took a pencil out of her smock and started scribbling. "She's not from around here, you know. She's from Los Angeles. Big surprise. The crazies in California."

"Right," said Bernadette.

Martini frowned at her drawing and erased part of it. "If I were you, I'd try to make the drive during the day. They live outside of town, practically *in* the forest."

"Paul Bunyan State Forest?"

With a dark face, Martini looked up from her drawing and nodded toward the photo of Lydia. "Same forest where the body was found. Now, how close to the exact same spot, I don't know."

"Hmmm."

Martini went back to the map. "Winter or summer, those back roads can be rough going. Half of them ain't marked worth a damn. Cell-phone reception in the woods is hit-or-miss. What I'm saying is, get stuck at night and you're screwed."

"You've been to their place?"

Barking a laugh, Martini said, "Wouldn't be caught dead. I just know where they live. Everyone knows. They're what you might call *infamous.*"

Bernadette stood up, taking the photo with her. "Thanks for the help, Delores."

Martini stopped writing and ran her eyes up and down Bernadette's slight figure. "Hope you ain't planning on going out there by yourself. Karl hunts, so he's got guns. They've got a pack of dogs, too. Call ahead so they lock them up. Everyone calls ahead before going over there."

Bernadette took the slip of paper from Martini and examined it. "I appreciate your concern, but I've got a gun—and a big partner."

"I seen him out in the hall," said Martini, tucking an errant band of hair behind her ear. "He could double for that Erik Estrada actor. A young Erik Estrada, from the *CHiPs* days. I suppose he hears that all the time."

"I'll make sure he hears it now," said Bernadette, jamming the slip of paper into her jacket pocket.

Hessler was at the end of a double shift, and Garcia and Bernadette agreed to get him out of the way next.

The size of a closet, Hessler's office was crowded with an old metal desk and floor-to-ceiling bookshelves. If there was a window, it was buried behind the walls of medical reference materials. Instead of hiding behind his metal clunker during the interview, the doctor propped his butt on the edge of it to talk to them. The agents sat in folding chairs. Most of their questions were about the storage room/morgue and its key.

"You said the nursing supervisor keeps the key," said Bernadette.

"I should have said *generally* keeps the key," he said quickly.

"Tonight, I had it. Sometimes at night, it's the physician on duty. It never left my pocket."

"What if the cafeteria needs to get something out of there?" asked Garcia.

"Cafeteria is closed at night."

"During the day," said Bernadette. "Do they have to hunt down the nursing supervisor, or does the cafeteria staff have access?"

"Cooks have a key," said Hessler.

"Where do they keep it?" asked Bernadette.

He hesitated. "Hanging up in the kitchen."

"So anyone can use it?" asked Garcia.

"When there's a body in the room, they don't enter," the doctor said defensively.

"Honor system?" asked Bernadette.

Hessler: "Well . . . I guess."

"I saw computer paper in there," said Bernadette. "Office staff have a key?"

Hessler rubbed his bloodshot eyes with his thumb and index finger. "Yes, but they know not to go in."

"No security guard on at night?" asked Bernadette.

"Budget cuts," Hessler said tiredly. "We've got a sign. Visitors use the desk phone to call ER for an escort."

"Anyone call tonight?" asked Garcia. "Anyone come to see a patient late? Anyone come by late for any reason? A pharmacy delivery or—"

Hessler shook his head. "No one."

"That you know of," said Garcia.

"That I know of," Hessler conceded.

"And during the day virtually anyone could have grabbed a key to that room," said Bernadette.

Hessler: "What do you want me to say?"

"One other question," said Bernadette. "Did Delores Martini disappear at all during her shift?"

Hessler rubbed his eyes again. "Agent Saint Clare, there are so few of us on at night, and this is such a small hospital. I not only cover the ER, I take care of all the patients on the floor. Same with the nurses. ER and the patients on the floor. Back and forth. We all wear many hats and do *everything*. We hardly have time to use the bathroom."

"You had time for birthday cake," Bernadette said dryly.

Hessler frowned. "Why are you focusing on Delores? Did she—"

"We're not focusing on anyone," Bernadette said quickly. "She's the only nurse we've interviewed so far. Trying to see who can vouch for whom. Anyone else disappear, even for a few minutes?"

He raised his right hand. "Swear to God, *no one* working under me tonight had opportunity to touch that body."

"Don't speak to anyone about the details of this conversation," said Bernadette as she and Garcia got up.

"I'd like to go home and go to bed," Hessler said. "Am I free to leave?"

"Go ahead," Bernadette said over her shoulder.

When they were down the hall and out of Hessler's earshot, Garcia asked, "Why'd you toss in that question about Martini specifically?"

"She was a little too helpful."

"A tight little group, this ER crew," said Garcia. "They're going to back each other up."

Bernadette looked into an empty patient room. Through the windows, she saw Hessler heading for his car. The tall man was bent over in a question mark as he walked. The long black coat hanging from his lean frame only added to his insectlike appearance. "He sure flew out of here," she said, pointing toward the window.

They saw Hessler get in a sedan, start up the car, and peel out of the lot without bothering to clear even his windshield.

"Wonder where he's going in such a hurry," said Garcia.

"Miss!" yelled a voice across the hall.

Both agents turned. An enormously pregnant woman was summoning them from her bed. She'd kicked off her covers and seemed to be struggling to sit up. Her hospital gown was hiked halfway up her generous thighs.

Bernadette headed for the room. "She needs a hand."

"I'm not going in there," said Garcia. "She said *Miss*, not *Mister*." One of the Minneapolis agents came up to him with a question, and the two men went down the hall together.

"Want help sitting up?" asked Bernadette, moving to the bedside.

"Ah, screw it. Isn't worth it." The woman dropped back against the pillows. She had a plump, rosy face and straight blond hair down to her shoulders.

"Want me to raise your head?"

"That'd be great, doll."

Bernadette pushed the controls on the bed rails. "When're you due?"

"First thing in the morning."

"A Cesarean?"

"Yup."

"Good luck."

"I saw deputies going up and down the hall," said the woman. "A bunch of guys in suits. Are you with them?"

"Yeah. I'm an FBI agent. Bernadette Saint Clare."

"This about that girl on the news?" The woman protectively put her hands on her mountainous belly. "Television said they cut out her baby."

The details had gotten out, and quickly. Bernadette took the photo from her jacket and showed it to the woman. "See her around town?"

The woman whipped the picture out of Bernadette's fingers. "So this is the poor thing. What's her name?"

"She look familiar?"

"I've been on bed rest. Stuck inside." The woman handed it back to Bernadette, and her eyes widened. "Christ. Did someone at the hospital do it?"

"No, no," said Bernadette, afraid to upset the expectant mother. "The body was brought here, that's all."

That lame explanation seemed to satisfy her, and she nodded. "Oh. Right."

"If this girl sought out prenatal care, any idea where she might have gone?"

The woman didn't hesitate. "Clinic in Akeley. West end of downtown, a couple of blocks off the main drag. It's close to the hospital, and the doctor there is the best. Eve Bossard. She's so popular, everybody loves her. Around here, you can't swing a dead cat by the tail without hitting a girl named Eve."

"Eve Bossard," Bernadette repeated.

"Really nice lady. Makes house calls. Can you imagine that in this day and age?"

"No, I can't."

"Operates a free clinic certain afternoons. Doesn't care how poor you are or what sort of health insurance you've got."

"That's wonderful," said Bernadette.

"Plus she's a specialist. Handles difficult pregnancies." The woman added proudly, "I'm having twins."

After Bernadette left the room, she took out her notebook and flipped to a clean page. Wrote down two words:

*Eve Bossard.*

Garcia came up to her with a cup of coffee in each hand. He passed her one.

She sipped. Scalding, black, and bitter, exactly how she liked it. She told Garcia about the Mother Teresa obstetrician.

"We can follow up tomorrow," he said. "She might have seen the kid in her clinic."

She checked her watch. "We've still got a lot to do here tonight."

Bernadette and Garcia went down the hall, strategizing. They had to talk to four more nurses, a janitor, and a radiology tech. Though the disinfectant smelled fresh, they didn't want to rule out anyone who'd been in the building the previous twenty-four hours, and who had knowledge of the storage room/morgue. They'd finish interviewing the second shift, catch the third as they were punching in, and stay for the morning crew.

Garcia dragged a hand down his face. "Let's have our Minneapolis guys do the cafeteria ladies and office folks. You and I will stick with the medical people."

"No cameras, spotty security at the door," said Bernadette. "Reality is, anyone could have walked in off the street, jimmied the lock, and slipped into the room."

"They'd have to know about the room," said Garcia. "It's kind of a secret."

"Try keeping a secret in a small town."

# CHAPTER SIX

It was shortly before midnight, in the cinder-block basement of a house on the edge of the forest. Twenty black-robed adults stood in a circle around an altar, which in its previous life had been an oak dining-room table. The rectangle was covered with a purple cloth, its center embroidered with a pentacle. Pillar candles flickered at each corner of the table. The altar stood in the center of a five-pointed star that had been drawn on the concrete floor.

Two robed couples stood at the altar, a set anchoring each end of the table. The younger couple carried a baby boy dressed in a black velour romper, gold pentacles embroidered on the front and back. The boy was crying and hiccuping, and his mother and father kept passing him back and forth to each other.

"Come on, sweetie pie, one burpy," cooed the mother, holding the infant over her shoulder, which was draped with a Winnie the Pooh spit rag. "Come on, Tommy."

"You shouldn't call him that," the father whispered into her ear.

"The ceremony hasn't started," she said. "He doesn't have his pagan name yet."

"You can still use it," he said, taking the boy from her.

"It's against the rules," she said, and looked across the table toward the older couple, the priest and the priestess. "Isn't it?"

The white-haired, bearded man shrugged, and his silver-haired female companion whispered to the younger pair, "We're not following a set form here, dears. This coven doesn't have hard-and-fast rules. We do our own thing. Just go with the flow."

"What about the ceremony?" asked the younger woman, adjusting the hood on her robe. "This isn't just a bunch of made-up stuff, is it? I want it to mean something."

"It will," the priest reassured her.

"We got the ritual from a coven out East," added the priestess. "Tweaked it a bit to make it our own."

The other adults ignored the discussion that was taking place inside the circle. Two of the robed men had pushed their hoods back to have an animated argument about the value of various ice-fishing electronics.

"If you ask me, a depth finder that goes for under five bills has gotta be shit."

"Any depth finder is shit if you don't know how to use it."

Three of the women were comparing corn-pudding recipes.

"A box of that corn-muffin mix, a can of creamed corn, a can of regular corn, three eggs, a carton of French onion dip from the dairy case, and a stick of melted butter." The woman tucked her hands into the voluminous velvet sleeves of her robe. "Make sure you spread the batter out in a wide pan or it'll never bake through."

"I like to use fresh corn when it's in season; otherwise I stick with frozen."

"Fresh, canned, or frozen, it all tastes the same if it's buried in a hot dish. This one time I tried substituting the onion dip for a carton of—"

"Time to get started," announced the priest, clapping his hands together.

"Quiet, please," said the priestess, stepping over to the wall and dimming the lights. The black-painted walls of the room became blacker.

Hoods that had been pushed off were put back up and the room fell silent, except for the sound of the hiccuping baby.

The silver-haired woman retrieved a bowl of salt from the altar. Standing with the bowl cupped between her hands, the priestess addressed the group in a clear, strong voice. "This child has chosen to be born to our sister Cerridwen and our brother Odin."

"In his past life, he played and worked and walked among us," continued the priest, fingering his beard while he spoke. "He has reincarnated, and elected to come back to those who knew and loved him before."

"Though his spirit is old, his body is brand-new," said the priestess.

"Therefore it must be introduced to the ancient ways," said the priest.

Tipping her head to the parents standing on the other end of the altar, the priestess whispered, "Go ahead, dears."

The man passed the baby back to the woman. Holding the boy under the armpits, the mother faced him to the north. The priestess went over to the infant, sprinkled salt on his downy head, and said, "I Isis, named for the consort of Osiris, call to the north. Creatures and powers of earth, welcome this babe with open arms. Bestow upon him your great blessings."

The mother turned her baby to face the east. The priestess returned the salt bowl to the altar while the priest retrieved a bowl smoking with incense. Moving the bowl in front of and under the dangling infant, so that the incense wafted around the baby, the priest said, "I Osiris, named for the beloved of Isis, call to the east. Creatures and powers of air, welcome this babe with open arms. Bestow upon him your great blessings."

The baby hiccuped loudly, and one of the corn-pudding witches chuckled. The mother passed the infant over to the father, who burped the child and turned him around again, this time to dangle facing the south.

The priest set down the incense and picked up a dagger from the table. He touched the flat of the blade to the baby's head and said, "I Osiris call to the south. Creatures and powers of fire, welcome this babe with open arms. Bestow upon him your great blessings."

While the priest set the dagger back, the priestess lifted a chalice from the altar. The child's father held him facing the west. The priestess dipped her fingertips into the water and sprinkled the infant's head. "I Isis call to the west. Creatures and powers of water, welcome this babe with open arms. Bestow upon him your great blessings."

The parents went back to their end of the altar with their baby while the priest and the priestess returned to theirs. The infant had stopped hiccuping and was starting to doze off in his father's arms.

The priestess: "Odin and Cerridwen, what Wiccan name have you selected for your boy child?"

The baby's mother took a small cup from the altar, dipped her fingertips into it, and traced a pentagram on the sleeping child's forehead. "With this blessing oil, we name thee Herne."

The infant's father: "God of the wild hunt, god who is celebrated in the autumn months when deer go into rut."

A murmur of approval from the males in the circle.

The priest: "Herne, you have honored your parents by choosing to be born to them. Now they honor you with these vows."

Together, the parents recited, "We promise to love, honor, and respect you. We shall protect you from all that is evil and leave you free to enjoy all that is good."

The priestess went around the table and gently lifted the sleeping child from his father's arms. "The gods and all present bear witness to the naming of this boy child."

As the priestess walked in a clockwise direction around the

circle, each person she passed touched a hand to the top of the baby's head. Some offered their own impromptu blessings.

"The gods be with you, Herne."

"Bless you, little boy."

"Live long, Herne."

"Be a good deer hunter like your old man, kid."

After the baby was returned to his parents, a chalice of red wine was passed around clockwise. Before sipping, each drinker raised the goblet toward the child and said, "I honor you, Herne."

After the naming ceremony, everyone went upstairs for cake and decaf coffee. Most removed their robes first, however, tossing the heaps of black velvet over the coats and jackets they'd deposited in the guest bedroom.

The three corn-pudding ladies plopped next to one another on a sofa, their cake plates balanced on their laps and their coffee mugs locked in their fists.

"Did you see the cake before they cut into it?" asked the one in the middle. "It was one of those photo cakes from that bakery in Park Rapids. It had his hospital picture on it. Adorable."

"I didn't get a chance to see it," said the witch on the right, taking a sip of coffee.

"My grandson had one of those for his graduation open house," said the witch on the left.

The one in the middle took a bite of cake and declared, "Marble. A little dry. I would have ordered the chocolate instead. That bakery does a good chocolate."

"I've got the best recipe for carrot cake," said the witch on the right, and the other two leaned toward her to hear it.

Herne, named for the god of the wild hunt, was in the bathroom getting his diaper changed.

Separated from the group, two of the men stood whispering in a corner. Both were tall. One was bony and haggard, and the other was carrying extra weight around his middle. Each had a paper coffee cup in his hand, but neither was drinking out of it. Neither seemed very happy.

"I warned her to leave it alone, but she did it anyway," growled the gaunt man.

"What's done is done," said the man with the gut.

"Should we tell the others?"

"No need to agitate them. We agitate them, one of them might do something rash and foolish."

The gaunt man chuckled dryly. "You mean more foolish than has already been done?"

"I don't want to talk about it anymore."

"We have to talk about it. What if the feds come after one of us? We all need to be telling the same story, otherwise they'll know." The narrow man swept the room with his eyes. "I say we tell the group. They're all here."

The man with the big gut finally took a sip of his coffee and shuddered. It was ice-cold. He tipped the cup back and swallowed. "We don't know who we can trust. Hell, for all I know you did it."

"You know for a fact that tonight I was—"

"I'm not talking about tonight. I'm talking about last night."

"What about you?" the gaunt man growled. "Where were you? It could have been you."

"That's my point. It could have been you. It could have been me. It could have been any of us."

He surveyed the room again, finding potential fiends instead of friends. "You really think one of ours did it? Why would they?"

"I don't know why." The fat fingers crushed the paper cup. "But if it was one of our own, I say we take care of it ourselves."

# CHAPTER SEVEN

That was a workout," said Bernadette as she and Garcia trudged to the truck. She checked her watch. It was ten in the morning. They'd spent fourteen hours in the hospital and she'd been without sleep for twenty-four. She'd also consumed about a gallon of coffee. She was both exhausted and wired.

"No solid suspects beyond the witch," said Garcia, squinting into the falling snow.

Seth's deputies had taken off at dawn, but the Minneapolis agents were staying behind to do some mop-up at the hospital. The ERT guys hadn't yet showed at the facility—they were still at the tented crime scene—and the Ramsey County Medical Examiner's wagon, though on the road, was an hour away. B.K. had been assigned to stay planted outside the storage room/morgue. "Maybe he should be relieved," said Bernadette as they came up to the truck. "Poor kid was standing in that hallway all night."

Garcia fished his keys out of his pocket. "What is it with you and Cahill?"

"It's just that he's so . . . I don't know . . . green."

"He'll be fine."

Bernadette yanked open the front passenger door and climbed in. Their next stop was the Ashe place. "Delores said we should call ahead because of the dogs."

"Like we're gonna give them some warning."

"I know. Just thought I'd point it out. Dogs and guns. Guns and dogs. Be ready."

"Imagine everyone up here has at least a shotgun," said Garcia, getting behind the wheel and starting up the Titan. "As far as dogs go, I like dogs."

Their breath filled the interior of the cab, and Bernadette clapped her gloved hands together. "The inside of this thing is colder than it is outside."

Garcia cranked the cab's heat on maximum. "It's got a great heater. We'll be toasty in no time." He reached behind his seat to grab an ice scraper and hopped out with it.

Watching Garcia's face through the windshield while he shaved the ice off the windows, Bernadette remembered Martini's comment. When he got back inside the truck, she passed it on.

"Erik Estrada?" Garcia navigated the truck out of the parking lot and headed for Paul Bunyan State Forest. "I wish."


While Garcia steered, Bernadette tried to navigate using the map Delores had scratched out for her. They were heading north on Minnesota 64, the highway that sliced vertically through the south section of the forest. As soon as they turned off the highway, they got into trouble.

"Maybe you're holding it upside down," offered Garcia as they reached the end of what appeared to be an old logging trail. The narrow, snow-clogged path came to a dead stop at a thick stand of trees. No houses or other vehicles were anywhere in sight.

Bernadette flipped the slip of paper, frowned, and flipped it back. "Have you got a map?"

"Look around."

She reached under her seat and pulled out an ice scraper, a flashlight, a stocking cap, and a first-aid kit. The only thing inside the glove box was the Titan's manual, another flashlight, and a bag of licorice, the red sticks as hard as icicles. With raised brows, she held up the sack of candy.

"Emergency Twizzlers." He took his arm off the square rest that sat between them on the bench. "Check in here."

Bernadette lifted the lid. Loose change, sunglasses, a box of Kleenex, and candy. She plucked out a Baby Ruth, peeled off the wrapper, and gnawed on the frozen candy bar.

He surveyed the woods around them. "Where in the hell are we?"

"Let's get back on the main road," she suggested.

Garcia tried to turn the truck around, but there wasn't enough room. He threw an arm over the top of the seat, looked behind him, and started backing up. "If we get stuck, I'm going to be pissed."

Bernadette looked through the windshield at the morning sky. The temperature was in the single digits, and snow was still falling. "Should have brought a GPS."

Garcia got them back on 64. "For sure it's on the east side of the highway?"

"According to Delores," said Bernadette, peering through her window. "She said the road is visible from the highway but not the house."

After two more wrong turns, they finally hung a right onto a road that looked as if it was meant for more than logging trucks. It was a little wider, and had been visited by a plow.

"This looks promising," said Garcia.

Bernadette studied Martini's scribbles. "There should be a sharp right pretty quick here."

They took the first right that came up, and immediately realized that it was another logging road. Garcia put the truck in reverse and backed out. "I'm getting pretty good at this."

The next right led them down a road that seemed better cleared than the highway. "This has gotta be their place," Bernadette said.

"Why do you say that?"

"The boyfriend drives a plow."

The snow was getting heavier, and Garcia activated the truck's windshield wipers. "Gonna be a busy boy today."

"A postal box and an address marker," said Bernadette, pointing.

"Since deer don't receive mail, that's a good sign," said Garcia.

The trees on either side of the road started thinning and then stopped altogether as they came to a clearing. Garcia braked so they could scope out the scene.

At the far end was a rambler with an attached two-car garage, and next to the garage was a barn. There was a plowed driveway in front of the garage and another in front of the barn's double doors, but no vehicles were parked in either of them. A collection of snow-covered heaps littered the yard, however: Rusty station wagon with fake wood paneling on the sides. Turquoise Volkswagen Beetle. Camper top resting on a set of blocks. Purple conversion van with plastic taped over the missing back windows. Cherry-red convertible, its cloth top in shreds and its interior filled with snow. A half-dozen ancient snowmobiles.

"The boyfriend must like to work on engines," said Bernadette.

"Let's see if anyone is minding witch headquarters," said Garcia, taking his foot off the brake and rolling toward the house.

Bernadette pointed to a massive woodpile alongside the barn. Another mountain was stacked against the side of the house. "I'll bet all that wood is for her kiln."

The road branched off, the right leading to the barn and the left to the house. Garcia took the left fork, pulling up to the garage. One of the garage doors had a plastic road sign nailed to it. Against the yellow background was the black silhouette of a witch on a broom, and the words SAVE A BROOM. RIDE A WITCH. On the other garage door was another road sign declaring, PROUD TO BE A PAGAN. Beneath the words was an upright five-pointed star with a circle around it.

"I remember that lawsuit over dead Wiccan vets not being allowed to have those symbols on their government-issued markers," said Bernadette.

"The one on the girl was inverted, though."

"That makes it satanic, not Wiccan."

"Doesn't exclude the witch from our short list," said Garcia.

"I agree," said Bernadette. "If Ashe doesn't have something to do with the murder and the star, she has to know someone who does. There's gotta be a connection."

"If nothing else, someone wanted us to land on her doorstep."

"Let's do this."

Both opened their doors and hopped out. With one hand still on the open passenger door, Bernadette caught a movement out of the corner of her eye. She glanced toward the area between the garage and the barn. Bounding out from behind the barn's woodpile were two thick-necked pit bulls.

"Tony! Dogs!" She jumped back into the cab and shut the door. The snarling animals hurled themselves against her side of the truck with such ferocity that the Titan rocked.

Garcia dived inside and slammed his door. "Jesus Christ!"

Two more pit bulls dashed out from between the garage and the barn, one of them running to Bernadette's door and the other circling around to Garcia's side. The agents had to yell in order to hear each other above the barking.

"Crap!" hollered Bernadette. "I was expecting hunting dogs!"

The pit bull on Garcia's side jumped so high, its front paws hit the middle of the window. "Hunting dogs, my ass!"

Wondering if someone would hear the racket and come out, Bernadette scanned the front of the house. "The windows are covered with black paper!"

"Pit bulls and blacked-out windows! You think there's something naughty going on inside?"

Two more dogs came running toward the truck to join in the frenzy. Bernadette instinctively looked up at the truck's ceiling for a shotgun and realized that it hadn't been fitted with a gun rack. "How many of these monsters do they have?"

Garcia took out his Glock and put his hand on the door. "I've had enough of this!"

The dogs on the passenger side were standing on their back paws and clawing madly with their front, as if trying to dig a hole through the metal. "God almighty!"

The instant Garcia opened his door a crack, one of the dogs shoved its head into the opening. As Garcia kicked at the snarling animal with his boot, the dog latched on to the heel. "Shit!" Garcia yelled, and aimed his weapon.

"Don't! You'll blow your foot off!"

"Fuck!" Garcia wiggled his foot out of the boot.

Bernadette threw herself across Garcia's lap, grabbed the door handle, and slammed the door against the animal's head. The pit bull fell away from the truck, the boot still clamped between its teeth. As Garcia and Bernadette both wrestled the door closed, two other dogs hurled themselves against the driver's side of the Nissan.

Panting, Bernadette collapsed against her seat. "Are you okay? Did he bite you?"

"I'm fine."

Glancing through the window, she saw that the dog with the

boot was shaking its head furiously. "I don't think your boot is going to make it."

"Funny," said Garcia, looking through Bernadette's window.

Bernadette ran a hand through her damp hair. She had worked up a sweat. "Let's get out of here and come back with animal control."

Garcia adjusted his grip on the gun and put his left hand on the controls for the driver's window. "Fuck animal control!"

Bernadette watched as Garcia rolled his window down an inch. "What are you going to do?"

Garcia poked the muzzle of his Glock through the gap. "Empty my gun!"

As if they knew Garcia's intent, a trio of barking dogs attacked the driver's window, their paws clawing at the glass and nearly reaching the gap.

"Tony, you can't!"

"Watch me." Garcia angled the barrel down toward the pack of pit bulls. "Eat this, assholes!"

# CHAPTER EIGHT

Tony, wait. Someone is coming," said Bernadette, nodding toward the barn.

A slender woman wearing tinted John Lennon eyeglasses and Bo Derek braids marched toward the truck. She was dressed in jeans, a flannel shirt with the sleeves pushed up to the elbows, and a down vest. Her jeans were tucked into lace-up black leather boots that reached her knees. She was wiping her hands on a work apron that was tied around her waist.

With a grumble, Garcia pulled his gun out of the window and rolled it back up. "Lucky dogs."

Instead of calling off the pit bulls, the woman stood behind them peering into the truck's cab. "Who are you?" she yelled to Bernadette's side.

Bernadette slapped her identification wallet against the window. "FBI!"

The woman grabbed one of the dogs by the collar, pulled him off Bernadette's door, and stepped closer to get a better look at the ID. As she studied the badge, she took off her glasses.

Through the window, Bernadette could see that the woman had multiple piercings: A nostril. Both eyebrows. Her chin just below her bottom lip. All the way up her ears. A tattoo snaked across her throat. It was a serpent swallowing its own head, the symbol of infinity or cyclicality. "Are you Jordan Ashe?" Bernadette yelled above the barking.

The woman's eyes narrowed. "What do you want?"

"We need to talk to you!" Bernadette hollered. "Put the dogs away!"

The woman didn't budge.

Garcia leaned across Bernadette's lap and shouted through the glass. "Lock up your animals!"

Her eyes darted from Garcia's angry face to the gun in his hand. She grabbed two of the dogs by the collar and started dragging them toward the barn. The others followed, tails wagging as if this were all part of a game. The woman wasn't big, but she was strong enough to handle the pit bulls with authority. When one of the dogs tried to bolt, she grabbed it by the collar and whipped it into the barn.

"I'll bet she's split her share of logs," said Bernadette.

Garcia watched as the woman slid the barn door closed. "I don't like this one damn bit."

They both scanned the yard to make sure there were no more loose dogs around, and then popped open their doors. When Bernadette hopped out of the truck, she landed on Garcia's mangled boot. Riddled with teeth marks and covered in drool, it resembled a hunk of chewed-up beef gristle. She picked it up with two fingers and took it over to him. "Can you identify the remains, sir?"

He took it from her, dropped it on the ground, and stepped into it. "Should have shot the motherfuckers. Every last one of them."

"I thought you liked dogs."

"Not those dogs."

"Maybe we need to get some backup," said Bernadette, her eyes focused on the black windows as they walked toward the house.

They both stood at the bottom of the front stoop, waiting for the woman to let them inside. She seemed in no hurry as she made her way from the barn toward the house.

"Before we call in the troops, let's uncover the nature of this particular illegal enterprise," Garcia said under his breath.


"Pit-bull rescue?" Bernadette sputtered.

"They should be put down," Garcia grumbled.

"Don't start that with me," Ashe warned.

Bernadette pointed to the windows. "And what is all the black paper about?"

"I do psychic readings and healing touch, and I need it dark for both."

They were all three standing in the middle of a small front room, its walls painted a nameless shade that could be achieved only by mixing leftover cans. The wood floor was covered by an area rug, its muddy color one that could be achieved only by a failure to vacuum. Under the blacked-out windows was a black leather couch with a coffee table in front of it. Against the opposite wall was a brick fireplace, a blaze popping behind a screen. Against the same wall, to the right of the hearth, was a doorway leading to a hall and the bedrooms. The house smelled of dogs and cigarette smoke. Beneath those was another aroma. Reefer? No, something else, thought Bernadette. Maybe it was pine. There was a tree, and ornament boxes on the floor around it. Someone was in the midst of taking down the decorations.

To the left of the fireplace, tucked into a corner, was a round table covered with a black cloth. Two metal folding chairs were parked across from each other, and between them, in the center of

the table, was a set of tarot cards. Bernadette went over to the
deck, picked it up, and shuffled through it. The colorful images—
apparently taken from paintings—were soft and beautiful. "I've seen
these before," she said, stopping at a card called the Ace of Pentacles. It depicted a nude woman reaching up toward a five-pointed
star. "Witches Tarot, right?"

"I'm impressed," Ashe said dryly, and then looked at Garcia. "I
need to·smoke. Can I reach for my smokes without getting shot?"

"Go ahead," said Garcia, keeping his eyes trained on her hands.

The woman unzipped her down vest. "Appreciate it, especially
since it's my house and all."

"Where's Karl Vizner?" asked Bernadette, setting down the cards.

Ashe took a pack of Camels and a lighter from the front pocket
of her flannel shirt. As she lit up, her attention shifted from Bernadette's blue left eye to her brown right one. "I'm not answering any
questions until you tell me what this is about."

"Where's Vizner?" repeated Garcia.

"Plowing." Ashe took a deep drag and exhaled in Garcia's direction. "Is this about that dead kid they found in Paul Bunyan? I heard
the FBI was coming to town. That's what this is about, isn't it?"

"You folks live close to the scene," said Garcia, his hands in his
jacket pockets.

Obviously remembering that Garcia had a gun, Ashe looked
nervously at his right arm. "So?"

"So did you see anything suspicious on New Year's Eve?"

Instead of answering, the woman took another pull on her cigarette.

Spotting a sagging bookcase, Bernadette went over to it and surveyed the contents. A Shakespeare anthology and a collection of
F. Scott Fitzgerald paperbacks shared space with a fat volume on
the Wicca religion. An entire shelf was jammed with books on alternative and holistic medicine. She lifted the lid off a clay jar, picked

it up, and took a whiff of what was inside. "Nice pot. What's inside of it?"

"Sage," Ashe said as she exhaled a cloud. "I use it for cleansing."

Next to the pot was a trio of figurines. They could have been garden gnomes, except they were a fraction of the size, fitting in the palm of a hand. Bernadette picked one up. "Cute."

"Wizards," Ashe said through a gray haze. "I've got those three and two out in the barn. My unholy quints. I'm not sure they're going to sell. People might find them too . . . what's the word?"

"Mystical?" asked Bernadette, setting it down.

"Ugly," Ashe said.

Garcia was getting impatient with the small talk. "We need you to answer some questions."

"I need a cup of tea first," Ashe said, and started for the kitchen.

"Sounds good." Bernadette was right behind her, and stood in the doorway.

Ashe turned the burner on under a teakettle, opened a cupboard, and took down a box of tea. "Want a cup?"

"No thanks." Bernadette ran her eyes around the galley, a cheerier space than the front room. The cupboards and walls were painted bright white, and the floor was tiled with black and white squares of linoleum. Bunches of dried herbs hung above the sink. Bernadette went over to the plants and examined them, crushing the leaves of one and smelling her gloved fingers.

"Thyme," said Ashe.

"For cleansing?"

"Cooking. I like to cook." She motioned toward the full sink with her cigarette. "Doing dishes, not so much."

"I can relate to that." Bernadette unzipped her jacket but kept on her gloves. "The dishes part, not the cooking part."

"I have to cook. If it were up to Karl, we'd be living off fried pork rinds and frozen pizza." The woman fished out a tea bag and dropped it into a cup decorated with a winged monkey from *The Wizard of Oz* and the words DON'T MAKE ME RELEASE THE FLYING MONKEYS.

"You aren't what I'd call a closeted witch," said Bernadette, nodding toward the cup.

Ashe leaned her back against the counter, facing Bernadette. "That's what this is really about, isn't it? Some sort of religious persecution. Dare I say it? A witch hunt."

"Are there any other Wiccans in the area?"

"I'm what's called a solitary practitioner." She took a puff and tapped the cigarette into a lopsided handmade ashtray on the counter.

"I thought you had to be in a coven to be a Wiccan, otherwise you're just a—"

"Otherwise I'm just a witch." She gave a dismissive wave. "I've heard that before, and it's nonsense. I honor and revere the earth. I celebrate the changing of the seasons, the phases of the moon, the gods and goddesses."

"What about Karl?"

"He's a lapsed Catholic. Sort of lapsed. He gets a Christmas tree every year. Goes to church on major holidays."

"He's a CEO, then," Bernadette said.

"Huh?" Ashe asked through a haze of smoke.

"Christmas and Easter Only."

She stepped next to Bernadette to drop the butt in the sink and returned to her resting spot opposite the agent. "Is that what you are?"

"Pretty much."

"So where did you learn about the Witches Tarot? It's a specialized deck."

"I have a little background," said Bernadette. "Spent time in Louisiana."

Ashe scrutinized Bernadette's mismatched eyes. "You should let me do a reading for you. You've got a yin-and-yang thing going on with the blue and the brown. I think we could have a cool outcome."

"I'm not a big believer."

"I know what you're thinking," said Ashe. "I'm not a charlatan. I *can* see. Intuit. I have premonitions. All the women in my clan have premonitions. It's a female thing. Most women are better at watching and listening than men are, don't you think? This is just an extension of that. I'll bet you could see stuff if you tried. At least let me read your palm."

Bernadette shoved her hands inside her jacket pockets. "I had my palm read in New Orleans. Once is enough."

"New Orleans." The teapot whistled, and Ashe took it off the stove. "There are some powerful sisters down there."

"I met a few characters. Witches. Voodoo priestesses. Satanists." Bernadette paused, waiting for a reaction. "Lots of Satanists."

"Takes all sorts." Ashe dropped a tea bag into her mug and poured water over it.

"The Wiccans in the area didn't like the Satanists, and I never quite understood why that was the case."

Ashe turned around with the mug in her hand. "An intelligent woman like yourself—someone who recognizes the Witches Tarot and hung out in New Orleans—I'll bet you could figure out why those two groups don't always see eye to eye."

"I'd like to hear your explanation."

Ashe blew on her tea. "Wiccans celebrate pre-Christian deities and do not—I repeat, *do not*—honor the Christian anti-God. Satanists see the Christian anti-God as a manifestation of their deity. They worship him. They worship the Devil."

"But in terms of visible differences—"

"Let me put it in a way that a nice ex-Catholic girl would understand," said Ashe, her voice hardening. "Satanists don't turn the other cheek, okay? There's no forgive and forget. Some practice black magic with the specific goal of nailing someone who has pissed them off. Their motto is pretty much, 'Do whatever the hell you want.' We say, 'Do whatever you want as long as you don't hurt someone, including yourself.' Wiccans don't try to dominate or control or harm others. The way I see it, we are the opposite of Satanists. The exact fucking opposite. The general, ignorant public thinks we're the same, and that gives us a bad name. Causes us all sorts of problems."

"But you both use the five-pointed star, don't you?" Bernadette asked evenly.

Ashe blinked twice and took a sip of tea. "Theirs is inverted."

"But—"

With a toss of her braids, Ashe turned her back on Bernadette and headed into the front room. "Let's get this interrogation over with. I've got work to do."

Ashe had apparently decided that she'd said too much. Bernadette followed her out of the kitchen.

Garcia had pulled one of the folding chairs away from the table and was sitting across from the couch. Ashe took the hint, went over to the couch, and dropped down with her tea in her hand. "Don't you people need some sort of paperwork? Seriously, should I even be talking to you without a lawyer?"

Bernadette sat down on the edge of the coffee table and folded her hands in front of her. "This isn't that big of a deal. We just want to know if you saw anything on New Year's Eve. Your residence is close to where the body was found."

"So are a lot of houses. Lots of people live in and around Paul Bunyan. Go talk to them." Ashe took a sip of tea and grinned tightly. "Oh, wait. They aren't a religious minority."

Bernadette: "We just want to know if you or Karl saw anything out of the ordinary that day."

"Karl was on the plow all night and into the next morning.

None of his jobs were anywhere near Paul Bunyan. They were all in town."

"What about earlier, before the snow started falling?" asked Garcia.

"He was busy getting his equipment ready. He was holed up in the garage all day."

"What about you?" asked Garcia.

"I didn't get outside." She set down her cup, pulled out another cigarette, and talked as she lit up. "I was in the barn, throwing pots. I have a big show coming up in the spring."

"What about the healing touch?" asked Bernadette.

Ashe released a cloud over the coffee table. "I've been cutting back on that, until the show is over."

"I understand you've been at the hospital offering your services," said Bernadette.

"I haven't been there in months," said Ashe, fingering her cigarette. "Why do you care about that, anyway? That has nothing to do with being in the woods."

Bernadette fished the dead girl's photo out of her jacket and extended it to Ashe. "Is she familiar?"

Ashe looked down at the picture without touching it. "So this is the dead kid. Who was she? What was her name?"

"Recognize her?" Bernadette asked.

"Nope," said Ashe.

Garcia: "Are you sure? Take a good look."

"That's enough," said Ashe, raising a palm. "You want anything else, I call an attorney."

"Are you guilty of anything?" asked Bernadette.

"No," Ashe snapped.

"Then you don't need a lawyer," said Bernadette.

"Talk to us now and we'll keep it low-key," said Garcia. "We just have a few more questions. You might have seen something that you don't even recognize as a clue."

"A girl was brutally murdered, a young girl," said Bernadette. "We could really use your help."

"I'm sorry, but I was inside all day. I can't help."

Garcia: "If you'll just—"

"No," said Ashe, bolting up from the couch. "I'm done."

Garcia and Bernadette exchanged glances. They both stood.

Ashe went over to the front door and yanked it open, sending a cold draft rolling into the room. "Hurry up. I'm not paying to heat the outside."

As Bernadette followed Garcia out the door, she extended a business card to Ashe. "In case something comes to you."

The woman looked at the card for several seconds and finally snatched it out of Bernadette's hand. "I'll let you know if I have a vision."

The door slammed after the two agents.

"See anything in the bedrooms?" asked Bernadette as they walked to the truck.

"Dirty laundry and sheets for curtains," said Garcia. "Balls of dog hair on the floor. Nice place."

Bernadette looked over her shoulder at the paper-covered windows. "She's hiding something."


Ashe peeked through a slit between the papers, watching until the two agents pulled away. As soon as they were out of sight, she left the windows and walked back and forth across the front room. When she got to the Christmas tree, she booted a box of glass balls. The carton slammed against the wall and the ornaments exploded in an eruption of red, green, gold, and silver.

She turned on her heel, marched into the kitchen, and flicked her cigarette into the sink. She studied the phone sitting on the kitchen counter. What if that male agent had planted bugs in her house while he was alone in the front room? What if they were tapping her landline? Could they tap her cell? She didn't think so. No wires. Have to have wires to wiretap, right?

She told herself she was being ridiculous. She locked her hands over the edge of the kitchen counter, closed her eyes, and took a deep, cleansing breath. "I am a stone in an ancient circle . . . I am a stone in an ancient circle . . . I am a stone in an ancient circle."

She stood straight, zipped up her vest, and went outside. As she jogged to the barn, she muttered a prayer under her breath: "Lady of the moon, lord of the sun, protect me and mine."

The dogs gathered around her as she entered. She contemplated letting them outside, in case the agents came back, but that man had a gun and seemed ready to use it. Bastard. She didn't want to put her precious puppies in harm's way. Putting her hand on one of the dogs' heads, she whispered, "Don't worry."

Ashe locked the barn door so that no one could surprise her and extracted her cell phone from her apron pocket. She punched in a number and with a trembling hand lifted the phone to her ear. An answering machine picked up, and she closed the phone with a snap. She couldn't leave a message. The wrong person might hear it.

She opened the phone and punched in another number. "Pick up, pick up, pick up," she chanted while pacing the length of the barn. She put a hand to her forehead. "Please pick up. Please. Mother Goddess, make someone pick up the fucking phone!"

Mother Goddess apparently heard. After ten rings, someone answered.

Her voice cracking, Ashe said into the phone, "We have a problem."

# CHAPTER NINE

Back on Minnesota 64.

Garcia's cell rang. He took it out, flipped it open, and looked at the screen. "Shit." Putting the phone to his ear, he slipped into his most buttoned-up voice. "Assistant Special Agent in Charge Anthony Garcia."

Bernadette watched Garcia's face. It tightened like an angry fist.

"Yes, sir," he said into the phone. "No, no, sir. But you have to understand . . ."

A double *sir*. It was either their bosses in D.C. or Mag Dunton's office finally returning Garcia's calls.

"I realize that, Senator. We're under direct orders from Washington."

It wasn't Dunton's people; it was the man himself.

"Apologize for that, sir. We couldn't wait . . . I'm sure it is, but we couldn't delay starting the investigation."

Bernadette could hear Dunton's raised voice on the other end of the cell. Something about his wife being upset.

The snow was coming down so heavily, the wipers were pretty

much useless. Visibility was about three car lengths and shrinking fast. Garcia looked in his rearview mirror and saw a plow bearing down on them. He hung a right on a logging road, slammed on the brakes, and put the truck in park. Behind them, the plow rumbled past in a cloud of snow.

Garcia checked his watch. "I'm sorry, but your daughter's body is already on the way to the Twin Cities . . . No idea, sir. ME would be able to tell you. These things typically take time . . . Days, possibly longer. After that, her remains can be released to a funeral home. I suggest you call . . ."

More yelling from Dunton. Garcia lowered the phone and shot Bernadette a grim smile. He returned the cell to his ear. From listening to what followed on Garcia's end, it seemed that Dunton was drilling him about the investigation.

"Don't know . . . Don't know that either, sir. We need a little more time . . . No arrests yet, but I'm certain we'll be able to . . ."

Bernadette heard the next four words as clearly as if Dunton had shouted them in her face: *"You people are useless!"*

Garcia again took the phone away from his ear. He and Bernadette both stared at the cell in his hand as if it were a hand grenade with the pin pulled. Too bad Garcia couldn't roll down his window and chuck it into a snowbank.

Garcia puffed out a breath of air and lifted the cell. Listened. "No one under me has permission to say anything to the press . . . No, sir. That wasn't from us."

Dunton was blaming them for the information released to the media. At least the girl's name hadn't been leaked. Yet.

"Sir . . . sir . . . please. Could we meet in town? If we could have a face-to-face. Where are you and Mrs. Dunton staying? . . . Uh-huh . . . I know exactly where that is. I could meet you . . ."

Bernadette gave Garcia a weak but encouraging smile.

"If you could fill me in on the last time she contacted you or anyone else, be it a family member or a friend or . . . Yes, sir . . . I also have questions about what she was doing up north in the first place. Who the father might be. Anything, any ideas, any names would . . . Yes, sir. I can appreciate that, but—"

Garcia blinked and snapped the cell closed. "Hung up on me."

"Why isn't he helping us instead of fighting with us?" sputtered Bernadette. "Doesn't he want his daughter's killer caught?"

"Not by the FBI. By anybody *but* the FBI. He'd actually have to admit we could be useful."

"We were assigned to this case to make a point, weren't we?"

"You just figured that out?"

"I don't like being used to make a point. I just want to do my job. Why can't I just work and do my job without all the bullshit?"

"Welcome to my world."

"I take it they're up here."

"Yeah. I'm going to meet them."

"What's this *I* stuff?"

"I'm paid to deal with this crap; you aren't. Just worry about solving the case."

"When're you seeing them?"

"Later. We've got plenty of time to check out that clinic."

She wanted to give Garcia something solid, a good lead to take to his meeting with Dunton. "Let's try my sight first. How close is Ed's cabin?"

"Close enough."

Garcia backed over the hump of snow created by the passing plow and steered the truck back onto the highway, heading south. He hung a right onto Minnesota 34. Then it was all county roads.

While Garcia hiked up the back steps and unlocked the cabin door—he had his own keys to his cousin's place—Bernadette went around to the back of the truck and grabbed their duffels. Garcia took both bags and led her up the steps.

They stepped into a tiny mudroom. Garcia kicked off his boots, and Bernadette did the same. The mudroom opened into a short hallway. She poked her head into the room at the end. A small bedroom. Next was a larger bedroom that faced the lake. Then a bathroom. She clawed some toilet paper off the roll, blew her nose, and followed Garcia into the main living space of the log A-frame.

The kitchen was open, with an island topped by a range. Beyond the kitchen was the front room and its redbrick fireplace. An open stairway, railed with skinned logs, led to a loft sleeping area. Nice, she thought.

Bernadette took some newspapers from a stack next to the hearth, bunched them up, and shoved the balls into the fireplace. She topped them with kindling and a log.

"I turned up the heat," said Garcia, coming up behind her as she lit the newspaper.

The cabin's basement was frigid. They should have kept their outdoor gear on, right down to their boots. A hunk of old gold shag carpet covered the bedroom's icy concrete floor. The wood-paneled walls were decorated with dead fish, most of them large-mouth bass. She assumed all of them were Ed's trophies. Their glassy eyes added to the chilly feel of the dank space.

Bernadette and her boss sat on opposite ends of a sagging sleeper sofa, a plaid piece that took up one wall of the cell. On each side of the couch was a table topped by a lamp, but only the light on Garcia's end worked. The shade depicted a stream with a buck standing onshore, drinking from the running waters. The shade slowly rotated so that the deer would phase out of view, its rump in a slow retreat. Against the opposite wall was a bed covered with a down spread. In the middle of the wall above the bed's headboard was an egress window with a ragged blanket tacked over it. The smallest bit of light bordered the edges of the curtain. It was not enough to distract her.

"This couch is shit," groused Garcia. He'd sunk so far down into the cushion that his knees were nearly at the same height as his head. "You sure you don't want to go back upstairs?"

"This is good." As she rotated her head, she noticed a hole in the ceiling the size of a fist and wondered what the hell that was about. A failed effort at putting in a ceiling fixture? The space smelled like sweaty men, and she wrinkled her nose. "Who usually sleeps down here?"

"Overflow parking for Ed's buddies in homicide. Not the nicest room in the house, but you wanted dark."

"It's perfect." Bernadette rubbed her arms over her shirt and blew a puff of air. Not quite cold enough to see her breath. On her lap was the plastic bag containing the sliver of flannel from Lydia's nightgown.

"Ready?" Garcia asked.

"Ready," she said.

"Here we go." He snapped off the lamp as the buck's butt was again fading out of view.

No airplane or traffic noise. No distant voices or music. Not even the wind broke the stillness. The only interruption to the quiet was a wooden groan. The cabin settling. She concentrated on her breathing. In and out. In. Out. She opened her hand on her lap and tipped the bag over her palm. As light as a feather, the fabric floated down to her fingers. She curled her hand into a fist, closed her eyes, and whispered her prayer.


Bernadette opens her eyes to . . . the storm.

The killer is looking out a window. Even with her hazy vision, she can tell that it's daytime and snow is falling. Beyond the white blur, green blurs. Pine trees. This could be virtually anywhere with a winter season, but she knows it's up north. She can feel it.

The murderer drops the blinds and cranks them so they shut tight. Why close them in the middle of the day? What is this person up to?

The killer turns away from the window and flicks on a table lamp but makes the move too quickly for her to study the hand—its size, whether there is jewelry or a watch. Whether this person has tattoos.

The room is small and butter-yellow. Rectangles decorate the walls. Color photos or paintings—she can't tell which. A bed with a nightstand and the lamp. Odd lamp. The base is bright yellow and in the shape of a duck.

Suddenly everything goes dark, but it isn't the same as when Bernadette loses a connection. There are shadows and vague shapes. Movement. A distant, throbbing light beyond the blackness. What is this? She's never been here before. Her sight has never done this sort of . . .

Inside the yellow room again, glancing toward a door beyond the bed. The murderer steps up to it, raises a fist, and knocks. Again, too fast for her to scrutinize the hand. The killer backs away, and the door pops open. Someone standing in the doorway. Bernadette can't make out the details of the face, a creamy round with dark slits for eyes. Long brown hair. A rose-colored robe or dress. Can't tell which. Doesn't matter. This is a woman. The killer puts a hand on her shoulder and they walk together to the bed. Is this the next . . . ?

•   •   •

That strange, shadowy world again. Gray shapes like amoebas, moving and undulating and pulsating. A hint of light behind them, or between them. Past them. What is this place? This is the weirdest thing she's ever . . .

The rosy woman is sitting on the edge of the mattress. She turns on it and brings her legs up. The killer is standing over her, concentrating on the woman's face. She's talking.

The woman lies back against the pillows, and the baby butcher puts both hands on her belly.

Black and gray again. Bernadette tries to will the shadowland away, but it stays in her eyes. Stays. Stays. Swimming gray shapes. A promise of light, but no light. She can't waste time with this nonsense. A woman is in danger.

Bernadette forced her fist open and tipped her hand, dropping the fabric.

She closed her eyes tight and opened them to a familiar darkness. The cabin's basement. She could see daylight oozing out from the edges of the makeshift curtain. Before she could speak, she had to take a gulp of air. "The killer's with a pregnant woman!"

# CHAPTER TEN

Garcia turned on the light. "Where?"

She jumped to her feet and ran up the stairs while stuffing the plastic bag into her pocket. "Could have been a private home, a clinic."

He followed her. "The hospital?"

"We were over every inch of that place, and I didn't recognize the room." She gave him a summary as they put on their outdoor gear. "A small yellow room with a bed. The murderer looked out the window and I saw snow coming down, so it's gotta be up here."

"The entire state and half of Wisconsin are under a blizzard warning," said Garcia.

"Fine. I *think* it's up here." Bernadette zipped her jacket. "A woman came out of another room. The bathroom, maybe. She had brown hair and wore a rose-colored outfit. After she stretched out on the bed, he put his hands on her stomach."

"Sure it was a *he*? What about Ashe? Could have been her hands doing that healing-touch bullshit. Potters have strong mitts, right?"

While Bernadette couldn't visualize the witch's hands at that moment, she did recall the woman's athleticism. She tossed those dogs around like puppies. "Could have been Ashe."

"Should we go back there?"

"Wasn't her house. No black paper or sheets on the window. Blinds."

"How do you know the gal on the bed was pregnant?" asked Garcia, pulling on his hat. "Did she have a bump?"

"Not really."

"Then how do you know?"

"I told you, he—or she—laid hands on her gut."

Garcia didn't say anything, but she knew that expression. She'd seen it before on him. He believed in her sight, but he didn't always agree with her interpretation. It frustrated her. "Tony, I *know.* I just know she was pregnant, just like I know the killer is up here."

He put his hand on the door. "Do you *know* where we're going?"

"OB clinic in Akeley. Let's start there."

As they drove, she told him about the strange dark interludes in between her visions.

"What was that about?"

"Haven't a clue," she said. "Let's worry about it later."

The storefronts lining the tiny town's main thoroughfare were all but invisible from the road. They passed the Akeley Historical Museum and a fifty-foot statue of Paul Bunyan. He was down on one knee and had his hand out. It was piled high with snow, making it appear as if he were in the process of forming a snowball.

"Akeley is definitely in touch with its inner lumberjack," Bernadette observed.

The town's grocery store—the Blue Ox Market—had a huge mural of Paul's blue ox, Babe, splashed across its exterior. The hair salon was called Babe's Cut and Curl. One of the gas stations was Bunyan's Gas Station. The ice-cream shop was named Paul's Purple Cow Ice Cream & Eatery.

"Where did she say it was?" asked Garcia, peering into the whiteness.

"West end of town, two blocks or so off the main street."

"I seem to remember some businesses down here," Garcia said, swinging a wide left and fishtailing a bit as he did so.

They drove two more blocks and Bernadette spotted a squat brick building across the road, sitting on a corner. Floodlights mounted at its entrance illuminated the front. Garcia made a U-turn, so that the truck was parked on the same side of the street. When Bernadette hopped out, she landed in snowbanks that went past her knees. Garcia was on point and she walked directly behind him, taking advantage of the path he made with his big boots. When they got to the front, they were able to read the sign on the glass door: NORTHERN PINES OBSTETRICS AND GYNECOLOGY. "Sounds like a resort," Bernadette said.

They stomped their boots on the stoop and pushed inside, going through a foyer and a second glass door. They stood just inside the second door, stomping again and unzipping their jackets. Bernadette saw a receptionist's window on the left, but there was no one at the counter. She spotted a box of Kleenex, grabbed a handful of tissues, and blew her nose. "Hello," she said, trying to see if there was anyone hidden among the filing cabinets behind the counter.

The lights were all on, but the waiting room was empty. "Think the clinic is closed?" Garcia asked.

"Patients must have canceled because of the storm," she said.

"So maybe this isn't what you saw." Garcia thumped around the room to take a look. Couches and chairs covered with a print depicting bears and pine trees. Framed pictures of loons on the water and ducks in flight. Magazines scattered on coffee tables and end tables. Opposite the receptionist's counter, a large room for kids with toddler-size tables and chairs. Tons of toys and puzzles. An aquarium and a television set mounted to the ceiling. *The Little Mermaid* was playing, and a toddler girl was sitting on the floor watching. "Hey, kid," said Garcia. "Didn't see you there. Where is everybody? Where're Mommy and Daddy?"

The girl looked up at him and giggled. "You're silly." She went back to staring at the screen, and Garcia joined her.

Bernadette tried the door to the receptionist's area and found it locked. She moved down to a door that she assumed led to the examining area. Locked again. She pounded on it. "Tony?"

"What?" he asked, still staring at the television.

He obviously didn't believe the clinic was going to give them anything, and his skepticism made her mad. "Want me to turn up the sound for you?"

A door marked PRIVATE popped open and a tall, plump blond woman came out into the waiting room. She wore a smock with a Hello Kitty print on it and matching slacks. The outfit was finished off by sneakers the size of skateboards. "I'm sorry, folks. Thought our receptionist got a hold of all our appointments to reschedule."

"You Dr. Bossard's nurse?" Garcia asked.

"For about a hundred years." The woman stared at Bernadette's face, and then at her midriff. "Are you a new patient?"

Bernadette: "I'm not—"

"You're not the one I talked to this morning? The triplets?"

Bernadette's mouth dropped open, and Garcia glanced over with a lopsided grin on his face.

The woman went to the receptionist's counter and reached over for some paperwork. "I'm sorry you hauled all the way over here for nothing. You and your hubby should have called first."

Garcia left the kiddie room and walked over to the woman. "Is Dr. Bossard expected back today?"

"Afraid not. We had back-to-back emergency surgeries. She's stuck at the hospital the rest of the day, finishing up with those ladies. It's only luck you caught *me* here." The woman tried to hand a stack of forms to Bernadette. "Why don't you take these home with you, fill them out, and bring them back. Be as accurate as possible. Did your old OB send your records with you? What due date did he give you?"

Bernadette didn't answer. The humiliating line of questioning didn't distract her as much as the woman's left arm: she had a stump at the end instead of a hand.

Garcia approached the woman with his identification wallet open. "We're with the Federal Bureau of Investigation."

As the woman took in the badge, her eyes widened. "This about that poor little girl they found in the woods? Whole county is talking about it, talking about the FBI coming. All sorts of talk."

"I imagine," Garcia said as he put away the wallet.

"Why'd you come to the clinic?"

"We were hoping to speak with the doctor," said Bernadette.

"Miss . . . I'm sorry . . . what's your name?" asked Garcia.

"Rachel. Rachel White."

Bernadette held up Lydia's photograph. "She look familiar? Might she have come into the clinic?"

White buried her hand and her stump in the pockets of her smock and studied the picture. "The poor sweetheart. Makes you sick just thinking about it."

"Take your time," said Garcia.

"Sorry." White shook her head. "Honest to God, how could someone kill a pregnant girl? Who'd do such a thing? Couldn't be anyone from around here."

"We don't know," said Garcia.

"The folks around here, they're good people," said White.

"They wouldn't. Got to be a stranger. Someone passing through town. A sicko from the cities."

Bernadette found her eyes flitting down to the stump and back to the woman's face. White caught her staring and smiled pleasantly. Bernadette felt her face redden. "Uh . . . I'd like to look around."

"Can't let you do that," said White, crossing her arms under her large breasts. "I've got a patient. Need to get back to her."

The little girl ran over to White and twined her arms around one of her legs. "I want Mamma."

"Go watch your show, sweet cheeks. Mamma will be right out." White tousled the girl's hair, and the child ran back to the mermaid movie.

"I thought you said you'd rescheduled all the patients," said Garcia.

"She wasn't scheduled, she's a drop-in. She was having some Braxton Hicks contractions. Her hubby freaked out and—" White cut herself off. "I shouldn't be telling you patient information."

A pregnant woman was back there with her husband, and *he* could be the killer, thought Bernadette. She ran over to the receptionist's counter, climbed over it, and darted into the back of the clinic.

"Hey!" the nurse yelled after her.

Bernadette ran down the hall, sticking her head into each examining room. Empty, empty, empty. The door at the end was closed. She drew her gun, put her hand on the knob, and pushed the door open.

A woman was half naked on an exam table, her knees raised and her feet in stirrups. She took one look at the weapon in Bernadette's hand and shrieked.

Bernadette holstered her Glock. It wasn't the same room or the same woman as in her sight. "FBI, ma'am. I'm sorry if I—"

A burly bearded man came out from behind the open door and stepped in front of Bernadette. With both hands, he pushed her backward into the hall. "Get away from my wife."

Bernadette shoved his hands down. "I'm—"

"I don't give a shit who you are!"

"She's got a gun!" the wife yelled from inside the room. "She pointed a gun at me!"

Garcia wedged himself between Bernadette and the angry husband. "FBI! Back off!"

Fists clenched at his sides, the man took two steps backward. "What's going on?"

"This the guy?" Garcia asked Bernadette.

"No," she said.

"What's this about?" asked the husband.

"We're with the FBI," said Garcia.

"Yeah. I got that part." He looked at Bernadette. "Why in the hell did you point a gun at my wife?"

"Sir, I didn't point it at her."

"Are you calling her a liar?" The husband was so mad, he was spewing spit while he talked.

Garcia raised a palm. "Sir. Please calm down."

"Calm down? I'm not the one who came charging in here with a—"

Behind him, his wife moaned. "They're coming again!"

White slipped past the trio in the hall and went into the examining room. "Honey, try to relax. Practice your breathing."

"I want Dr. Bossard," the woman whimpered.

"I've been doing this forever and a day, honey. These are just Braxton Hicks. Believe me."

The husband glared at the two agents, turned around, and followed the nurse into the room, slamming the door after him.

"Is this place even remotely like the one you saw?" asked Garcia.

None of the rooms had blinds or yellow paint. "No."

White came out of the examining room, gently closing the door behind her. "You two need to leave," she said in a low voice.

Garcia looked past her, toward the room. "Is she okay?"

"False labor," said White. "All the commotion didn't help."

Bernadette dug a business card out of her jacket. "If the doctor could call us, we'd appreciate it."

"I'll tell her." White snatched the card and tucked it into her smock. "There *are* other clinics in the area. Maybe one of them saw the girl."

"We'll try them," said Garcia.

White eyed Bernadette. "None of them will want someone running around with a gun, either. I guarantee it. When Dr. Bossard hears about this, she's going to lose it. I mean it. She is going to completely flip."

"I apologize," said Garcia.

"Who sent you here, anyway?" asked White, putting a hand on one hip and a stump on the other. "Why did you decide you needed to barge in and—"

The door opened behind the nurse. "Come on!" barked the husband. "Who in the hell is the patient here? Let's have some closure."

White went back into the room.

Bernadette and Garcia headed for the exit. "I'm not really happy with the way this went down," said Garcia.

"I thought—"

"I know what you thought."

"She didn't ask for the girl's name," said Bernadette as they walked outside. "Did you notice that? Wouldn't that be someone's first question, unless they already knew the name? Dippy Delores asked. The witch lady asked."

"You're reading too much into stupid shit."

Bernadette frowned but let the insult pass. "She was real interested in knowing how we'd gotten on to their clinic."

"Not unusual."

"I didn't like the woman," Bernadette said flatly.

"Because she accused you of triplets."

"That's not why." Fuming, Bernadette pulled open the passenger door and jumped inside the Nissan.

Garcia got behind the wheel and started up the truck. "Is she a suspect?"

"No," Bernadette admitted. "You saw her stump."

"Now where?" asked Garcia, pulling away from the curb.

"The hospital."

"She's probably calling Bossard right now," said Garcia. "Doc's gonna be madder than hell."


After the false-labor couple and their child left, Rachel White went around the waiting room shutting off the television and the lights. After the front of the building was dark, she went to the glass doors and looked outside. Saw only the snow.

As she walked toward the rear of the clinic, her face was knotted with anger. In a back office, she picked up the telephone and punched in a number with her stump. Walked the length of the office twice while waiting for her call to be picked up. "You're not going to believe what just happened here," she said into the phone.

# CHAPTER ELEVEN

Eve Bossard was exactly what Bernadette expected in a do-gooder small-town doc: a slightly frumpy lady with a hippy, Earth Mother aura about her.

Bossard's jean skirt went down well past her knees. Instead of nylons, she wore black tights that sagged a bit at the ankles. On her feet were the requisite Birkenstock clogs. Her long brown hair was pulled away from her face by a single fat braid that dangled halfway down her back. Strands of gray streaked the brown.

The woman was probably in her late forties—about a decade older than Bernadette—but not a dot of makeup decorated her face. Bernadette suspected that she was one of those driven professionals who couldn't find the time for frivolous niceties. The doctor walked and talked with the speed of someone who needed more hours in the day to get things done.

While the two agents leaned their backs against a wall, waiting for Bossard to finish examining a woman behind the closed door of a hospital room, Bernadette offered her initial opinion of the doctor. "She's cool."

Garcia bounced his back against the wall. "We met her for two seconds, while she was going from one room to the other."

"She looks like my high school home-ec teacher."

"Did she have that unibrow thing going, too?"

"You're mean."

"Probably wears those opaque tights because she doesn't shave her legs."

"That's a shitty thing to say."

"Hey, some men like that hirsute stuff."

She checked her watch. "Can't believe we're back here. We spend any more time in this joint, they're going to start billing us."

The door popped open and Bossard walked into the hallway, her clogs clopping on the linoleum floor. They peeled their backs off the wall and made a beeline for the obstetrician. Garcia opened his mouth to speak and Bossard held up a long index finger. "Give me one minute."

While the physician wrote in a folder, Bernadette studied the woman's hands. Were they large enough? Didn't matter. Couldn't have been her; she'd been at the hospital all day.

"There," said Bossard, closing the folder. "What do you want to know?"

She didn't sound madder than hell. Bernadette figured White hadn't yet told Bossard what had happened at the clinic. Good. "Did you take care of this girl?" asked Bernadette, holding up the photograph of Lydia.

The doctor looked past the photo at the two agents. "Come on, guys. I can't talk about my patients. You know that."

"Please, just look," said Garcia.

Bossard hesitated, and then examined the picture. "Sorry," she said, glancing up from the photograph. "She's never been a patient."

"You're certain?"

Bossard's eyes widened. "That's the girl they found in the woods?"

"Yes," said Garcia.

Bossard took a step back from the two agents and hugged the paperwork to her chest. "Why would you think she came to see *me*?"

"We were told you have clinic hours for poor folks," said Bernadette. "We were hoping she might have stopped by."

"Not all teenagers seek prenatal care," said Bossard.

"At some point they have to go in," said Garcia. "This girl was pretty far along."

"A few manage to hide the fact they're pregnant, and even deny to themselves that they're carrying a child. End up delivering on the bathroom floor of their parents' home. In a gas-station toilet. Sometimes the baby makes it. Sometimes not." Bossard's voice and lashes dropped. "Teen pregnancy can be—"

"You're certain this pregnant teen was never seen at your clinic," Bernadette interrupted, holding the photo higher.

"I have a small practice, and I know all my patients quite well. I've never seen her before. I'm sorry."

"So are we," said Bernadette, putting the picture back inside her pocket.

"We get lots of tourists, especially on weekends. She could have gotten lost in the crowds. During the week, there's a chance she would have been noticed. The streets aren't so busy then. Red hair would have made her stand out."

"Do you have any suggestions on other clinics or docs we could try?" asked Garcia. "Was there a place a runaway would have hung out?"

"We don't get a lot of runaways up here. As far as other physicians go . . ." She bit down on her bottom lip.

Bossard didn't want to piss off her colleagues. Tough, thought Bernadette. "Is there a man OB around here?"

"Not anywhere close. To find a male obstetrician, you'd have to drive all the way to . . ." Bossard stopped herself, and her eyes got as big as saucers. "You can't possibly think one of *us* did it! That's crazy! We spend all day trying to *save* babies and mothers!"

Now she's madder than hell, thought Bernadette. "Dr. Bossard—"

"I don't believe this!"

"Ma'am," said Garcia.

"If you think I'm going to send you after another obstetrician, you're mistaken. We rely on each other up here. They'd never speak to me again! My name would be mud!" She paused in her diatribe and her eyes narrowed. She looked from one agent to the other. "What evidence do you have? I'd really like to know. Was the procedure—"

"The *procedure* was a bloody mess," Bernadette said.

Bossard opened her mouth to say something and promptly clamped it shut.

Garcia: "Dr. Bossard, if you know something—"

"Oh, boy," the physician said under her breath. "I really shouldn't. I've got no reason to believe she'd be involved."

"Who?" Bernadette asked.

Bossard's mouth stretched into a straight, hard line. "She's not a medical doctor."

Bernadette could practically see the woman's mind cranking away, working to justify the betrayal. "A name . . ."

"I like Sonia very much," said Bossard. "Really, I do. But she has a hard time acknowledging her limits. She isn't a physician."

"Who?" asked Garcia.

"Sonia Graham," said Bossard.

The doc surrendered the name a little too quickly, thought Bernadette. No love lost between these two women.

"She promotes some . . . positive things," Bossard said grudgingly. "Drug-free births, breast-feeding, proper nutrition. She's a midwife. Was a midwife."

*"Was?"* asked Bernadette.

The straight, hard mouth again. "She agreed to do a home birth. I don't approve of home births. Like many OBs, I believe midwives should deliver in a hospital setting. Then if something goes awry—"

"What happened?" asked Bernadette.

"The mother was a VBAC. Vaginal birth after Cesarean. Poor candidate for a home birth, and I told Sonia that repeatedly. The risk of a uterine rupture was too great."

"What happened?" asked Bernadette.

"The mother hemorrhaged postpartum."

"She died?" asked Garcia.

"She made it to the hospital. The baby lived. The mother lived. But it was a *bloody mess,*" said Bossard. "No other way to describe it."

"You were the one who came to the rescue?" asked Bernadette.

Bossard nodded grimly.

"Did Graham lose her license?" asked Garcia.

"She agreed to stop practicing." Bossard smiled tightly. "After I insisted."

"We'll have to run this down," said Garcia.

"Do you think she's capable of murder?" Bernadette asked. "I mean, a home birth turned sour is one thing, but—"

"How do you know it didn't start out as a home birth turned sour?" asked Bossard.

Bernadette didn't want to get into the fact that the girl's head was bashed in—not usually part of a home birth, turned sour or not. "Well, that's a good point."

"We won't know until after we talk to the ME," added Garcia.

"A teenage girl, a stranger to town—how would she have hooked up with Graham?" asked Bernadette.

"Everyone knows her," said Bossard. "She's got her followers. She has a yoga studio in Walker. Conducts special exercise classes for pregnant mothers. Dispenses advice on nutrition and breast-feeding."

Bernadette thought back to what she'd observed with her sight: hands placed on a woman's abdomen. "Is it possible she's still making house calls on the side?"

"Would she risk another delivery?" asked Garcia.

Bossard shrugged. "Maybe. I know she misses it. Midwives are a strange breed. They see birth as a spiritual event."

*Spiritual.* Intriguing word to use, especially in light of the satanic symbol, Bernadette figured. "What about her home life? Does she have a family, go to church? Who are her friends?"

"Don't know her all that well personally," said Bossard. "She's not from Minnesota originally. She's from . . . I don't know . . . Vermont, I think. Very active midwife culture there."

Because Bernadette couldn't tell Bossard why she really wanted the information, she carefully framed her next request. "This girl might have confided in another pregnant woman. I'd appreciate a list of expectant mothers in the area. We'd keep it confidential."

Bossard stared at Bernadette with disbelief. "That will *never* happen."

Garcia knew the request crossed a line and kept his mouth shut.

"They could be in danger," Bernadette added.

"A serial killer?" Bossard mulled over the possibility. "I don't believe it."

"If we could warn them—"

"You think they're not on alert after watching the news?"

Bernadette handed the doctor a card. "Call if you think of something else."

Bossard slipped the card into her smock. "You *won't* tell Sonia I gave you her name, correct?"

Bernadette made the zipper sign across her lips.

"My mention of her possible involvement, all speculation. Just thought you should know there's someone out there besides a medical doctor." She checked her watch. "I really need to—"

"One more question," said Bernadette. "We've been talking about an alternative birthing method—"

"One I don't oppose, as long as it's in the proper setting."

"Gotcha," said Bernadette. "What about alternative religions around here?"

Bossard slowly shook her head. "I'm not understanding you."

"Witchcraft. Satanism. Ever come across a patient or anyone else who practices either?" Garcia asked.

"I don't pay attention to that sort of thing," Bossard said with a sniff. "Catholic. Lutheran. Witch. I could care less. I'm all about science, not superstition."

Garcia's cell started ringing and he fumbled around to find it. "Excuse me."

"Mr. Garcia, we like visitors to the hospital to turn off their phones."

"Right," Garcia said shortly, and answered it.

Bossard seemed perturbed by Garcia's response, and Bernadette stifled a grin while he talked into the cell. Like Bernadette's home-ec teacher, Dr. Bossard wasn't used to having her orders ignored.

"Hey, Seth. Yeah. We just saw her this morning, her and her damn dogs . . . What can you tell me about that little operation of hers?"

Bossard had stepped away from them and was studying a chart posted outside a patient's room.

By the time Garcia got off the phone, Bossard was gone from the corridor. Bernadette walked across the hall.

"What're you doing?" Garcia asked with irritation. "We gotta get going."

"Give me a minute." She lifted the patient chart hanging to the left of the door and quickly scanned the first page. With a frown, she put the chart back in the holder.

"What's wrong?"

As they started to walk down the hall, Bernadette looked over her shoulder. "I trust her and I don't."

"Thought she reminded you of your hairy home-ec teacher."

"Did you notice the questions she *didn't* ask about the dead girl? Didn't ask her name or what had happened to the fetus."

"Big deal," he said. "You made the same observations about her nurse at the clinic. Like I said before, you're reading too much into dumb shit."

He was really starting to tick her off. "Tell me if I'm reading too much into this: you know the chart I was just checking?"

"Breaking about two hundred federal laws. What was up with that?"

"While you were on the phone with the sheriff, Bossard was standing nearby, going over that paperwork."

"So? She had another patient."

"It was a guy, and he gave birth to a bouncing baby appendix," said Bernadette.

One side of Garcia's mouth turned up. "The chart-checking was a ruse. Bossard was staying in the hall to eavesdrop."

"Granted, she could have been nosy and nothing more," Bernadette conceded.

"I like her tip about the midwife," said Garcia.

"OBs don't like midwives. Here's Bossard's chance to get back at one who crossed her."

"It's still a good tip."

"It is," she acknowledged.

They stepped outside. It was snowing hard. "Let's head on over to Walker and check her out," said Garcia. "Check out the tatt shop while we're at it."

Bernadette hopped inside the truck. "What did Wharten have to say about Ashe?"

Garcia got behind the wheel and started up the Titan. "He was kind of weird about it."

"How so?"

"The whole witch subject, I think it makes him uncomfortable."

"He's mortified that he's got that sort of thing going on around here," said Bernadette.

"Maybe that's it."

From the hospital, they headed northeast, taking Minnesota 34 East toward Walker. In good weather, it would have been a fifteen-minute drive. In the snow, it would take a bit longer.

On a trail on the left side of the road, a gang of snowmobilers were tearing in the opposite direction as the truck. "That looks like fun," said Bernadette.

"I could use some fun," Garcia said tiredly.

She checked the dashboard clock. "I haven't slept for—"

"I know, I know. Me, too." .

"And we need to eat."

"We'll grab something in Walker, on the way to yoga class."

## CHAPTER TWELVE

Downtown Walker's backyard was a bay of Leech Lake, a massive body of water that had shores lined with resorts and lake homes. In the winter, a village of shacks—many of them complete with heaters, electricity, toilets, beds, and television sets—sprang up on the lake's frozen surface. Anglers drilled holes and fished through the ice with the comforts of home around them. Temporary streets were plowed around the houses, and the community was trafficked by snowmobiles, ATVs, and even full-size trucks.

"Third-largest lake entirely within the boundaries of Minnesota," said Garcia, ticking off Leech Lake facts as they made their way down the sidewalk, shoving burgers into their mouths. "More than a hundred thousand surface acres."

They tossed their wrappers in the trash. The sun had gone down, the snow was falling steadily, and the wind had picked up. The sidewalks were emptying of pedestrians.

"This town is going to roll up the pavement quick," said Garcia. "Tatts or tummies? Your pick."

"The fallen midwife is more urgent. Tatt shop is a long shot."

While they waited to cross the street, Bernadette studied the ads and flyers in a storefront window. Our Lady of the Pines Catholic Church gave early notice of its fish-fry dinners. *Every Friday night during Lent!* The annual polar plunge was coming up in February. A spaghetti supper was being held for a family that had suffered a house fire.

Bernadette suddenly felt nostalgic for rural life, and the sense of neighborliness that came with living in a small, tight community. At the same time, she had to be pragmatic. Were she working as a cop in Mayberry, its citizens would long ago have eviscerated her for being bizarre. Was that the witch's biggest sin—being odd? What about the midwife? She remembered what might have been the biggest criticism of the two women:

*She's not from Minnesota originally. She's from . . . I don't know . . . Vermont, I think.*

*She's not from around here, you know. She's from Los Angeles.*

Minnesotans. If you weren't born in the state, you weren't one of them. At least Bernadette had her birthright going for her.

Despite the weather, Sonia Graham's studio was full. About twenty women were packed into the long, narrow room. They were a variety of shapes and sizes, and wore everything from tights to sweats. Bernadette searched for an obviously pregnant belly but didn't see one. They were all sitting cross-legged on the floor and had their eyes closed.

Walking the length of the room was the instructor, a big-boned woman with a taut, muscled body that stopped just short of belonging on a female bodybuilder's circuit. She could have whipped Bernadette's butt without straining the seams of her spandex, and given Garcia a hard time in a bar fight.

"Breathe in through the nose and out through the mouth," she told the women as she marched toward the back of the room. Instrumental Christmas music was playing in the background. She turned on the heels of her sneakers and walked toward the front of the room. Noticing Garcia and Bernadette standing at the counter, she smiled and held up her hand while continuing to give instructions to the women. "Gradually deepen the breath. Elongate your spine. Elongate."

"I'll be with you folks in a minute," she said in a low voice when she reached the two agents. She spun around and returned to the back of the room.

The woman's long brown hair was tied back so tightly from her head, it pulled on her eyebrows, giving her a slightly crazed expression. A dark shadow colored her upper lip. Deep and raspy, her voice sounded like that of a man imitating a tough woman.

"She's my junior-high gym teacher," Bernadette whispered into Garcia's ear.

"Mine, too," Garcia whispered back. "And he was a prick."

Now the woman stood in the middle of the room with her hands on her hips. "Do our chant."

The entire room went, "Ooommm."

Someone giggled.

"Marie," the instructor said. "That didn't sound like our chant."

The entire room laughed.

She was back to Garcia and Bernadette. Scrutinizing Bernadette's jacketed midriff, she asked, "How can I help?"

Garcia started to answer. "We're with—"

"Child!" the woman spouted. "Of course. Congratulations!"

Bernadette gritted her teeth and said nothing.

Graham smiled at Garcia. "And this gentleman is . . . Dad?"

Before Garcia could answer, the woman turned back to her clients. "Keep chanting."

"Ooommm," hummed the room.

Behind the woman's back, Garcia gave Bernadette a sympathetic smile. "You can't possibly believe you're even remotely—"

"I hate this jacket," Bernadette hissed, unzipping the down. "It makes me look fat."

"I'm Sonia Graham," the woman said, extending her hand to Bernadette.

"Nice to meet you."

Graham trapped Bernadette's gloved fingers between her own massive mitts. "How about a cup of hot tea? It's a special herbal blend for expectant moms. No caffeine."

"I'm good." Bernadette examined the woman's hands. Definitely large enough. No jewelry or tattoos but a rubber band around the left wrist.

Graham went behind the front counter and slapped a clipboard and a handful of brochures on top of it. A pen in the shape of a candy cane was added to the pile. "I can sign you up for an informational appointment. How far along are you?"

Bernadette: "I'm not—"

"I can hook you up with some fantastic exercise wear that grows with you," said the woman, ducking down behind the counter and digging around. "Let me get you a catalog. Where did I put it? I can't remember anything, I swear. I have the worst memory."

"Stop her now, before I shoot her," Bernadette whispered to Garcia.

"I have exercise wear for kiddies, too. I offer postpartum classes for new moms and their babies . . . here it is. I knew I put it back here."

Garcia stepped up to the counter, leaned over it, and said in a low voice, "We need to talk privately, Ms. Graham."

Graham stood up with a catalog in her hand. She looked from Garcia to Bernadette and back to Garcia. "I apologize if I came on too—"

"We're with the FBI," said Bernadette, more than happy to shut the woman up with a flash of her identification badge.

The woman dropped the catalog on the counter. The gym teacher's voice suddenly became demure and soft. "My office is in back."

Graham sat behind her desk with her hands resting atop a copy of *Fit Pregnancy* magazine. This month's cover stories: "How to Select a Nursing Bra" and "Sex in the Third Trimester." Graham nervously snapped the rubber band around her wrist. "Can I get you something to drink? Coffee? A soda?"

"I'm good," said Bernadette.

"No thanks," said Garcia.

The agents sat on the opposite side of the desk on a set of webbed lawn chairs. The office was the size of a closet and felt as hot as an incubator. Its walls were tacked with posters of exercising women, many of them pregnant. Garcia's eyes darted this way and that as he frantically searched for a focal point that wouldn't get him into trouble. He settled on the paper decorations that were dangling from the ceiling. Stars, with five points.

Bernadette tried to start off with small talk. "Business looks like it's going good."

"It is," Graham said, and snapped the rubber band.

"Did you have an exercise studio in Vermont?" asked Garcia.

"No. This is new for me." She paused, snapped again, and asked, "Who told you I was from Vermont? Has someone been talking about me?"

Instead of answering, Bernadette slid Lydia Dunton's photo across the desk. "Have you seen this young lady around town recently?"

Graham looked down and quickly looked up again. "No."

"Take your time," said Garcia, his eyes finally surrendering to the object that was sitting on a corner of the woman's desk: a model of a uterus. The cutaway was resting on its side, and harbored a curled fetus.

Graham raised her hand to her throat. "The girl who was killed!"

"That's right," said Bernadette.

*Snap.* "Who suggested that I might know this girl? Why did you stop in here?"

Garcia took the uterus off Graham's desk and examined it as he spoke. "We're going up and down the street with the picture. Saw all the gals through the window. Thought we'd take a chance. Maybe this young lady came by."

"News said she was pregnant," Graham said evenly.

"Yes," Bernadette answered.

"Maybe you should try the hospital," Graham said.

"Mind if we showed her picture to the ladies out on the floor?" asked Garcia. He took the fetus out of the model and set the empty uterus back on the desk. "Won't take long."

"I really don't want my clients to think I'm in some sort of trouble with the law. It could hurt my business." Two snaps of the rubber band. "Please don't."

"Have you had problems in the past?" asked Bernadette, wanting to hear Graham's take on the story.

*Snap. Snap. Snap.* "I'm also a midwife. One of my patients had issues during a home delivery. Mother and child turned out fine, but it was . . . complicated."

"What happened, exactly?" asked Garcia, the fetus cupped in his hand.

"There was some excessive bleeding, that's all. Nothing my fault. They got to the hospital in plenty of time."

Bernadette: "We were told a different version of events."

"By Dr. Bossard, I'll bet," said Graham, her face reddening. "That's who you've been talking to."

"You aren't best friends, I take it," said Garcia.

"I offer an alternative to traditional hospital delivery. Many physicians are uncomfortable with that, including Eve. She's a brilliant, brilliant medical professional who has done a world of good in the area, but she has problems with . . ." The woman stopped herself.

Bernadette raised her brows. "Yes?"

Graham sat straighter in her chair. "Every year, midwives in this state attend thousands of births. Thousands. Did you even know that?"

Bernadette didn't like getting a lecture. "We're not here to—"

"We've got our own registry and professional groups. When people hear the word *midwife,* they think *home delivery.* In fact, ninety-nine percent of nurse-midwife deliveries actually take place in an institutional setting."

Bernadette wondered if the woman's latest delivery had taken place in the vicinity of Paul Bunyan State Forest. Graham looked muscular enough to overpower a small girl. "Where are most of *your* births?" Bernadette asked. "At the hospital? At home?"

Graham's fingers meshed together atop her desk and tightened. "Dr. Bossard has . . . derailed my practice for the time being."

As he tossed the fetus back and forth between his two hands like a flesh-colored baseball, Garcia lobbed the big question at her. "Where were you New Year's Eve?"

Graham's eyes widened. She unclasped her hands and locked them over the edge of her desk. "I had nothing to do with that! Why would you think I had something to do with that?"

"No one is accusing you of anything, ma'am," said Bernadette. "Please answer the question."

"I was here. I had an open house."

"What time?" Garcia asked.

"It ran all day. People floated in and out."

Garcia asked, "Any witches or Satanists on the invite list?"

"What?"

Garcia glanced up at the paper stars again. Some were hung upside down. "Oh, and those five-pointed . . . what are those called again, Agent Saint Clare?"

"Pentagrams," said Bernadette.

"Know anything about those?" asked Garcia.

Graham leaned forward and smiled. "I think Eve might be a better person to ask."

Bernadette and Garcia exchanged glances. Bernadette asked, "Is Dr. Bossard a—"

Graham stood up. "Unlike Eve, I'm not a Judas. You want to ask her about her extracurriculars, go right ahead. It's not my place."

"That isn't an answer," said Garcia.

Graham walked around the desk, went to the door, and opened it. "I'm not answering any more questions without an attorney. Please leave."

The two agents didn't move.

Graham's eyes went to the barren uterus on the corner of her desktop. "That's an expensive model. Where's the fetus? What did you do with it?"

Garcia set the fetus inside the model with its legs crossed. "Did I do that right?" he asked dryly.

"No," said Graham. "It's in complete breech."

"Mother and child could die, right?" asked Bernadette, as she plucked Lydia Dunton's photo off the desk.

They exited the office and Graham followed them to the front door, locking it after them. Bernadette thought back to her vision earlier in the day. It had been before lunch. She checked the hours painted on the glass door.

The studio was closed two mornings a week, including that morning. Bernadette pointed this out to Garcia.

"Interesting. But what about the bombshell she dropped about Bossard?" he asked.

"Bullshit, I'll bet. But we'll have to check it out."

"What about her own background?" asked Garcia. "Think she's really from Vermont?"

"She's not from here," said Bernadette. "She offered us a soda. No one from Minnesota says *soda*. We say *pop*."

"Let's have Cahill run the background on her, Bossard—" Garcia's cell rang. He took it out, flipped it open, checked the screen. Sighed and put the phone to his ear. "Assistant Special Agent in Charge Anthony Garcia . . . Yes, Senator."

While her boss spoke into the phone, Bernadette saw a group of women turn the lock and let themselves out of the studio. They'd changed into their street clothes and had their gym bags slung over their shoulders or in their hands. Graham was nowhere in sight. Bernadette pulled out Lydia's photo. Held it out to the first woman in the line of escapees and identified herself as an FBI agent. All six women formed a circle around Bernadette.

They passed the photo around, each taking her time studying it. The last woman handed it back to Bernadette. "Who is she?"

"Did any of you spot her around town? Recognize her at all?"

None of them had seen Lydia. Then a woman put a mitten to her mouth. "You're investigating that dead body in the woods. That girl is the dead body."

A plump older lady in a peacoat—she was able to fasten only the top button—asked, "Do you have any suspects? Have you arrested anybody?"

That let loose a string of other questions from the circle:

"Why'd they do it?"

"Did they rape her, too?"

"What was her name?"

"She wasn't from around here, was she?"

"Who're her parents?"

"What happened to the baby?"

"Pipe down," the peacoat said to her friends. Then to Bernadette: "Inquiring minds want to know what you were doing in Sonia's studio. Don't tell me you think she's got something to do with—"

"We were shopping the photo around, going up and down the street," Bernadette said quickly. While she had suspicions about Sonia Graham, she didn't want to torpedo the woman's business just yet. "Ms. Graham's establishment happened to be one of the few still operating during the bad weather."

"You do know that Sonia has a . . . history," said the peacoat.

"Eleanor," gasped a woman in a hunting jacket. "Don't."

"Why not?" the peacoat snapped.

"Ms. Graham told me she had complications during a home birth," said Bernadette. "She said there was some bleeding but that the mother and child made it to the hospital and everything worked out."

All the women nodded and the hunting jacket said, "That was my cousin's dippy wife. Bad deal, but it wasn't Sonia's fault. The dip thought a home birth would get her out of another C-section."

"See," said a skinny woman in a down jacket. "Sonia told the FBI people everything. Sonia's a good person."

"What about her *other* activities?" asked the peacoat.

Silence from the gang of women.

Then one said, "I have to go."

"Me, too," said another, hiking her bag over her shoulder.

"Wait," said Bernadette, holding up a hand to halt any exits. "This is a murder investigation."

"She's a lesbian," the peacoat blurted.

"God, Eleanor," said the hunting jacket. "You had to tear the top off that can of worms, didn't you?"

"Things should be out in the open, that's all," said the peacoat, trying to pull the garment tighter around her body as a wind rolled down the street.

"She came out to a few of us," said the peacoat. "Asked us to keep it quiet."

"Good job with that, Eleanor," sneered the down vest.

"But is she a Wiccan?" asked Bernadette.

Half of the women frowned with confusion.

"A witch," Bernadette said. "Is she a witch?"

"Oh, you mean like Jordan," said one.

"Right," said Bernadette. "Know of *any* witches around town, besides Jordan Ashe? Any Satanists?"

One shrugged. "Sonia can be a bitch, but I don't think she's a witch."

The down vest laughed.

The peacoat: "How can Sonia be a witch? She plays Christmas music. She throws a Christmas party every year."

"When does she throw it?"

"New Year's Eve," volunteered the hunting jacket.

"She was here all day New Year's Eve?"

"I helped make the punch with her in the morning," said the down vest.

"I was here in the afternoon and saw her," said the hunting jacket.

"Me, too," said another.

"Were any of you with her at the studio, and she disappeared for a while?" asked Bernadette.

The women looked at one another and shook their heads.

"What's this about?" asked the peacoat.

Garcia came up to Bernadette and put his hand on her arm. "Let's go."

Bernadette slipped the photo back inside her jacket and took out a handful of business cards. Passed them out. "Call me if something else comes to mind. You suddenly remember seeing this young lady somewhere. Whatever." Her eyes met the eyes of the peacoat lady. "Anything."

"I showed them Lydia's photo," Bernadette said as she and Garcia got into the truck.

"No luck?"

"No luck." Bernadette reached over and turned up the heat. She told Garcia that Graham was in the studio on New Year's Eve, at least for the most part, and that none of her clients believed she was a witch. She also revealed that Graham was a lesbian.

"Knock me over with a feather on that one," said Garcia. "Did you ask about the doc being a witch?"

"I didn't want to throw her name out there. I think Graham made it up to make trouble."

"Since this ain't seventeenth-century Salem, we can't lock up someone based on rumor and innuendo. That's about all we have right now. As much as the bosses in D.C. want to impress the senator with a quick arrest . . ." His voice trailed off.

She eyed the dashboard clock. It was nearly suppertime. "Shouldn't you and Dunton be getting together soon? Is that what that phone call was about?"

"Meeting switched to tomorrow. Said he's too pooped to meet today. Took too much effort to haul up here."

"That's a good excuse," said Bernadette.

"He apparently thought so."

They drove past the tatt shop. It was closed for the night. "So much for that idea," said Garcia. "Let's regroup at the cabin."

Bernadette opened the storage box between them and eyed the candy bars. The sight of them turned her stomach. "I need some real food," she said, slamming it shut.

# CHAPTER THIRTEEN

Garcia thawed some walleye fillets in the microwave, coated them with cracker crumbs, and started pan-frying them on the range. "Talk to me," he said, his lids drooping. "I'm falling asleep at the wheel."

Bernadette closed the fireplace doors, dusted off her hands, and launched into a to-do list. "Let's get some of the Minneapolis guys to check around at the other clinics. Cahill needs to start those background checks we talked about. Oh, then tomorrow morning you and I can—"

"Not the case," he said. "Anything but the case. Tell me about . . . tell me about your stint in New Orleans. What was that like?"

She dropped onto the couch and accommodated him, rambling on. "When I needed a quick lesson on anything weird—spells, rituals, chicken decapitations—all I had to do was walk up and down the streets of the French Quarter. Poke my head into a shop. They knew everything about voodoo dolls, potions, gris-gris bags."

"Gris-gris bags?"

"Sacks filled with roots and herbs, for good mojo. Attract a mate, get rid of an enemy, have a safe trip."

"I'll stick with my Saint Christopher medal." He adjusted the heat under the pan. "That's where you became the big expert on witchcraft and all that."

She put her feet up on the cushions. "I wouldn't call myself an expert."

"Tell me about this star stuff," he said, flipping the fish. "I get the pentagram. Pointing down, it's satanic. Pointing up . . ."

"Pointing up, it's a symbol for witches representing Mother Earth plus the four basic elements of wind, water, earth, and fire. Add a point and you've got a hexagram. Represents the interaction of God with humanity. With seven points, well, there're a ton of seven-based belief systems. The seven heads of the beast in the Book of Revelation. In Galician folklore, the seventh son born into a family will be a werewolf."

"Stars can mean a lot of things," he said, and popped a sampler into his mouth.

"Or nothing at all. Remember those two little girls supposedly kidnapped from their own beds? Letter found in the house said don't try looking for them. At the bottom of the note was a pentagram."

"That's right. Girls turned up dead in a swamp. Mom and Dad did it. They were abusers. Used the satanic junk as a smokescreen." He pointed the spatula at her. "You broke that case."

"Did such a bang-up job, they gave me beach time."

"Saw that suspension in your file. Something about backdating a memo to cover up the fact that you delayed starting the investigation. Didn't sound like you. I usually have to hold you back."

A small compliment from him. She hadn't had many of those this assignment. "It was bullshit. As soon as I was assigned to the case, I dug in—and my sight led us straight to the parents. When people started asking questions about how I'd figured it out, my ASAC cooked up a misconduct story to get rid of me." As she talked about it, she got mad all over again. "Even when I get the job done, I'm an embarrassment."

"Didn't mean to hit a nerve," said Garcia, taking the pan off the stove.

She wondered if she was an embarrassment to *him*.

He started dishing out the fish. "Want to eat in front of the fire? We could open a bottle of wine."

In light of their history, both of those options sounded too comfy. She got up and took a stool at the kitchen island. Had a sip of water. "This is good."

He stood across from her and ate at the counter.

While they were cleaning up, his phone rang. He wiped his hands on the thighs of his jeans and picked up. "Yeah . . . Hey, Forbes . . . Get anything good?"

Forbes was one of the ERT guys.

"That's what I figured," said Garcia, pacing the kitchen floor as he talked. "What about the storage room / morgue?"

Garcia sounded like he was going to be on for a while. There was something she wanted to check before they called it a night. She dropped down on the couch, opened her laptop, and started pecking.

There'd been a handful of fetus thefts over the years, the babies stolen by acquaintances or family members who wanted to pass the children off as their own. The cases had been quickly solved—all but one.

She went to the Division of Criminal Investigation, part of the Wisconsin Department of Justice. Its Special Assignments Bureau had a cold-case unit assisting local law-enforcement agencies in resolving unsolved Wisconsin homicides. She clicked on the link for Unsolved Homicides around Wisconsin. Half a dozen cases were listed under the heading UNSOLVED . . . SEEKING INFORMATION FROM THE PUBLIC. She couldn't find the case there, and then saw another link to Missing from Wisconsin.

That brought up several thumbnail photos of missing adults and kids, and one black-and-white sketch—of an unidentified dead woman. Black-and-white police sketches could appear so generic, she could be looking at a drawing of her own face and not realize it. Bernadette put the cursor over the thumbnail and brought up a large poster.

UNIDENTIFIED was the heading above the sketch. To the right of the drawing were the bare-bones details: Age. Sex. Race. Height. Weight. Location found. Date found.

Below that was a narrative:

A female estimated to be in her mid-twenties was found dead in Brule River State Forest in northwestern Wisconsin. A fetus had been cut from her womb. The infant's body has not been found. The victim was nude. Her ears were pierced, but she was wearing no jewelry. No identification or other personal items were found near the body. Anyone with information is asked to call Lt. Jerry Dupray of the Douglas County Sheriff's Department.

Garcia was still in the kitchen, talking and pacing and sounding frustrated. She picked up her cell and called Douglas County to see if she could put her hands on the file. The deputy on the other end of the line asked her to call back on Monday, when the records folks were around. She made a stink and the deputy transferred her to a sergeant. The sergeant transferred her to Dupray's desk, telling her to leave a message on the lieutenant's voice mail.

Dupray was still there, working late on some paperwork, and

picked up after two rings. He offered to buy her coffee on Saturday morning in Brule, a tiny town in the middle of Brule River State Forest. He lived around there and said he would be happy to bring the file home with him. The guy who'd originally worked the case had died and Dupray had inherited it.

Garcia closed his phone just as she was closing hers. "Nothing from the wedding tent. Too much from the storage room/morgue. Too many prints. Too much hair."

She was back to reading. "No surprise."

"Our Minneapolis crew is going to hit the other clinics around here, show the girl's photo around. I told Forbes to tell B.K. to get going on some background checks. Ashe and Graham to start. The two out-of-towners."

"Good, good," she mumbled as she scrolled down her screen.

"What're you looking up?"

"That thing in Wisconsin."

He closed the dishwasher and started it. "We can take a steam later. They've got a steam room down in the basement."

"I didn't bring a swimsuit," she said distractedly.

"Neither did I. We can figure something out."

*We* again. She couldn't hold it in any longer; she had to ask about his cold shoulder at the bureau bash. "You get all cozy here, but you ignored me at the party. What's the deal?"

"Don't want to talk about that stupid party."

"Why not?"

He leaned a hand against the counter. "You were loaded, that's why. You were loaded and I'm your boss, and it wouldn't have looked good if we'd been together or left together."

"I drank too much because you were ignoring me."

"Are we in junior high? Jesus!"

"On top of that, you've been an asshole to me when it comes

to work." She knew that was an exaggeration, but he'd gotten her wound up. "Questioning everything I come up with and—"

"What have you come up with, Cat? We're looking for a guy with two hands. No. Wait. Could be a big chick with two hands. He or she is someplace where it's snowing. Stop the fucking presses."

"Go to hell!"

"Watch your mouth, Agent!"

"Oh, now you're the big boss. You just invited me to get naked with you in the steam room!"

"I did not." His phone rang again, and he ignored it.

"Why did you want me to crash here instead of at a hotel with the others?" Another, more disturbing question occurred to her. "Do they know we're here together?"

"No," he said quickly. "They don't know. Everyone's at different hotels. Nobody's comparing notes."

"You hope." She took a calming breath. "Tony, I think I should drive to Wisconsin tonight."

"That other stolen-fetus case? It was years ago. No connection. A waste of time."

There he was, dismissing her ideas again. She grit her teeth and continued. "There are some similarities. Found in a state forest, like our girl."

He ran a hand through his hair. "If this is about—"

"It's about work," she said.

"All we've got is the truck."

He was reaching for arguments to this plan, and she wasn't going to let him stop her. She needed to get out of there. "I can handle the truck. Have one of the Minneapolis guys come by for you in the morning. Use his wheels."

His cell rang again, and he picked it up. "Garcia . . . No, Senator. This is fine . . ."

While he talked, she started to gather her things together.

"No apology necessary, sir . . . No offense taken. I can't begin to imagine what you and your wife are going through."

Dunton was sorry for taking Garcia's head off earlier. Good, she thought.

"As a matter of fact, I have an agent working on an angle right now. There's a case similar to your daughter's, and she's heading on over there." Garcia looked over at her and offered a weak smile. "Bernadette Saint Clare . . . Yes, sir. She's the best."

There was Garcia's apology to her.

## CHAPTER FOURTEEN

Bernadette caught a break: it stopped snowing.

She took Minnesota 200 to U.S. Highway 2 East. She gassed up after crossing the border into Wisconsin and got back on the highway. During the entire drive, she suppressed her worries about Garcia and thought about the northwestern Wisconsin murder. Radio stations along the way provided background music, mostly country-and-western dirges.

About the time Tim McGraw's "Don't Take the Girl" made her consider slitting her wrists, she pulled into Brule. It had one motel, one restaurant, two gas stations, two bars, two churches, and a white clapboard town hall. Bernadette checked the dashboard clock. It was a quarter past ten. She'd made the drive in exactly three hours and twenty minutes.

She turned in to the parking lot of the Brown Trout Inn, a motel with a strip of rooms that faced the highway. The only other vehicle was a rusty Chevy sedan parked in front of the office. She pulled in next to the beater and hopped out.

The door to the office was open and the lights were on.

Bernadette went inside. "Hello?" A door behind the counter was open to a front room. She heard machine-gun fire and the voice of Edward G. Robinson. An old gangster flick. She yelled louder. "Hello!"

A man wearing white chin stubble and black-framed eyeglasses shuffled out and leaned his arms on the counter. The night clerk was dressed in jeans and a thermal top, with the sleeves pushed up to his bony elbows. His wispy gray hair was matted on one side. He looked as if he'd been sleeping, and sounded like it, too. "What?" he croaked.

"A room."

He hacked a couple of times and popped a cherry cough drop into his mouth. "You've got the place to yourself."

"How about a room at the end?"

The clerk turned around and eyed the keys hanging on the wall behind him. "Which end?"

He reeked of menthol chest ointment, and her nose wrinkled. "Either."

He plucked Room 8 off its hook and slapped it on the counter. "Twenty-nine a night plus tax."

She picked up the key. "You need it now?"

Grinning, he revealed a gold top tooth. "Think I can trust you, little lady. Pay as you leave." He slid a guest register across the counter and she signed it.

She parked the truck in front of her room and went inside. It smelled musky and salty, like the bedroom in Ed's basement. The walls were aqua blue, and an acrylic-framed poster of a jumping trout hung above the headboard of each of the twin beds. Checking the bathroom, she was surprised to find the shower clean. So was the sink, and there was a night-light plugged into the outlet next to it.

She pulled down the pea-green spread of one of the beds; the sheets underneath looked and smelled questionable. Bernadette kicked off her boots but kept the rest of her clothes on. Her jacket and the rest of her gear went on the other bed.

Sitting cross-legged on the mattress, she picked up the television remote and pressed the power button. The set stayed dead, and she was too beat to walk across the room and turn it on manually. It had been thirty-six hours since Garcia called her at home about a dead girl and a missing fetus. Thirty-six hours since she'd slept.

Five minutes after she turned off the lights, she was asleep.

In the middle of the night, her eyes snapped open and she bolted upright in bed. Sitting motionless, she listened. Someone was jiggling the doorknob. Unless a motorist had pulled in even later than she, there were no other motel guests. The creepy clerk?

There was no peephole on the door, and the drapes of the windows on either side of the door were closed. She slid off the mattress, padded over to the other bed, and felt around until she found her Glock. Hunkering down low, Bernadette went over to the door and listened. The night-light provided just enough illumination. The knob moved again.

She'd put the security chain in place. Slowly, she raised her arm over her head, felt the chain, and gently slid it out of the slot. The instant she grabbed the knob, it stopped moving. The intruder had felt her hand on it. She stood up and threw the door open.

By the floodlights of a building across the street, she could see a figure running across the motel parking lot. She didn't want to lose him. Dressed in only socks, jeans, and a sweater, she took off after him. "Stop! FBI! Stop now!"

As he ran across the road, he glanced at her over his shoulder.

He had a ski mask pulled over his face. Given the distance and the darkness, she had a tough time judging his size, and had no clue whether he carried a weapon.

He darted behind a gas station that faced the highway.

"FBI!" she yelled. "Stop!"

Behind the station was a residential street lined with small houses. He ran alongside a rambler and she thought she saw him hook around to the home's backyard. She followed, her gun in her hand. With each bounding step in the snow, her stocking feet stung.

Pitch-black behind the home. Neither it nor any of its neighbors had outside lights. Squinting in the darkness, she tried to look for a shape or movement against the white of the snow. Her lungs burned from the freezing air, and her feet and hands were growing numb.

"Fuck!" she said in a cloudy puff of air. She pointed her gun into the darkness. "FBI! Come out now, hands over your head!"

Nothing.

She yelled a less professional warning: "Don't try anything, asshole! I've got a gun!"

The lights went on inside the rambler, and the back door opened. A rotund man with a jacket pulled over boxers and T-shirt came out on the back stoop, a shotgun in his meaty fists.

She lowered her Glock and raised her free hand. "FBI, sir."

The first thing he noticed was her lack of outerwear. "Where in the hell's your clothes?"

His question confused her. "What?"

"What're you doing in my yard?"

"Chasing a suspect."

"Bullshit!" He noticed the pistol in her hand and started raising the barrel.

"Don't! I'm an FBI agent!"

"My ass!" He pointed the gun at her.

Bernadette dropped to the snow, and a shot rang out over her head.

"Jerry Dupray from the sheriff's office!" Bernadette hollered from the ground. "I'm meeting him tomorrow!"

Another blast over her head. "Next one's gonna be for real!"

A woman in a bathrobe and hair rollers stuck her head outside. "Boyd! Put it down! We know Jerry!"

He lowered the barrel. "She's making it up!"

The woman yanked the gun out of his hands. "I'm sorry, miss. Kids broke in to the garage last fall."

Bernadette got to her feet. "Call nine-one-one! Send them to the Brown Trout!"

Those instructions seemed to impress the man. "Crap."

"Is Boyd in trouble?" asked the woman. "He really wouldn't have shot nobody."

Bernadette was freezing, and she wanted to return to her stuff. She'd left the door to her room wide open. "Call!" she yelled, and started running back to the motel.

As she dashed across the highway, she glanced over her shoulder. No one following her, neither an armed homeowner nor a guy in a ski mask.


When she got back to her room, she called the cops herself. Minutes later, a young male deputy came to her door and took notes while a female deputy roused the caretaker and questioned him. Patrol cars were out in the neighborhood, looking for the intruder. Deputies were also at the Zastrow residence.

"I don't want him arrested," said Bernadette.

"He shot at an FBI agent," said the deputy.

Bernadette was angry about being forced to drop, but she'd

been without a jacket or identification. It had to have looked suspicious. "Scare the crap out of him and let him off with a warning," she suggested. She was sitting on the edge of the bed, rubbing her bare feet to get the sensation back.

"We'll see what the bosses want to do." The deputy clicked his pen. "You think someone came after you specifically? Who knew you were in town?"

"Jerry's the only one," she said. "Meeting with him on a case tomorrow."

The deputy grinned. "Wasn't Jerry messing with you. I know that."

She grimaced as she asked, "Got a registered sex offender living around here?"

"Not for fifty miles."

"Good," she said.

"You think someone followed you here? Did you stop at a wayside rest and see some scumbag giving you the eye as you were leaving?" The deputy tipped his head toward the parking lot. "Maybe someone coming down the highway spotted the nice truck all by itself and, I don't know . . ."

"I don't know either," she said tiredly.

"How about we leave a man outside your door tonight?"

"That's not necessary," she said, and got up to see him out. "Thanks, though."

Bernadette contemplated getting a different hotel but figured at that hour she could have trouble finding something, and she was dead tired. She went to the office to have the clerk give her a different room. The guy still had the television blaring. "Anyone call for me tonight?" she asked.

"No calls," he said groggily.

While he took down another room key, she eyed the guest register. It was sitting open on the counter. Anyone could have sneaked into the unlocked office and figured out that she was there. She chastised herself for signing her real name, but she never would have guessed that she needed to be so clandestine in this tiny town.

He handed her a key. "You okay?"

"I'm okay."

"Good." He turned around and went back to his program.

While pacing the new room, she called Garcia. Even though she'd wakened him in the middle of the night, he was paying complete attention. "Are you all right?" he asked.

In an attempt to lighten things, she laughed and said, "My feet feel like ice cubes."

"I want that Zastrow character charged."

"No," she said. "Absolutely not. Please, Tony. Promise."

"Fine, fine." Back to talking about the intruder: "Ski mask. Sounds like he had a plan."

"Burglary plan? Robbery plan? Scare-the-agent plan?" She didn't want to verbalize a possible rape plan.

"You're obviously getting too close to something, and the killer figured eliminating the main agent in the case could slow us down."

She didn't like hearing that. "You think they would have gone all the way and killed me?"

"I do," he said.

She wished he had sugarcoated it a little. "Why didn't they go through with it?"

"I suppose the asshole thought he'd have an easy time busting into your room and taking you before you could put up a fight."

"When he realized I was awake and ready for him, he panicked and ran," she said.

"Think someone tailed you all the way from the cabin?"

"I would have noticed," she said. At the same time, she wasn't sure. Her head had been wrapped around the case. Didn't help that the big truck would make such an easy tail; it was probably visible from Mars. "Besides you and Dupray, who knew I was going to Brule?"

"Haven't mentioned Brule to anyone," he said. "Haven't mentioned Wisconsin to anyone."

She stopped pacing and peeked outside from behind the drapes. "If I wasn't followed and no one was told I was going to Brule, that means someone guessed I was coming here."

"Why would they guess that?"

She resumed her pacing. "They know the two cases are connected. Knew it'd be just a matter of time before we drew a line from one to the other."

"Why would they pick *tonight* to look for you in Brule? It'd have to be a lucky guess."

She looked outside again. Again saw only the lights of the commercial building across the street. "What if the killer lives in Brule? He kills a woman here years ago. No one catches him. Time passes. He goes over to Minnesota. Slices up another pregnant woman on New Year's Eve. Comes back home. Hopes no one figures it out. Then he hears we're on the case. Getting too close. Waits and readies himself."

"I don't know, Cat. A little far-fetched. I'd have an easier time believing someone followed you, be it from Walker or from the gas station down the street from the motel."

She sat down on the bed, mustard yellow instead of pea green. "You might be right."

"You sound absolutely shot," he said.

"So do you."

"You should have taken the deputies up on their offer."

"No one's coming back tonight," she said.

"Hey, about that fight we had earlier—"

"My fault, forget it," she said.

"Get some sleep, and check in regularly tomorrow," he said. "Don't take any chances. Please."

She had no intention of taking any chances. Bernadette slept with her gun by her side and a chair wedged under the doorknob. As wound up as she was, she managed to sleep deeply enough to dream.

*This time she isn't a participant in a dream; she's a watcher.*

*Bernadette was in a large, shadowy space, the only illumination coming from a massive stone fireplace. The oversized blaze lent a decidedly satanic quality to the pair occupying the room. Though the fire animated their faces with dancing light, Bernadette's nightmare didn't allow her to see their features. They could have been men or women or genderless demons.*

*The hellish picture was thrown off-kilter by the Charlie Brown Christmas. The top of the mantel was crowded with winter-themed Peanuts figurines and music boxes. A balsam fir weighted down by more Peanuts characters—heavy on Snoopy and Woodstock—sat against the wall to the right of the hearth. From somewhere in this strange hell came the voice of Burl Ives singing "A Holly Jolly Christmas."*

*One of the figures walked back and forth in front of the fireplace. The pacing had a practiced rhythm, like that of a zoo animal accustomed to getting exercise by going back and forth across the width of its cage. Again, Bernadette's dream allowed no details. She couldn't tell what the pacer was wearing. He or she was a dark blur. The moving figure was speaking, but Bernadette could make out only four words. They were repeated over and over with the rhythm of a drumbeat.*

*"Should've killed the bitch . . . Should've killed the bitch . . . Should've killed the bitch."*

*No name was mentioned, but Bernadette knew she was the bitch. She was the one who should have been killed.*

The pacer stopped moving, raised a hand, wiped his or her face with a rag, and dropped the cloth on the floor. Bernadette got a flash of an impression. The rag was black and had eyeholes in it. A ski mask.

The pacing resumed.

"Should've killed the bitch . . . Should've killed the bitch . . . Should've killed the bitch."

The other person in the room was seated on a couch parked between the pacer and the fire. He or she offered up a different chant.

"She's too close . . . She's too close . . . She's too close."

The two genderless voices merged into one:

"Should've killed the bitch . . . She's too close . . . Should've killed the bitch . . . She's too close . . ."

The voice trailed off, and was replaced by Burl Ives. "Rudolph the Red-Nosed Reindeer."

The blur on the couch raised an arm toward the fire. Wait. Not an arm. Something else. A tool of some sort. A chain saw?

The pacer followed the pointing tool, went over to a pile next to the hearth, and carried a log over to the fire. As it was set on the glowing embers, Bernadette got a good look at the wood. It wasn't a log; it was an arm.

The pacer turned around and went over to the figure on the couch. Extended both palms and tipped them. Coins rained down, landing at the seated figure's feet. The silver turned to blue and green and red and white. Poker chips.

Back to the fireplace. The pacer stared hard at the mantel, and the Peanuts characters came into focus for Bernadette. Charlie Brown carrying the sad tree bereft of needles. Schroeder seated at his piano with a sheet of Christmas music. Peppermint Patty armed with a peppermint stick. Long fingers plucked a music box out of the collection. Snoopy resting atop his doghouse, the roofline strung with tiny lights. When the hinged roof was opened, the tune "Christmas Time Is Here" tinkled delicately. The top of the doghouse was closed and the music box set back on the mantel.

*Suddenly a hand swept across the mantel.*

"No! No! No!" yelled the figure on the couch while statues and music boxes tumbled onto the wood floor, making a racket like shattering dishes. Amid the rubble, "Christmas Time Is Here" resumed its tinkle for a few seconds and then stopped.

Bernadette followed the destructive pacer as he or she left the living room and went into the kitchen. It had a fireplace, and a dog curled up on a rug in front of the hearth. The blur bent over the animal and scratched it on the head.

"Good boy . . . Good boy . . . Good boy."

The dog's tail thumped on the rug.

The figure went over to a basket set alongside the hearth. Did it contain more limb logs? The top was covered with a pink blanket. A blurry hand reached down and peeled back one corner of the cover.

"Good girl . . . Good girl . . . Good girl."

# CHAPTER FIFTEEN

Dupray woke her up the next morning with his phone call. "I got a jingle from one of the guys. What the hell happened last night? Who tried to break in?"

"Could have been random," she said, not really believing it but not wanting to dwell on it, either.

"Boyd Zastrow, I know him. Didn't think he'd ever haul off and—"

"Don't worry about it," she said quickly. "I was on his property and I must have looked like a nut. Didn't have boots or a jacket. Had a big gun in my hand. Middle of the night."

"You okay?"

"I'm okay," she said, though she felt groggy and a little confused after an evening of weird happenings followed by a night of weird dreams.

Instead of meeting her at the café in town, he gave her directions to his place. He lived just outside Brule.

"I make good coffee," he said.

•   •   •

It was terrible coffee.

They sat in his kitchen and sipped the watery stuff, with parts of the file spread out on the table in front of them. It was a small, square kitchen in a small, square house, and seemed a tight fit for such a big guy. Dupray was well over six feet tall and had an impressive gut. His ash-brown hair brushed the collar of his flannel shirt, and his bushy mustache needed a trim. Though he was about her age, he was already twice divorced and had three young sons from the two wives.

He'd just started with Douglas County when the body turned up in the woods, and as a young deputy hadn't had anything to do with the initial investigation. Now it was his, however, and he'd obviously been over the file many times.

She took notes and asked questions as she read. Campers had discovered the corpse. "Campers? In January?"

"Calling them campers was being generous," said Dupray. "I knew those slackers and they were looking for a place to drink and screw, pardon my French. Otherwise, that time of year and with no snow, those woods would have been deader than a doornail. She could have been out there until spring thaw. Was dumb fucking luck they found her."

She continued reading. "Says here the kids didn't hear or see anything."

"They'd just pulled into the campground when they found her." He took a sip of coffee. "Parked their party van and were taking a hike after lunch. My guess is the menu was Bud Light and reefer."

An autopsy determined that the woman had bled to death after sustaining an abdominal wound from a sharp object. It was believed she was knocked unconscious before she was sliced open. Because of the brutality of the attack, the baby was assumed injured or dead. The cut had been vertical, right through the navel. When she read that, Bernadette frowned. "My victim was sliced vertically through the navel, too."

He shrugged. "Not sure that means anything. How else would you do it if you were an amateur?"

She took a sip of coffee. "No chance the baby survived?"

"The hospitals were checked. No newborn was brought in. The thinking at the time was that without medical attention, well . . ."

"No sign of the baby's remains anywhere?"

"My feeling has always been that it was dumped in the woods, too, probably around the same time as the mother. The forest contains the entire forty-four miles of the Bois Brule River, eight miles of frontage on Lake Superior. Could have been disposed of in the water, though a search turned up zip. It's also quite likely some critters got it." He cleared his throat. "Being a father myself, I do my best to avoid thinking about that particular likelihood."

Crime-scene investigators found no fingerprints, and thought the perpetrator had worn gloves. With the lack of snow and the rock-hard ground, there were no shoe prints or tire marks. She didn't see anything that indicated they had a particular suspect in mind. "Jerry, was there anybody liked for the crime? A village sociopath? Someone who isn't mentioned in the official records?"

He nodded at the mess on the table. "It's all there. No suspects. No motive. No nothing. Nobody came out of the woodwork to claim the woman, either. She's resting in a cheap pine crate under a Jane Doe marker."

She fingered the handle of her coffee mug. "A sad way to be buried."

"Worse way to die. Who would do that to a woman and her little baby? Why?"

"We're asking those very same questions, Jerry."

"That star stuff, I don't know. Your deal sounds more like a cult thing. A different animal altogether."

He was right. The similarities between the two cases weren't all that compelling. The attempted break-in could have been truly random. She eyed the mess on the table to see if there was anything else of interest and held up a morgue photo of the woman. It wasn't very clear. There was an evidence bag, the only thing inside it a length of yarn with the ends knotted together. "What's this?"

"Found in the general vicinity of the body. Park trash."

She opened her mouth to ask if they'd run a DNA test and instead said, "Hate to trouble you, but I'd love another cup for the road."

"Let me make another pot." He got up and turned his back to fuss with the coffee.

"I'll pull this stuff together." She stood to gather the papers and quickly took the evidence bag and tucked it into her jacket pocket. She sat back down, squaring the pile of materials.

"There you go." He refilled her mug and returned to his chair, pouring himself another cup. As he set the pot down, he looked pointedly at her gloved hands.

"I'm always cold," she explained.

"My ex—uh, one of them—was the same way. Kept a heating pad on her feet all winter." He took a sip. "What else do you need?"

She turned her notebook to a clean page and slid it across the table. "Could you give me a layout of the woods, a rough sketch?"

"I can do one better." He got up and went to a kitchen drawer, rummaged around, and came back with a park map. He sat down next to her and pointed, explaining that the forest was a vertical swatch, thirty miles north to south, with U.S. Highway 2 slicing it in half. There were two campgrounds: the Boise Brule, just south of Highway 2, and the Copper Range, four miles north of the highway.

"The goofs who discovered the body were at the second campground, but they'd gone a ways into the woods before finding her," said Dupray, marking an X on the map. "In the fall, these trails

would be walked by hunters, but in January there'd be nobody. I figure whoever did it parked at the campground and carried the body
into the woods via one of those trails. Dumped her and hightailed
it out of there."

Bernadette shuffled through the papers. "How long did the ME
say she'd been out there?"

"Killed the day before she was found, and dumped shortly after
death. Could have been in the woods a full twenty-four hours."

"Would you have to know those woods well?"

"To dump her where she was dumped?" He shrugged. "It's a popular recreation area. The bastard who did her could have hunted
there. Snowmobilers would know the area. Campers. Real campers,
not the morons."

She thought about asking him to take her to the spot but decided she'd rather go it alone.

As he accompanied her to the door, she showed him the photo
of her victim. "Poor kid," he said. "Hope you get the fucker, pardon my French."

They shook hands. "Thanks for everything, Jerry."

"Keep me posted. Wish I could have been more help."

She slipped her hand inside her jacket pocket and felt the evidence bag. "Actually, you were a lot of help."

There'd be nothing to see after all these years. All she wanted to
do was get a feel for the place.

The main roads through the forest had been plowed. With the
snow, there'd be cross-country skiing, snowmobiling, and snow-
shoeing. She parked at one of the campsites and hopped out of the
truck. She took her Glock out of the holster tucked into her waist,
checked it, and put it back. Hiked into the woods. According to the
map, she was on Casey-Percival Creek, a fourteen-mile trail.

There was no wind or snowfall, and the sun was out. The temperature was in the teens below zero, but the sunshine made it

bearable. In the distance, she heard engines. Snowmobiles. She came to a clearing and looked down at the map. This appeared to be the location. She stood in the middle and did a complete turn, scoping it out. It was well hidden from any road.

She heard a rustling and put her hand inside her jacket, over her gun. Two deer stepped into the clearing, twenty yards from where she stood. They stared at her for a few seconds and disappeared into the trees.

"Paranoid," she said under her breath.

Still, as she returned to the truck she kept her hand over the gun.

Driving back to Brule, she remembered the Presbyterian Church in town. That's where she would try her sight.


The church—white clapboard with a single steeple topped by a simple cross—had services posted outside. Worship was at nine in the morning on Sundays, followed by fellowship. The front was locked, so she went around and tried a side door. Open.

She went inside the small church and took a seat in the back pew. With tall windows on each side of her, it wasn't as dark as she normally preferred. The quiet made up for it, however. Bernadette unzipped her jacket and peeled off her hat and gloves. Took out the bag and opened it. She closed her eyes tight. Breathing deeply, she took in the scents of the church. Old wood and lemon furniture polish. She opened her hand and tipped the bag. Wrapped her hand around the length of yarn.

"Lord," she whispered. "Help me see clearly."

Slowly, she opened her eyes. All she saw was the inside of the country church.

Bernadette returned the yarn to the bag, pulled her gloves back on, and got up. She'd never been inside a Presbyterian Church be-

fore and wasn't sure of protocol, but on her way out she genu-
flected and made the sign of the cross.

Burying her hands in her jacket pockets as she walked, she felt
the bag and told herself she'd give it one more chance later.

Jerry's wimpy brew wasn't going to get her through the day. She
spotted a pair of storefronts across the street and prayed that one
of them was a coffee shop.

One was a sporting-goods dealer, and the other was a secondhand store. That reminded her that Lydia must have been selling
her parents' things during her travels, and she made a mental note
to look for a similar shop in Walker. As she glanced inside the window of the store, something told her to check the place out.

She pushed open the door, and a set of Christmas bells hanging
from the knob announced her presence. A woman a decade or so
younger than Bernadette, with a tight Fender-guitar T-shirt stretched
over massive breasts, came out of the back room. She greeted her only
customer with a big smile. "Spending some of that Christmas money?"

"You betcha," said Bernadette.

The shop was the length and width of a bowling lane. Waist-
high glass cases ran along each side and at the end, where the pins
would have been, was a set of shelves containing musical instru-
ments: guitars, a saxophone, and a trumpet. There were also floor-
to-ceiling shelves behind the glass cases, and these were stuffed
with dusty trinkets: plates and figurines and shot glasses.

The woman went behind one of the counters and rested her
forearms and breasts atop the glass. "Let me know if I can take
something out for you."

Bernadette went up to a case containing necklaces, earrings,
and rings. The St. Paul police report about Lydia listed what the girl
had taken before running away, and none of the stuff in the case

was high-end enough to have come from Mrs. Dunton's jewelry box. It was all thin gold chains, fake pearls, zircon earrings. Fat vintage brooches with colorful stones.

One thing caught Bernadette's eye, however. She put her finger on the glass and pointed. "That, please."

The woman went over to Bernadette's end of the counter, reached into the case, and put her hand on a pearl ring. "This?"

"The one next to it."

"This?" the woman asked.

"Yeah."

The woman took it out and set it atop the glass. "I think it's more for a boy."

"It is." Bernadette had recognized it as a class ring, and immediately zeroed in on the name of the school.

"I can give you a deal on it," the woman said.

Picking it up, Bernadette examined the engraving inside the band. "I need to see the paperwork on this thing."

The big smile evaporated. "You a cop?"

Bernadette set down the ring and produced her ID wallet. "FBI."

"Sure. I got records." The woman went into the back room and came out a minute later with a sheet of paper.

Bernadette ripped the document out of the woman's hand and examined it. The name of the ring's seller was wrong, but she could have carried fake ID. "Do you remember what this girl looked like?"

The woman chewed her bottom lip. "Well . . . I . . . not really."

"This is a murder investigation."

That got the woman's attention. "Redhead. She was a redhead."

Bernadette slapped Lydia's photo atop the glass. "This her?"

"Yeah. That's the chick. What'd she do?" A pause. "Shit. Is she the one they found dead over in Paul Bunyan?"

"Did she say what she was doing in town?" asked Bernadette. "Think hard. This is important."

"I only bought it from her because I felt sorry for her. Who in the hell wants someone else's class ring? I'm such a sucker. I knew I should have—"

"What was she doing in town?" Bernadette repeated.

"I didn't ask, and she didn't tell."

"Where was she headed?"

"Don't know."

"Was she with someone?"

"Not that I saw."

"How'd she get here?"

"What do you mean?"

"Did she have someone driving her, or did she thumb it or . . ."

"I haven't a clue, Officer."

"Where was she staying while she was in town?"

The woman held out her palms and shook her head. "I'm sorry."

"Ma'am, you'd better be telling me the truth."

"I swear to God I am," said the woman, dropping down onto a stool behind the counter.

Bernadette fished out her cell and called Garcia. "Tony . . . You are not going to believe this. Lydia was in Brule in early December. Yeah . . . Sold a ring here, a boy's class ring." She picked up the ring and tipped it so she could read the name engraved inside the band. "David Strandelunder . . . That's gotta be the boyfriend, and maybe the MIA daddy."

Taking the ring and the paperwork with her, Bernadette left the shop. Garcia told her he'd track down Strandelunder so she could question the boy by the end of the day. Meantime, she shopped Lydia's photo around town, starting with her own motel.

"Never seen her before," said the clerk, still popping cherry lozenges in between coughs.

He stood on the opposite side of the counter while Bernadette flipped through the grimy registration book. There were few visitors in December, and none offered a name that resembled Lydia's real or fake one. Bernadette held the pawnshop papers next to the guest signatures from early in the month and found identical handwriting beside one name. She looked up at him and said through her teeth, "You don't remember her, huh?"

The guy shifted his feet nervously. "Well . . . we get a lot of people through here."

"This is a murder investigation," she told him for the third time.

He glanced down at the photo of the girl and back at Bernadette. Wiped his nose with a ball of tissue. "You know, maybe she does look a tad familiar."

Bernadette ran through the same questions that she'd posed to the woman at the secondhand store. Got the same answers.

She took the photo to the gas stations and sporting-goods dealer. None of the employees recognized the girl. A waitress at the restaurant remembered her but hadn't had any sort of conversation with her.

Bernadette checked her watch as she left the restaurant. It was already two in the afternoon, and it would be a three-hour drive or so to the Twin Cities. She'd established that Lydia had been in Brule. No one who saw the girl seemed to know why she was in the tiny town, but Bernadette had a theory. The boyfriend might be able to confirm it. Because what he told her could send her running elsewhere, she wanted to get to the kid before it got too late in the day.

As Bernadette drove, she checked in with Garcia. The first thing he asked was whether she'd had any more trouble, and she assured him that she hadn't. At the same time, she was keeping a close watch in her rearview mirror.

"You call even if you don't like the looks of the grandma in the station wagon behind you," he said.

"I will," she promised.

Noticing the time on the dashboard clock, she asked about his meeting with Dunton. It had been postponed—again. They discussed whether to tell the senator that his daughter had been spotted in Brule and decided to hold off until they could ascertain why she'd been in the town.

Garcia: "If she was chasing after that old murder case and that's what got her killed . . ."

"We have to know *why* she went after it," finished Bernadette. She wasn't ready to share her theory with him. She wanted to talk to the boyfriend first.

Garcia told her the agents checking the other women's clinics in the Walker area had come up with nothing. The ME hadn't yet gotten back with a report.

"Did B.K. come up with anything juicy on Ashe or Graham?"

"Nothing much." Both women were from the states they'd claimed. Graham's record was spotless. From her days in California, Ashe had two misdemeanors on her record—both for possession of less than an ounce of marijuana.

"That isn't exactly a shocker," said Bernadette.

They were refusing to talk any further, and Garcia asked how far Bernadette wanted to push the two women.

"Let me see what I come up with on this boyfriend," said Bernadette.

Garcia gave her some background on David Strandelunder. The kid was two years older than Lydia. He'd dropped out of school after finishing his junior year. Shortly after that, his mother had kicked him out of the house for doing drugs. He was living on his own and working at his uncle's foundry in St. Paul.

"Guess we know what the big attraction was," said Bernadette.

"Bad boys do get the girls," said Garcia.

# CHAPTER SIXTEEN

The bad boy's uncle was a tall, thin man with slate hair clipped close to his head. His stiff gray work pants and shirt matched, and nearly blended into his taut gray skin. His cheeks were sunken and deep lines formed a parenthesis around his thin-lipped mouth. The gray brows over his gray eyes were knit in what appeared to be a permanent expression of worry. The brows knitted even tighter when she flashed her identification.

"What'd he do? Rob a bank?" Russell Hague asked, sounding as if he were only half joking.

"He may have knowledge of a crime."

"What kind of crime?"

"Murder."

"Crap," he said, and stopped asking questions. He started leading her down the long, narrow hallway that would take them to the foundry. Along the way, Hague put on a pair of safety glasses and handed her a set. "These are for your baby blues. Uh, I mean . . ."

She slipped the specs over her eyes. "Thanks."

"Actually, your eyes are kind of neat," said the nervous Hague, struggling to make conversation. "I had a hunting dog with one blue eye and one brown. He could spot a tick on the back of a field mouse."

One side of her mouth turned up. "That's neat."

"Sure you don't want to wait for him in the office?"

Bernadette feared that Hague would let the nephew out the back door while she was waiting up front. "That's okay," she said pleasantly. "Never set foot in a foundry before. Kind of curious."

"We've got a partial crew on Saturdays, but it's still crazy busy." Hague opened the door to the shop. "Stay close. Don't want any accidents."

Steam and smoke. Men wearing silver suits and face shields pouring molten metal into buckets. A space-age version of Dante's Inferno. She'd had a college-lit professor who insisted that his students memorize the circles of hell, and she put this scene right around the sixth. The one with the heretics trapped in flaming tombs. "When you *do* have an accident, I imagine it's pretty horrific."

"Never had anything serious, thank the Lord. A foundry across the river had a bad one a few years back. There was a spill. Poor bastard melted like a candle." They stopped in the middle of the shop floor and Hague yelled to a trio of men standing together. "Hey, shithead!"

The middle man raised his face shield. "Yeah."

"Somebody wants to talk to you."

Bernadette started to interview Strandelunder in the foundry, but it was too hard to talk above the racket of the equipment. They walked back to the office.

The boy was tall and lean and gray-skinned like his uncle. He wore his long black hair tied into a ponytail and had a gold loop in his left ear. Though he was only eighteen, a five o'clock shadow darkened the hollows of his cheeks and colored his high cheekbones. He slouched in a metal folding chair while she sat behind the uncle's desk in the small, hot office. Hague stood off to the side, leaning his back against shelves filled with foundry books and binders. *OSHA Reference Manual. Welding Data. Filtering Info. Foundry Seminar. Government Specs. Mold-Pour Log.* While they talked, it became obvious to Bernadette that she'd misjudged the uncle. Hague was perfectly willing to throw his nephew to the federal wolves.

"Jesus H. Christ, Davy! You're as stupid as they come. Just answer the goddamn question."

"I'll say it again; I didn't do nothing," said Strandelunder.

The young man refused to acknowledge Lydia or her pregnancy, and showed no reaction when Bernadette told him how his girlfriend had died. His answer to every question was a denial.

Bernadette reached into her pocket and held out Strandelunder's class ring. "Recognize this?"

He sat up straighter but didn't say anything.

"Evidence," said Bernadette, examining the inside of the band.

Eyes locked on the ring, Strandelunder squirmed in his seat. "Evidence of what?"

"Know where we found this?" asked Bernadette, letting the boy's imagination run wild.

"Didn't kill her," said Strandelunder. "Didn't kill no baby."

The uncle looked at Bernadette. "He *has* been working here steady since the fall. Now, whether he took off over a weekend and drove up north—"

"Thanks a whole fucking lot, Uncle Russ!" The boy bent in half and dropped his face in his folded arms. Started crying.

"Davy!" barked Hague. "Be a man!"

"Lyd!" the boy sobbed.

Bernadette didn't believe the boy did it. "When did you see her last, David?"

"She came in here Thanksgiving week," volunteered the uncle.

He tipped his head toward his nephew. "She waltzed onto the floor while shithead was in the middle of a pour. Bawling her eyes out. Major scene."

"Did she have a fight with her parents?" Bernadette asked the figure hunched in the folding chair.

Strandelunder sat up and dragged a sleeve across his nose. "That mother of hers was an old bitch. She found out Lyd was pregnant, and she wanted her to go get an abortion. An abortion! Lyd told her to go fuck herself, and the old bitch threw her out."

Bernadette's mouth hardened. The Duntons had lied; they knew about the pregnancy. "What did Lydia do?"

"You know why that old bitch wanted to kill it?" Strandelunder poked a finger into his chest. "Because it was my baby! Mine! Old bitch hated my guts! I wasn't good enough!"

"David, what did Lydia do after they kicked her out?"

The boy wrapped his arms around his gut and started rocking. "My baby! Mine."

"David," said Bernadette. "What did Lydia do? Where did she go?"

He sniffed. "She came over to my place. I got a duplex with some guys. South Minneapolis."

"Scary pigsty," editorialized Hague.

"After the old bitch and her husband left for the weekend, Lyd broke in to . . . uh, got back into the house to get some . . . stuff," said Strandelunder. "Clothes and whatever."

"This is over Thanksgiving?" asked Bernadette.

"That weekend," the boy said. "Saturday."

"Keep going," said Bernadette.

"While Lyd was digging around, she found something."

Bernadette leaned forward. Now it was getting juicy. "What? What did she find?"

"Letters or something. She found them in the . . ." He cut himself off and looked down at his hands.

Bernadette: "I don't really care where Lydia was digging."

"She found them tied together in the safe."

"Did you read them?"

The boy shook his head. "Told her to mess with them later because we had to get the hell out of—" He stopped short again and looked from Bernadette to his uncle.

Strandelunder had just admitted to busting into the Dunton house with Lydia. "Keep going," said Bernadette.

Hague nodded, and Strandelunder continued. "She . . . we left, and while I was driving she was reading the stuff—the letters, or whatever they were. Lyd started freaking out in the car."

"What did she say?" asked Bernadette.

"She was, like, screaming, 'Oh, my God! Oh, my God! I can't believe this shit!' And I'm, like, 'What shit? What is it?' She wouldn't tell me. She kept saying, 'I can't believe it! I can't believe it! This is fucking unreal!' I tried to look, and she shoved the stuff in her backpack. She told me it was none of my damn business." He shook his head. "I'm her kid's father, and it's none of my damn business. How do you like that?"

"Then what happened?" asked Bernadette.

"We got back to the duplex and she's so freaked out, I'm afraid she's gonna pop the kid out then and there. She's walking back and forth and yelling, 'Those fuckers! Those fuckers! I can't believe it!' I told her to tell me, and she says it again. 'It's none of your damn business.' Nice, huh?" He looked from one of his listeners to the other. "Tell you the problem: That old bitch mother of hers was always working on Lyd, telling her I'm a loser. Telling her I'm too stupid. Lyd started to buy into that shit."

"Couldn't have been too hard of a sell," said Hague.

"Uncle Russ! Jesus! You're supposed to be on my side!" The boy put his hand to his forehead. "Nobody's on my side."

"I'm on your side," said Bernadette.

"Right," the boy said. "Fucking FBI's on my side. Have to be real stupid to swallow that one, lady."

"David, I know you didn't do it," said Bernadette.

His body relaxed a little. "You know?"

"I know," she said. "Now, what happened next?"

"I went to the liquor store."

The uncle: "Your pregnant woman is having conniptions and you left to go get a six-pack?"

"Can you think of a better time to make a beer run?"

The uncle: "Boy might be smarter than he looks."

"I got back and she was gone. No note, no nothing. Gone. Took her backpack and her share of the . . . her stuff that she got from the house."

"Share?" snapped the uncle. "Did you goddamn steal from the home of a United States senator, son?"

The boy looked over at him with a sneer. "I ain't your son."

"Did she call while she was on the road?" asked Bernadette.

"Twice," the boy said.

According to the St. Paul police files, the Duntons claimed their daughter had no cell. Was that another lie from the parents? "Did she have a phone on her?" asked Bernadette.

He shook his head. "Called from pay phones."

"When?"

"First time was, I don't know, a week or so after she left. She wanted to know if it was okay to sell my class ring. She wanted to wait on selling the other stuff because it would attract attention. I told her to go ahead and sell the ring. I never liked high school."

"Did she say where she was calling from?" asked Bernadette.

"Somewhere in Wisconsin. Rule? Something like that."

Close enough, Bernadette figured. "What else did she say?"

"She told me she tried talking to her mother, but the old bitch hung up on her."

They had indeed had contact with their daughter after she left home. More information left out by the Duntons, thought Bernadette. "So Lydia's mother didn't ask her to come back or ask her where—"

"Old bitch didn't do nothing but tell Lyd she was stupid for going to Wisconsin." He wiped his nose with his shirtsleeve. "Lyd said after talking to her mother she felt like a fugitive."

Bernadette wondered if the boy was getting his words mixed up. "You sure she said *fugitive*?"

"Something like that. Maybe it was *refugee*, like that Tom Petty song." Under his breath, he sang a few words. "Yeah. Could have been *refugee*."

This boy was not smart enough to carry out a murder, thought Bernadette. She was surprised that he could successfully execute a trip to the liquor store. "When did she call again?"

He looked up at the ceiling, thinking. "Four days before Christmas. We talked about that, how it was four days away."

"Where did she call from then?"

"She was back in Minnesota."

"Why did she call?"

He smiled. "To tell me the baby had just kicked her a good one."

"What else did she say?" asked Bernadette. "Did she say where she was or who she was with?"

"She said she was up north, looking for somebody."

"Who? Who was she looking for?"

"Don't you remember, lady? It's none of my motherfucking business."

"Davy," Hague said sternly.

"She didn't say, okay? She wouldn't tell me. All she said was she was looking for someone, and she felt like a fugitive. A refugee. Whatever."

"David, is there anything else she said? A name or—"

"Did somebody really cut her open and take my baby and kill it?" The boy's eyes started to well up. "Did that really happen, lady? Is my little baby dead?"

Bernadette hesitated. "Afraid it's true. I'm sorry."

"You know who did it?" he yelled through his tears. "That old bitch mother of hers, that's who! She didn't want that baby around! She did her own fucking abortion on Lyd!"

Another hour of questioning didn't get much more from David Strandelunder. Bernadette would have his cell records checked, but she believed him when he said Lydia had called only twice. Getting phone records out of the Duntons would be another matter. It would require some diplomacy. Up Garcia's alley, not hers. Why had they lied or omitted information? Embarrassment? Michelle Dunton's behavior wasn't going to earn her the Mother of the Year award.

Bernadette had the police pick up Strandelunder for burglarizing the Duntons. Until the case was cleared, she wanted someone sitting on him. She might have more questions for him later. Bernadette and Hague stood watching on the sidewalk while Strandelunder was loaded into a squad, his eyes red from bawling over his lost infant.

"Better call that loser sister of mine," said the uncle, heading back to the foundry.

Bernadette vowed to herself that she'd watch Strandelunder's case and help the kid out. He really did need someone on his side.

Before she pulled out of the foundry parking lot, she phoned Garcia to give him an update.

He wasn't ready to give credence to Strandelunder's version of events. "Has it occurred to you that the boy genius has a faulty memory, especially since he despises the Duntons? For all you know, Michelle Dunton begged Lydia to come back. Hell, maybe the girl never called home at all."

"What about the Duntons' phone records?"

"I'll work on it. This is . . . delicate."

"That's why *you're* doing it," she said.

Garcia did admit that he was intrigued by the mysterious documents Lydia found at her parents' home. "Boyfriend didn't sound sharp enough to make that up."

"Whatever she found, it had to have something to do with the earlier murder," said Bernadette.

"Maybe not. Maybe the papers just had to do with Brule."

"I don't follow."

Garcia theorized that the letters could have taken Lydia to Brule for reasons completely unrelated to the earlier murder. While she was in the small town, she got the attention of the Brule resident who'd killed the pregnant woman years ago. Very pregnant and all alone, she would have been tempting. He followed Lydia to Walker—perhaps even picked her up while she was thumbing it—and killed her and dumped her in Paul Bunyan. "He goes back to Brule. Sees you poking around there. Knows the FBI is on Lydia's case. Tries to scare you off."

"Why did Lydia go to Walker?"

"Why did she go to Brule?" he countered. "Answer is in those letters."

"What about my sight?"

"Nothing you saw clashes with my idea. There's snow in Brule.

Those hands on a pregnant woman could have been on a pregnant woman in Wisconsin instead of Minnesota."

"You're saying this is about a sick north-woods maniac who targets pregnant women and their fetuses, but he's only killed twice."

"Yeah."

"The pentagram?"

"He got religion between victims, or he knew there was witch stuff going on in Walker and used the star to throw us off. Take your pick."

Bernadette didn't like the randomness of Garcia's scenario. Plus, she had trouble admitting that they'd wasted days harassing a pagan and a former midwife, women whose only sin might be that they were outsiders. "I'll chew on it while I drive," she said.

"Coming back up here tonight?"

"I've got one more stop, and then I'll head north."

"Don't waste too much time before hitting the road," he warned. "Another blizzard is on the way. It's already starting here."

She glanced through the windshield. Flakes were starting to fall. "I'll leave soon," she said, and hung up.

It was already dark out. She checked the dashboard clock. Saturday services at most churches would be over.


At the outskirts of downtown St. Paul, she found a Catholic church and went inside. A handful of people were scattered around the pews, saying Rosaries and paging through prayer books. She took a seat in the back, took off her gloves, reached into her pocket, and took out the bag. She went down on her knees and said her own prayers before beginning.

# CHAPTER SEVENTEEN

As Jordan Ashe put her hand on the barn door, the dogs gathered around her, whining and wiggling. She'd kept them inside since morning, and now they wanted out. When Ashe slid the door open, they almost knocked her over in the stampede. Following them outside, she blinked in the snowfall as she watched them gallop into the early-evening darkness.

The weather was supposed to get much worse. Good time to let the puppies have one last run for the day. The acreage behind the barn was fenced, and they could only get so far. They'd head back home when they got hungry. If there were stragglers, Karl would fetch them as soon as he got back from plowing—whenever the hell that would be.

She'd thought about phoning him to tell him about the latest FBI call—that Garcia guy wanting to talk to her again—but decided she didn't want to distract him while he was working.

Reaching into her apron, she took out her pack of Camels. Two left. She fished one out, put it to her lips, and lit up. Inhaling like it was her last breath on the planet, she filled her lungs with smoke and held it. As she put the pack back in her apron, she felt something else. She withdrew the female agent's business card. The woman had done a good job of sucking up to her the other day. For a second in the kitchen, Ashe had considered telling Saint Clare about the others. Then she came to her senses. The woman was just another cop.

"Cunt," Ashe cursed, releasing a cloud of cigarette smoke. She snapped the lighter and held the flame under the card. The fire licked at her fingertips before she finally dropped the burning paper on the driveway. Putting her boot over the black rectangle, she pressed it into the snow. She went back inside the barn but left the door open a crack in case some of her puppies came back early.

She went over to her workbench and punched on the radio.

". . . *should expect blizzard conditions. Winds of up to forty-five miles per hour are expected, causing blowing snow and low visibility. By early Sunday morning, everything north of the Twin Cities will . . .*"

"Suck," said Ashe, shutting off the radio. She flipped through her CD folder, popped a weathered Melissa Etheridge disc into the clay-splattered player, and cranked the volume as high as it would go. Pulling out a stool, she sat down and rested her elbows on the bench, every once in a while tapping a gray snake into a lopsided ashtray. She sucked on her cigarette until the embers reached the filter, tossed the butt into the tray, and hopped off the stool. Rubbed her arms. For her comfort and that of the dogs, she'd had Karl install assorted space heaters and a wood-burning stove, but the massive old building remained cold and drafty.

Ashe pushed the sleeves of her shirt past her elbows and sat down at her wheel to throw one last pot. She hadn't lied to the FBI agents about having a show coming up. The wooden shelves lining the walls of the barn were bending under the weight of the work she'd already completed. Tourists bought the stuff, not collectors, but at least she was making a living.

That's why she'd relocated to the Midwest from California. It was easier to make a living. The downside: fitting in was tough. She'd found a group, but they were afraid to be themselves in public. Because they were natives of the area, they felt the burden of having to behave. If only their neighbors knew. If only the folks in the towns knew what was going on in the woods. Whenever she contemplated blowing the top off the secrets and lies, she talked herself out of it. Could be the FBI agents would do the job for her. She'd felt obligated to warn her friends with phone calls during the past couple of days. That accomplished, she could get her head back into her work.

Starting out with a slow spin, she worked the wedge of clay into a smooth ball. Ashe forced the material down with her right hand while her left worked as the guide. After moistening her hands and the clay, she jacked up the speed. She enjoyed the feel of the wet clay moving between her hands. Moving, moving, moving in a circle like Mother Earth. Spinning, spinning. The music in the background gave her rhythm and energy.

Behind her, the barn door slid open a few inches wider and a figure in a hooded parka stepped inside. Slowly and gently, the intruder shut the door all the way.

Lost in the music and the clay, Ashe had her eyes closed and her hands occupied. She never heard the vehicle pull down the driveway, the barn door move, or the booted feet come up behind her. By the time she felt gloved hands wrapping around her neck from behind, it was too late.

As the intruder started to pull the potter down from her stool, Ashe clung to the partially formed vase as if it were a lifeline. For an instant, the clay's seal against the wheel was enough to keep her from being unseated. Then the vase surrendered, tearing in two. The bottom stayed stuck to the wheel and the top remained in the artist's hands as she went sailing backward off her chair.

Ashe felt the wind leave her lungs as she landed on her back. She instinctively tightened her hold on the clay that remained between her hands. Cranking her arm back, she threw the lump at the figure standing over her. With one step to the side, the parka dodged the missile.

Ashe rolled over and scrambled to her feet. "Get away!" she panted.

Without saying a word, the parka thumped after her.

Ashe ran to her bench. Where was her phone? Where had she set it down? Unable to find the cell, she grabbed a large pot, raised it over her head, and spun around. Tossed it at the intruder. The pot landed behind the parka, shattering and scattering cerulean shards.

The parka continued marching toward her.

The dogs were at the door now. Ashe could hear them barking. Trying to get inside the barn. They knew. They knew something was wrong. If she could get to the door and let them in. Ashe hurled another pot, this one crashing at the intruder's feet and stalling the big boots. Ashe dashed past the parka and headed for the door. The dogs. The dogs would save her.

Her hand was on the door when she felt those gloves again, wrapped around her waist from behind. "No!" she screamed, and clawed at the door, sliding it open an inch. A dog's muzzle tried to push through. A second muzzle stacked on top of the first. Behind the pair, the other dogs snarled and scratched at the door.

The intruder swung her around like a rag doll, throwing Ashe against one of the barn's beams. Ashe grunted upon impact and crumpled against the wood. She curled into a ball at the base of the pillar. "Why?" she whispered to the floor, and covered her head with her arms.

Ashe heard her attacker's boots march over to the barn door. The slab of wood slammed shut, causing a cacophony of yelps.

The monster had hurt her puppies.

Furious, Ashe uncurled her body and used the barn's beam to help her climb to her feet. She hobbled toward the hooded figure. "You fucker!"

The parka came at her and fell on top of her like a tumbling brick wall, throwing Ashe onto her back. As the weight bore down on her, Ashe pushed against the wall with both palms. "No!"

The dogs barked and growled and hurled themselves against the other side of the barn door, the wood vibrating with their fury.

The leather-clad fingers tightened around the throat of their mistress. Tightened. Tightened.

Panting and perspiring from the exertion, the intruder stood up and pushed back the hood of the parka. Swiped a layer of sweat off the forehead. Ashe was sprawled on her back with her eyes wide open and bulging and red, like the exaggerated eyes of a comic-book character. Half a dozen times, the intruder prodded Ashe in the side with the toe of a large boot. With each poke came a snarled word.

"Witch . . . bitch . . . are . . . you . . . dead . . . bitch?"

The body rocked, but there was no sign of life. The killer's nostrils flared. The witch bitch had wet herself and crapped in her pants. She was definitely dead.

"Good." Then to the barking dogs on the other side of the door: "No!"

The gloved hands reached into the deep pockets of the parka and withdrew a length of clothesline, the end fashioned into a sloppy noose. The circle of rope was dropped over Ashe's head and tightened around her throat. The original plan had been to take the corpse into the woods and use a tree. Witches worshipped trees or the woods or some such shit, right? It would have been a fitting setting for suicide. That idea was scrapped as soon as the snow started, however. The storm would have made the going too difficult, and would have raised questions about the death. Who hangs themselves outside during a blizzard?

The barn had a massive beam that ran down the middle, from the back of the building to above the front door. Twenty feet off the ground or better, it would take some work to get the rope over it. After searching the barn for something with weight, the intruder spotted the clay that Ashe had so ineffectually hurled. Good deal. It even had the witch's prints all over it. The lump was squeezed around the free end of the clothesline and pressed into a neat ball. After several tosses—and losing the clay once—the ball carried the end of the rope over the beam.

The intruder plucked the clay ball off the rope. Gloved hands worked fist over fist, pulling on the rope and raising the body to a standing position. Now, how high off the floor would be credible? The eyes went to the stool sitting under the bench. *That high.*

The free end of the line was anchored to one of the legs of the bench and the stool was positioned under the body so that Ashe's feet were dangling a few inches over the seat. The parka stood back to admire the scene. Something crucial was missing.

The body was lowered back to the floor. The potter's workbench was surveyed. A cluster of jars, jugs, and bottles sat at one end, along with some brushes. The gloved hands reached for a container of something red and a small brush. The intruder opened the jar and squatted at the head of the body, brush poised. A master waiting to begin work on a virgin canvas. Slowly and carefully, an inverted star was painted on Ashe's forehead.

# CHAPTER EIGHTEEN

Bernadette's sight is acting screwy again, switching from a scene to that strange, fluid blackness.

Back to the scene. She sees hands drawing a pentagram. The face on the floor is too blurry for her to recognize, but she knows the mop of braids surrounding the victim's head. Those eyes, wide and unblinking. She's familiar with them, too. They're the eyes of the dead.

That blackness again. She doesn't have time to waste with that nonsense.

Forcing her hand open, Bernadette released the knotted yarn. As she blinked repeatedly to clear her eyes, she felt around her jacket for her cell. It seemed to take forever for her to see well enough to punch in Garcia's number.

He answered, but he was breaking up badly. Crackling and fading. "Cat . . . what . . ."

"Tony!" she yelled into the cell. Everyone in the church turned and looked at her. She didn't care. "Jordan Ashe is dead! Go to the Ashe place!"

Nothing on the other end now.

Using the plastic bag to shield her hand, she scooped up the yarn, shoved it inside her pocket, and bounded out of the church. As she ran across the church parking lot, she tried Garcia again. Couldn't get through. Couldn't get through to the other agents up there, either. They were together in a hole without reception.

"Fuck!" she yelled into the night air, and banged the side of the truck with her hand.

She thought of one other person she could try. Even though they had yet to meet, he knew her boss. He'd be easier to convince than an anonymous emergency dispatcher.

"Sheriff Wharten? This is Agent Bernadette Saint Clare . . ."

The parka stood straight to admire the artwork and issue a critique. "Nice."

The jar and brush were returned to the bench. The body was raised and tied off again. As a final touch, the stool was kicked over.

*Perfect.*

Noticing that the animals had stopped barking, the intruder looked toward the barn door. Were they gone? They must have found the treats dumped at the far end of the property. The dogs had been figured into the plan.

To neaten up the scene, pieces of busted pots were picked up and tossed into a trash can under the bench. The tipped stool in front of the pottery wheel was set upright. Every so often, an ear was tilted toward the barn door. Still quiet.

While cleaning up, the intruder eyed the pottery lining the shelves and found most of the items ugly and unworthy. Two pieces weren't bad, however: a pair of little men wearing pointed hats. They were lost amid the other, larger objects. One of the fellows was scooped up and dropped into a pocket of the parka.

One last survey of the place, like checking a motel room to make sure nothing had been left behind. Eyes landed on the cell phone hiding behind an ashtray on the bench. Nothing on the witch's cell would tell the cops what had happened here just now, or what had transpired elsewhere a couple of days earlier. Better to leave it alone.

The hood went back up over the head. A test, before the barn door was opened: "Here, boy! Come on, boy! Good dog!"

Silence.

The barn door was opened a crack. No animal snouts tried to bust through. A whistle was issued, followed by a clap of hands. No response, not even a distant bark. The treats had distracted them.

Ashe's killer slid the barn door open and went back into the snowstorm. The boyfriend would be working through the night. On his way in, Vizner would clear his own road and driveway, thereby plowing away any telling tire tracks.

Like the dogs, the weather had been figured into the plan, and it had held up its end of the operation beautifully.


When Karl Vizner tried Jordan's cell and didn't have any luck, he decided to take a break and head home. He always worried that those damn dogs of hers were going to haul off and eat her someday for supper. Even a witch couldn't charm the teeth off a hungry pit bull.

A private plow operator with a full-size truck and attached plow, Vizner made a good living clearing parking lots for businesses in the surrounding towns. He also picked up work doing plowing for cabin owners in the area. The big highway jobs were left up to the monster Minnesota Department of Transportation machines, however. As he drove along the state highway, he noticed that they'd managed to do a good job in the midst of the storm. Like him, however, they'd have to keep working it.

Once he turned down his own road, he lowered the blade and plowed his way home. When he got to the fork, he veered to the right and did the driveway in front of the barn. The dogs were milling by the doors. Jordan had to be in there, working on her pots. Then he went to the left and cleared the driveway leading to the garage. As he plowed, he noticed fresh tire tracks. Had the FBI stopped by the house because he'd refused to return their calls? He felt bad if she'd had to contend with them alone again. *Assholes.*

After he finished plowing, he hopped out of the truck and headed for the barn. A gust rolled down his back and he pulled up the collar of his work coat. He nudged the animals out of the way as he tried to get to the doors. "Make a hole, you monsters."

Vizner froze in the middle of the pack of dogs. Drops of red splattered the snow. A couple of the bitches had gashes running down their muzzles. Had Jordan left them outside for too long? Had they tangled with one another, some wild animal, or the fence? No. She took better care of the animals than she did of her old man. Something was wrong. Terribly, fucking wrong.

The two largest males were digging under the door and steaming up the air like a couple of engines. They'd scratched away all the snow and had gotten down to the frozen dirt. Though it was as hard as concrete, the pair had managed to dig a shallow trench in the soil. The other dogs were standing behind the excavators, whimpering and wiggling their asses, anxious as hell to get inside the barn. Vizner clamped a hand over the collar of the biggest digger and pulled the dog off the door. The dog sat in the snow and looked at him.

"Fuck!" said Vizner. The dog's snout was ground beef. "What the fuck is going on?"

Vizner put his hand on the door, took a deep breath, and slid it wide open. Barking and yelping, the dogs went around him to rush inside. He stood in the threshold with one hand on the edge of the door. His grip over the wood tightened, and for a second he wondered if he was going to puke or pass out or do both. He squared his shoulders, went inside, and closed the door after him.

On wobbly legs, he walked into the middle of the barn while pulling off his hat. "Jordan, no," he whispered up to the dangling figure. "No, no, no, no, no."

When he reached the tipped stool, he cranked his foot back and booted it. The stool was airborne for a few seconds, and then landed on the wood floor with a clatter. The closest dogs yelped and scattered.

Vizner ran to the anchored end of the rope and squatted next to the workbench leg. Gloves still on his fingers, he started to undo the knot. "Fuck!" He pulled off his gloves with his teeth, spit them out, and continued untying with his bare, trembling fingers. "Jesus, Mary, and Joseph. Help me. Forgive her. Please forgive her."

The smallest female was sniffing around Vizner as he struggled to undo the knot, tears welling in his eyes. The bitch licked his cheeks. "That's enough, girl," he said with a sniffle. "Sit. Go on. Sit." With a whine, she did as she was told.

One of the big males was standing beneath the body, barking and standing on his hind legs. The rest—the fucking four-legged mercenaries—were in back of the barn, preoccupied with digging into their food. They didn't give a shit about the one who had filled their bowls that morning. Every morning.

*"Come on, puppies. Here you go. Momma's got food."*

*"Chow wagon's here, you big mooches."*

*"Hey, fellas. Let the ladies have some."*

Gathering up his end of the rope, Vizner stood straight and pivoted around to face the suspended figure. Her back was to him. She could have been a scarecrow, those arms and legs so heavy and lifeless. Those braids in such disarray. Quickly, he let the rope run through his hands and lowered Jordan to the floor. With a soft thud, she landed in a heap and then flopped onto her back, tangled legs still under her. Her hair all over her face. A scarecrow cut down.

Vizner dropped the rope and ran to the body, kicking a dog out of the way as he went. He fell to his knees by her shoulders. He knew she was dead, but he went through the motions anyway. He loosened the noose and slipped it off her head. Put his fingers to her neck. Lifted her wrist and checked for a pulse. He dropped her hand and pushed aside the braids to look at her face.

Her forehead.

He reached out an index finger to touch it, but then pulled his hand away. He sat back on his heels and rubbed his eyes with his palms to make sure he wasn't delusional. Seeing things topsy-turvy because he was so freaked out.

He took down his hands, leaned over her, and checked her face again. There it was, an upside-down star. Painted in red. Jordan hadn't done this. She hadn't committed suicide. One weight was lifted off his heart, only to be replaced by another.

As he got to his feet, an icy draft rolled through the barn and wrapped itself around his body. Shuddering, his attention was drawn to the door. It was open a crack. Had he left it that way? Had the wind blown it open?

Boots thumping like a bouncing rubber ball, he ran to the door, slid it shut, and locked it. More thumping as he ran to the back of the barn and took an old double-barreled shotgun down from a shelf. He fumbled around the dusty boxes of shells until he came to the right one. He ripped off the top of the box and took out two shells, dropping them both on the floor. "Fuck me," he muttered, and took out two more.

He hadn't used or cleaned the old hinge-action shotgun in a long time. He had to work the release to get the action to open, revealing the empty chambers. As he fed a shell into each rusty chamber, he wished like hell he had more dependable firepower. The rifle was in the house, and he didn't want to make the run across the yard. He needed to stay and protect Jordan's body. That's what he told himself as he stuffed more shells into his jacket pocket.

He went over to the door and stood there with the gun. The two big males followed, one standing on each side of him. The pair didn't bark or whine or wag their tails. They just stood at the door, staring at the wood and breathing hard. Smart bastards. They knew something wicked could be going down and they wanted in on the mayhem. The others were busy eating and licking their crotches. A female was nosing around the body. Vizner would have to keep one eye on that situation. If the animal looked like it was going to start sampling Jordan, he'd put a hole in the dog. Any excuse and he'd put holes in all of them. Where had the pack of ungrateful fuckers been while Jordan was being killed? Were they too busy fighting with one another to fight for her? Why hadn't they saved the woman who'd saved them?

*My little witch.*

Vizner stifled a sob and put his ear to the barn door. All he heard on the other side was the wind whipping through the yard, yowling like a cat that was being kicked to death.

He looked back at the lifeless heap in the middle of the floor. "No!" he yelled at the sniffing dog. "Bad!" Reprimanded, the bitch retreated to the back of the barn to join the other chickenshits. Only the two large males stayed at the front. Soldiers flanking their leader.

"Good boys." With his free hand, Vizner reached into his coat pocket and withdrew his cell.


The sheriff was already pulling down the driveway. It had taken Bernadette a while, but she'd convinced him to check on Jordan Ashe. She told the sheriff she had a hunch.

She figured Garcia's buddy would believe a hunch before he believed her second sight.

# CHAPTER NINETEEN

While she was on the highway headed north, Bernadette's cell rang. It was Garcia calling. She picked up and asked, "Did you get the bastard?"

"Too late."

She pounded the steering wheel. "Fuck!"

"Seth said you sent him over there based on a bad feeling."

"My sight."

"I figured."

She steered around a slow-moving minivan. The weather and the traffic were both bad, but she was making good time. Flying in the monster truck. "So Wharten is the one who found her."

"Boyfriend found her, hanging from a beam in the barn. Lowered her to the floor. Called the sheriff just as Seth was pulling in. I'm on my way over there now."

"I tried calling you as soon as I saw."

"What did you see?"

"I saw the star being painted on Ashe's forehead." Before he could ask about identifying marks, she added, "The painter wore gloves."

"Obviously we can't tell them what you saw," said Garcia. "We'll be tap-dancing as it is trying to explain how you've got this great gut."

"I don't want that poor man thinking his girlfriend killed herself, but I don't want my sight outed, either."

Garcia assured her that she wouldn't have to reveal anything about her abilities. The inverted pentagram alone convinced Vizner that his girlfriend hadn't committed suicide: a Wiccan wouldn't have painted a satanic symbol on herself as one of her final acts. The sheriff agreed that it was a murder set up to look like a suicide. The ERT guys, already at the scene, concurred. The Ramsey County ME had agreed to do the autopsy and was sending a wagon up north. Again.

"Why was she killed, Tony? You think she knew something? Was someone afraid she was going to give up and spill it to us?"

"That's what I'm thinking."

"Did the boyfriend name any names for the sheriff? What'd he tell Wharten?"

"Seth found him awfully fucking reticent for a guy who'd just discovered the love of his life dangling from the end of a clothesline. Wharten doesn't believe Vizner did it, but he thinks the guy knows something. Afraid to open his mouth about it."

"Scared it will implicate him in something?"

"Scared period," said Garcia. "When they got to the place, he was holed up in the barn with the door locked and a shotgun in his hands."

"Thought he was a big guy," said Bernadette. "Plus, they have all those dogs. Why didn't the dogs protect Ashe?"

"Might have gotten preoccupied with some wild animal. Seth said they were all clawed up."

"Have a hard time believing those dogs just happened to come across a raccoon at the same time their owner was being attacked," said Bernadette. "Somebody baited them. Got them away from the barn."

"We could have B.K. check the perimeter of the property. That'd be a good job for him."

"Tony, something else."

"Yeah."

"When I used my sight this last time, I wasn't holding that scrap from Lydia's gown. I . . . borrowed something from the files of that old case."

"What are you saying?"

He was having trouble processing this. She was having difficulty herself. She spoke more slowly. "I found a hunk of yarn in the old file, in an evidence bag. I took it."

"Illegal, but keep going."

"When I held on to it, it took me to the eyes of Ashe's murderer."

"A piece of string from the Wisconsin murder case took you to Minnesota," he said.

"Right."

"So that seals it."

"Exactly," she said. "The two cases *are* connected."

"Doesn't rule out my two-note serial-killer theory," he said.

"Let's go over that goofy scenario. The maniac kills a pregnant woman and her fetus in Brule. Sees Lydia in Brule years later. Follows her to Walker and kills her. Goes back to Brule. Tries to scare me off when I get there. Goes back to Walker and kills Ashe."

"It's only a three-hour drive or so between the two towns. Plenty of time."

"Why kill Ashe?"

"My serial-killer guy could have found out she was a witch. She was famous around these parts. Killing Ashe was a red herring, like Lydia's pentagram."

"Your theory sucks," she said. "The randomness of it pisses me off."

"Come up with your own theory, then."

"We still need to know what was in those letters Lydia found. We still need to find her backpack."

"Then hurry and get your ass up here."

"I will," she said, and hung up to concentrate on her driving.


About three hours later, she reached the turnoff leading to Ashe's place. Wharten's deputies lifted the yellow tape and let the truck through. She bumped past the bureau's ERT van, a white monolith parked to one side of the narrow road. The back end was sticking out, forcing any vehicle going in either direction to swerve into a snowbank to get around the van.

The lights of the Nissan shined down the driveway leading to the barn, illuminating a plastic evidence bag being held up by one of the crime-scene guys. Whatever was inside the bag used to be covered in striped orange fur and wear a collar with tags. Another crime-scene guy came up with a second sack; the contents were similar.

The pit-bull bait, she thought.

As she hopped out of the truck and headed for the barn, Bernadette noticed Cahill standing on one side of the building, next to the woodpile. Another agent from Minneapolis was facing him, and they were both shaking their heads. Bernadette wondered if B.K. was the one who'd made the bloody find. She suddenly remembered that he liked cats—he owned two or three of them—and she felt bad for him. She clung to the possibility that the evidence bags contained the remains of some woodland creatures. Mutant raccoons with striped orange fur, collars, and nametags.

Garcia was standing outside the barn, talking to a tall, slender man with a thick mane of white hair and a white mustache. He wore a sheriff's jacket and heavy leather gloves, but he had pulled off one glove and his cap and was vigorously scratching his head with the tips of his bare fingers. *Hat hair.* In Minnesota in the winter, everybody had it. When she came up to them, they were taking a break from crime talk.

"So how's the fishing been up here?" asked Garcia.

"Crappies have been good on shiners, mostly late afternoon," said Wharten, still scratching his scalp. "Northerns have been hitting steady on sucker minnows."

"I gotta get out with you," said Garcia.

"Yeah, you do," said Wharten, pulling his hat and glove back on.

"I'll call you," Garcia said.

"Don't be making promises you can't keep, Antonia. Don't be breaking my heart." Wharten looked at Bernadette and winked. "He's always breaking my heart, this one."

"My agent, Bernadette Saint Clare," said Garcia.

Wharten shook Bernadette's hand. "Quite a hunch you had today. What precipitated it?"

At that instant, two ERT guys exited the barn, slamming the door loudly after them. They were talking and laughing. One of the pair spotted Garcia and nudged his partner. They stopped yapping. "Sir," one of them said to Garcia.

"Agent," Garcia responded stiffly. As the pair headed for the ERT van down the road, Garcia glared at them.

Bernadette smiled pleasantly at the sheriff. "Thanks for putting up with us, sir."

Wharten grinned, revealing straight teeth as white as his hair. "Are you kidding me? I'm happy as hell the bureau is taking the lead on this quagmire. I got plenty else to do that doesn't involve a politician's dead daughter, a dead witch, and a sack of dead cats."

"A sack?" Bernadette asked with a curled lip.

"Makes me sick," said Wharten. "Don't get me wrong. I'm a dog man all the way. But this was so barbaric."

"Do we know where the cats might have come from?" asked Bernadette.

"Was just telling Antonia here that hardly anybody up here puts collars and ID on their felines," said Wharten. "But these tabbies were special. They belonged to a particular elderly woman in town who treated them like . . . well . . . this is gonna put her straight in the grave. Deputies did rock, paper, scissors to see who had to go to her house and break the news."

"I wonder if she saw someone skulking around, waiting to take them," said Bernadette.

"As much as she doted on them, she did let them run around outside at all hours," said Wharten. "She had one of those pet doors on her back door."

"So anyone could have snatched them," said Garcia.

"Who found them?" asked Bernadette.

Wharten looked toward the woodpile. "Your guy. The young fella. Carson. He found a bloody shredded gunnysack tied to the back fence and the carcasses nearby. More of your crew is working on getting footprints. Didn't have a chance, the poor kitties. Fucking dogs must have had a field day ripping open the bag and having at them. A couple of the mutts did have scratches and bites, but for all I know they did it to each other in the frenzy. Entire breed should be eradicated, if you ask me."

Bernadette looked over the sheriff's shoulder toward the closed barn door. "Ashe liked the dogs enough to rescue them."

"They sure as shit didn't do anything to rescue *her,* now did they?" asked Wharten, following Bernadette's gaze to the barn. "Imagine that: a pack of these brutes between her and whoever killed her. Didn't do her a damn bit of good. All the murderer had to do was distract the four-legged morons with a sack of cats. It's a cliché, for Christ's sake. Pit bulls and a sack of cats."

A wary Bernadette ran her eyes around the yard. "Where are the four-legged morons right now?"

"They've been hauled away to a veterinarian. He'll tend to their wounds and keep them caged until we figure all this out." Wharten pointed a finger at Garcia. "Correction: until *you* figure this out, Antonia."

"And the boyfriend isn't talking?" asked Bernadette.

"Not yet," said Wharten. "He's in the house with a couple of my men. They had to pry his hands off the barn door, he was so afraid to move. I suppose he's thinking whoever did this to her is coming back for him."

"Why'd he come home in the first place?" asked Bernadette. "With all the plowing he had to do tonight—"

"He kept calling her and getting no answer," said Wharten.

"Did you know her at all?" Bernadette asked.

Wharten shrugged. "Him more than her. She was odd, even without the witch business."

"This star stuff—first on the dead girl and now on Ashe—what do you make of it?" asked Garcia.

"I think I could do without it," said Wharten. "I could do without some Satanist running around, trying to start trouble with our law-abiding witches."

Garcia and Bernadette looked at each other. Garcia said, "You used the plural, Seth."

"Yes, I did, Antonia. They sure teach you good at that fancy FBI training academy."

Bernadette's brows arched. "How many witches are we talking?"

"Loads," Wharten said.

This was a revelation. Not one or two. *Loads.* "Does the general population know?" she asked.

"Not if I can help it," said Wharten.

"Why?" asked Garcia.

"Persecution," said Wharten.

The pagan landscape was suddenly changing. "Do you think this is about Satanists versus Wiccans?" asked Bernadette.

"I don't know if it's Devil worshippers versus witches, witches versus witches, or a pack of foaming-at-the-mouth Lutherans trying to pin something on an outsider," said the sheriff, adjusting his brimmed hat so that it sat lower on his head. "What I do know is the murder rate in my county has shot up by about a billion percent since New Year's Eve and you need to do something about it. You need to solve this, and quickly."

"We're working on it," said Garcia.

"Did you know Dunton's people called me today? You think I need that?"

"I didn't know," said Garcia.

Each man's voice suddenly carried an edge that cut through the buddy-buddy fishing banter, and Bernadette instinctively took one step back. As the two men continued, the steam pouring out of their mouths made them appear even angrier.

Wharten thumbed over his shoulder toward the barn. "You've got an army of men and piles of equipment that most of us in law enforcement only dream about. Your budget for paper clips is fatter than my annual payroll."

Garcia's jaw tensed. "We're making progress. You've gotta give us a chance."

"You're sucking air." The sheriff pointed a fat gloved finger at Bernadette. "And what about her? I've been told she's one of your big deals. How about getting one of those hunches *before* my people are killed?"

"This is a federal investigation. We'll conduct it the way we see fit. How we utilize Agent Saint Clare or any of our other personnel is our call."

"Sheriff?" somebody called from the darkness.

"Pardon me," Wharten said stiffly, and left to talk to someone down the driveway.

Bernadette whistled. "Man."

"I don't blame him," said Garcia.

"I guess," she said.

"Loads of witches," said Garcia, opening the barn door. "How does that change things?"

"I'm not sure," said Bernadette.


The barn was thick with crime-scene guys dressed in identical dark blue hooded jackets and latex gloves. Emblazoned on the back of each jacket in huge yellow letters: FBI EVIDENCE RESPONSE TEAM. For the heck of it, she'd love to go up to one of them and ask, "Is there anyone here from the FBI Evidence Response Team?"

Garcia and Bernadette both stayed where they were, just inside the door. They didn't want to mess up the crime scene. One of the blue men was bent over the body. When he looked up and saw Garcia, he waved the boss over. "No, it's okay. You're good."

"Let's see what you got there, Tuckert," said Garcia, stuffing his leather drivers into one pocket and pulling his work gloves out of the other.

Also exchanging the leather for latex, Bernadette followed at Garcia's heels. A couple of the blue men stopped what they were doing to gawk at the newcomers. A tired-looking young guy with a camera lifted his right hand, and she returned the greeting. He'd been at the New Year's Eve party. In fact, he might have been the one distributing the Jell-O shooters. For every two he'd given out, he'd downed one. No wonder he still looked beat-up.

She and Garcia stood over the body while Tuckert, squatting next to it, pointed with a gloved finger. "See these here?" he asked, pointing to disk-shaped marks around the witch's neck. "These are *not* from a rope or some other device. This is manual strangulation."

"Takes a strong person," said Garcia.

"How long would it take to do something like that, to keep up the pressure and strangle a woman with your hands?" asked Bernadette.

Bobby Tuckert—a brown-haired, barrel-chested fellow from the South who was new to Minneapolis Division—looked up at her. His attention darted between her blue and brown. "Uh . . . I'm sorry . . . what was the question?" he asked in a slight drawl.

"Forget it," Garcia said impatiently.

Shifting her focus to the artwork on the dead woman's forehead, Bernadette said, "That doesn't look like blood."

Tuckert pointed across the room to a workbench, which was taped off. "She had a bunch of paints and brushes. We figure the star was painted with one of those."

The noose was on the floor next to the body, no doubt where Vizner had dropped it after freeing her neck. "So someone killed her first, then put the noose over her head and hoisted her up," said Garcia, walking over to where the other end of the rope was hanging from a beam.

Bernadette joined Garcia. The line was dangling at her eye level and swaying slightly from the wind seeping through the gaping cracks in the barn's walls. "What's this stuff at the end of it?"

"Clay, we think," said Tuckert. "We found a lump of it in the middle of the floor. We're figuring it was used to get the rope over the beam."

"Sounds feasible," said Garcia, walking back to the body.

"We're betting the lady's assailant wore gloves, sir. We found what look like glove prints in the clay."

"Good work," said Garcia, hunkering down next to the body, across from Tuckert.

Bernadette went over to the potter's wheel and saw the remains of something in the middle. Ashe was working on a project when she was interrupted. Hands clasped behind her back, Bernadette stepped over to the shelves filled with finished pieces. "Hope the victim got some licks in before she was killed."

"No blood or skin under her nails, but broken pottery in a trash can," said Tuckert. "That could be something, or maybe not."

Nodding, Bernadette continued touring the pottery display. "Barn door wasn't busted or anything?"

"No sign of a break-in," said Tuckert. "Dogs clawed up the outside of it, though."

"So maybe they did try to protect her," said Garcia.

"Cell phone?" Bernadette asked.

"Left on the workbench," said Tuckert. "B.K. . . . Agent Cahill should be able to get some good stuff off it."

"Tire tracks? Footprints?" Garcia asked.

"The boyfriend plowed the road to his house and the driveways before he found her, so that didn't help," said Tuckert. "Then there's the blizzard. That blowing and drifting didn't help much, either."

"Sheriff said some of our guys are checking out footprints by the back fence, near the dead cats," said Garcia.

"Again, the weather isn't helping." Tuckert released a barely audible sigh, a commentary on the climate of his new home and its lack of cooperation as he tried to do his work. "We're doing what we can, sir. It's been every bit as challenging as that crime scene in Blue Ox Park."

Garcia didn't bother correcting him on the name of the state forest.

While listening to the dismal report, Bernadette continued to survey Ashe's shelves. She spotted a wizard like the ones she'd seen in the house. What had Ashe said about them?

*"I've got those three and two out in the barn. My unholy quints."*

There was only one wizard on the dusty shelf, and a circle of clean wood next to it. That's where the second one had stood. Someone had pilfered it. The killer? In case it had been moved rather than taken, Bernadette quickly scanned the shelves again, from top to bottom. No. No second wizard.

Bernadette, turning to face Garcia and Tuckert: "Something was taken. One thing."

"What?" asked Garcia.

"Ashe made these small wizard statues, and the killer took one as a souvenir. Took it from the shelf here."

"Good," Garcia said. "If we find one of those little dudes on someone's buffet, we'll have our killer."

"Exactly." The blue men were staring at her. Their freak colleague had showed them up. *Tough.*

"Anything else?" Garcia asked hopefully.

Bernadette peeled off the latex and stuffed the gloves into her pocket. "Going to go outside and talk to Carson about his find along the back fence. See if the phone came up with anything juicy."

Garcia stood up. "I'm heading to the house to try the boyfriend. Join me when you finish with Cahill."

Bernadette started for the door, pulling her leather gloves tighter over her fingers. As she exited the barn, she felt the eyes of the blue men burning a hole in her back. It made her smile.

# CHAPTER TWENTY

B.K. had left his station next to the woodpile. Bernadette couldn't see any of the other agents, so she asked a deputy if he knew where Cahill had gone.

"Which one was he?" asked the youngster, who was the size and shape of an oak tree. They grew them big up north.

"He's the one who found the dead animals," she said.

"Cat Man Do. Sure."

She cringed at the nickname they'd given him. "Yeah. Carson Cahill. Where is he?"

"He went to your RV," the deputy said with a smirk. "How many folks does that thing sleep, by the way? Does it come standard with HDTV?"

"Hilarious," she said, and started down the driveway.

"My grandpa's shopping around for one to take down to Arizona," he yelled after her. "What kind of mileage does it get?"

Turning around, she hollered over her shoulder, "One on the highway and zero in the city." She heard him laugh, and she had to do the same.

The wind had died down and the snow had stopped, but the temp was dropping. Her boots squeaked as she walked on the snow.

She caught up with B.K. as he was getting out of the van. "Hey, Carson."

"Hey, Bern," he said, zipping his jacket to his neck.

As she stepped up to him, she could see that his face was knotted with tension. Was it the mangled cats or the crime scene in general? She decided to ask about something safe. "How'd you make out with the victim's phone? Come up with anything decent?"

"A lot," he said, leaning his butt against the side of the van. "She made a bunch of calls today. A bunch yesterday. Boom, boom, boom, one after another."

"Hmm. That's fascinating as hell. All local numbers?"

"Yup. All local. She was up to something. Trying to organize something or track someone down."

"Or warn people," she said.

"About what?"

"About us—or someone else—coming after them."

"Then the outgoing calls stopped and she missed a bunch of incoming, all from a Karl Vizner."

"Let's go for a hike," she said, nodding away from the commotion.

For several minutes, they walked without talking. The new snow made the road glow bright white. He broke the silence with a voice that sounded forced in its casualness. "Heard you ran into some trouble in Brule."

"Long story." She sensed that he didn't want to hear it, and that he in fact wanted to get back to the well-lit homestead.

Something rustled in the woods. "What was that?" he asked, his head snapping to look behind them.

"Maybe we should start walking back," she offered, thinking it was nothing more than a deer.

"No, I'm good," he said quickly, then added, "If you're good."

"I'm sorry you had to be the one to find the cats," she said.

"It'll be a long time before I forget that," he said, burying his hands in his jacket pockets. "There was blood and fur and guts all over the snow, like a horror movie. I won't be sleeping tonight."

"I've been there," she said, thinking back to her worse murder scenes.

"I suppose you think getting so worked up over dead animals is ridiculous," he said.

"Not at all," she said sympathetically.

"I imagine you've seen a lot worse, with all the years you've been in law enforcement."

"Now you're making me sound old."

A branch snapped and Cahill's arm shot out. "Bern," he whispered, clutching her forearm.

They both froze and she put her fingers to her lips to silence him. Something large was moving through the woods, not far from the road. Slowly, she unzipped her jacket and reached inside. Unsnapped her holster and drew her gun. Cahill did the same.

Bernadette crouched low, pulling him down with her. She peered into the trees on her side of the road, and he surveyed his side. They heard nothing for a minute or two, and slowly started to straighten up. Another crack caused them both to stop in a semi-crouched position. The noise was coming from the left, from her side of the road. Cahill looked over his shoulder, back toward the house. Bernadette shook her head. She didn't want to risk losing the culprit. She pointed to a gap between the trees and Cahill hesitated. Nodded. She stood up and slipped into the forest, and he followed.

Slowly, she wove between the trees and bushes on a path of sorts. A couple of feet wide, it cut a meandering swath through the

woods. Deer or humans could have made it. Maybe one had created it first and then the other took advantage. Regardless, it allowed her and B.K. to make their way in the darkness without
walking straight into a tree or tripping over a fallen branch.

Whatever they were tracking, it sounded as if it were making its
own path through the woods. They could hear it barreling ahead of
them, snapping twigs and rattling bushes. A frightened animal, or a
panic-stricken human?

Every minute or so, she glanced behind to make sure B.K. was
keeping up. Cahill was staying back about ten feet. His gun was no
longer in his hand. He'd put it back in either his holster or his jacket
pocket. She was glad; she didn't want to be the victim of friendly
fire. She kept her Glock in her fist.

The noise was fading; they were going to lose it. She picked up
the pace, going from a jog to a run. Behind her, she could hear
Cahill increasing his speed. She ran into the branches of a bush or a
tree and pushed the limb aside without snapping it. She stopped for
a second to hold it for B.K.

Winded, he came up beside her in a cloud of steam. "We should
call," he said in a hoarse whisper.

"Not yet," she whispered back, and continued running. She
wanted to make sure it wasn't just a deer.

He went after her. "Bern. Wait."

The path emptied out into a clearing. She stumbled into it a few
yards and stopped dead. Was she seeing this, or was the darkness
playing tricks? A chill deeper than the night's dropping tempera-
tures invaded her belly, and she instinctively tightened her grip on
the gun.

Panting, Cahill came up beside her. He rested his hand against a
tree while he caught his breath and took in the scene. "This looks
like some sort of—"

"Get out your light," she whispered.

He fished his Mag out of his jacket, clicked it on, and ran the light around the clearing. "Holy crap," he muttered.

"Yeah," she said.

Arranged around the perimeter were backless benches, the legs made of tree stumps and the seats made of rough-cut lumber. The benches were set in a perfect circle and resembled the sort of thing found at a group campground. The arrangement of rustic furniture had nothing to do with campfires and roasting marshmallows, however. In the center of the space was a table, the legs a little taller than those of a dining-room table and made of skinned logs. The top consisted of a thin slab of flat, irregularly shaped stone. It was decorated with a set of candles.

Cahill trained the beam on the table. "Some sort of altar."

"I'd say so." Bernadette took out her own flashlight. Walking the perimeter of the clearing, she held her Glock in one hand and shined the beam into the woods with the other. She saw no movement.

"Bern," said Cahill, swallowing hard. "Uh . . . there's something on top of the table, between the candles."

She spun around and shined the light on the altar. "Please let it be another cat," she said under her breath.

"What?" asked Cahill, staying at the perimeter.

"Sorry," she said, stepping slowly toward the center. "It's just that . . . well . . . that'd be better than some alternatives."

"I'm calling for backup," he said.

"Please do," she said, shining the light on the mound in the center of the slab. The object was covered with a towel or a small blanket, neatly arranged so that the edges of the cloth were straight and all four corners pointed out. At each tip was a large, partially melted pillar candle. The candles were positioned at the north, east, south, and west—the four cardinal points, important in pagan ceremonies.

Behind her, she heard Cahill talking, trying to give directions. His voice was tremulous. "I don't know how far in we are, but you should be able to see . . ."

Bernadette moved closer to the altar and stretched out her arms. With the barrel of her gun, she lifted one corner of the blanket, which was the size of a pillowcase. Her mind was filled with the horrific possibilities of what could fit under such a small drape. "Dear God," she whispered. "Let it be an animal. Please, please, please."

Cahill came up behind her. "What is it, Bern?"

She lifted the corner higher while shining the light underneath. "It doesn't look frozen. It must have been left here a few minutes ago."

"What is it?" He also trained his flashlight on the object, but maintained his distance.

"We interrupted something, I think."

"But what is it?" he rasped.

"I don't know . . . something . . . turned inside out."

"Jesus," he said, and took a step back.

She lowered her gun, letting the blanket drop onto the bloody mess. "I think it's some kind of animal. I hope it is."

"Is there fur?"

She didn't want to answer.

He squeaked his next question. "What else could it be? It's so small. Oh, God. Maybe it's a—"

"Stop." She didn't want Cahill to voice her biggest fear.

"But—"

"Shut up." Bernadette shivered. They were being observed. She could feel someone's eyes on the clearing. On her and Cahill. A rustling in the woods confirmed it. Spinning around, she aimed her gun and flashlight into the trees.

"What is it?" he whispered. That was becoming his mantra.

"Carson," she said evenly.

"Yeah?"

"Get out your weapon."

He pulled his gun from his jacket pocket. "Now what?"

"Stay here. Guard the . . . thing on the altar."

"Bern. No. Don't go."

"I'm not going far," she said, and slipped between two tall pines.

There was no path to make the hunt easy, but she wasn't afraid to use her flashlight this time. The element of surprise was gone; now it was a footrace. She pocketed her gun to free up her hands as she threaded through the forest. She came upon a fallen tree limb and jumped over it, stumbling as she landed but staying on her feet. Her breath clouded the air in front of her. "Stop!" she yelled into the woods. "FBI!"

The sound was getting louder. A bull barreling through the forest, stomping on bushes and snapping branches. This had to be a big, clumsy man, and she was closing in on him. Shining the flashlight ahead, she still couldn't see him through the pines and aspens. "Stop now!" she yelled. "FBI!"

As she pushed a low-hanging branch out of her way, another one slapped her across the face. She kicked her way through a thicket of wild berries, the bushes pulling and scratching at her clothing and slowing her down. Despite the subzero temperature, she was perspiring under her jacket.

She wove between a thick stand of aspens. As soon as she cleared the trees, she stepped onto the shore of a snow-covered oval. She ran the beam around her side of the pond, a body of water the size of a kids' hockey rink. She couldn't see any marks on the surface of the pond, which had to be frozen under the layer of snow. Aiming the light down, she walked the shoreline searching for footprints. All she saw were the tops of cattails poking up through the white blanket like whiskers. Scanning the surrounding woods for signs of the bull, she spotted no broken twigs or trampled bushes.

Bernadette finished her circuit where she'd started it. "Fuck!" she said under her breath. She'd lost him.

Turning away from the pond, she headed back into the aspens. She didn't know how long she'd been gone from B.K. He was probably hysterical, and sending everyone else into a panic. Diving into the woods without backup was exactly the kind of cowgirl crap that made Garcia's face turn purple.

Bernadette kept the flashlight trained ahead of her as she jogged through the woods, retracing her steps back to the outdoor worship space. Satanic campground. Whatever the hell it was called.

Behind her, someone emerged from between two trees and swung a branch with the force of a lumberjack chopping a tree. The limb caught Bernadette between the shoulder blades and she stumbled forward with a grunt. The toe of her boot caught under a fallen branch and she went flying face-first onto the ground. Her forehead hit a flat stone poking up through the snow.

The hooded figure raised the branch to take a second chop, this time aiming for the back of the head.

The sound of an approaching helicopter vibrated the night sky.

Branch still in hand, the assailant ducked down and vanished between the trees.

# CHAPTER TWENTY-ONE

Bernadette woke up flat on her back, with Garcia's face hovering over her and a blanket under her. There were others standing around on the narrow path, but she couldn't make out their features. Lights were shining in her eyes, and she put her hand in front of her face. "Tony—"

"Stay still." He was kneeling at her side. "I've got a stretcher coming."

"I don't need a damn stretcher," she said, and propped herself up on her elbows in an attempt to rise. Her head was throbbing.

"Take it easy." He put an arm around her to support her as she sat up. "Do you remember what happened?"

She had to think hard. It was foggy. "Someone hit me from behind. Nailed me in the back with a bat or something." She put her fingers to her forehead. "I must have landed on something hard."

"You're lucky he didn't finish the job and crack your skull open." Garcia looked up at the cluster of lights and people. "You heard her. Get moving. Tell the searchers we're looking for a weapon in addition to a suspect."

The sound of men mumbling and boots on the snow. The lights didn't leave her face, though, and she covered her eyes with her hand. She heard a helicopter overhead but doubted that her assailant could be found easily, especially at night. This was someone who knew the woods. Did the bastard get B.K., too? "Cahill?" she asked. "Is he okay?"

"He led us to you," said Garcia.

Cahill's voice from behind the lights: "I'm here, Bern . . ."

"I'm sorry I left you," she said. "I shouldn't have left you."

"You're right," Garcia said flatly, and then tightened his hold around her shoulders. "This wasn't a good deal for either one of you."

"We were on the road when we heard something in the woods," she said, leaning back against Garcia. "We . . . I . . . decided to check it out."

"Agent Cahill told us. Did you get a look at him?"

Again, her memory wasn't clear. "No . . . I'm pretty sure I didn't . . . I didn't see him. He sounded big, though. A big ox crashing around."

"What else?" asked Garcia.

She took her hand down from her eyes. The frozen oval. She remembered walking around it. "I tracked him to the pond over there and lost him. I was on my way back to B.K. when . . . I guess that's when the fucker got me."

"That's quite a find you and B.K. made," said Garcia.

"One of my deputies would have come across it eventually," said the sheriff from behind the lights. He sounded defensive.

Bernadette recalled the worship space. "I think the big ox led us there. He wanted us to find it, to find that mess on the altar. It was fresh."

"We saw," said Garcia.

She bit down on her bottom lip. "What was it? Do we know?"

"Baby pig, we think," said Garcia.

"Good. I was afraid it was . . ." Her voice trailed off.

"That mangled animal—what does it mean?" Cahill asked.

The bloody spectacle. Being left alone in the woods with it. Finding her unconscious. All of it had obviously shaken the young agent, and she felt terrible about putting B.K. through it. "I don't know what it means, Carson," she said gently. "People associate animal sacrifice with certain pagan religions."

"The witches didn't do it," said Wharten.

"The investigation will determine who is responsible, Seth," said Garcia.

Wharten stepped out from behind the lights and hunkered down next to Bernadette. He asked in a softened voice, "How are you feeling?"

"I'll live," she said.

As he squatted by her side, he folded his big hands in front of him. "I know all these people, and they wouldn't kill and gut a young girl. They wouldn't kill and hang one of their own. They wouldn't attack a member of law enforcement. They sure as hell wouldn't waste good livestock on animal sacrifice."

Growing up on a farm, she found that last comment reasonable. "Then what do you think is going on, Sheriff?"

"Someone is setting them up," Wharten said. "That's all I can figure."

"But the event that started this whole thing, the murder of a senator's daughter and her missing fetus, that can't just be about setting someone up," said Bernadette. "And what about the dead girl's amazing disappearing pentagram?"

"There's gotta be more to it," Garcia agreed.

By the sound of it, Garcia had abandoned his goofy serial-killer theory. Good riddance. He'd been interviewing Vizner while she and B.K. were having their big adventure. "The boyfriend, did he have a clue about any of that?"

"He wasn't any help," said Garcia. "Maybe tomorrow. He's still a wreck."

Bernadette looked at the sheriff. "You said Ashe was one of their own? By that, you meant—"

"One of the coven's own." Wharten stood up. "Difference between her and the rest of them was she was more flamboyant about it. Seemed to enjoy being the lightning rod for attention and criticism." He paused. "We can see what that got her."

"I wonder if that's who she was calling like crazy, right before she was killed," said Bernadette. "She was trying to warn them about something."

"About what?" asked Wharten.

"A killer coming after them," said Bernadette. "The FBI coming after them."

"They aren't afraid of the law," said Wharten. "They have nothing to hide."

Garcia looked up at him with raised brows. "Nothing to hide? Seth, you said yourself you were trying to keep their existence under wraps. If nothing else, they've been hiding their religious practices."

"What if those secretive ceremonies included not only the sacrifice of that baby animal but also the sacrifice of a human fetus?" asked Bernadette. "Having a pregnant runaway in their midst would have been hard to resist. Easy pickings. Who would miss her? They didn't know she was a senator's daughter."

"They wouldn't do those things," said the sheriff.

"Who put that ceremonial space in the woods, close to Ashe's house?" asked Bernadette. "It took a lot of hands, and it sure wasn't Lutheran hands."

"Then why would they also kill one of their own?" asked Wharten, this time not sounding so defensive. This time, sounding as if there might be a possibility.

Garcia: "Maybe she was so freaked out by our visit, making all those panicky calls . . ."

"They worried she was going to turn on them," said Wharten, finishing the thought. He rubbed his chin. "We have to see who Jordan called."

"Cahill has Ashe's cell," said Bernadette.

Cahill materialized at Wharten's elbow and flipped open the dead woman's phone.

Wharten stared at the cell for a moment and then sighed heavily. "I can tell you if they're all members of the coven."

Bernadette: "If that's who Ashe was calling right before she was killed . . ."

"We need a serious come-to-Jesus meeting," said Wharten.

With Garcia's assistance, Bernadette got on her feet. She was dizzy, but she didn't want to tell him that. "I want to be in on this get-together."

"Not tonight," said Garcia, putting an arm around her back. "I want you checked out."

She touched her forehead again. "They're going to tell me to ice it and take plenty of Tylenol or some such shit."

"You're going in," said Garcia.

"I'm not."

"They're already here," said Wharten, stepping to one side.

A pair of paramedics—a man and a woman—came through with a stretcher. The man ran his eyes around the half-dozen people on the path. "Where's the injured party?"

"I am not going in on my back," Bernadette said to Garcia.

Garcia addressed the medics. "Thanks, but I'll drive her in."

"You sure?" asked the woman. She tipped her head toward the homestead. "Rig is ready and waiting."

"I'm sorry for your trouble," said Bernadette. She peeled herself away from Garcia, walked around the paramedics and their gear, and started hobbling down the path.

Wharten looked after her. "She's a stubborn one, isn't she?"

"Yup," said Garcia. He turned to Cahill. "While we're at the hospital, sit down with the sheriff and go over those phone numbers."

"Yes, sir," said Cahill.

Garcia told Wharten, "Then, sometime tomorrow, we'll host an intervention."

Wharten grinned tightly and nodded. "Sounds good, Antonia."

"Thanks, Seth." Garcia turned to start down the path.

Wharten snagged him by the shoulder. "Tony . . ."

Garcia turned to face him. "Yeah?"

"About my going ballistic earlier . . ."

Garcia: "You can buy the bait."

"Then we're square?"

"We're square," Garcia said, and went after Bernadette.

Wharten slapped B.K. on the back. "Let's do this, young man."

"Yes, sir."

The two men went down the path, the sheriff taking the lead. He checked his watch. "My favorite greasy spoon's open all night. You can spring for a cup of java."

"Yes, sir."

# CHAPTER TWENTY-TWO

H ow long were you unconscious?"

"Did you vomit on the way to the hospital?"

"Are you nauseous or sleepy or dizzy?"

"What do you remember immediately before and after the impact?"

"Have you suffered any sort of head trauma before?"

After bombarding her with questions, Dr. Hessler shined a penlight into her eyes. "What are you checking for?" she asked.

"Pupils equal and reactive to light," he said. "PERL, we call it."

"The blue and brown throw you off?" she asked.

"Seen it before," he said distractedly. "Not that unusual."

If only he knew how bizarre her eyes really were, Bernadette mused. He clicked off the light and turned around to write something down on his chart. "Can I go now?" she asked his narrow back.

"Not yet," he muttered as he scribbled.

She had a headache, and her back was sore from taking the hit. Otherwise she felt more foolish than injured. "What else do you need to do?" she asked.

"I'd like to order a CT scan of your brain, just to be sure."

"How long is that going to take?"

"This time of night . . ." Rather than finish the sentence, he continued writing.

*This time of night* promised to be a long wait. She hopped off the examining table, stepped into her boots, grabbed her jacket, and went for the exit.

"Wait," Hessler said after her. "We're not through with you."

"Thank you," Bernadette said over her shoulder, and pushed through the doors into the waiting area.

Garcia was the only one sitting in the small, stuffy room. He closed a magazine and stood up. "What did they say?"

"I'm fine." She started to put on her jacket, and he quickly moved to help her with it. He was treating her like an invalid.

"What are you supposed to do about the forehead?"

She'd bolted before the doctor could give her instructions. She fabricated something, figuring it was medically accurate. "Ice it and take Tylenol for the pain."

Garcia zipped up his jacket. "Tylenol? I think all I've got back at the cabin is—"

"I'm sure whatever it is, it'll work," she said, zipping up.

Carrying a clipboard stacked with paperwork, Hessler came out of the emergency room. "We're not finished with her yet."

Garcia looked at Bernadette. "You told me they said—"

"I'm fine." She fished her gloves out of her jacket pockets and pulled them on.

"I'm sure you are," said Hessler. "But there are still some tests I would like to—"

"Doc," she said, putting a hand on his arm. "I'm good. I gotta hit the road."

Hessler: "A CT scan of your brain, and then you can leave with my blessing."

"If the doctor wants to check your brain, let him check your brain."

"We've been here forever." She yanked a stocking cap on over her head and winced.

"How serious is this, Doctor?" asked Garcia. "Shouldn't she be hospitalized overnight?"

Bernadette took a step back from both men and folded her arms in front of her. "That will never happen."

"There are something like a million cases of concussions in the United States annually. Some of those require hospitalization, but most people are treated in the ER or doctor's office." Hessler tucked the chart under his arm. "It all depends upon the seriousness of the injury."

"Where would you rank this one?" asked Garcia.

"How long a person remains unconscious can be an indicator of the severity of the concussion," said Hessler. "Unfortunately—"

"We don't know how long she was out," said Garcia.

"Sure we do," said Bernadette, talking quickly to derail any attempts to keep her at the hospital. "Agent Cahill told you I was gone from him for just a few minutes. Most of that time, I was chasing after the suspect. Ergo . . . well . . . you guys do the math. I was unconscious for less than a minute. A second or two. I was knocked out for a couple of seconds."

"You weren't out for long, but it was more than two seconds, Cat," said Garcia.

"But—"

"Ergo, put a lid on it."

"She was evasive when I asked about previous head injuries," said Hessler, treating Garcia like the father of an uncooperative pediatric patient. "Has she lost consciousness before? Any other recent incidents on or off the job?"

Garcia hesitated before answering. "In the fall, she got knocked into the river by a guy. I'd call that an incident."

Hessler looked at his patient with raised brows.

"Bad dinner date," she said.

Hessler went back to asking Garcia the questions. "He hit her on the head?"

"No, on the back. The suspect whacked her on the back with a board or a bat. Then she went into the water."

"Her head didn't strike anything on the way down?" Hessler asked Garcia.

"You can ask me—I'm standing right here," interjected Bernadette. "And no, my head didn't hit anything. It was a clean dive."

Hessler continued, still addressing Garcia. "The reason I ask is there's been evidence of an increased rate of brain injury and even death among those who have had previous concussions with loss of consciousness."

"What about repeated back injuries? Do you think I should take her in and have her back looked at when we get home?"

"I don't think it would hurt to have her family physician give her a thorough exam."

Surrendering to her exclusion from the discussion, Bernadette took Garcia's former seat in the waiting room.

"What should I expect tonight?"

"There may be some irritability."

"That'd be something new."

Bernadette glared at Garcia, but both men continued to ignore her.

"Some dizziness. A headache. Those are not unusual following an injury of this nature. If she demonstrates more serious symptoms, you need to bring her back in immediately. I'm talking persistent confusion, repeated vomiting, convulsions, slurred speech.

Weakness or decreased coordination. If her headache gets worse."

"I've heard of head-injury victims going to sleep and never waking up," Garcia said.

"It happens," said Hessler.

Bernadette didn't like the sound of that.

"So do I have to keep her up all night?" asked Garcia.

"She can go to bed tonight, but I want you to wake her up every two hours. You might want to stay in the room with her, to keep a close watch."

The right side of Bernadette's mouth turned up. This could be quite the evening.

"Tylenol for the pain," continued Hessler. "She absolutely needs to take it easy. No runs through the woods for a while. She'll be fine."

"That's what I've been saying." Bernadette stood up.

Garcia pumped the doctor's hand. "Appreciate it."

Hessler shook his head grimly. "The things going on around here. Murdered girl. That poor Ashe woman. Your agent getting attacked. Hope you catch the person or persons responsible."

"Don't worry," said Bernadette, pulling her gloves tighter over her fingers. "We will."

Hessler buried his hands in the pockets of his medical jacket. "So . . . any suspects?"

"Would you like to nominate someone?" Bernadette asked lightly.

"Can't be someone from around here," Hessler said.

"He knows the woods, this guy," said Bernadette. "It's gotta be someone from around here."

Hessler took the chart he'd been carrying under his arm and started flipping through it. "Talk is you came upon an interesting sight out in the forest this evening."

"What did you hear, exactly?" Bernadette asked.

The doctor kept his eyes on the chart, which seemed to be growing more engrossing by the second. "Uh . . . nothing . . . I just heard you found some . . . strange things. Some unusual . . . furniture."

"Furniture," she repeated. "A strangely benign word for a satanic altar topped by a blood sacrifice."

Hessler turned to the last page of his chart and said nothing in response.

"Any thoughts on who arranged such *furniture?*" Bernadette asked.

Hessler looked up from his paperwork. "Not my area of expertise, Miss Saint Clare. I imagine you and Mr. Garcia have your own ideas."

"Have to believe it was the local witches," said Bernadette. "Jordan Ashe's cohorts."

"Again, it's not my area," said Hessler. "But my understanding is that practitioners of the Wiccan faith don't kill things as part of their tradition."

"You think the furniture was put there by another group?" asked Bernadette. "A Scout troop?"

The doctor tucked the clipboard under his arm. "If you're clear on your after-care instructions—"

"I am," she said pleasantly.

"Then I really need to get back to work," said Hessler, turning on his heel.

"Thanks again," she said after him as he disappeared behind the ER doors.


Bernadette and Garcia saved their analysis for the stroll across the parking lot. It was bitterly cold, but there was no wind. Thinking the frigid night air might numb the pain in her head, she pulled off her stocking cap as they walked.

"Another defender of the local witches," said Garcia.

"I think he's more than that," said Bernadette. "I got some spooky vibes from him."

"Think he keeps some eye of newt in his medical bag?"

"That certainly wasn't politically correct," she said as they got to the Titan. "And yes, that's exactly what I think. I think he's one of the witches."

"Sven the witch," said Garcia, pulling open the driver's door. "Doesn't really roll off the tongue, does it?"

"Not exactly."

"Wait," said Garcia. "That means he's a . . . witch doctor."

"You had to say it, didn't you?" Bernadette laughed and then groaned. "Owie. My head."

They got inside the truck and Garcia started it up. "I did think it was telling the way he accepted your plural description of those folks. If my fishing buddy is to be believed, Jordan Ashe was the only Wiccan who let it all hang out. Everyone else is under wraps."

"If Hessler *is* one of them, he would have had access to Lydia's body," she said. "He could have been the one who removed the inverted pentagram."

"Why would he do that?"

"Public relations?"

"That would mean he put on a big performance for us in the basement, feigning surprise, pretending he didn't know shit about shit."

"A good act," she said.

"I don't know," Garcia said slowly. "His shock seemed genuine. I'm not sure he's the one."

"Plus, you'd think a medical professional—a doctor—would be

smarter than that," she conceded. "And he did take good care of me. I didn't pick up on any hostility or nervousness."

Garcia reached under the driver's seat, pulled out the ice scraper, and hopped out of the cab. While he cleared off the windows, she fooled with the heater and the vents. She felt guilty for not helping him outside, but her headache wasn't getting any better.

Garcia hopped back in and steered the truck out of the parking lot. "Let's go back to the cabin. I'll make you a late supper and then we can get some sleep—in two-hour doses. Come morning, we'll be able to think more clearly about Sven."

"I've got one thing left to do yet tonight on the case."

"What?"

"You know what," she said.

"You're not feeling well enough to do that," he said. "Save it for tomorrow."

"Bullshit."

"Cat . . ."

"Get some red meat in me and a beer and I'll be ready to rock."

# CHAPTER TWENTY-THREE

Garcia thawed some venison steaks and cooked them up for her. After she ate, they sat on the couch in front of the fireplace.

"Need anything else?"

"A beer or a glass of wine would be nice."

"Be right back." He returned a minute later.

She looked at what was in his hands. "That isn't what I ordered."

He passed her the pills and water. "You're going to follow the doctor's instructions."

"That guy is a twit," she said, downing the Tylenol. "A twit witch doctor."

Garcia set another log in the hearth. "He wasn't a dummy, and that witch part is open for debate. I'm not sure you're right about his involvement. Like Seth, he could simply be protective of the locals, be they Wiccan, Lutherans, or Methodists. And even if he is a witch—hell, even if everyone in the county is a witch—that still doesn't mean we've got our killer."

"We could settle it if I do my deal tonight."

•  •  •

He dropped onto the couch next to her. "Your head—"

"Is much better," she said, and patted her stomach. "And look how much food I put away."

"First sign of trouble, you pull out," he said.

"Agreed."

"Where do we do this?"

While she wanted it as dark as possible, she didn't want to go back to the stinky man-basement. She looked toward the loft. The light from the fireplace would still be visible from up there, but barely. "We can do it upstairs."

"All there is up there is a chair and a bed."

"That's fine." Bernadette also figured if she passed out, at least she'd be in bed already—not that she could tell Garcia that.

"Okay," he said hesitantly, and stood up. "I'll start turning off the lights."

She knew he was worried about temptation—on both their parts—but she wasn't going to let anything happen.


She sat on the bed with her shoes off and her back against the headboard, cushioned by pillows. Garcia pulled the chair—a rocker—over to the bedside. He looked uncomfortable in it, sitting on the edge so that it wouldn't teeter backward on him.

Every light—save the one on the nightstand next to the bed—was off. On her lap was the plastic bag containing the sliver from Lydia's nightgown. She'd picked the flannel scrap over the string because it was more substantial. There was no doubt in her mind that each would lead to the same set of eyes.

"Ready?" Garcia asked.

"Ready," she said.

He reached over and switched off the lamp. "Remember, if anything goes wrong—"

"I'll put on the brakes," she said.

She heard a loud creak: Garcia trying to keep his balance on the edge of the rocker.

"Sorry," he whispered, and creaked again.

She couldn't see his face in the darkness, but there was enough ambient lighting from the distant fire that she could make out his profile. He was bent over like a question mark on the rocker. "Tony, sit on the damn mattress."

He didn't say anything.

"Promise I can keep my hands off you. You're not George Clooney, for God's sake."

"That nurse said I looked like that other actor."

"I was never a *CHiPs* fan."

"You burst my little bubble." Another creak as he got up, and a squeak as he perched on the end of the mattress.

She rolled her head one way and then the other. Bent it forward and back. She noticed the skylight above the bed; it was filled with stars. She pointed at it. "Beautiful."

"Very," he said in a low voice.

Even in the dark, she could tell he was staring at her, and it rattled her. She closed her eyes tight.

"Cat," he whispered a minute later. "I don't think this is a good place for your deal."

She whispered back, "Just be still."

They both sat frozen and silent. The quiet was interrupted by a distant groan. The cabin settling. She concentrated on her breathing. In and out. In. Out. She opened her hand on her lap and tipped the bag over her palm. As light as a feather, the fabric floated down to her fingers. She curled her hand into a fist and whispered the words she always said: "Lord, help me see clearly."

She opened her eyes to the skylight. The stars fell away, replaced by . . . a charging buffalo.

The killer is sitting in front of the stuffed animal, its humped shape unmistakable. The murderer raises his eyes, and Bernadette is startled by what comes into view next. A massive trophy is mounted on the wall above the buffalo. It isn't a buck but some other large animal with an enormous rack. A moose, she figures. Another prize is standing to the right of the buffalo, and this creature she recognizes immediately: a bear standing on its hind legs, front paws raised menacingly. The room is dimly lit, and her vision is hampered by its usual blurriness. Nevertheless, she can make out the log walls behind the stuffed animals. This has to be a north-woods retreat.

A figure crosses in front of the killer's line of sight, going from left to right. Then right to left. Back again. Despite the quick movement, Bernadette is able to get a general impression of size and gender: short man. A bit of a gut, but not fat. The killer keeps his gaze low. If only the short guy would look up so Bernadette could see more of him. She tries to note as much as possible of the marching man. What is he wearing? She has a good view of his shoes. They're black and narrow and small. His legs are dressed in black, too. Trousers, or possibly jeans, topped by a dark sweater or a sweatshirt. Something long-sleeved. His hands are stuffed in the front pockets of his pants.

The man steps closer and extends his hands to the murderer, palms up. He's pleading a case. There's a gold band on the ring finger; that means the guy is . . .

Bernadette blinks, and suddenly she's in another room. How did that happen? The murderer couldn't have moved that quickly. Is she mistaken? Is this simply a different view of the same place? No. This is a kitchen. Even the lighting is different from that of the trophy room. It's bright. Bernadette realizes what happened, why the view changed so swiftly and thoroughly, and it makes her heart race.

Bernadette can see that killer number two is moving toward a wall of stainless steel. He—or she—pulls open the door and reaches inside, giving Bernadette a view of the right hand by the light of the refrigerator. Large, milky fingers wrap around a jar. The murderer slams the fridge door and takes the late-night snack over to a black box. A microwave oven. Sets the jar inside, slams the door. Bernadette gets a quick glimpse of the glowing numbers before the oven timer is set. This is real time!

The killer pops open the oven and takes out the jar. Carries it to a nearby table. Sets it down. Reaches toward the center of the table and pulls a laundry basket close. Must be doing some folding. Peels back the edges of a pink cloth.

A tiny hand reaches out.

Bernadette can't believe what she's seeing. She blinks twice, and suddenly she's back to the first room. Back staring at the damn dead animals.

The murderer gets up and starts walking across the room but is intercepted by the short guy. They stand close. Bernadette can't make out the short guy's face, but she can see that he's got a round, smooth head. Shaved?

The egghead's mouth is moving. He raises a hand with all five fingers extended. Does that mean something? The killer takes a step back and sits down again. Maybe the short guy was asking for five more minutes. Bernadette can see other people milling around behind the short guy, but she can't get a good look. If only he'd get the hell out of the . . .

Back in the kitchen, facing the fridge. Bernadette didn't even blink this time. What is up with this bouncing between scenes?

Killer number two looks away from the fridge. Seated at the table, holding that jar up and examining it. Bernadette can see that a nipple tops the bottle. He tips it down and . . .

Back in the trophy room. Everyone is gone. The killer stands and crosses the room. Goes to a set of patio doors to the right of the trophies. The drapes are open and the killer looks out. It's night out, but Bernadette can make out a snow-covered deck with rails. Beyond that, a flat white surface dotted with lights and little boxes. Fish houses on a frozen lake. Lights are moving between the shacks. Snowmobiles or all-terrain vehicles. Where? Up north? It has to be up here.

Back in the kitchen, seated at the table. There's something resting in the murderer's left arm. He or she adjusts the bundle. A hand reaches up. Pink, like the blanket. So tiny. That baby has to belong to . . .

Everything goes black.

Bernadette inhaled sharply and tightened her hold over the flannel fabric. "Come back to me!"

Garcia's voice in her ear: "What is it?"

"It's alive!"

"What's alive?"

"The baby," Bernadette panted. "Lydia's baby. It has to be hers."

"Where? What do you see?"

"Nothing now." She tossed the fabric down. "I fucking lost it."

"Cat . . ."

"Give me a minute," she said, and blinked to try to clear her eyes. "This is unbelievable," Garcia said.

She felt him get up from the bed. "There are two killers," she said to the darkness.

"What? How do you know?"

She closed her eyes tight and opened them slowly. "I switched from one set of eyes to another. Went from one room to another. Back and forth. Might have been in two different houses."

"Crap! Has that ever happened before?"

"I don't . . . I can't . . . I don't remember." She was distracted by his questions as she tried to get her regular sight back. Tipping her head up, she hoped the skylight and its stars would come into view.

"Is the baby in any danger?"

"Not that I can tell. The killer was feeding her . . . giving her a bottle."

"Her? You know it's a girl?"

"She was swaddled in pink."

"What else?" Garcia asked excitedly.

"A short guy with a shaved head was talking to the other killer. It was in a room filled with big-game trophies. It had a window looking out over a lake filled with ice shacks on it."

"Was it happening right now or—"

"Yes. I think so." She rubbed her eyes with the heels of her hands.

"Where? Somewhere close? Every lake in the state is covered with fish shacks. Was it up here?"

"Stop asking so many questions!" She could hear him stomping around her. Angry and frustrated, she didn't know if it was the killers' emotions rising up in her or her own. "Leave me alone for a minute!"

"What is it, Cat?"

"I can't see," she whispered, more to herself than to Garcia.

"I know," he said, putting a hand on her shoulder. "You just told me you lost the connection."

"No," she said hoarsely, and brushed his hand off her. "That's not what I mean."

"What're you saying?"

"I can't see anything with my regular eyesight. I'm completely blind."

# CHAPTER TWENTY-FOUR

Garcia brought new meaning to the phrase "freaked out."

"Son of a bitch!" he bellowed.

Before Bernadette could raise an argument, he scooped her up from the bed. Wrapping her arms around his neck, she hung on tight as he bounded down the stairs. The sensation of getting jostled around in complete darkness was terrifying and a little exciting. A carnival ride controlled by a drunken operator.

When they landed on the first floor, Garcia dropped her on the couch. She heard his truck keys jingling. "What do you think you're doing?" she asked.

"I'm warming up the Titan."

The possibility of being left alone like this infused her with terror. She struggled to keep her voice calm. "Where are you going?"

"We're going back to the hospital."

She could hear fabric rustling. He was putting on his coat. "We were just there a couple of hours ago."

"This has got to have something to do with your concussion.

They said if your symptoms got worse I was supposed to bring you back in."

"Sudden blindness was not on the list of things to watch for," she said. "I really don't think this has anything to do with it."

"Shaken infants go blind."

"I wasn't shaken, and I'm not an infant."

"Can't be a coincidence."

The prospect of revealing her unnatural abilities to a layman unhinged her more than losing her eyesight. "Tony. Think about it, when Hessler asks what I was doing right before this happened, what are we going to tell him?"

"So what if he knows? He's a medical doctor. Patient privacy. He has to keep it confidential."

"He won't. By morning, everyone will know. I'll be turned into a circus act."

"We don't have to tell him shit then," said Garcia. "We'll say you were getting ready for bed when everything went black."

She heard him pull the door open. "Tony. No. I am not going to spend another three hours in that damn—"

The door slammed.

Her heart was pounding, and she had to force herself to sit motionless on the couch. She needed to derail another trip to the ER. As shaken as she was by the loss of her regular sight, she didn't want to go back to the hospital and risk being exposed. Even if Garcia was correct in assuming that this had something to do with her head injury, she couldn't imagine there was anything Hessler could do about it at this hour. He worked at a small hospital in the middle of the woods. If her sight didn't return by dawn, she'd have Garcia drive her to a medical center in the Twin Cities. Besides, if Hessler did have something to do with the killings, he was the last person she wanted to trust with something as precious as her eyes. Keeping her blind could only help his cause.

She heard the door open and Garcia stomp his feet. He brought a cold draft inside with him, and she rubbed her arms. "Were you raised in a barn?" she asked, working to lighten her voice and defuse the situation.

"Love it when you talk farm talk to me," he said, and closed the door. He walked next to her. "I've got your coat. Stand up and I'll help you with it."

She shook her head and fastened her hands over the edge of the cushions. "I am not moving from this couch."

"I'll throw you over my shoulder and haul you out of here like a sack of potatoes."

"Oh yeah, big shot? I'd really like to see you . . ." She stopped herself, and laughed dryly.

"That isn't funny," he said.

"You're smiling, aren't you? I can hear it in your voice. You're cracking up."

"I am not," he said stiffly.

Bernadette felt the couch sag as he sat down beside her. Making like Helen Keller, she put her hands on his face and ran her fingertips over his mouth. "You are. You're ready to crack up, you sick bastard."

"You're tickling me." He put his fingers over hers and pulled her hands down. "You're trembling. You're scared."

"I'm cold." She yanked her hands away from him. "Now go shut off the truck and come back inside. Put another log on."

"Then what?"

"Then we have a glass of wine in front of the fire and relax."

"Your sight—"

"Is going to come back," she said. "I'm absolutely certain."

"How?"

"I have a plan," she said.

"Let's hear it. If it's not good, we're going with my plan. The sane plan."

"You're wasting gas."

She felt him get up from the couch, heard the door open and close. She fell back against the cushions and tried to quickly come up with some bullshit that would satisfy him. Only one thing came to mind, and she wasn't looking forward to it. Her head still ached, and she was exhausted. At the same time, she was curious in a clinical sort of way. Would it work, or would it screw her up even further? Would it cause something temporary to become something permanent? There was only one way to find out.

"Absolutely not," said Garcia. "That's how you lost your eyesight in the first place."

"Hear me out," she said.

"I'm listening," he said, and sat down next to her.

Garcia was fiddling with his keys. He wasn't going to roll over on this one. She talked fast. "The blackness I saw before when I used my vision, that must have been my sight struggling to get a lock on two sets of eyes. Well, it finally did it. It figured out how to go back and forth."

"So . . ."

"So . . ." She was making this up as she went along. "So I got a sort of whiplash from whipping back and forth between homicidal maniacs. I've . . . I don't know . . . disturbed something related to my special sight. Knocked something loose. Thrown something off balance."

"But your concussion . . ."

"Could have made me more vulnerable to damage. I'll give you that one."

"How in the hell is returning to the front lines going to fix it?"

She had to admit that the more she explained her plan, the less sense it made. Then again, her special sight didn't make sense, either. Instinct told her that this idea of hers could work. "Trust me on this."

"If it doesn't pan out, we're going back to the ER."

"When the sun comes up."

"Immediately."

She chewed her bottom lip. "I don't trust Hessler as far as I can throw him and his cauldron."

"I'll drive you to Minneapolis. University of Minnesota Medical Center."

If her scheme didn't work, she'd be ready to go back to the cities. The longer this lasted, the more anxious she became. "Agreed," she said.

"Where do you want to do it?"

She didn't want to move around the cabin, with him leading her. Demoralizing. "Right here would work," she said. "But you'll have to find that sliver of cloth. I think we dropped it on the floor in all the commotion."

He got up from the couch and returned a minute later. Sat down next to her. "Let me know when."

Holding up her right palm, she announced, "I'm ready."

"You're shivering." He started to get up. "I'm going to turn up the heat."

She reached for him and felt his shirt. Pulled him back down. "I lied," she said. "I *am* afraid."

"You sure you want to go through with this? We could hop in the truck right now and head south. Mayo Clinic. We could drive straight through. We'd be in Rochester before—"

"Give it," she said.

Garcia placed his hand under hers to steady her and dropped the fabric into her palm. Curling his fist over hers, he said, "Good luck."

Even though she was blind, she closed her eyes. She inhaled deeply and exhaled slowly. They both sat in silence, neither moving. A log tumbled in the hearth, and the sound seemed to fill the entire cabin. She opened her eyes.

"What do you see?" Garcia whispered.

"Nothing," she said, fighting the panic that was building inside.

"So this isn't working," he said, shifting his weight on the cushions.

She put her left hand on his thigh. "Give me some time. I'm distracted."

He put his hand over hers. "You feel like an icicle. I'm putting more wood on the fire."

As he opened the glass doors, she felt a rush of heat on her face. She wondered what it would be like never again to see the flames. Never again to see anything. Could she live that way? Maybe it was the price she paid for wielding supernatural tools. One sense exchanged for another. If only the choice had been laid out to her at the onset, she would never have opted to keep this gift. A mundane life with normal eyesight and no psychic upgrades, that would have been her first pick.

As if cuing in on that thought, she was suddenly back again, in the kitchen.

Then back in the trophy room.

Back to the kitchen.

Trophy room.

Kitchen.

"Stop!" she yelled, and closed her eyes. Unfurled her fist. Tipped the fabric onto her lap.

Garcia: "Cat?"

Slowly, she opened her eyes and saw that he was standing in front of her. She looked up at him. "Tony."

"Can you see me?"

She blinked twice and rose to her feet. "I can see you."

"Is stuff out of focus or blurry or—"

"It's good. Like before." She took a step forward and started to sway. "I'm just a little woozy."

He wrapped his arms around her shoulders. "Take it easy."

"I'm just worried that—"

"What?"

"I think my sight, my special sight . . . I was jerking back and forth between the two killers' eyes . . . It's not supposed to work that way. I think it's permanently screwed up."

"If it is, we'll manage."

"But what good would I be to you?"

He rubbed her back. "You're an excellent agent, with or without it."

"The only reason the bureau keeps me around is because I can do things the others can't. If I've lost it, they're going to send me packing."

"Not if I have anything to say about it."

"You'd put yourself at risk, and I can't let you do that." She started to pull away from him, and he tightened his hold. "What're you doing?"

"Read my mind."

"Funny."

He bent down and kissed her along the side of the neck. "This was a long time coming, Cat."

"We can't do this," she said, and in the same instant found herself leaning into him.

"Didn't this scare teach you?" he growled into her neck. "Life's too fucking short."

"What about our jobs? This case? The work?"

"It'll all be there in the morning," he said.

•  •  •

They returned to the bed in the loft.

It was too bright, so she threw her panties over the shade. She was glad she'd worn something lacy instead of her usual Jockey briefs.

He'd been working out with weights for years, and had the big arms and rippled abdominal muscles to show for it. He wasn't excessively pumped but, rather, looked like someone who'd been working on a farm all his life. It was a look that aroused her and made her nostalgic; she wanted the night to last.

He went down on top of her, and his mouth went to her breasts. She buried her hands in the top of his dark head. He smelled clean and fresh. Someone who'd been outside all day. She opened her legs to him, but he held back. He lifted his mouth off her breasts and breathed into her ear: "Let me know if I'm too rough. It's been so long."

"For me, too." Running her hands over his back, she enjoyed how hard and smooth he was under her palms. She gently grazed the back of his neck with her nails.

"Feels good," he said.

She ran her fingers down the length of his body, dragging her nails from his shoulder blades down to his lower back. Raking his buttocks, she whispered, "What about that?"

"Yeah," he moaned, and returned his mouth to her breasts.

She cupped the back of his head with her hand and arched her back. "Tony."

He pulled his mouth off her and grabbed her breasts, bunching them in his hands and kneading them. The entire time, he kept his attention focused on her face. "Am I hurting you?"

"It's good," she said, looking up at him with narrow eyes.

He lowered his lips to hers and kissed her. His tongue darted into her mouth. As he withdrew it, she scraped his tongue with her teeth. "You are so beautiful," he said.

As he increased the force of his thrusts, she locked her arms and legs around him. "I'm going to come."

"Not yet," he said, and raised his body off hers.

"No," she said.

"I'm not done." Ducking his head down, he disappeared under the covers.

She felt him kissing the inside of her thighs. He came up from under the covers and entered her again. They climaxed together, and fell asleep at the same time.

In the middle of the night, she was shaken awake. "I'm good, I'm not dead," she croaked. "You don't have to get me up."

He climbed on top of her, and they made love twice before falling back asleep.

# CHAPTER TWENTY-FIVE

Shivering, she awoke on her back just before dawn to sheets damp with sweat. Collapsed facedown on the bed, Garcia was snoring into the pillow. One of his long legs was thrown carelessly across her body. What would he think of her after last night? What did she think of herself? Sex had a way of ruining more things than it fixed.

Stirring and mumbling, he flipped onto his back. "Cat?"

"Yeah?" She held her breath, waiting for him to blurt something about how they'd made a massive mistake. Their careers were in jeopardy. It can never happen again. The sky was falling. Their world had turned to shit.

Instead, he rolled on top of her and buried his mouth in the crook of her neck. "Good morning," he said against her skin.

"Good morning," she said softly.

"That was fun last night," he said, lifting his face off her neck.

She smiled at him; he looked like a sleepy puppy. "You hungry?"

"Yeah, I am." He pushed her legs apart with his thighs.

She inhaled sharply. "Wait . . ."

"I'm sorry," he stammered. "I hurt you. I'm . . ."

She pressed against his lower back, holding him where he was. "No. It's okay. It's good."

He lowered his mouth to hers and kissed her on her bottom lip. "You and I . . ."

*Here it comes,* she thought. "Yeah?"

"We really needed it."

"We did," she said.

He rocked gently and returned to nibbling on her neck.

He fell back asleep. Typical guy. She slipped out of bed, stepped into her panties, pulled a sweatshirt on over her head and socks on her feet. Padded down the stairs. The cabin was cold, and she wanted to get a fire going. Get breakfast going, too.

He came down half an hour later wearing boxers, a tank T-shirt, black socks, and his cabin slippers. "That coffee smells good."

She eyed his attire and stifled a laugh. "Uh . . . Decaf, unfortunately. It's all Ed had on hand."

"This place is fucking freezing," he said, rubbing his arms.

"I stoked the fire," she said as she stood at the stove, stirring some scrambled eggs.

"Ed's not gonna like his next heating bill, but what the hell." He hobbled over to the thermostat and turned up the furnace. "You checked the date on those eggs, I hope."

She examined the carton. "Expired two weeks ago."

"Won't kill us." Garcia opened the freezer, took out a slab of bacon, and put it in the microwave. "Let's have some of this pork action, too."

She slapped another pan on the stove. "Grab some coffee and sit down. My turn to play house."

"How's the head?" he asked as he poured himself a cup.

"Perfectly fine," she said, and it was.

"I shouldn't have let you sleep through the night."

"You didn't," she said.

"What do you mean?"

She pointed the spatula at him. "You don't remember, do you?"

Leaning a hand against the counter, he took a sip of coffee. "Remember?"

"Amazing," she said, taking the bacon out of the microwave. "I mean, I've heard of people doing it, but I always thought it was an urban legend."

"What?"

"You sleep-screwed."

"I did not," he said, but his face reddened.

"Did too," she said, dropping the thawed slab into the skillet. "You made love to me in the middle of the night, and you don't even remember."

He grinned sheepishly. "So what if I did? Are you complaining?"

"Not at all," she said.

He took another sip of java and propped his butt against the counter. "So . . . how was I?"

"Great—both times."

He raised his brows and nodded. "I did it twice. Impressive."

"Go sit down, stud," she said. "I'll call you when breakfast is ready."

Before following her instructions, he came up behind her and wrapped his arms around her waist. Planted a kiss on the back of her neck. His hands moved up, traveled under her shirt, and cupped her breasts. "How about we go for a record?"

"Not while I'm frying bacon."

"I can't hear you," he said, and started to snore.

• • •

As they ate, they rehashed what Bernadette had seen with her ricocheting sight.

"So behind door number one we have a short man pacing in a
taxidermy room in a house on a lake. Behind door number two—"

"We have Lydia's baby getting bottle-fed in somebody's
kitchen."

"What makes you so sure it was the Dunton girl's baby?"

"It had tiny pink hands. Newborn hands."

"Could have been someone else's newborn. You saw someone
else's pregnant belly earlier."

"I'm positive it was Lydia's."

"What do we do with what you saw? Where does it take the investigation? Should we be putting out a bulletin on this baby? What
if someone knows of folks around town who suddenly turned up
with an infant?"

"The way these small towns are, people would have reported
such a thing already. I think whoever is holding her is sly enough to
avoid taking her out in public. Putting the baby on the news could
even endanger her. The bozos could panic and decide to dump
her."

"Why are they keeping her? There's been no ransom demand, at
least none that Dunton has revealed."

Bernadette took a bite of her eggs and pointed the fork at Garcia. "If it was a kidnapping for money, why not take both the
mother and the child? Why kill one and snatch the other? Wouldn't
the senator have paid more to get both back? It doesn't make
sense."

"What about the short guy? Do you have enough for a sketch?"

She buttered a triangle of toast. She'd burned it. "Short—"

"I got the short part."

"He had a little bit of a gut, but not too bad. Dark clothing. Small feet. Egg head, possibly shaved."

"Not enough for an artist."

"But if I saw him walking down the street, I might be able to identify him as my guy."

"Should we circulate something with Seth's people?"

"Let's keep it low-key," she said. "Talk to Wharten and see if he knows someone in the area who fits that description. Maybe the senator has an enemy with that build and noggin."

"I've gotta get together with Dunton and his people this morning," Garcia said, and chomped a slice of bacon in half.

"Do we tell him his granddaughter is alive?"

"Not until we've got her in our arms," he said.

She pushed her eggs around with her fork. Garcia was being cautious, and she couldn't blame him. Maybe he was still unconvinced that it was indeed Dunton's granddaughter. "Where're you meeting them?"

"Private home outside Walker. He has a buddy on the lake."

"Want me to come with you?"

"Why don't you drop me off and go do that tattoo parlor in town?"

"Doubt it's going to lead anywhere."

"It's worth a shot." He dragged a napkin across his mouth and dropped it on the table. "It's the only tatt shop I know of around these parts. If she got the heart while she was up here, it's gotta be them."

Bernadette figured he was giving her busywork to keep her away from the Dunton meeting. If it didn't go well, Garcia didn't want to be flogged in front of her. "Sure. You're right. Definitely worth a try."

He picked up a slice of toast and frowned at it. Set it back down.

"At some point today, we've got to check in with your little buddy. See what progress he made in matching Ashe's outgoing calls to witches."

She stood up and took her plate to the kitchen. "Let's get moving. We're burning daylight."

"What is it with you and that guy, by the way?" asked Garcia, following her.

Trying to avoid his eyes, she turned her back to load the dishwasher. "I have no idea what you're talking about."

After a long silence, he said, "Please tell me you didn't sleep with Cahill after the New Year's Eve party."

She froze with a set of silverware in her hands. Is that the real reason he was pissed about the party? Part of her wanted to snap that it wasn't any of his business, and another part of her wanted to stab Garcia with a fork. Instead, she answered calmly and honestly: "I had a little too much to drink."

"We've established that."

Her hands tightened around the utensils. "He drove me home in my truck."

"He spent the night?"

Before she could commit a crime with them, she dropped the forks into the dishwasher. "On my couch. Is that okay?"

"Yeah."

"Why did you wait to ask?"

He shrugged. "Thought you'd be mad . . . and you are. So I guess I should have kept my trap shut."

"Forget it," she said, and slammed the dishwasher closed.

He put his hands on her shoulders and massaged them. "Look. I'm insecure. He's a young guy and . . . I don't know . . . I was jealous."

She turned around and faced him. "You are my first man since I came back to Minnesota. Actually, my first in quite a while. It's not because I haven't been asked. I've been asked."

"I'm sure you have."

"I was waiting for someone worth the hassle."

He kissed her on the forehead. "You want to shower first, or should I?"

That wasn't what she was hoping to hear out of his mouth at that moment. "Uh . . . why don't you go first? I'm going to clean up a little more in the kitchen."

"You could join me," he said, wrapping his arms around her. "The shower in the basement has room enough for two."

"You go ahead." She patted his chest. "Don't use up all the hot water."

She watched his back as he headed for the basement door. Obviously he didn't think she was worth the hassle.


So that he could make some calls and take notes, Garcia let her pilot the Titan. His first call was to the Ramsey County Medical Examiner. His people had retrieved Ashe's body and driven it to St. Paul. The ME also expected to have some news on the Dunton girl's autopsy later in the day.

She gave Garcia a sideways glance while he spoke with B.K. Now that she and the boss had slept together, she feared everyone knew or at least suspected. At the same time, she told herself to stop worrying about that bullshit and concentrate on the case.

"All of them are?" Garcia asked into the phone, and scribbled on a notepad. "Good work."

Cahill and the sheriff must have matched all the calls from Ashe's cell to the phone numbers of coven members. Bernadette was excited.

"Why don't you give me the names and numbers right now? . . . How many are you talking? . . . That many, huh?"

Sounded like northern Minnesota was thick with witches.

"Agent Saint Clare is good," said Garcia. "She's with me right now. She's dropping me off to a meeting and then checking out a tatt shop."

Crap, thought Bernadette. B.K. is going to wonder why she and Garcia are together so early in the morning.

"It's in downtown Walker, on the main drag . . . I don't know. Twenty minutes, maybe. We're on Minnesota 34, just west of Walker . . . Sure . . . I'm certain she'd appreciate the update. I'll let her know." Garcia closed the phone.

"*All* those outgoing calls were to fellow witches," said Bernadette.

"Yup. Cahill is going to join you at the tatt shop this morning. Give you a rundown of our witch roster."

"Great," she said, but her brows were knotted.

"What's wrong?"

"Do you think he knows?"

"Knows what?"

She looked at him in disbelief. "Do I have to draw you an X-rated picture?"

"Oh," said Garcia.

She slowed behind a truck pulling a trailer loaded with snow-mobiles. "I'm being paranoid."

"No. You're right, Cat. We'll have to be careful from now on."

*From now on.* Garcia was talking as if their intimacy wasn't a quick fling, and she found some comfort in that. "Watch what you say, that's all."

"I'm not going to be talking you up in the locker room or anything."

"That's gallant of you," she said dryly, and stopped behind the snowmobile trailer as it hung a left into the woods. "What I mean is, don't mention that the two of us hashed something over during dinner or breakfast. People will start putting two and two together.

Maybe I should check in to a hotel. I'll find one where nobody else is staying. They'll think I was there all along."

"That's dumb."

"Let's stop talking about this," she said. "I'm starting to go crazy."

"Back to the sane subject of witches: what should we do with them?"

"They must have a leader," said Bernadette. "Let's go to his house. Her house. We'll start the questioning there."

"Tonight?"

"Sooner, if we can get to it. How long is this Dunton meeting going to take?"

Garcia ripped off his stocking cap and scratched his scalp. "I wish I knew."

"Get as much as you can about Lydia."

Garcia bunched the cap in his hand. "I will."

"I'd like to know why she went to Brule and then Walker. Why didn't the Duntons tell the St. Paul cops that their runaway daughter was pregnant, and that they'd thrown her out of the house? What about those mysterious letters she found? What did she say to her mom when she called home, and what did Michelle Dunton say to her? Did Lydia try calling home any other times?"

"We don't know that the boyfriend was telling the truth."

"Two more things. Don't forget to ask about their phone records and—"

Garcia's ringing cell interrupted her list. He flipped it open. "Garcia here . . . Oh, hey, Seth."

Bernadette reached over and cranked up the heat. The sky was clear and blue, belying the temperature of twenty below zero. When they'd first gotten into the truck that morning, it felt like crawling inside a chest freezer.

"I just got off the phone with Cahill. He's going to brief Saint

Clare this morning. She's fine . . . We did. Hessler saw her." Garcia paused. "Uh, is he one of them, by the way?"

Garcia looked over at Bernadette and nodded. She'd pegged him: Sven was a witch doctor.

"I forgot to ask my agent: Anything more come of the boot prints? Yup, yup . . . That's what I figured . . . A partial's better than nothing. Did my guys or yours find anything more in the woods? . . . That's disappointing."

Bernadette gathered that the footprints around Ashe's place weren't clear enough to produce anything spectacular, and that a search of the forest had come up empty. Neither surprised her.

"One more question, Seth. Is there a guy around the towns who looks like . . . well . . . short, little bit of a gut, shaved head . . . Funny, Seth. Very funny . . . I don't know. Probably a cross between the two. Never mind. Forget I asked, okay?"

Garcia seemed embarrassed. Tough. Bernadette saw the guy, and he could lead them to their killers.

"We're following up on some stuff this morning." Garcia switched the phone to his other ear. "I realize that . . . We've already had this conversation . . . No. I'm outta commission until this afternoon. Try me this afternoon." Garcia closed his cell.

She had to ask: "He wanted to know if my egghead guy was—"

"Dr. Evil or Mini-Me."

"Hilarious."

"They got some partials from the boot prints. Nothing that's going to rock our world."

"I heard."

"But Hessler. A medical professional. That should make him a strong candidate. We still don't have a reasonable motive, though."

"We do. We talked around the edges of it with Lydia. Now we've got a live baby being held somewhere. Being kept alive for some purpose."

"What purpose?"

Bernadette swallowed hard. "What if the baby is needed for a ceremony?"

"Fuck!" spat Garcia. "That would be monstrous. A human sacrifice? An infant?"

"Wiccans don't do that sort of thing," said Bernadette. "But there could be renegades in their midst. Same person or persons who left that pig on the altar."

"What about the woman and fetus killed in Brule years ago? Same thing? Some sort of sacrifice?"

"Could be."

"Again, what was Lydia doing in Brule? Where's the connection?"

"It goes back to those letters," she said. "We have to find them."

She hung a right off Minnesota 34, turning the truck in to town. She didn't know where to go from downtown Walker. Garcia waved his hand straight ahead. "Other side of downtown. Keep going. House is on Walker Bay, in a gated community. Practically walking distance from town."

"Are you sure you don't want me to go in with you?"

"Why would you want to put yourself through that?" Garcia asked.

"He's probably got people there. You should have people. I can be your people."

"My people should drop me off and go back to town to get some work done."

The dozen or so homes in the gated community were all large, modern, and constructed of massive pine logs—not the fake kind but the real deal. The one belonging to Dunton's buddy sat at the end of the community's private road, atop a hill along the bay. Like its neighbors, it sat on a couple of acres of wooded land. A stone chimney rose up along one side of the house and along the other side was a three-stall garage. The driveway coming down to the street was made of brick pavers set in a herringbone design. A black Lexus sedan and a white Cadillac Escalade were parked in the driveway in front of the garage doors.

She hung a left to turn onto the paved circular drive that looped past the front of the house and braked at the bottom of the steps leading up to the entrance.

"I'll call for a ride," he said, and hopped out.

"Good luck," she said.

He gave her a little salute and slammed the truck door.

Pulling out of the circular drive, she looked in her rearview mirror. Garcia's shoulders were slumped as he went up the steps slowly but purposefully, one foot in front of the other. He was moving like a man going to a wake. She hung a right and headed back to town.

# CHAPTER TWENTY-SIX

The tattoo parlor was on the outskirts of the downtown, anchoring the end of a block. It occupied the bottom half of a two-story brick building. She pulled the truck around to the side, parked in a small lot, and hopped out.

She peered into the storefront windows, which were hand-painted with the name of the tatt shop—Northern Inklings—and its hours. It operated on Sundays, but she had some time to kill before the business opened.

She walked down the sidewalk to check out the neighbors. The sunshine bounced off the snowbanks, white mountain ranges lining the road. A man dressed in flannel shirtsleeves, camo hunting pants, and a fur bomber hat was sprinkling salt at the entrance to the hardware store next door. "Good to see the sun," he said, pausing in his work to blink into the sky.

"Sure is," she said through the fog of her own breath.

She spotted Cahill coming down the sidewalk. He raised his hand, and the two met in front of a coffee shop. He'd eschewed his office clothes for jeans and a sweatshirt, which looked less ridiculous with his puffy coat and clunky boots. "How's the skull, Bern?"

"Great. Thanks for asking." She pointed to the coffee shop. "How about we grab a cup?"

They went inside and took a table. She thought he looked tired. He must have had dead-cat dreams. "Did you sleep okay?"

"I guess."

"A lot happened last night."

"I'd rather not talk about it." He pulled off his hat and gloves and scratched his head. "Hat hair."

"Tell me about it," said Bernadette, running a hand through her own messy mop.

The waitress came up with a pad and pen. "What can I get you?"

"Mocha latte," said B.K.

"Whipped cream?" asked the waitress.

"Lots," said Cahill.

"Anything from the bakery?"

"Well, I already—"

"We have great muffins."

Cahill paused while he admired her muffins. "Sure."

"Which would you like? Cranberry's my favorite."

"Cranberry," Cahill repeated numbly.

"You, ma'am?"

"Coffee. Black."

Carson stared at the girl as she went back to the counter. Bernadette couldn't believe Garcia had worried about her and B.K., a youngster obsessed with big, young bosoms. Beside muffin girl, Bernadette felt old and flat-chested. She looked at the file Cahill had dropped on the table. "What's that?"

"Oh, almost forgot." He handed it to her. "Wharten said this is for you and Antonia. Who is Antonia?"

Bernadette opened the folder and some gruesome crime-scene photos started to slide out. She caught them. The file contained the work the sheriff's office and the BCA had already done on the Dunton case. "Good. This is good."

"Who's this Antonia?"

She flipped through the materials. Skimmed the interview with Landon Guthrie, the hunter who'd discovered the body. Report from the county coroner. Nothing in the folder would bust the case wide open. She closed it and set it down. "So I hear you and the sheriff had good luck matching witches to phone numbers."

Cahill reached behind him and pulled a notebook out of his back pants pocket. Slapped it on the table. "It's all there."

"Fantastic." She grabbed the pad and started flipping through it. In neat printing, Cahill had profiled one witch per page. At the top was the phone number and below that were the name, age, and residence. That was followed by the individual's profession and other background information.

> Frederick Cleveland, 39. Akeley. Self-emp. carpenter. Divorced, 3
> kids: 2 speed viol. last 5 yrs. Hunts w/bow + black powder.
> Aka Drachen.
> Aleck Johansonn, 50. Nevis. Butcher. Married, 4 kids + 2 grand.
> Rifle hunter. Aka Lord Valdeth. One DWI 8 yrs ago. Wife,
> Meredith Johansonn, 48, homemaker. Aka Lady Bronwyn. No
> crime/traffic.
> Irene Edwalters, 27. Walker. Home hairdresser/electrolysis. Sin-
> gle. 1 kid. No guns. Aka Sapphyre. No crime/traffic.

Bernadette stopped when she got to Dr. Sven Hessler's name and number. "This guy worked on me last night."

"What?" asked Cahill.

She pointed to the page. "Remember that ER doc who was hanging around the hospital morgue?"

"Tall, skinny dude with glasses?"

"Yup. He was on duty last night." Bernadette ran her eyes over her physician's information:

> Sven Hessler, 36. Park Rapids. Doc. Single. No kids. Angler. No
> guns. Aka Lord Blade. Speed viol. last year.

"So the aliases are their coven names," said Bernadette, continuing to flip through the notebook.

"Right," said Cahill. "Some are lords and ladies. Seth said it has to do with reaching a certain level. Second-degree initiation—whatever that means. Sounds a little Dungeons & Dragons."

As she continued flipping through the notebook, Bernadette spotted Bossard's name. Graham hadn't lied after all.

> Eve Bossard, 47. Walker. OB/GYN. Single. No kids. Anti-gun.
> Aka Lady Morgana. No crime/traffic.

The obstetrician just got bumped up to Bernadette's short list.

The waitress came by and set the muffin and mocha latte in front of B.K. and the black coffee in front of Bernadette. "Can I get you anything else?"

"I'm good," said Bernadette.

"Thanks," mumbled Cahill. He watched intently as the girl went over to another table, leaned over, and wiped it down, her muffins spilling out of her sweater.

"Did Wharten mention whether any of these lords and ladies are the coven leaders?"

"What?"

"Carson?" Bernadette snapped her fingers in front of him.

"Sorry. What?"

"Did the sheriff identify the coven leaders?"

"Not really."

"Is he the one who gave you the criminal and traffic background?"

"Some of it. Some of it I pulled up from the usual databases. That's not to say I couldn't have missed something."

"There's got to be twenty names here."

"Twenty-five exactly."

"Not *that* many, are there?"

"Count," he said, pointing to the notebook.

She returned to the beginning and started turning pages. Two sheets in the middle were stuck together with something purple. "You and the sheriff went out for pie last night?"

"Yeah."

"Blueberry?"

"How'd you guess?"

"That's why they pay me the big bucks," she said, gently separating the pages. She stared at the sheet she'd initially missed. Smiled tightly. "That lying, conniving—"

"Who?" asked Cahill.

"I think I know who erased the pentagram from Lydia Dunton's forehead."

"Really?" His eyes went to the notebook. "Which one?"

"Nurse Delores Martini, aka Lady Willow."


"You sure she's the one?" asked Cahill, leaning across the table.

"She was at the hospital the night Tony . . . the night Garcia and I saw the star was gone from the body. She's the one who pointed us to Ashe."

"You think she's the killer?"

Bernadette closed the pad and put it into her jacket pocket. "She just graduated to my short list, along with a couple of other coven members with medical expertise."

Bernadette was excited by what she'd found, but unless she was calling to tell Garcia she had the killers in cuffs she couldn't interrupt his meeting. She checked her watch. A tad too early to head over to the tatt shop, too. Reaching over to a neighboring table, she snagged a coffee-stained copy of the *Star Tribune*. She paged through it, scanning for anything on the girl who'd been found dead in the forest, or the woman discovered hanging in her barn. She didn't find a word on either, but there was plenty on the cold snap, as well as some post-blizzard analysis. Minnesotans loved to wallow in their bad weather.

Cahill bit his muffin in half, chewed three times, and swallowed. Licked his fingers. "Sheriff said the witches are all meeting tonight in the woods because it's a full moon. A little full-moon soirée. Plan is we slide in, watch them awhile to see if they're up to no good, and then crash the bash. Scare the heck out of them and see who squeals first. See who squeals like a stuck pig."

She took a sip of coffee. "You're sounding like . . . I don't know."

"Sheriff Wharten?"

"No. Barney Fife." She took another drink. "What's everyone else doing today?"

"Some of the guys are still trying to get something out of the witch lady's boyfriend. The crime-scene dudes—who knows what the hell they're doing? Jerking off in that big trailer of theirs."

"Do I detect a little resentment?"

"They get all the glory." He took a sip of his mocha latte, getting whipped cream on his nose. "There's what, three of those CSI shows on TV now? Four?"

•   •   •

They finished their drinks and Bernadette threw down some bills. "My treat."

"Now what?" he asked.

She stood up and put on her jacket. "I'm heading over to the tattoo parlor. Should be open by now."

"Run this tatt thing by me. Why are you checking it out?"

She told him about Lydia's heart, and the possibility that she'd gotten it while she was in Walker. "A long shot," she admitted.

"Want some company?" he asked, putting on his coat.

"Sure. Why not?"

They walked a couple of doors down to the shop. She pulled on the door handle. Still locked.

Cahill checked the hours posted against his watch. "Should be open."

She peered through the glass and saw a wooden counter with an old-fashioned cash register. Behind that was an Oriental folding screen used as a room divider. The work was probably done on the other side. Was someone behind the screen? She tapped on the glass door. A ruddy-faced man poked his head out from behind the divider and mouthed something to them, but she couldn't understand it. He disappeared behind the screen again. "There's someone inside," she said.

"Here he comes," said Cahill.

The guy came out from behind the screen, went around the counter, and unlocked the door. "Sorry, folks," he said, and held it open for them.

She stepped inside. "Don't worry about it."

"Can you give me another minute?" he asked. Before they could answer, he went back behind the screen. "Had a puker in here yesterday. Cleaned it up, but it still stinks."

Bernadette's nose wrinkled. She did smell vomit. She heard him spraying. Vomit and floral air freshener. "Are you the owner?"

"Sole proprietor. Sole artist. Sole inmate of the asylum." More spraying. "Go ahead and look for your tatts. See if anything speaks to you. I do custom work, too. Just give me a rough drawing."

She saw that the walls to the right and left of the entrance were lined with rows of framed pictures. Within each rectangle was either a close-up color photo of a tattoo adorning various body parts—arms, chests, shoulders, legs, backs, breasts—or a color sketch of a tattoo design. Wild tropical birds and flowers. Skulls. Fantastic butterflies. Fairies. Nude, winged women. Flaming motorcycles. Flaming cars. Tigers and lions and leopards. Barbed wire and chains. Unicorns. A flying pig.

"See anything you like?" he asked from behind the screen.

"There's too much to choose from," she said as she unzipped her jacket and pulled off her hat.

Cahill was studying the naked back and butt of a curvaceous tattooed woman. "Cool," he muttered.

One of the framed photos was of the man behind the screen. LEONARD "LENNY" NAVARE, it said under the picture. RESIDENT LUNATIC. It showed him from the waist up, in a black leather vest. His exposed chest and arms were covered with a little bit of everything. In the photo, he was sporting a set of long blond braids.

"You cut your hair," Bernadette said.

He came out from behind the screen. He was wearing the same vest as in the photo, but it was pulled over a T-shirt. A bow to the cold weather. He ran a meaty hand through his buzz cut. "Getting too old for that stuff. Starting to get gray in it. Chicks don't dig that gray."

The stink was getting to her, and she wanted to make this quick. She pulled out her wallet and flashed her ID. "Agent Bernadette Saint Clare. FBI."

"Whoa," he said, taking a step back from her. "Didn't see that coming. My taxes are up-to-date, ma'am."

"That's good to know, but I'm not here to talk taxes." She pulled Lydia's photo out of her jacket and held it up. "Recognize her?"

He took a set of reading glasses out of his jeans and slipped them on. "Chicks don't dig these much, either." He took the photo from her and held it up to his nose.

"Take a good look," she said. "This is important."

"No," he said, lowering the picture and handing it back to her. "Never . . . never seen her before."

Bernadette didn't believe him. "She got a tattoo from you."

"I don't think so," he said.

"A heart tatt," she said.

"I'd remember if I'd—"

"Your DNA will show up on the ink," interjected Cahill.

Bernadette was pretty sure that was bullshit, and had to give the kid points for creativity. "That's right," she said evenly. *Your* DNA, Lenny."

Navare swallowed hard and extended his hand. "Let me have another look."

She smiled tightly and handed him the photo. "Think hard, Lenny. If we catch you covering up anything—"

"I had a senior moment is all. That's right. Gave her an itty-bitty heart tatt." He pointed to the right side of his face, just below the outside of his eye.

"When?" asked Cahill.

He pulled off his cheaters and handed the photo back to Bernadette. "What did she do? Rob a bank?"

Cahill came up next to Bernadette. "When did you see her last?"

"That don't sound too good," he said. "What happened to her?"

"Sir, if you could answer the question . . ." said Cahill.

"She came in here Christmas Eve. I was getting ready to close."

"Did she tell you her story?" asked Bernadette. "What did she say?"

He folded his big arms in front of him. "I'm not sure I should be telling tales out of school."

"She was a minor, Lenny," said Bernadette.

"Did you have written parental permission to give her that tatt?" asked Cahill.

"She told me she was eighteen. She had ID."

"Did she look like she was eighteen?" asked Bernadette.

He unfolded his arms but didn't answer.

Bernadette put her hands behind her back and walked back and forth in front of the counter. "You sold a tatt to a minor without parental permission. A misdemeanor under state statutes."

"I didn't know," he said. "She had ID."

Bernadette stopped pacing and pointed a finger at him. "On top of that, she was pregnant."

He blanched. "Goddamn. I didn't know. She looked chubby. I didn't think she was—"

"What did she tell you?" asked Cahill.

He rubbed his chin. "She didn't tell me anything."

Bernadette was sure he was lying again. "Show me your records. You do keep records, don't you?"

"For two years, on each and every person tattooed. I photocopy their driver's license or ID, and then I have them fill out a form: name, address, phone, date of birth, and their signature. She signed for that tatt."

"What name did she give you?" asked Bernadette.

"I . . . don't remember her name."

"Let's see the records," said Cahill.

"Don't you need a search warrant or some such shit?"

"If I have to get one, I swear to God I'll come back with a small army and rip this place apart," said Bernadette. "It'll take a month for you to get back to business."

"Fuck. All that for a little girl? Did she kill someone or what?"

His eyes widened. "She was the one who was killed. Son of a bitch. She's the kid they found in the woods."

"Are you looking to be named an accessory to murder, Lenny?" asked Cahill.

"Christ, no."

"Where're your files?" asked Bernadette.

He thumbed over his shoulder. "In the back."

"Lead the way," said Cahill.

"It's really a mess," said Navare. "Why don't you two wait out here?"

"Lead the way," Cahill repeated.

Bernadette liked double-teaming with the kid. When he wanted, he could be an intimidating prick.

The two agents followed the shop owner behind the counter and screen, and went past the work area. Puke and floral odors aside, it looked as pristine as a dentist's lab. To the left of the table and tools was a door. Navare pushed it open and turned on the overhead light, a naked bulb mounted to the ceiling.

The walls of the ten-by-ten cube were tacked with motorcycle posters, nude centerfolds ripped out of magazines, and enlargements of tattooed people. Bernadette assumed they were past clients. A battered metal desk was shoved up against the wall opposite the door, and an ancient wooden file cabinet was crammed into a corner to the left of the desk. Navare went to the cabinet and pulled open the middle drawer. "Give me a minute," he said, and started poking around the files. Every once in a while, he looked over his shoulder at them. He seemed nervous as hell.

"If you can't remember her name, how are you going to look her up?" asked Cahill.

Navare didn't answer.

The two agents exchanged glances. Bernadette walked deeper

inside. Between the desk and the cabinet stood a life-size cardboard cutout of Lucy Lawless as Xena, the warrior princess. That brought to mind another tough broad, and her tattoo of a snake swallowing its own tail. "Did you do Jordan Ashe's tatt?"

"Nah," Navare said. "She got that ink before she moved to Minnesota. She's not from around here, you know."

"I heard," said Bernadette.

"Too bad she offed herself. Never would have pegged her to be the type. I'm not saying she was Little Miss Mary Sunshine or anything, but . . ." His voice trailed off as he continued digging.

Bernadette found it interesting that a suicide story was already being circulated around the towns.

Navare turned around. "How'd you know her? Was she part of this mess?"

Cahill nodded toward the cabinet. "Please. We're on a tight schedule."

He turned around and resumed his search. Bernadette kept running her eyes around the room. She eyed the space under his desk. There was something sitting on the floor next to the legs of the chair. It was lavender. This man didn't look like a lavender sort of fellow.

He wrestled a folder out of the tightly packed drawer. "Here she is. Heart girl."

Bernadette ripped the file out of his hand and opened it. Two pages. The first was a photocopy of a driver's license. It had Lydia's mug shot and then a bunch of bullshit lifted off a Massachusetts ID, starting with the name Angela Schmidt. Bernadette had seen similar fake licenses a thousand times. She turned to the second page and saw that Lydia had carefully copied the fictitious information from the plastic. When the kid signed at the bottom of the form, however, she changed the spelling of the last name, going with *Schmitt*. Bernadette smiled sadly. Lydia was just a goofy kid.

"What's up?" Navare asked.

"I'm keeping this," she said, closing the folder.

"Uh . . . sure." Navare shut the cabinet drawer.

"What else did she tell you? Did she say how long she'd been in town? Did she say where she was headed after your shop?" asked Cahill.

He shrugged. "I got the impression she'd just gotten to town. She asked a lot of questions."

"About?" asked Cahill.

"Where she could crash for cheap. Where she could eat for cheap."

"You didn't think any of that was worth reporting to the police?" asked Bernadette.

"I didn't know she was the dead kid," he said.

"Even before that happened," said Cahill. "Especially before that happened. Why didn't you tell the police you had a pregnant minor in your shop? A girl who sounded like she was in trouble?"

"I told you, I didn't—"

"You didn't know." Bernadette waved a hand toward the cutout. "And I'm Xena."

"I get all sorts in here, lady. I can't be calling the cops every time someone turns up with a story. No one would ever give me their business."

"You could have contacted a social worker," said Bernadette. "You could have called the hospital. You could have done something. She was vulnerable."

"She looked like she could handle herself," said Navare.

"She's dead, so I guess she couldn't handle shit," said Cahill.

He hung his head. "I'm . . . sorry. I didn't . . . I'm sorry."

"Where did you send her to eat or stay?" asked Bernadette.

"The restaurants were already closed for Christmas, and I told her that. Far as hotels go, I gave her a phone book so she could make some calls."

"She had a cell?" asked Cahill.

"I told her she could use mine."

Phone records would be invaluable, thought Bernadette. "So she took it and called?"

"No, but she did use the phone book to look up an address. Said she wanted to surprise them."

"Them? It was plural?" asked Cahill.

Navare pursed his lips. "Uh . . . I'm not a hundred percent positive. Could have been a him or a her."

"Were they friends, relatives?" asked Bernadette.

"She didn't say."

"Did she tell you where the person or persons lived?" asked Bernadette. "Think hard. Maybe she asked you how to get there."

Navare shook his head.

"Were they in Walker? Did they live around here?" asked Cahill.

"Maybe. I don't know for sure."

"But she was checking a Walker phone book," said Bernadette. "Where is the book?"

Navare lifted a few papers off his desk. Extracted a warped, mildewed phone book. "Here."

Bernadette grabbed it and examined the cover. The thing covered multiple communities. She started flipping through it. "Did she fold a page or write something down out of this thing?"

"She had a pen in her hand, but I wasn't really paying attention."

Bernadette looked for taxi or bus listings in the immediate area and found none. The towns were too small. "How was she going to get there? Get to wherever she was going?"

"Haven't a clue. Maybe she was going to thumb it."

Bernadette, still riffling through the book: "After she left, in which direction did she go?"

Navare shook his head. "Sorry."

She tucked the phone directory under her arm. "You just let her leave? You didn't even offer to give her a—"

"I'm not a taxi service. I'm not the welfare office. I run a tatt shop. She came in, she got her ink, she . . . paid. She skedaddled."

Bernadette sensed some hesitation in his voice about the paid part. "How'd she pay?"

Navare ran a hand across the buzz cut. "Well, she didn't pay. Pisses me off."

Bernadette couldn't see this guy letting someone walk out of his shop with a freebie. "What did you do?"

"Did you do something to her?" asked Cahill.

Navare backed away from the two agents and raised his palms. "Now wait a minute. Don't you be accusing me of nothing."

Bernadette went over to the desk, bent down, and pulled out the lavender object that was hiding underneath. She held it up. A girl's backpack, decorated with heart decals. "What the fuck is this?"

Navare's mouth dropped open.

"Son of a bitch," said Cahill.

Navare spun around and sprinted through the office door.

Bernadette was on his heels. "Stop!"

Navare tripped over his own equipment, knocking a tray of needles and ink to the floor with a clatter. He pushed a table toward Bernadette and she shoved it out of her way. Cahill bounded past her and went after the big man. "Stop, now!"

Navare went around the screen and tipped it onto Cahill. Bernadette dodged Cahill and the falling screen and jumped on Navare's back as he was clambering over the front counter. They both fell to the floor, with Bernadette riding Navare's back. "Bitch!" he hollered, and bucked her off. Scrambled to his feet and climbed over the counter.

"Stop or I'll shoot!" she hollered, getting on her feet with her Glock between her hands.

Navare was almost to the door. He looked behind him and saw the gun. Threw up his hands and froze. "I didn't," he said over his shoulder.

"Don't move!" snapped Bernadette, coming around the counter.

"Didn't kill anyone, swear to God!" Navare yelled to the glass door.

Behind her, Cahill was on his cell.

"Why'd you do it?" she asked. "Why'd you kill her?"

"I didn't!"

Keeping her gun trained on his back, she itched to put a bullet in him. "Then why'd you run, huh? Why'd you run, Lenny? Tell me. I'd really like to know."

# CHAPTER TWENTY-SEVEN

Wharten and his deputies were first on the scene, and the sheriff personally loaded the handcuffed shop owner into the back of a squad. "You're in a world of trouble now, Lenny," said Wharten, his hand on the open door of the car.

"I didn't do nothing!" Navare said. "I was holding the stuff until she came back with the money she owed me, that's all. I was holding it!"

Wharten slammed the door and watched the squad as it pulled away. "Dumbass," said the sheriff.

Navare had run for a very good reason. In addition to Lydia's backpack, he was keeping a pile of jewelry the girl had taken from her parents. Bernadette didn't think he'd killed anyone—he could prove that he was out of town when Lydia was murdered—but he'd sat on a backpack filled with stunning information. What angered Bernadette even more was that he could have summoned the authorities while Lydia was in his shop and prevented her from falling into the hands that eventually killed her.

Cahill joined Wharten on the sidewalk. "Thanks for the assist, sir."

Wharten slapped the agent on the back. "Good work, young man."

Bernadette was sitting on a bench behind them, talking to Tuckert. He'd come by to bag the backpack and its contents: dirty clothes, toiletries, letters.

The letters.

The boyfriend hadn't been lying. Lydia had uncovered an ugly secret when she found those papers.

"From reading them, it sure is hard to figure out what they've got over the senator," said Tuckert.

"Whatever it is, they think it's worth a fortune," Bernadette said.

"You'll figure it out," he said. "That was a good catch on that missing statue in the barn."

Kudos from other agents were rare. "Thanks," she said with a small smile.

"Thank *you*." Tuckert got up off the bench and left with his booty. There'd be DNA tests to run and handwriting to be analyzed.

Her phone rang, and she checked the screen. Garcia. "Yeah."

Garcia: "Agent Saint Clare?"

The formal stuff. He wasn't alone. "Want me to pick you up out front?" she asked evenly.

"You need to come inside," Garcia said.

"Why?"

"Are you still on the line, Agent Saint Clare? You're breaking up. Can you hear me?"

He was telling her to pay attention. "I'm here, sir," she said.

"I want you to review the case with the senator and his wife, Agent Saint Clare. We'd like to *see* you here as soon as possible."

Garcia had something she needed to see. "Yes, sir."

"How long will it take for you to get here?" he asked. "Where are you right now?"

"Agent Cahill is with me, sir." She snagged B.K.'s jacket and pulled him down onto the bench. "Do I have time to get rid of him first, or should I bring him along?"

Silence on Garcia's end. Then: "He can wait in the truck. This won't take long."

"Need me to bring over anything additional for the meeting, sir? I could call the Minneapolis crew and have them come by with it."

"No. Just you. Make it quick, Agent. I don't want to keep the senator and his people waiting."

"Yes, sir," she said, and closed the phone.

"What's going on?" asked Cahill.

"Come on." Bernadette ran to the truck, with B.K. trailing after her.

"What's going on?" he repeated.

She threw open the door and got behind the wheel. "Garcia wants me. He's got something I need to see."

Cahill jumped into the front passenger seat. "Is he in trouble?"

"I don't know. Probably not." She reached inside her jacket, took her Glock out of its holster, checked it, and put it back.

"That looks more like a *yes.*"

"Better to be prepared." She started up the truck and squealed out of the parking lot.

"I thought he was meeting with the Duntons."

"He is." She put the pedal to the floor.

Cahill fumbled with his phone. "Should I call for backup?"

"I gave him the opportunity to signal for more troops and he declined." As they came up on a red light, she quickly scouted for other cars and blew through the intersection.

"If he's in hot water, why wouldn't he want more bodies?"

"Like I said, I don't know that he's got a problem. He might not be sure he's got a problem. Plus, it would not help our relationship with Dunton if the entire Minneapolis Division descended on his pal's place with guns drawn."

"Then why do you need me?"

"I did indicate to him that you would be outside if we needed you."

"So I'm the backup."

"Essentially, yes."

"That's what I was afraid of." He put away his cell and reached inside his jacket for his gun. Took it out and checked it. "I've never fired this thing, except on the range."

B.K. was as pale as the snowbanks. Once again, she was dragging the young techie into a dicey situation. The poor kid was going to turn gray by the time she finished with him. "Word around the campfire is you're an excellent shot."

He stared at the gun. "Which fucked-up campfire did you get that information from?"

"Carson, you were a great help in that tatt shop. Played it just right."

"You're the one who made the tackle. I was along for the ride, like now." He holstered his Glock. "What did Garcia say, exactly? What did he find?"

"I'm not as worried about what *he* found," she said. "I'm more worried about what *we* found."

"They wouldn't do anything to Garcia." A pause. "Would they? How could they?"

"Those letters tell me the Duntons are in a jam, and people in a jam do crazy things."

As Bernadette pulled the truck up the circular drive, Cahill gawked at the massive lake home. "Lincoln Logs on steroids."

When she dropped Garcia off that morning, she'd hardly taken notice of the mansion's log construction. The north woods were littered with log homes, large and small. It never occurred to her that this one might contain the trophy room from her vision. She suspected that Garcia wanted her to see the interior of the home, to determine if it contained at least one of the rooms she'd observed with her sight.

Bernadette parked the truck just past the steps leading to the front door and turned off the engine. "He told me to have you wait in the truck."

"Which was code for . . ."

"Having you wait in the truck."

"At least let me get out and walk around outside." He pulled his gloves tighter over his hands. "Do we have a plan? I'd like to know the plan."

"You don't need to know everything, Carson."

"I don't know anything. Nobody ever tells me stuff. I'm always operating in a fog."

"The sooner you find peace with that, the better off you'll be. Don't ask questions. Don't worry about what anybody else is doing. Stay where I put you. Shoot when I tell you. Maintain your inner calm and go with the flow."

"What the heck is that, FBI Zen?" He ran a trembling hand through his hair. "Too bad we didn't have time to pull some equipment together to monitor this deal. That's what I'm good at. Could have slapped a couple of mikes and a transmitter on Garcia before his meeting. Could have wired you."

"That would have been overkill for this situation." Even as she said that, she didn't know if it was true. The letters changed everything.

Since they were expected, there was no sneaking up on the house. Nevertheless, she wanted to get the lay of the land. The

Lexus and the Escalade were parked in the driveway, in front of the garage doors. She took down their license numbers. If necessary, she could run the plates later, but she figured they belonged to Dunton and his entourage. Through the truck's rear and side mirrors, she studied the front of the house. Stickers plastered on the windows indicated that the place had alarms, but she didn't see any security cameras. Maybe those were deemed excessive since the homes were already behind gates.

She wondered if she could get away with having B.K. posted near a door. The trophy room she'd observed through her special sight had a patio door with a view of the frozen lake, and Garcia knew that. He'd try to steer the meeting to that room so she could check it out. That being the case, Cahill would be closest to them if he hung around in back of the house.

"Let's go," she said, opening her door.

They hopped out, walked up the drive, and stopped at the foot of the stairs leading up to the front door. "Where?" he asked.

"Let's go around back." She motioned toward a shoveled path that peeled off from the walk and looped around toward the back of the two-story house. "I'll go with you and get you situated."

They hiked along the side of the cabin with the stone chimney. Smoke was pouring out of the top, and she could smell the burning wood. Someone was having an afternoon fire. She ran her eyes over that side of the house. The shades were up, but she didn't see any movement in any of the windows. They got to the far corner of the house and stayed there, surveying like a couple of confused meter readers wondering where the utility box was located.

A gradual slope led to the shore. She looked down the hill toward the frozen body of water. Like the lake she'd observed through her sight, it was dotted with fishing shacks and snowmobiles. Certainly every other cabin in northern Minnesota enjoyed such a view.

Scanning the back of the house, she saw that the sprawling deck ran the entire width, with steps at each end leading up to it from the backyard. Beneath the deck, firewood was stacked against the house. She also saw a couple of snowmobiles covered with canvas, and a wheelbarrow. The basement windows that faced the storage area were dark.

Topside, three sets of patio doors opened onto the deck. The sliders closest to them led to a kitchen or dining area, she deduced, because a massive grill anchored that end of the deck. If this was indeed the correct house, the middle patio doors or the ones on the opposite end led to the trophy room.

"Where should I park my ass?" Cahill asked impatiently.

"My guess is we're going to be meeting in one of the rooms with the patio doors. Not the sliders that open to the grill but one of the other two."

"That's a pretty specific guess," he said.

"I'll step close to the window and look out, so you'll know for sure which one."

"What if they notice me?"

"I hope they do." If Cahill was spotted skulking around, it would give the impression that she and Garcia had the rest of the bureau watching their backs. At the same time, a lone agent couldn't possibly piss off the senator.

"Do you want me to go up on the deck?"

"First make a show of strolling around and checking out the backyard. Then come up on the deck. Walk back and forth. Keep your eyes on my window." She thought of something that would rattle the folks in the room. "Every so often, put your right hand inside your jacket. Just the right, so it's obvious you're not trying to keep your mitts warm."

"They'll think I've got a gun in my pocket."

"That's the point."

"When should I make a move?"

"Only if all hell breaks loose."

"Define."

"A thug slams me into the window. A body crashes through the glass and lands at your feet. The back half of the house blows up. You hear gunshots. You see or hear anything like that, call for backup and kick down a door. Come inside with your weapon drawn."

"Otherwise my main job is to hang around outside and look vaguely threatening."

"Pretty much."

"I feel like that guy in *The Godfather.* The baker who goes to the hospital with flowers for the Don. What was his name?"

"I don't remember. Enzo? Mario? Something ending with an *o*."

"That poor chump. He goes to the hospital with flowers for the Don, and Michael has him stand outside with his hands in his pockets, acting all tough like he has a gun. Pretending the little baker dude is one of the Godfather's bodyguards."

She was impressed. B.K. had actually figured it out. That was his role exactly. "There's one big difference between you and the baker dude."

"Yeah?"

"You really do have a gun."

Bernadette returned to the front of the house. Before ascending the steps, she ran her eyes around. All the shades on that side were down. As Bernadette mounted the steps, she put her hand over her gun. The only person she could trust inside the house was her boss, and for all she knew he had a pistol jammed into his side. Her backup was a scared kid who'd never fired a weapon under duress. This case was turning out to be even more fun than she'd hoped.

# CHAPTER TWENTY-EIGHT

She pushed the bell and heard it chime inside. The door popped open immediately. They must have seen son of Enzo roaming the grounds.

A guy who resembled a well-dressed bar bouncer blocked the doorway. She held up her ID wallet. "Agent Bernadette Saint Clare."

"This way," he said, throwing a hand toward the back of the house.

Staring at his meaty fists, Bernadette thought back to the hands from her sight. Touching a pregnant woman. Reaching into the refrigerator to retrieve the baby bottle. Feeding Lydia's baby. They could be the same hands. Maybe.

As she jogged to keep up with him, she looked around. While Ed's place was nice, there was no mistaking it was a cabin. The furniture wasn't coordinated, the couch cushions sagged, and the kitchen dishes were mismatched. Except for the log walls, the interior of this Walker Bay home could have been lifted from a decorating magazine. Plush area rugs and runners. Wide-plank wood floors. Dried-flower arrangements, tapered candles, and bowls of potpourri. Distressed country furniture. An open staircase in the middle of the main floor led up to a true second story instead of a loft.

She followed the bouncer down a hall to a room facing the lake. After quickly sweeping the space with her eyes, she looked at Garcia and nodded. "Sir." He knew what that meant: this was indeed one of the two rooms that she'd visited with her sight.

Her boss was standing with his back to the menacing bear, and it looked as if the thing were poised to pounce on him. A metaphor for the meeting with the senator. Even though he'd been at the house since morning, Garcia was still carrying his jacket. They'd obviously made a point of making him feel unwelcome. Bastards.

Garcia crossed the room and stepped up to a couch parked against the wall. "Senator and Mrs. Dunton, this is the lead agent working on your daughter's case. Bernadette Saint Clare."

A tall, trim, auburn-haired man with a lantern jaw got up from the couch and Bernadette recognized him immediately from his newspaper photos. Senator Magnus Dunton. Dressed in starched khakis and a cashmere crewneck, he could have stepped out of a Brooks Brothers catalog. Dunton offered his hand, and it was too late for Bernadette to remove her gloves. "Thank you for everything you're trying to do," he said tiredly.

"Senator," Bernadette said, and tipped her head to his seated wife. "Mrs. Dunton."

Ash-blond hair tied back from her narrow face, Michelle Dunton was the Ralph Lauren model. Hollow cheeks. Peach lipstick. Skinny jeans. Yellow cable-knit sweater. Half-spent cigarette dangling from long, pale fingers. She nodded at Bernadette and tapped a gray snake. The ashtray in front of her was filled with peach-stained butts.

Dunton glanced through the slider. "Who's that?"

Through the glass, Bernadette could see Cahill coming into view. He caught her eye and then turned around. Walked up to the deck railing and looked out over the lake. "Agent Carson Cahill," she said, and left her boss to fill in the rest.

Garcia: "He's assisting Agent Saint Clare on the case, but he doesn't need to be a part of this briefing."

While Dunton was studying Cahill's back, the young agent slipped a hand inside his jacket pocket. The senator opened his mouth as if to make a comment, and then closed it. He sat back down on the couch. A cushion separated the couple, and Bernadette took note: this tragedy had not brought the Duntons closer together.

"I'd like some coffee," Mrs. Dunton said to the bouncer. With her hoarse chain-smoker's voice, she sounded as if she were sitting at a bar ordering another Manhattan.

"Would you like a cup, Miss Saint Clare?" asked the senator.

"Love one," said Bernadette, unzipping her jacket.

Michelle Dunton snuffed her cigarette out in the ashtray, took the pack off the coffee table, and got up. Proceeded to follow the bouncer out of the room.

"Don't you want to stay and hear this?" Dunton asked after her.

Michelle Dunton stopped in the doorway and spun on her heel. While withdrawing another smoke from the pack, she looked from Bernadette to Garcia. "Have you arrested the person who killed my Lydia?"

Garcia: "No, but like I said before—"

"Do you have a name?" she asked, and put the cigarette to her lips.

"No," Bernadette said shortly.

Michelle Dunton flicked her lighter, took a long pull, and expelled a cloud into the room.

"Mickey," the senator said. "At least listen to what they have to say."

"They've got nothing." His wife turned around and exited the room, leaving behind a wisp of smoke and a hint of Chanel No. 5.

Dunton sat forward on the couch and folded his hands in front of him. "I apologize," he said to the floor. "She . . . we're having a hard time understanding all of this."

Bernadette had dealt with many grieving relatives over the years. The silent sufferers displayed nothing more than red-rimmed eyes and knotted tissues. At the other end were the screamers and wailers. While Magnus Dunton seemed to fit the quiet end of the spectrum, Bernadette had no idea where Michelle fell. She appeared more irritated than grief-stricken, but then everyone handled it differently.

"Let's hear it," Dunton said to no one in particular.

Wing-backed chairs were at each end of the couch, but Bernadette didn't feel comfortable taking a seat unless it was offered. Garcia came up next to her, and they both stood facing the senator. A pair of delinquents meeting with the assistant principal. Bernadette started. "First, let me say how sorry I am for your loss."

"Thank you." Dunton crossed his arms in front of him and fell back against the cushions. "What have you come up with?"

Bernadette wished she'd had a minute alone with Garcia, to tell him what she'd found in the backpack. She had no idea whether he'd want her to reveal their discovery to the Duntons. Bernadette decided to give the senator an opportunity to spill the beans on his own. "I believe we've made . . . substantial progress," she said, selecting her words carefully. "But we need your help to . . . take the investigation to the next level."

"Next level? What's that supposed to mean?"

"Let me ask you this, did your daughter contact you or your wife at all while she was on the road?"

"No." He motioned toward Garcia. "Already told him that."

Dunton had already told a lie, at least if Lydia's boyfriend was to be believed. "Sir, why would your daughter have traveled up north in the first place?" asked Bernadette. "What drew her here? Who did she have in the Walker area?"

"She didn't know a soul around here."

"But you obviously know people up here if they're hosting you," said Bernadette.

"This cabin belongs to a business associate of mine. Lydia had never been here, never been to the area." Dunton got up from the couch. "If all you're going to do is ask me the same questions—"

"Did she know anyone in Brule?" Bernadette asked.

"Where?"

"The identity of the baby's father," continued Bernadette. "If we could have some help with that. What about a boyfriend? Was she seeing anyone from the neighborhood or . . . her school?"

"I . . . I don't know who got her pregnant," said Dunton.

Bernadette detected a slight hesitation in his voice. He did know that David Strandelunder had fathered the child. More lying.

Dunton went over to the slider and looked out at the agent pacing the deck. Son of Enzo had made an impression on the senator. "Why is that important?"

Garcia: "If we knew—"

"If I knew, I'd wring his neck," said Dunton in a low growl.

"Sir, someone has stepped forward," she said. "If you could confirm that he's a possibility, that he knew your daughter."

Dunton sighed to the glass. "Davy Strandelunder?"

Bernadette blinked. She was stunned that he'd suddenly offered up the name. "Yes. Can you tell us if he's—"

"A lowlife with absolutely no future."

"Did he father Lydia's baby?" asked Bernadette.

"That boy caused this family a whole lot of heartache, and I don't want my daughter's name . . ." Dunton put his hand over his mouth for a moment. "I don't want Lydia's name associated with his. He wasn't . . . good enough for her."

"Why didn't you volunteer his name earlier, Senator?" asked Garcia.

"What difference does it make who got her pregnant?"

Garcia: "The person who killed her—"

"He didn't do it," said Dunton. "He doesn't have much going for him, but he's not a . . . Davy wouldn't have done that, not to Lydia."

"Why didn't you and Mrs. Dunton tell the police that you'd kicked Lydia out of the house?" asked Bernadette. "Why didn't you inform them that she was pregnant?"

"Come on, Miss Saint Clare." He walked into the middle of the room and stood between the two agents. *"Miss* Saint Clare. Kids?"

"No."

"You don't either, do you?" he asked Garcia.

"No, sir."

"Neither one of you has a clue. Did we do the best job? Hell, no." Then, in a much lower voice, "We tried."

"We aren't judging you, sir," Garcia said. "But by withholding information, you've hindered our investigation and endangered others."

"Are you aware that another person was murdered yesterday?" Bernadette asked.

"A potter woman. Mr. Garcia has already informed me, and I'll tell you exactly what I told him: I didn't know the individual and I have not the slightest inkling what her connection to my daughter was. Her death must be completely unrelated."

Bernadette: "Senator, if there is anything you could—"

"That's enough," he said tiredly, and put his hand to his forehead. "I've had enough."

Garcia: "Sir, we're—"

"You're wasting time. I never wanted you people on the case in the first place. I knew this would happen. I want the FBI off the case and I want my daughter's body released so we can plan a proper . . ." His voice started breaking.

"We can't do that yet, sir," said Garcia.

"If you could please answer our questions," said Bernadette.

A maid rattled into the room with a serving tray. She set the tray down on the coffee table and waited with her hands folded in front of her apron. Bernadette noticed that there was only one cup on the tray, along with the pot and a creamer. Michelle Dunton came in after the young woman. "Thank you, Rose. That'll be all."

After the servant exited, Michelle Dunton sat down and poured herself a cup. Took a sip and addressed her husband as if the agents weren't in the room. "Maggie, you look beat. Tell them to come back tomorrow."

The bouncer walked in, followed by a second bruiser in a suit. "Is everything all right, sir?"

The senator returned to the patio window and looked out. Cahill had stopped moving and was leaning against the deck rails, one hand buried in his jacket pocket. "Their colleague must be getting cold," Dunton said. "See if he needs anything."

Garcia's jaw tensed. "Agent Cahill doesn't need a thing. Thank you anyway, Senator."

The bureau had displayed some muscle, and the senator was attempting to push back. Maybe instigate a tussle and manufacture a reason to throw them out. Bernadette wondered how far Dunton was willing to take this.

Not that far, apparently.

Dunton said to the two bouncers, "Why don't you fill up the cars. We'll be leaving tomorrow."

The pair exited, taking a layer of tension with them.

Michelle Dunton got up from the couch and went over to her

husband. "Maggie?" she asked her husband's back, and took a sip of coffee.

"What?"

"Tell them to go."

Dunton didn't say anything.

She made an exasperated noise, went back to the coffee table, and poured herself another cup. Took a sip and frowned. "Rose!" she yelled to the door. When no one materialized, she picked up the tray herself. An excuse to flee the room.

Bernadette decided to drop the bomb. "Senator. Mrs. Dunton. Who has been blackmailing you?"

Michelle Dunton froze with the tray in her hands. Her husband turned from the window. "What?"

"We found Lydia's backpack," said Bernadette. "It was filled with letters. Someone has been milking you for large sums of money."

Garcia looked at Bernadette with wide eyes.

"You found Lydia's things?" Michelle Dunton inhaled sharply and released the tray. Glass and coffee exploded on the floor.

"What in the hell are you talking about?" Dunton rushed past the two agents to get to his wife.

Michelle Dunton dropped down on her knees next to the mess and began talking to the broken dishes. To herself. "They found my baby's things."

Dunton extended a hand down to her. "Mickey, it's fine," he said through his teeth. "Please, get up."

The mumbling woman sat back on her heels, half of a broken cup in each hand. "Maggie, make them give us Lydia's things. I want them back."

"Senator, who has been blackmailing you?" asked Bernadette. "What do they know?"

"Get out," said Dunton. Then a shout toward the door: "Ben!"

A short man with an egg head stepped into the room, and Bernadette and Garcia looked at each other.

The guy from her vision.

Dunton went down next to his wife while giving orders to the man. "See them out. Get Rose in here."

The new arrival took a step toward Bernadette with his hand extended. "I'm Benjamin Rathers, the senator's chief of—"

"They don't need to know who you are," said Dunton, rising with his wife, an arm around her waist. "Get them out of here."

"Senator," said Bernadette. "We need to know who is blackmailing—"

"No one," the senator snapped. "No one is blackmailing us."

Eyes darting between Bernadette and his boss, Rathers seemed dazed and confused.

"But the letters . . ." Bernadette continued.

"I have no idea what you're talking about," said Dunton. "Letters. What letters? That's a load of nonsense. Good God. I can't believe I'm even having this conversation."

"Lydia," croaked Michelle Dunton, falling against her husband and burying her face in his shirt. Her narrow shoulders started shaking.

Dunton wrapped his arms around his sobbing wife. "Why are you wasting time harassing the only people you know *didn't* kill Lydia? Why don't you go after those Satanists or witches or whatever they are?"

Garcia and Bernadette exchanged quick glances. Garcia shook his head.

"Senator," Bernadette said. "Who told you we were investigating those folks?"

Ignoring the question, Dunton walked his wife toward the door. "Get out," he said, and glanced over his shoulder at the patio door. "And take your bodyguard with you."

"I want to go to bed," Michelle Dunton croaked.

"Let's get you upstairs," Dunton said, and the couple left the room.

Rathers was alone with the agents, and the mess on the floor. He didn't make a move toward disposing of either, but instead buried his hands in his pants pockets and rocked back and forth on the balls of his feet.

Seeing an opportunity, Bernadette made a beeline for the debris. "Let me help before we leave."

"You don't have to do that," said Rathers, pulling his hands out of his pockets and stepping over to the scene of the accident.

Bernadette started picking up pieces of stoneware and setting them on the tray. She looked up at him with concern. "The coffee is going to stain, and this area rug looks like an antique."

"What should I do?" asked Rathers.

She stood up with the tray. "Do they have any soda water in the kitchen?"

"I'll check," he said, and thumped out of the room.

Bernadette wondered how much of the couple's act was authentic. The wife's distress over the loss of her daughter appeared genuine, but the emotional meltdown over the backpack was way over the top. Michelle had staged it to allow them a quick exit. Who was blackmailing them, and why? It had to have something to do with Lydia's murder. Why didn't they want to cooperate with the bureau in finding their daughter's killer? Was it simply because Dunton's disdain for the FBI ran so deep? That seemed as implausible as Michelle's big scene. What would they have done if Bernadette had dropped the big bomb on them and told them that their grandbaby was alive?

She whispered to Garcia, "Have a quick look around, and then meet me in the truck with B.K."

She followed Rathers to the kitchen. It was nothing like the kitchen she'd observed through her sight. As she dumped the broken cups into a wastebasket, Bernadette studied the man rummaging around the refrigerator.

Benjamin Rathers was one of those guys who shaved his head to achieve a certain look. As if to emphasize that the pristine scalp was not an accident but a radical statement, he also sported a diamond stud in one lobe. She hadn't noticed that when using her sight. He was a rebel, but a quiet, well-groomed one. He was around her age, and just a couple of inches taller. He was dressed in dark slacks, a dark sweater, and black little shoes—the same outfit she'd spied on him when she was using her sight. This guy was pretty high up in the food chain, and he'd met with one of the killers. Did he realize it? Surely the killers and the blackmailers were the same people. She had to find out about the letters and who'd visited the night before.

"No soda water," said Rathers.

Bernadette figured she could work on this guy. He seemed decent, and was obviously taken aback by the melodrama that had unfolded. She continued with the helpful hausfrau routine. "What's that green bottle on the second shelf?" she asked, looking over his shoulder.

"Perrier."

"That'll work."

He fished it out and handed it to her. "What else do you need?"

She opened the cabinet under the sink and pulled out a roll of paper towels. "These."

Bernadette headed back toward the trophy room, with Rathers following her and whispering, "I really need to see you out."

Garcia was gone from the room, and Cahill had left the deck. She was glad to get Rathers alone. She kneeled over the brown amoeba, poured the fizzy beverage into the middle of it, and dropped some towels on top of the puddle. "This works like a charm every time."

He shuffled his feet as he stood over her. "I'll have to remember that one. We have a lot of spills at home. Little kids. You know."

She stood up and handed the empty bottle and towel roll to Rathers. "That should do it."

"Uh . . . thank you." Almost apologizing for his boss and the earlier scene, he added, "The Duntons have been without sleep since . . . since the news."

"Ben, do you know anything about Lydia and those letters? Who has been wringing money out of the Duntons?"

Rathers seemed genuinely perplexed. "Letters?"

"When Lydia and her boyfriend broke in to the house—"

"Lydia lived there," Rathers said defensively. "It wasn't a break-in if it was her house."

"When they entered the house on Thanksgiving weekend, they took some things, including a set of letters. Correspondence between the Duntons and someone asking for money."

"The senator receives lots of requests from constituents," said Rathers. "They want money for projects, for their causes."

"They threatened to reveal something unless they were paid. Does that sound like someone asking him to vote for a piece of legislation?"

Rathers adjusted his grip on the bottle and the paper towels. "You need to get out of here."

"What's going on here, Benjamin?"

"I can't," he said, shaking his head.

"We can protect you."

He looked down at his feet.

"Who was over to the house last night?" she asked.

"What do you . . . what are you getting at?"

"Who was here late last night?"

"Why?"

"Under this roof, last night. Name them."

"I was here. The senator and his wife. The two drivers."

"Rose?"

"She'd left. She's not a live-in."

"Who else? What about the owners of the house?"

"They're in Europe."

"Was anyone else here late last night?"

He looked down again. "I'm not sure what you're getting at. What happened last night?"

She had to show him that she had enough information to do some damage. "A meeting was held here last night, in this very room. You were involved."

"How would you know?" His gaze swiveled this way and that, finally landing on the windows.

Rathers was worried that the bureau was spying on them. Bernadette saw no good reason to ease his concerns, and in fact anticipated only good things resulting from that sort of paranoia. "We believe the murderer was one of those in attendance," she said authoritatively. "He's probably the one who's been blackmailing the Duntons."

He tore a sheet off the paper-towel roll and patted his forehead.

"If you withhold vital information and a third person is murdered, we could come after you. We *will* come after you. That's a promise."

Rathers started babbling. "Agent Saint Clare, you have to believe me. I'd like to help, but I don't see how I can. I work for a man who . . . I work for a man of some rank and power. He lost his daughter . . . I can't . . . I don't know what I can do to help you . . . It's out of my control . . . It's . . . I don't know."

"What gave the senator the idea that we were investigating a coven?"

"I'd never heard that before in my life. That was news to me. You have got to believe me, Agent Saint Clare. I don't know anything about witches and Satanists relative to this case. Relative to anything! And this whole blackmail thing!" He dropped the bottle and the towels on an end table. "Gotta get you out of here before the senator comes back down."

"Ben, don't force us to take you in for questioning."

"But I don't know anything!"

"I think you know more than—"

"That's enough!" bellowed a voice behind Bernadette.

She turned and saw the senator, his face red with anger. "Sir," she said. "This is—"

"This is outrageous," he said, marching toward her. "I want you out of this house right now!"

"Senator, I'm sorry, but—"

"You bet you're sorry." He put a hand on her shoulder and started steering her to the door. "I just got off the phone with Washington."

"I'll see her out, sir."

"Don't say another word to her," snarled Dunton.

Rathers walked her outside and to the truck, where Garcia was waiting behind the wheel and Cahill was sitting in back. Before Bernadette got in, she passed Rathers a card. "Call me."

He didn't say anything more, but slipped the card inside his pocket. Turned around and headed up the steps.

As Garcia steered the truck down the drive, Bernadette glanced at the front of the house. The drapes of a second-story window moved. Who was spying on whom?

## CHAPTER TWENTY-NINE

No one in the truck said a word until the closed gates of the gated community were in the rearview mirror. The first one to speak was Garcia, and he wasn't happy.

"The next time you decide to pull a rabbit out of your ass, I'd appreciate some warning."

Bernadette didn't need to look in the backseat to know B.K. was squirming. The kid had no idea what had transpired in the house, but he was smart enough to keep his mouth shut while Garcia ranted.

"Sir, I'm sorry," she said, keeping it formal for Cahill's benefit. "I couldn't let the senator kick us out before I asked those questions. I wish I'd had time to brief you first, but I didn't."

"And what was that bit with Carson parading around, his hand on his gun?"

"My brain fart," she blurted.

B.K. leaned forward and stuck his head between the two front-seat passengers. "But I went along with it, sir."

Bernadette cringed. Maybe he wasn't smart enough.

"Close it, Carson!" snapped Garcia.

"Yes, sir," said Cahill, falling back against the seat.

"What did you two think was going to happen in there? He's a United States senator and I'm an agent of the federal government. Was he going to bump us off and dump us in a snowbank in the middle of the day?"

"I was just being cautious, sir," she said. "When we spoke over the phone, you sounded guarded, and I was concerned."

"I'm still alive and it's all good," said Garcia, steering the truck through downtown Walker. "Now tell me what happened this morning."

"Cahill and I went to the tatt shop together. After we pressed him on it, the scumbag owner admitted that he recognized Lydia's photo. Said he gave her that heart tatt on Christmas Eve."

"What was she doing up here? Did he say?"

"Hunting for someone. She even asked to use his phone book, to look up an address or name," said Bernadette.

"Who? Who'd she look up?"

"The guy didn't know. Lydia did ask him where she could find cheap eats and a place to stay."

Garcia braked for a red light and looked over at her. "Where did he send her?"

"He didn't. Sounds like he wasn't particularly helpful to her. On top of that, she couldn't pay for the tattoo, so he kept her backpack and her mom's jewelry. We arrested his ass, of course."

"You should have seen the tackle Bern made," added Cahill.

Bernadette offered Garcia a weak smile. "Yeah. You should have seen it."

Garcia frowned. "Keep going."

"The backpack was filled with letters."

"The ones the boyfriend talked about, apparently."

"Someone has been blackmailing the Duntons," she said.

The light turned green, but Garcia kept his foot on the brake. The driver behind him honked, and he accelerated. "Blackmailing them over what?"

"We need to do more checking, sir," said a small voice in the backseat.

"From reading them, it's not entirely clear," she said.

"Where are they?"

"Tuckert took them," she said. "He's so excited about the tests he's gonna run, he's peeing all over himself."

"I'd like to look at them."

"I took photos and sent them to my laptop. We'll read them at the—" She cut herself off, not wanting B.K. to know where she was staying. "We can read them later."

"You are really going to want to see those letters," interjected Cahill. "We're talking big bucks. One asked for a million."

"Dunton doesn't have that kind of money, does he?" asked Garcia.

"He's got to be sitting on a fortune from his days as a developer," she said. "Plus, remember her family is loaded."

"The letters didn't indicate what they were holding over him?" asked Garcia.

"The threats were very veiled."

"Any clue where they were mailed from? Any envelopes with postal stamps?"

"Afraid not. Maybe Lydia trashed them during her travels, or maybe the Duntons didn't keep them."

"Why would the Duntons keep any of that around their place?" asked Garcia.

"In case they decided to report their blackmailers to the cops?" she guessed.

"It sure turned around and bit them on the ass," said Garcia.

"Something bigger has been biting them on the ass over the

years," said Bernadette. "We've gotta find out what it was. It sent their daughter to Brule and then to Walker. Probably caused her death. Ashe's death, too."

"Anything in the writing indicate the connection to witches, pentagrams, any of that?"

"Nothing. If only the Duntons would cooperate and work with us. Put aside their feelings about the bureau."

"Don't hold your breath on that," said Garcia. "While you were inside playing house with Rathers, I got a call from D.C. Dunton bitched to the bosses in Washington. Told them he wants us off the case because we're incompetent."

"Incompetent? Based on what?"

"Our lack of progress."

"We're making progress," she protested. "What happened to-day was huge. Finding the bag and the letters was huge."

"He claimed that the guy who stole Lydia's stuff planted some shit in her bag in some sort of extortion plot—and that we're falling for it."

"That's not even a good lie," she said. "That's lame."

"The word of a United States senator against a thieving slime-ball who runs a tatt shop," said Garcia. "Gee, who're they gonna be-lieve? We need more before we can force the Duntons to talk to us about this blackmail business."

"Rathers knows something, but he's afraid to open his mouth," she said.

"Back up a minute. You're a hundred percent certain about Rathers and the room where we had the meeting today. They're the same man and the same room you saw—" Garcia stopped himself short, remembering that there was a third person in the cab.

Aware that Garcia was referring to her vision, Bernadette looked at her boss and nodded in affirmation. "Yeah. Absolutely certain."

Cahill: "What are you two saying? I'm lost. *Absolutely certain* about what?"

"Carson, what did we talk about?" asked Bernadette.

The young agent recited: "Don't ask questions. Don't worry about what everyone else is doing. Maintain my inner calm. Go with the flow."

Garcia frowned.

"I'm teaching Carson the art of FBI Zen," she explained.

"Nice," said Garcia.

"Sir," said Cahill. "You just passed—"

"Stop talking," said Garcia. "There's my FBI Zen lesson for the day."

"But you just passed my car, sir."

"Next time, spit it out."

"Yes, sir."

There was too much traffic on the street to back up. Garcia went around the block and pulled up next to the Crown Victoria. The sun was already going down, and soon the afternoon would surrender to another long winter night. Before Cahill hopped out of the truck, they talked about the witches' meeting later that evening. Cahill was charged with collecting some of the Minneapolis guys from their various hotels. They'd all meet in Walker with the sheriff's crew before heading to the forest, where the full-moon ceremony was being held.

"Need me to pick you up, Bern?" he asked before closing the door.

"I'll fetch her," said Garcia.

"Right," said B.K., and he went to his car.

Bernadette watched Cahill fiddling with the lock of his car door. It was giving him trouble. He dropped the keys, picked them up, and tried again. "Big goof."

"His size came in handy this afternoon," said Garcia.

Her eyes widened. "Hey. You said—"

"I didn't mind the display of firepower," Garcia conceded. "It was a good brain fart, actually. Dunton got the message not to screw with us, and at the same time we didn't put enough agents on the property that he could get righteously indignant about it."

"We're walking a fine line here, aren't we?"

"A fucking tightrope," said Garcia, pulling away as the young agent finally got inside his sedan.

"Did you notice Carson didn't ask where we were going?"

"Because it's none of his concern," Garcia said.

"I think he suspects," she said. "For all we know, they all suspect. They're all back at their hotels talking about us poolside."

"If that's the case, I hope they say only good things. 'That Garcia. He sure must have an impressive—' "

"Stop," she said.

At the outskirts of downtown Walker was a large grocery store. Garcia hung a left off the main drag and hung another left into the market's parking lot. He pulled a fistful of bills out of his jacket pocket. "I'm gonna run inside and buy some meat. What do you feel like? Steaks? Chicken?"

"Anything that'll fit on a grill."

"Want to come with?"

"Go ahead," she said. "I loathe grocery shopping almost as much as clothes shopping."

"You are one weird woman."

"No argument here. Look who I'm screwing."

"I'll leave the truck running," he said with a grin, and jumped out of the cab.

While he was in the store, she fiddled with the heating vents and played with the radio. The only stations that were coming in clear were country and western and hard rock. Though she'd already visited his CD wallet, she picked it up again and started from the back.

Discovered some music she'd missed during the drive up north. An Edith Piaf disc, followed by some Roy Orbison and Cowboy Junkies. Patsy Cline. The music from *O Brother, Where Art Thou?* and a CD put out by a band that hailed from Ecuador. She pulled out one disc and stared at it in disbelief. *Cher's Greatest Hits.*

Individually, there was nothing wrong with the tunes, but they made for a strange, almost disturbing, collection. "And you call me weird," she muttered.

Maybe it was their mutual weirdness that helped make them so comfortable with each other. At the same time, getting *too* comfortable worried her. Was she being set up for a big disappointment? What would happen to their relationship once they returned to the cities? Was it going to be like one of those summer flings that ended the minute the cabin was closed up? If so, maybe it was all for the better. Sleeping with the boss wasn't going to make her life simpler or easier. On the other hand, he was so good in bed. She'd heard about men who managed to sleep-screw but figured they were a myth. She'd actually found such a lover. How could she let him go? It would be like turning her back on a unicorn.

By the time he returned to the truck, she had "Gypsies, Tramps and Thieves" blaring.

"I can explain that," he said as he opened the back and set the groceries inside.

"I'm listening, Anthony," she said, swaying to the music.

He climbed in and slammed the door. "Ah, fuck it. It isn't worth it."

She turned off the tunes. "What did you buy us for dinner?"

The Titan bumped out of the parking lot. "Chicken. Steak. Ground beef. Pork loins. Pork chops. Enough for a month."

"We'd better not be here that long," she grumbled. "I miss my junk."

"Me, too," he said, and turned onto the highway. As he drove, he pulled at the neck of his dress shirt. "I'm changing into jeans as soon as I get to the cabin."

"Did the suit help your game?"

"Nothing could have helped my game with the Duntons," said Garcia.

# CHAPTER THIRTY

As soon as they got to the cabin, Bernadette set the laptop on the coffee table, pulled up the letters, and turned it over to Garcia to read while they sat on the couch.

"Veiled is right," he said, shaking his head.

"I suppose in case they were read by a third party." She pointed to the screen. "This one references his election."

"Appears so," said Garcia.

Your new status requires different terms. This is non-negotiable. A response is needed immediately. Any delay in payment will mean higher fees.

"Reads like a damn credit-card contract," said Bernadette.

"If the Duntons made payments, there's got to be a paper trail," said Garcia. "Cash-withdrawal records from the bank. Transfer notices."

She got up and walked back and forth between the table and the fireplace. "What did they have on him?"

"Lydia must have known what they were talking about," said Garcia.

Bernadette tossed another log on the fire. "Maybe the girl had more letters on her but lost or destroyed them. Hid them somewhere."

"Is that what took her to Brule and then to Walker? Did she confront the blackmailers and threaten to go to the police and that's what got her killed?"

"Where does that Brule murder fit in? Where do the witches fit in?" continued Bernadette, staring into the blaze.

Behind her, Garcia closed the laptop. "My head hurts."

They were both famished, and agreed to save the rest of the discussion until after dinner hit the table. While she peeled the potatoes, Garcia pulled on a stocking cap. "You're going to freeze your ass off," she said. "Why don't we cook them inside?"

"Because Tony wants to grill," he said petulantly, and went outside.

As she stood at the island stovetop adjusting the heat under the potatoes, she watched Garcia through the windows. Standing on the porch that ran across the lake side of the cabin, he was hunched over an old Weber. He finally got the coals going just as she got the water boiling. He covered the grill and came inside to warm up and watch her poke at the potatoes.

"Aren't you going to ask me how I like my steak?" she asked.

"I'll tell you exactly how you like it: burned on the outside and raw on the inside."

While he went outside to flip the burning steaks, Bernadette mashed the potatoes and lugged the kettle over to the table. He came in with a platter of black T-bones, blood swimming beneath them. "God, those look wonderful," she said. She dropped down onto a chair and started scooping mashed potatoes onto their plates.

Garcia sat down across from her, stabbed the smallest steak, and deposited it on her plate. Took the biggest for himself. There was one left. They both stared at it. "Arm-wrestle you for it," he said.

"Let's see how I do with this," she said, and started cutting into her meat.

They sawed and chewed and made happy sounds for several minutes. Garcia dragged a napkin across his mouth. "You want to go first or should I?"

"You go," she said.

Picking up his steak knife, he resumed his hacking at the T-bone while raising the big question that he couldn't ask with Cahill in the truck. "Do you realize where your sight is taking this investigation, Cat? You're implying that someone who was in that house last night, a member of the senator's entourage or a visitor—"

"I'm not implying shit—I'm saying that flat out," she said, pointing a fork at him. "Someone in *that* house killed his daughter and stole her baby. Otherwise I wouldn't have been able to see Rathers and that trophy room. You know how it works. I see through the eyes of murderers, not . . . pizza-delivery guys."

"Is that same person the blackmailer?"

"If the killer isn't the actual blackmailer, they have something to do with each other. They're working in tandem."

"So who was there last night?" Garcia asked.

"Rathers said the Duntons were there last night—and he was there, obviously. The maid was gone . . ."

"What about those two goons Dunton tried to send after Cahill?"

"They were there last night," said Bernadette.

"What do you think of those two? Do you like them for the killings?"

"I like them for their sheer size," said Bernadette, dipping a wedge of meat into a puddle of A1. "They would have been fully capable of handling a little girl and a lady witch."

"You think one of them tried to break in to your hotel room in Brule? What about the guy who attacked you?"

"I didn't get a good look at the motel guy. The guy in the woods sounded big, and either one of them would fit the bill." She popped some meat into her mouth and chewed.

"What about the baby?" asked Garcia. "Who was feeding the baby last night, in your vision?"

"Rathers said both goons were at the house last night, so—"

"So if Dunton's drivers *are* involved—"

"Someone is helping them, watching the baby while they're out and about."

"A third maniac we need to worry about," said Garcia. "Great."

"If the thugs are responsible, they were acting pretty cool." She took a sip of water. "You'd think they'd be sweating a little. Here they are, standing around the parents of the kid they killed. The grandparents of the baby they're holding. In walks the FBI agent that one of them bonked on the head."

"Good actors?" offered Garcia.

"No, those guys didn't look smart enough to pull it off, especially if the blackmail has been going on for years. There was someone else in that house last night, and I was seeing through his or her eyes." She dabbed her mouth and threw down her napkin. "Why don't they just tell us about the blackmailer? They must know their daughter's death is connected to the extortion."

"Whatever is being held over their heads, it's got to be enormous." He rifled a hunk of meat into his mouth. Chewed and swallowed. "We should get some answers when we crash the party tonight. Sounds like half the county is going to be there."

"The OB. Did I tell you that? Graham wasn't lying. Bossard *is* a member of the coven. Nurse Martini, too."

He lowered his utensils and blinked. "Isn't she the one who pointed you to Ashe in the first place?"

"She was one of the coven members Jordan called before she was killed."

"I'm still wondering about Dunton's crack regarding the witches," he said, and stabbed the third steak with his fork. "You want some of this?"

"No way. I'm full." She pushed her chair back and crossed one leg over the other. Thought about it. "Say the witches are the extortionists. If Dunton wants the fact that he's being blackmailed kept quiet, why would he have blurted out stuff about us investigating them? Why would he encourage us to go after them?"

"He wouldn't." Garcia stared at the T-bone he'd dropped onto his plate as if facing an uphill climb. Took a deep breath and started cutting into it.

"Whether they're really involved or not, how would he know that we're checking into them? Do you suppose someone let it slip while Dunton or his people were calling around trying to get the body released? They were bugging Wharten, the coroner, the ME."

"Maybe that's how they found out," said Garcia.

Garcia's cell rang while they were cleaning up. He picked it up and examined the screen. Answered it. "Yeah, Seth . . . really?" Garcia checked his watch. "That late? You sure? Okay. You're the expert. You still know where? . . . Wait, wait, wait. You lost me already. We'll stick with the original plan and all meet up and head in together . . . Good . . . Let me flag my people." Garcia hung up and punched a number in his cell.

"What's up?" asked Bernadette.

Garcia held up his hand while he talked into his phone. "Cahill, I'm gonna let you be my point man on this."

Bernadette smiled to herself. B.K. was going to enjoy being Garcia's anything.

"Tell the rest of the crew we've had a change of plans. Seth . . . Sheriff Wharten thinks the witches aren't getting together until midnight. Still in the woods. North section of Paul Bunyan. We'll meet up with Seth and his men in Walker a half hour beforehand, and we'll all go in together. Otherwise we'll never find it—I don't know north unit the way I know south. Got it? Good. Spread the word. See you there."

As soon as Garcia hung up, Bernadette asked, "How does Wharten know so much about the witches and their meeting?"

"Ashe's boyfriend."

"Karl Vizner?"

"He's still a wreck and isn't talking to our people, but Seth has been getting some information out of the guy. A lot of it Seth already knows. He knew this full-moon thing was coming up. It's one of their regular ceremonies. Vizner was able to tell him where the backup worship space is located, being that their main outdoor worship space was desecrated by the pig fetus, and by the presence of a bunch of FBI agents."

"I wonder which they found more odious," she said.

Garcia opened his mouth to offer an opinion, and his phone rang again.

"You're a busy man," said Bernadette, loading the dishwasher.

Garcia picked up his cell and checked the screen. "This should be good."

She closed the dishwasher and leaned a hand against the counter to listen.

Garcia: "Yeah, Doc. What's the skinny? Got anything yet? The senator has been asking about the release of her body."

The Ramsey County Medical Examiner with some autopsy results.

"Are you certain?" Garcia stood at the island and pulled a notepad toward him. Started taking frantic notes. "Damn. That is . . .

yeah . . . wow. Anything else to back that up? Uh-huh . . . It sure as shit does."

Bernadette was dying to know what the ME had found.

Garcia turned to a fresh page. Continued writing. "Yeah . . . yeah. What makes you think that?"

She craned her neck in an attempt to read what he was writing, but she couldn't decipher most of his scribbles.

"A what?" asked Garcia, pausing in his writing. "A *low-segment transverse incision*? What does that mean, exactly? . . . Uh-huh. Interesting."

Bernadette looked at his notes. One word was legible, but it was enough to get her heart racing:

*Scalpel.*

Garcia asked the ME the same questions she would have asked: "Doc, could someone other than an OB have done this? What about an ER doc or a nurse or—"

"A midwife," she whispered.

"Or a midwife?" Garcia listened and scribbled some more.

Bernadette was dancing around Garcia, trying to read his notes.

"Uh-huh . . . No, that's fine . . . I wasn't expecting any guarantees," Garcia said into the phone. "Why would someone use that procedure instead of going with the single incision, especially if they're trying to misdirect us? Yeah, I completely get what you're saying. That makes perfect sense. Yeah, yeah . . . Thanks, Doc."

As soon as Garcia closed his phone, Bernadette jumped on him. "Tell me."

"ME said we shouldn't assume the slice job was done by an amateur," said Garcia. "In other words, it might have looked like a mess, but it wasn't."

"What do you mean? Whoever did it cut through the navel, for Christ's sake. That sounds like the definition of amateur."

"That could have been an effort to throw us off."

"Keep talking."

"For starters, it was done with a sharp tool. Possibly a scalpel. Possibly."

"That isn't enough to convince me. Homicidal maniacs have sharp tools. What else did he say?"

"I'm probably screwing this up, losing something in the translation," said Garcia.

"Basically . . ."

"Basically, he said a true amateur would have done a vertical incision on the skin, all the way through to the uterus."

"That's not what was done?"

"No. Not exactly. This is where I might screw it up, so bear with me." He looked at his notes. "What was done was a vertical incision on the skin, and then a low-segment transverse incision into the uterus."

"How is that different?"

"In order to do this low-segment transverse incision thing, the bladder has to be pushed down so it isn't cut." He looked at his notes again. "This is done by cutting a transverse incision in the serosa and pushing it down by blunt—meaning fingers—and sharp—meaning scissors—dissection."

"What is a serosa?"

"It's the outer lining"—he flipped to the second page—"of the organs and body cavities of the abdomen. It's a membrane."

"So the bottom line is it was done by an OB?"

"He wouldn't say that with a hundred percent certainty. It could be someone who has seen the procedure done, been in an operating room for it."

"An ER doc? A nurse?"

"Only if he or she has OB experience, and that's pushing it."

"Midwife?"

"Not likely. But again, depends upon her experience."

"Why would someone who wants to throw us off use a procedure that points to a professional?"

"You heard me—that's what I asked," said Garcia. "ME thinks it's someone for whom the procedure is completely automatic. They've done it a million times. It's like breathing. Even if they start sloppy, cutting through the navel and all, they have to do it right once they get inside the mother."

"Couldn't it also be someone who has carefully memorized the procedure and doesn't know how to safely deliver a baby any other way?"

"Works for me. Take your pick."

"I didn't see anything in the Brule murder file about a low-segment whatever. Gotta put my hands on a more detailed autopsy report."

"They've gotta be related," he said.

As Bernadette walked back and forth across the kitchen floor, she felt as if an electric current were running through her body. "Lots of questions. So many questions."

"Like I said, we could get the answers at the witches' deal tonight. I say we stick with the plan. Drop in unannounced for some toad soup. Rattle our sabers and scare the hell out of them."

"What's this ceremony called again?"

"It's some sort of ritual celebrating the full moon." Garcia rubbed his chin. "What did Seth call it? The Lestat rite?"

"Lestat is a character in a vampire novel. He's pretty cool, but I doubt they built a whole rite around him."

"Maybe it was Esbat. Yeah. The Esbat rite."

Night had fallen hours ago. She stepped over to the windows facing the lake and looked out. The sky was clear. The moon looked as white and round as a snowball. "Good night for an Esbat rite, I'd say."

Garcia looked down at his sweatpants and sweatshirt. "What do you wear to an Esbat rite?"

She turned away from the window. "I don't know. Black jeans?"

"What do you think we're going to see there?"

She chewed her bottom lip. "I know what I *don't* want to see."

"Seth insists that his witches—"

"*His* witches," she repeated, shaking her head in dry amusement.

"He says they aren't into animal sacrifice, human sacrifice, ritual abuse. None of that. If he thought that was going on, he'd be all over them. He knows where they all live, Cat, and they know he knows."

"We've already talked about the possibility there's a renegade," she said. "I'm really worried about that little baby. Whether it's being watched by a coven of blackmailing witches, or a couple of greedy kidnappers, we've got to get to it."

"What are you saying?"

"I'm saying we have some time. We should go upstairs and give it another go."

His face darkened. "I don't need you going blind right before the big dance."

"The instant I have trouble, I'll pull out. I swear."

"I heard that tune before."

Bernadette started moving around the cabin, shutting off lights. "I'm going to win this one, Anthony."

"No, you're not."

She started for the loft. "I'm not listening."

## CHAPTER THIRTY-ONE

Benjamin Rathers wished he'd listened.

As he clomped around the frozen shores of Walker Bay in a set of borrowed snowshoes with a borrowed headlamp strapped to his head, he wished to God that he'd listened to his statistics teacher, and that he'd taken Uncle Joe up on his generous offer.

In high school, Rathers had displayed a talent for numbers—especially statistics—and his instructor had encouraged him to pursue a career as an actuary. His uncle Joe, a senior assistant actuary for an automobile-insurance company, had offered to find him a position, provided he attended college and passed the Society of Actuaries exam.

Looking for excitement beyond an insurance-company cubicle, Rathers had instead chased a degree in journalism at the University of Minnesota. He'd gotten on with a law journal. That had led to political contacts, and that had led to a mid-level job with the senator's office in Minnesota. Mid-level in Minnesota morphed into high-level in Washington, and in no time at all he was chief of staff for Mad Maggie.

It wasn't until after Rathers took the top job that he fully grasped how Dunton had earned his nickname. Outsiders thought the senator was called "mad" because he was so angry, constantly railing against his own government and its agencies. The denizens of Dunton's innermost circle knew that the noun was more applicable than the adjective: Magnus Dunton was not so much a *mad man* as a *madman*.

Rathers should have known better than to share with Dunton his suspicions that the FBI had the house under surveillance. The news sent the senator into a tailspin of paranoia. A meeting that had been scheduled for later that evening was deemed out of the question because the FBI was watching. Canceling the meeting via phone wasn't possible because the FBI was listening. Dunton didn't want anyone driving to the individual's home to deliver the cancellation notice because the FBI would follow the car once it left the gated community. The black helicopters had not only landed but were minutes away from disgorging an army of black-suited men. Come morning, Dunton and everyone he'd ever met would be eating off cafeteria trays and standing in line to use the urinals at Gitmo.

The only person remotely capable of calling Dunton off the ledge—Mrs. Mad Maggie—was curled up in her bed with her loyal and ever-present companion, Prince Valium.

End result: Rathers was ordered to sneak out back like a criminal, schlep around the lake, and knock on the person's door to deliver a sealed envelope.

Rathers had no idea why this particular constituent was so important. He'd only met the individual the night before. "A personal matter," Mad Maggie had said that evening, and chased everyone else out so that he could be alone with the visitor. More cloak-and-dagger crap. Dunton attracted other black-helicopter enthusiasts, and they were always coming to his office with cardboard boxes.

Evidence of government malfeasance. Plots within plots. Corruption at the highest levels.

Marybeth had been after him to quit the job, and this messenger-pigeon assignment convinced Rathers that his wife was right. Spending his workdays in a warm cubicle, pricing auto insurance in the southeastern United States, was preferable to crunching through the woods in snowshoes with a sealed envelope stuffed inside his jacket.

As he trudged, he thought about the questions raised by the FBI lady. Her claim that someone had been blackmailing the Duntons had thrown Rathers for a loop, as had the senator's comment about witches and Satanists. Was that just Mad Maggie tossing something bizarre out there, seeing if it'd stick or cause a stir—he approached legislation that way—or was something more insidious going on? When Dunton came down and found that the woman was still in the house, his reaction had been extreme, even for Mad Maggie.

Definitely time to leave Dunton's employment.

Certainly Rathers felt terrible about what had happened to Lydia, but she'd been headed for trouble for years. Spoiled rotten. Always on her father's lap. Always dressed in designer duds, like a miniature of Michelle. Enrolled in that artsy academy when she should have been sent to a more disciplined school. Then came the sleazy boyfriend and the pregnancy. The big fight with her parents. Whether they'd tossed Lydia out or she'd run off, Rathers didn't know for sure. Didn't matter. There was no blackmail plot. There were no witches or Devil worshippers. The girl had fallen victim to a random nut job, a whacked-out woodsman. It was as brutally simple as that.

Rathers huffed and puffed around the frozen bay. He'd originally planned to take a snowmobile, and had gotten as far as driving one down to the shoreline behind Dunton's pal's house. Rathers had been intimidated by the power of the thing, however. He'd never used a sled and decided that he wasn't comfortable trying to take a crash course in the dark. He switched to the snowshoes. Though he hadn't been on a set in years, he knew for a fact that they couldn't toss you off or drive you into a tree at fifty miles an hour. The webbing helped him float above the snow, rather than sink knee-deep into it. All he had to do was walk slightly bowlegged and remember that he couldn't back up in them because the metal cleats on the bottom would catch. He also borrowed a set of ski poles, and those helped him keep his balance and make good progress.

There was no wind and the sky was clear, but it was in the double digits below zero. Rathers had a headlamp strapped over his stocking cap, but he wouldn't need to turn it on yet. The moon was full and bright. With the shore on his right, he took in the cluster of fish houses on his left. A couple of them were strung with rope lights, and a few of the cabins on the lake had their yard lights going.

After he put the fishing village behind him, he stopped and stabbed his poles into the snow. Swiped his dripping nose with the back of his glove. Reached up and clicked on the headlamp. He pulled out the written instructions and held them in front of his face, so that the lamp illuminated the paper. Like the cabin where the Duntons were staying, the home was on the bay. It sat farther south, however, away from downtown Walker. It was also set back from the lake, which would make it more difficult to spot from the shore. He put the map back in his pocket and kept going.

Rathers came upon a compact cabin sitting close to shore, at the bottom of an incline. Its interior was lit and its small windows glowed like gold squares. He was supposed to pass a small cabin, its outhouse painted with a peace sign. He looked up at the dinky home. Sure enough, it had an outhouse set back from the lake. He tipped his head this way and that, and thought he could make out something painted on the side of the biffy. That meant the target house was six cabins down. He adjusted his grip on the ski poles and resumed his trek.

He thought he had the right place. The incline was thinly wooded, and he was sure that he saw lights at the top. He walked toward the shore and started the long hike up the hill. On snow-shoes, the best way to tackle a hill was to go straight up, utilizing the poles for balance and added traction. The cleats on the bottom grabbed the surface nicely and kept him from sliding backward.

A third of the way up, Rathers realized that he'd underestimated the steepness of the hill and overestimated his physical capabilities. Leaning heavily against the poles, he stopped to catch his breath, and to contemplate the very real possibility that he was having a heart attack. His chest was pounding like crazy, and he felt the sweat collecting under his armpits. The outdoor wear that he'd bor-rowed—a set of snowmobile pants and a ski jacket—didn't fit prop-erly. Dunton's buddy was built like Dunton. Tall and skinny. The pants sagged at the bottom and cut into him at the waist, and the jacket was compressing his chest. Or was that the heart attack?

"Fuck!" he wheezed, standing in the cloud of his labored breaths.

Could he even call for help from here? He pulled out his cell and checked the screen. Dead.

"Fuck!" he wheezed again, and put the phone back.

He had no choice but to continue the climb. He had to stop twice more, and each time took advantage of the trees, propping a hand against a trunk for support.

By the time he got to ground that wasn't so steep, he was drenched and his legs felt like jelly. The clearing ahead of him was angled but not as steep. At the top of it was the house. The win-dows facing the lake were lit, and he could see a deck running across the width of the place. Another log structure. People up north couldn't get enough of them. He'd had his fill of them, and made a mental note to cover his own cabin in vinyl siding, were he ever to buy a lake home.

When he got to the cabin, he saw that there were steps along one side leading up to the deck and a bright yard light mounted above the door.

"More climbing," he groaned.

Rathers took off the snowshoes, nearly falling over as he bent down to undo the straps from his boots. He leaned the snowshoes and poles against the side of the house. As he went up the steps, he hung on to the rail. When he got to the top, he took another break. He was light-headed, and starting to feel slightly chilled. Maybe he'd have the constituent drive him back. Screw Dunton and his FBI phobia.

Energized by the thought of an easy return trip, Rathers went over to the door and raised his fist to knock.

A peculiar sound made his hand freeze.

The curtains at the patio doors along the deck were closed, but he spotted a gap between the drapes. He carefully stepped over to the glass and peeked inside. All he saw was a figure dressed in jeans and a pink sweater, back turned toward the window. The person was shuffling side to side and jiggling. Rathers had three kids, and readily recognized the odd movement.

Baby dance.

The dancer turned around with a bawling bundle. The infant was obviously only a day or two old, but what brought back that heart-attack sensation was the child's head.

Orange fuzz.

Rathers slapped a hand over his mouth and fell back from the window. Turned and tiptoed toward the stairs. Stood at the top, wondering what to do and where to go. He remembered that he was wearing a headlamp and clicked it off. Had someone inside noticed the beam? No. They would have come outside. He reached inside his jacket and pulled out his cell. Still dead. Dropped it back in his pocket. He looked to the right and left and could see the lights of the other cabins. He'd go to them for help. What would he tell the senator?

He'd found Lydia's killer, and his grandchild.

A chilling revelation washed over the chief of staff. Rathers pulled off his stocking cap and dragged a gloved hand over the top of his sweaty scalp. He couldn't tell the senator anything. He'd have to call the cops.

Rathers dropped one foot on the step, intending to run next door.

A large figure in a parka came up behind him and slammed a shovel over the top of his head. Rathers grunted loudly and stumbled down a step with his hands out in front of him. The shovel came down a second time, and he fell forward, his face planted at the bottom step and his booted feet on the top.

## CHAPTER THIRTY-TWO

Bernadette is shuttling back and forth, looking through the eyes of one killer and then the other. This time the murderers aren't operating in different houses or even in separate rooms but are positioned less than six feet apart from each other. One is kneeling at a man's stocking feet, flashlight in hand, and the other is at the man's illuminated head. The light trained on the face of the man gives him a spooky glow. A severed head floating in the woods.

The rapidly shifting viewpoints, so close together, are making her head ache again. But she refuses to release the scrap of fabric that connects her to this death scene. She has no doubt that it is a death scene. She's equally certain of the dead man's identity; she'd recognize that shaved head anywhere.

Benjamin Rathers.

Rathers is on his back, sprawled against a blue background. A blanket or a sheet of plastic. While his head is bare and his feet are shoeless, the rest of him is clothed in outdoor gear. Ski jacket and pants, or a snowmobile suit. He was outside when he was killed.

The two murderers are so tightly focused on the corpse that they don't look at each other. Still, Bernadette can make out trees and nighttime blackness around the periphery of this jerky, morbid movie. This is happening right now, somewhere in the woods.

The killer positioned at Rathers' head reaches down. There is something in the gloved hand. It's a pen or a marker. Slowly and carefully, the murderer sets the tip on the pale forehead of Benjamin Rathers and begins to draw. A repeat of what happened to Jordan Ashe!

Bernadette gasped and opened her fist, releasing the sliver of fabric and breaking the connection. Eyes closed tight, she collapsed back against the headboard.

"Cat?" asked Garcia, putting a hand on her shoulder. "Can you see?"

Bernadette wasn't certain which sight Garcia was inquiring about, but she knew which one she valued more deeply. Slowly, she raised her lids. A crack at first. A kid afraid to watch the evisceration scene in a horror flick. As she discerned Garcia's reassuring profile in the darkness of the bedroom, she opened her eyes all the way and released a relieved breath. "I can see you."

"What did you see?" asked Garcia, perched on the edge of the mattress.

She leaned forward and dropped her face in her palms. "Give me a minute," she said through her fingers.

He slid off the bed and went over to the bedside lamp. Clicked it on. "Does your head hurt again?"

"No," she said, lying. "I'm trying to collect my thoughts is all."

"Bullshit."

She sat straight and wrapped her arms around her torso. Shivered. The killers were cold from working outside. Her gut was in a knot, indicating that they were also nervous. Or was it her own anxiety?

Garcia stood over her, arms crossed in front of him. "See anything we can use?"

"Benjamin Rathers is dead," she said numbly.

"Fuck! Are you sure?"

"They're in the woods with him, drawing a star on his forehead, just like was done to Ashe."

"The witches," said Garcia.

"Why would they pick him?" she asked, questioning herself as much as Garcia.

"Dunton's daughter, and now his chief of staff. The coven's got a vendetta against the senator."

Slowly, she shook her head. "I'm not sure . . ."

"Are you sure about what you witnessed?"

"The guy was definitely dead, and it was definitely Rathers."

"And it was taking place in real time?"

"Real time. Right now. The killers are in the woods, kneeling over Rathers' body, and one of them is drawing on his forehead."

"Then what is it you're not sure about?"

"Whether the witches are the culprits."

"You keep using the plural."

"I was doing that ping-pong thing. Ricocheting back and forth between both sets of eyes."

"Did one look at the other?"

"Sorry."

"If you didn't see one or the other, why are you so sure it wasn't the witches?"

"I'm not saying it wasn't them," she said with irritation. "I can't make any guarantees one way or the other."

"I can," he said, and whipped out his cell. "It was the witches."

"What makes you so confident?"

"Do you know of anyone else with a thing for pentagrams who happens to be in the woods tonight?"

Swinging her legs over the side of the mattress, Bernadette jumped down. She felt nauseous and dizzy, but she resisted the urge to clutch something for support. She didn't want Garcia to concern himself with her; they had a nighttime raid in the woods to worry about.

Garcia jogged down the stairs, punching his cell as he went. "Do you feel well enough to do this?" he asked her.

"I'm fine." When Bernadette was certain Garcia was out of eyesight, she went to her suitcase and fished some Tylenol out of her toiletry kit. Swallowed the pills dry. As she went after Garcia, she held on to the rails to steady her descent. The top of her head felt ready to explode, and her dinner was crawling up her throat. It was as if she'd just stepped off a Tilt-A-Whirl.

He was in the kitchen, talking on his cell. "Seth? I've received some information about tonight. We need to pull this thing together right now . . . I can't tell you that. You've got to trust me. Here's the plan . . ."

Bernadette went into the bathroom, closing and locking the door after her. She fell down in front of the toilet and vomited. Coughed and puked again. Put her hand to her forehead. "God," she moaned, and got on her feet. Grabbed a towel bar to keep from falling backward.

Garcia banged on the door as she was flushing the toilet. "Are you okay?"

"I took a pee," she said. "Is that okay?"

"Hurry up," he said. "We gotta get moving."

Bernadette clawed a wad of toilet paper off the roll and blew her nose. She opened the medicine cabinet and found an ancient bottle of a generic painkiller. Turned on the tap and swallowed three pills with a handful of water. Rinsed out her sour mouth. Splashed cold water on her face.

Through the door, Garcia said, "I just tried Rathers' cell and got nothing."

"Have you got a direct number for the senator?" she asked, clutching the edge of the sink.

Half a minute later: "I got Dunton out of bed. He said Rathers is in bed." Garcia banged on the door again. "Did you hear me? Are you dead or what?"

She unlocked the door and whipped it open. "Did he ask why in the hell we wanted to know about Rathers this time of night?"

"No. He hung up on me." Garcia's brows knotted. "You look like a ghost."

She patted her face with a towel. "You know using the sight drains me a little at first. I'll recharge in no time."

"Do you want to stay here?"

"Kiss my ass," she snapped, and threw down the towel. Squeezed past him.


"What's the story?" she asked as they got into the Titan.

Garcia started up the truck. "You and I are going to hop on Minnesota 64, drive through the south section of Paul Bunyan, connect with Minnesota 200, and take that into the north unit."

"I thought you didn't know the north."

Garcia reached under the driver's seat for the ice scraper. "Seth gave me good directions."

He hopped out of the truck to clear off the windows. When he got back in, she asked, "What about the rest of the gang?"

"Seth and his men are still meeting up with our folks in Walker. They're going to get hooked up with equipment and coordinate their—"

"Why aren't we joining that caravan?" she interrupted, skittish that she and Garcia were venturing off on their own. They didn't have proper communication equipment in the truck, and all they had for weapons were their handguns.

"I figured you wouldn't want to wait," he said, steering the Titan down the driveway.

"Right," she muttered. They'd switched roles, and she had to admit that she didn't approve of the way Garcia looked in a cowboy hat. She hoped this wasn't about showing off for his friend. At least they were wearing vests.

"Since it's the two of us going in together, I really need to know if you're going to be okay," he said, turning out of the driveway and heading for the highway.

"I'm feeling better," she said, and she wasn't lying. She reached forward and turned up the heater. "By the time we get to the party, I'll be a hundred percent."

"This is going down a lot sooner than Seth figured, isn't it?"

Bernadette looked at the time on the dashboard and double-checked it against her watch. If the scene she'd observed was indeed part of the Esbat rite, the witches were conducting their ceremony hours earlier than the time given by Wharten's informant.

Someone had been trying to mislead them, and Bernadette was afraid to point that out to Garcia. For all she knew, his fishing buddy was the problem.

# CHAPTER THIRTY-THREE

Trees ringed the flat worship space like silent participants in the ritual, and the full moon looked down with the bright indifference befitting a deity.

One after another, two hooded figures walked a circle. The hems of their black velvet robes dragged in the snow, making a softly slithering sound like some winter-hardy snake. Each carried a lit pillar raised to the nighttime sky.

Twenty other coven members stood outside the round, raising their own candles to the darkness. As usual, a few members were missing. Cerridwen and Odin were home with colicky baby Herne. Irene Edwalters, also known as Sapphyre, had a hot date with a nice Catholic man from Bemidji.

All the celebrants wore thick-soled boots on their feet and heavy jackets under their robes, creating distinctively bulky witches. Their hoods were pulled up over a variety of headgear, including blaze-orange stocking caps and fur bomber hats, and insulated gloves and mittens covered their hands. Practicing witchcraft outdoors in Minnesota in the winter required a substantial amount of sensible layering.

Pillar candles had been placed atop tree stumps positioned at the north, south, east, and west quarters of the circle. The north candle was green, representing the earth, and the south one was red for fire. East was yellow, in honor of air, and the west pillar was aqua blue, symbolizing water. In the center of the round was a makeshift altar: two sawhorses bridged by a sheet of plywood and draped by a ceremonial cloth with a pentacle embroidered in the center.

The light that topped the altar—a battery-operated Coleman lantern—wasn't exactly regulation for Wiccans. Some of the coven's more safety-conscious members insisted that they couldn't worship in the deep woods at night with only candles for illumination, especially when the ceremonial ground was one the coven didn't regularly utilize. Someone could trip and break a hip. Next to the Coleman was a more standard white pillar candle, and beside that was a bowl of cheap vodka. Water was the norm, but it would have frozen within a matter of minutes. Other objects on the altar were an obvious bow to the moon: Crescent-shaped silver medallions. Round crystals the size of golf balls. A platter of frosted sugar cookies in both crescent and round shapes. A child's picture book with the smiling face of the moon on the cover. A yellow crescent-moon stuffed toy.

After one complete rotation, the priest and the priestess took their stations, one at each end of the altar.

The priestess raised her candle high. "I Isis, named for the consort of Osiris, say the circle is about to be cast. May all those who enter it do so with complete trust and love." The priestess looked across the altar at the man and nodded once.

Taking the cue, the priest began lighting the candles at the four cardinal points, starting with the one in the east. "I Osiris, named for the beloved of Isis, call to the guardians of the east. Creatures and powers of air, watch over our rites so that we may enter the circle with complete trust and love."

As the priest bent down to light the yellow candle with his pillar, the flame quit on him. "Shoot," he muttered.

One of the worshippers reached into her robes and produced a Zippo. The woman held it out to the priest, but his back was turned. "Psst . . . Roger . . . here you go."

Osiris turned around, went over to the worshipper, and accepted the lighter. "Thanks, Delores."

The priest flicked the Zippo and restored his candle's flame, and used the lighter to ignite the yellow pillar. He moved on to the next element. "I Osiris, named for the beloved of Isis, call to the guardians of the south. Creatures and powers of fire, watch over our rites so that we may enter the circle with complete trust and love." He bent over the red candle and flicked the Zippo.


Hiding among the trees was an angry, grief-stricken man who had no intention of entering the circle with complete trust and love. He was hunkered down behind a boulder, about a hundred yards from the south quarter of the witches' circle. He knew when and where they'd be meeting because they'd invited him. They were going to honor her in some way during the ceremony. He'd politely informed them that they could fuck off. The sheriff knew the ritual was going to take place that night in the park, but he didn't know the exact time or place. He'd given Wharten bogus details. He knew the cops would get him that night, but he wanted to buy himself enough time to get the job done.

He'd driven into the park a good hour before their ritual, and parked where they'd never see his vehicle. Found the perfect spot to wait. He was dressed in his winter hunting camo, and his face was smeared with hunter's mud-brown camo cream. In his hands was his favorite deer rifle—a Browning semiautomatic thirty-ought-six. She'd saved and scrimped to buy it for his birthday two years ago. The attached scope was her gift to him just this past Christmas. The extra clips he carried that night were going to be his gift to the witches.

He wasn't on a hunt so much as a mission. This was about revenge. He'd take down as many as he could before the law found him and took him down. He didn't care anymore. The love of his life had been killed. The FBI had descended on his house, trampled all over his property, and threatened him. Accused him! All the while, these fools were out romping around in their ridiculous Halloween costumes, free to do as they pleased—and they were the real murderers. Each and every one of them was responsible. They might as well have taken turns wrapping their hands around her throat and squeezing the life out of her. She'd died for their sins, and now they were going to return the favor.

He poked his head over the rock and peered through the trees toward the glow. They all had their backs turned toward the woods, and it was difficult to distinguish tree trunk from black robe. He'd observed their rites before, and knew from their positions that the priest and the priestess were casting the circle right about now. When they were through with that, they'd all move in tighter. He'd move in closer and start picking them off. It'd be like ambushing yearlings at a salt lick.

The candles at all the quarters were lit. The first coven member—a big man with monster mukluks on his feet—entered the circle and approached the altar, gloved hands wrapped around his candle and head bowed.

"Speak the truth," the priestess ordered him, and laid her hand on his massive shoulder. "How do you come into this circle?"

"With complete trust and love," answered a gruff voice.

"I bless you and invite you to take your place among us, brother," said the priestess, removing her hand. The man stepped away from the altar and took a spot just inside the circle.

A female celebrant came up to the priest, her head down. "Speak the truth," the priest ordered her, and laid one of his hands on her shoulder. "How do you come into this circle?"

"With complete trust and love."

"I bless you and invite you to take your place among us, sister," said the priest, removing his hand.

One at a time, each of the coven members went up for a blessing before assuming a position inside the circle. As the last celebrant joined the circle, a shot rang out and one of the hooded figures folded.

Bernadette and Garcia were headed north on Minnesota 64, driving through the south section of Paul Bunyan, when Bernadette's cell rang. They were edgy, and the sound jarred both of them.

"Finally, someone calling for me," she said with a nervous grin, and flipped open her phone. She put the cell to her ear, and what she heard sent a chill running from her hand down to her heart.

Gunshots, and screaming.

"Help! He's trying to kill us! He's killing us!" screamed a man's voice. "Help!"

"Who is this?" Bernadette yelled back.

"Hessler! This is Sven Hessler! There's someone . . . he's in the trees! He's shooting!"

"Someone's shooting at the witches!" Bernadette told Garcia.

"Jesus!" he said, and accelerated.

Bernadette heard more gunshots and screaming. Her hand tightened over the phone. "Sven—"

"He's shooting at us!" Hessler yelled. "He's shooting!"

"Who?" she asked.

"I don't know! We can't see him!"

There was a break in the shooting, but the screaming continued. "Where are you?" she asked.

"Paul Bunyan!"

"The north section? We're on our way to—"

"No, not the north! The south!"

Bernadette looked at Garcia. "They're in the south unit!"

Garcia braked and the truck shuddered. "Wharten said they were in the—"

"It was a trick! The witches are being ambushed!" She heard the shooting resume, and it was rapid.

"Oh, God!" Hessler yelled over the screams in the background. "Hurry!"

"Where?" she asked. "Where in the south?"

"Oh, no!" Hessler yelled. "Two people! We've got two hit! We need an ambulance!"

"Sven . . . Dr. Hessler . . . I need to know where. We're on Minnesota 64 heading—"

Hessler yelled back, "We're on the east side of the . . ."

Hessler's end went dead, and Bernadette looked at the cell with horror. "Two down, and I don't know where the fuck they are!"

Garcia pulled out his cell, punched in a number, and put the phone to his ear. "Come on, come on, come on. Answer . . . Seth? The witches are in the south section, and someone's taking shots at them and . . . No, the south! Hessler called! We need ambulances! We need backup!"

She looked out her window. Had Hessler meant to tell her they were on the east side of the highway? She rolled down her window, but she couldn't hear anything coming out of the woods. She called up Hessler's number and dialed it. A busy signal. "Fuck!" she yelled into the darkness.

Next to her, Garcia was struggling to pull directions out of Wharten. "Where would they worship in the south unit?" he yelled into his cell. "We're on sixty-four, heading north! Where should we go? Tell us!"

"What if they're on the east side of the highway?" she hollered to Garcia. "Where do they worship on the east side?"

Garcia repeated the question to Wharten: "If they're on the east side of the highway, where would they be in the park? South unit, east side . . . Uh-huh . . . Yeah, yeah . . . Where I missed that ten-pointer last fall?"

Bernadette knew Garcia could find them; a man never forgets where he lost a ten-point buck.

"Got it! Call an ambulance, Seth! Call two of them! You've got people down!" Garcia snapped his cell shut and threw it down on the seat. Did a U-turn in the middle of the highway and aimed them south. "We missed the turnoff, but not by much." He drove half a mile and hung a mad left.

"Jesus, Tony! Jesus! Hurry!"

The truck barreled down a minimally plowed road, bucking like a bronco trying to throw them off. "I know exactly where this is," he said.

She tried calling Hessler on her cell again. No luck. She kept her window down, listening for the crack of rifle fire. "How far?"

"Not that far," he said, peering through the windshield. The truck's high beams fell on a long, narrow trail crowded by trees and bushes.

"How in the hell is the ambulance going to get through?" she wondered out loud.

"It'll get through," mumbled Garcia, his eyes trained ahead.

"Christ!" she breathed, as they took a massive mogul and bounced. She clutched the armrest.

"At least they've got an ER physician with them," said Garcia.

Bernadette kept her mouth closed but wondered: *Is the doctor dead? How many others are dead? Who is firing? Why?*

Nurse Delores Martini asked herself all four of those questions as she dove for cover behind a boulder. From her spot, she'd watched Sven Hessler make a dash toward the trees, take a bullet in the back, and collapse facedown in the snow. From where she was crouched, she could almost reach out and touch his outstretched arm. Three others were down in the south quadrant of the circle, also struck from behind. In the chaos, all the elemental candles had been knocked over and their flames extinguished in the snow. The Coleman lantern continued to shine, lending an eerie, almost ethereal glow to the carnage. Red splattered the white circle. The black robes of the prostrate celebrants looked like blankets draped over the bodies of the dead. All around them were footprints and discarded candles.

The shooting had stopped and the screaming had subsided, but in the woods behind her she could hear soft weeping and wailing. Someone coughing. Another person groaning. At least three of those who'd made it to the trees had been wounded while fleeing. She'd watched them jerk and go down, and then crawl into the blackness of the forest like injured animals.

Martini prayed that someone had reached the cars, parked about half a mile away on a narrow, snow-clogged trail. Maybe one of their members had managed to call for help. Hessler had a phone in his hand when he was hit, but she had no idea if he'd had a chance to use it. Nor could she see what had happened to the cell. Like many of the coven members, she hadn't brought her cell with her. This was supposed to be their quiet, meditative time away from ringing phones and the stresses of everyday living.

Who could have predicted they'd be dying?

Hessler lifted the index finger of his outstretched hand and moaned. Raised his face off the snow. The light at the edge of the circle was dim, but Martini swore that his eyes were trained on her. She told herself she had to do something. She'd grown up down the road from the Hesslers and babysat Sven when he was a kid. He'd come back to his hometown to practice medicine when he could have gone elsewhere and made more money. They'd worked side by side for years. She'd given him shit when he deserved it— and doctors always deserved it—but instead of being offended he'd given it right back. If he was going to die, he should do it in his hospital surrounded by his people, not on the frozen ground in the middle of the woods.

Taking a deep, bracing breath, Martini uncoiled her body and reached out from behind the boulder. Staying as low as her large figure allowed, she reached past the voluminous sleeves of Hessler's robe and latched on to his jacket cuff. Started backing up into the trees with the wounded man.

He moaned as she dragged him.

"Be quiet," she hissed.

A bullet sailed over her head and slammed into one of the trees behind her, sending bark and wood splinters flying.

"Jesus!" she yelped, and dropped Hessler's arm. Retreated back behind the rock.

Hessler raised his head again, and this time there was no doubt: he was looking at her as she peeked out from behind the boulder.

"Help me," he wheezed. "Delores, please . . ."

Martini slapped a hand over her mouth and started to weep. She turned her back on the injured man and rested her back against the rock. Shivered from fright, and the cold.

"Delores . . ."

Three more shots cracked the night air, and she heard someone in the woods grunt. Had another member of their coven been hit? Martini curled her knees up to her chest, wrapped her arms around her knees, and buried her face in the soft folds of her velvet robe. She wished she'd never laid eyes on that dead girl and the pentagram on her forehead. Really, all this was that girl's fault, Martini reassured herself.

"Delores . . ." Hessler said, this time hissing her name. A tire losing air. A man breathing his last. "Please . . . help . . . me . . ."

She clapped her gloved hands over her ears and rocked back and forth. She prayed a silent prayer, not to the gods and goddesses of her newly adopted faith but to the God of her childhood.

*Our Father who art in heaven . . .*

Through her hands, Martini heard another gunshot. It would be the last.

## CHAPTER THIRTY-FOUR

A pair of robed figures came crashing out of the woods and onto the road, collapsing in heaps of black velvet in front of the Titan's headlights. Garcia slammed on the brakes and Bernadette threw open her door. Ran toward the lumps. "Are you injured?"

The witches, both pretty blond girls, were on all fours. "Our friends . . ." one panted.

Garcia helped Bernadette raise the young women to a standing position. They looked to be in their early twenties. "Is either of you hurt?" Garcia asked.

"No," the girls answered in unison.

"How many were hit?" asked Bernadette, looking from one mascara-streaked face to the other.

"I don't know!" wailed the shorter one, collapsing against Bernadette and burying her face in the agent's chest.

"Our priest and priestess. Roger and Yvonne," said the taller girl, clutching Garcia's arm. "They got Roger and Yvonne."

Bernadette gently raised the young woman off her. "Who was it? Who attacked you?"

"We don't know!" screamed Garcia's girl.

"How many shooters were there?" asked Garcia.

"I don't know! I don't know!" said Bernadette's witch, and the young woman grabbed the agent by the shoulders. "Do something! Call an ambulance! Call the cops!"

"We are the cops," said Garcia.

"Thank God!" sobbed Bernadette's girl, and she started to crumple.

Bernadette tightened her hold on the young woman and walked her to the truck. Garcia followed with his clinging witch. The two agents piled the shivering, sniffling young women into the back of the Titan.

Garcia stepped away while Bernadette continued talking to the girls. "What are your names?"

"Britni Jensen," said the taller one.

"Anna Roseau," hiccuped the shorter one, brushing damp bangs off her forehead. Her hands were shaking.

"Can either of you give us directions?" asked Bernadette.

Roseau looked through the windshield. By the glare of the truck's headlights, Garcia was checking his gun. Seeing that her rescuers were armed calmed the witch. She took a deep breath and let it out. "About half a mile down the road. It looks like a dead end, but if you keep going through the trees and bushes you'll come to a clearing."

"Got it," said Bernadette, nodding. "The shooter or shooters. Any guess where the gunfire was coming from?"

"The opposite end of the clearing. Opposite from where you'll enter. You'll enter from the north and he was shooting from the south." Roseau dragged a hand across her nose. "I think it was one guy."

"I'm pretty sure he had a semiautomatic rifle," offered Jensen. "There'd be rapid fire—but not quick enough to be an automatic—and then a pause."

"While he reloaded?"

"Exactly," Jensen said, nodding.

This was hunting country, and even pretty young things knew a lot about guns, thought Bernadette. "Did he yell anything? Do you have any idea who it was? Who outside the coven knew you'd be here tonight?"

Roseau bit down on her top lip and then blurted one word: "Shit."

"Who?" asked Bernadette.

Jensen looked at her friend with raised brows. "Who are you thinking?"

"Who?" Bernadette asked more loudly.

Roseau swallowed once and answered. "Karl Vizner."

"We invited him to the Esbat and he pretty much flipped us off," said Jensen.

"He thought it was our fault that Jordan . . ." Roseau's voice trailed off.

Garcia came up behind Bernadette, talking into his cell and telling the rest of the crew where they'd come across survivors. "Correct. Take the turnoff after that."

Bernadette looked at him over her shoulder. "They think it's Vizner."

Garcia repeated the information into the phone. "Our survivors think Karl Vizner is the shooter . . . Yeah . . . Right."

"Get down on the floor of the truck," Bernadette ordered the two women.

The girls blinked at each other and then at the agent. The instructions weren't registering. "What?" asked Jensen.

Garcia opened the driver's door and killed the headlights. "Let's go, Cat."

Bernadette started to close the back passenger door. Roseau thrust out her hand and stopped the door from shutting. "Don't leave us without a gun! For Christ's sake, give us a gun!"

Bernadette disengaged Roseau's hand. "Help is coming," she said, and slammed the door.

Through the window, Jensen mouthed a curse at Bernadette, and Roseau followed with a flip of the bird. Then the feisty young witches dropped down onto the floor of the truck. Bernadette didn't like leaving them alone, but she and Garcia had to get to the shooting site.

Guns in hand, the two agents went down the dark road. Garcia took point, training a flashlight on the ground ahead of them. They came to the dead end and entered the trees, threading quietly between the trunks. The only sound was that of their footsteps in the snow and the occasional scrape of fabric against a bush. As thick as smoke, their breath hung in the air in front of their faces.

Spotting a glow up ahead, they immediately crouched down. Garcia punched off the flashlight, and the pair moved more slowly through the wooded maze. Just outside the clearing, they took cover behind tree trunks. What they saw would have made a surreal still life for an outdoor catalog.

Illuminating the round space was a Coleman lantern, sitting in the middle of a table draped with a cloth. A pillar candle sat next to the lantern, but it had burned out. A bowl and some other paraphernalia also topped the altar. Scattered on the ground around the table were more candles, and mounds of black velvet. Fallen worshippers. One was on her back, and Bernadette recognized her immediately. The others had gone down on their faces. No one was moving. No one was groaning. Bernadette prayed that they were simply playing possum for the shooter.

Where was Karl Vizner?

Garcia pointed to the right, and she nodded. Bernadette worked her way through the trees one way and Garcia circled around the other. At the south point where they met, they found Vizner behind a large boulder.

He was on his back, dressed in camo. He'd swallowed his own rifle and pulled the trigger.

"Crap," spat Bernadette, holstering her Glock.

Garcia put away his gun while shining the flashlight over the mess of blood and bone and brain matter. From what was left of Vizner's face, they could see that he'd worn camo paint. "This guy meant business," Garcia whispered.

Bernadette heard a moan coming from the trees. "Survivors," she said.

"FBI!" Garcia yelled into the night. "Call out your positions!"

"Over here!" a woman's voice yelled. "I've got an injured man!"

"Here, too!" yelled a man's voice. "My wife! Hurry! Please, hurry!"

Someone coughed and said weakly, "I'm shot."

Garcia worked the woods while Bernadette went to the fallen in the clearing. Eve Bossard was dead, her wide eyes staring up into the night sky. Had the obstetrician played any role in the drama that had taken place over the past few days? Someone else would have to answer that question.

Bernadette moved on to the next two victims: an older man with a white beard and an older woman. The priest and the priestess? Both were dead. The man had his arm extended, as if reaching out for the woman. She guessed that they were husband and wife.

Sven Hessler was sprawled on his belly. His head was turned to one side and his eyes were shut, but he was moaning. Bernadette kneeled at his head. The back of his robe was wet over the left shoulder. His right arm was outstretched, and his gloved hand seemed to be pointing to the woods. Bernadette leaned down and whispered into his ear, "Ambulances are coming."

"Delores," he groaned, and lifted his right hand.

Bernadette pulled out a penlight and entered the woods where he was pointing. She found Martini squatting behind a rock, shaking and crying.

Glancing up at the agent, the woman started babbling. "I'm sorry. I'm so sorry. It's not my fault. I didn't know. If I'd known, I wouldn't have. Honest to God, I wouldn't have . . ."

Bernadette cupped a hand under the big woman's elbow and raised her to her feet. "You wouldn't have *what*, Delores?"

Three dead and eight wounded. Hessler's injury was the most severe, and required that he be airlifted to a medical center in Fargo. The other patients were divided up between Crow Wing Lakes Memorial and hospitals in Park Rapids and Bemidji.

Martini's story came out while she was in the back of the sheriff's squad, one of a fleet of vehicles that had lined up behind the Titan. Garcia and Wharten were in the front seat, and Bernadette sat next to the ER nurse while she told her story.

Martini said she was there when the Dunton girl's body came through the doors of the hospital. She saw the inverted pentagram and feared that her coven would be blamed. She took the key to the storage room/morgue from its hook in the cafeteria and sneaked inside to remove the star. It was a visceral, impulsive reaction, and one that she immediately regretted. She learned that the mark had been viewed and documented not only by local first responders and the area's coroner but also by the Minnesota Bureau of Criminal Apprehension.

Martini didn't completely panic until she found out that the FBI was involved—and that its agents were well aware of the star's existence and its removal. She tried to steer the bureau toward the only witch who was open about her faith, counting on Ashe to take the fall for the whole coven.

"It was at least partially her own fault," said Martini, twisting a wad of tissue between her trembling hands.

"How do you figure?" asked Bernadette, one brow raised skeptically.

"She was so . . . I don't know . . . out there," said Martini, looking from Bernadette to the two men staring at her over the front seat. "If she'd been more discreet like the rest of us . . ." Martini's voice trailed off.

Wharten shook his head slowly. "Jesus H. Christmas, Delores."

"Am I going to be charged with anything?" she whined.

"You tampered with evidence, Delores," said Wharten. "You interfered with a murder investigation."

"I want a lawyer," Martini blurted, and started tearing up. "I'm not saying anything more without a lawyer."

Garcia and Bernadette slid out of the car while Wharten stayed with his weeping passenger.

The two agents walked to the Titan and leaned their butts against the driver's side while the crime-scene crew, other FBI personnel, sheriff's deputies, and medical guys moved around them. They watched as an emergency sled, pulled by a snowmobile, came out of the woods for the third time. The rig glided past the Titan and the other parked cars, heading for an ambulance that was waiting at the end of the road.

Garcia kicked at a lump of snow. "Do you suppose Vizner figured the witches killed his girlfriend?"

"My guess is he blamed them for bringing the killer to her door." She buried her hands in her pockets. "Either way, it was a fucking disaster."

Garcia pulled off his stocking cap and vigorously rubbed his head. "We need to sort this thing through, Cat."

She peeled her backside off the side of the truck and turned to face him. She thought he looked tired, and she felt the same. Finding so many dead, including the shooter, had been a shock, and then a drain. "Fine. Let's sort."

"For starters, do you believe Martini?"

"I do. And you?"

"Yeah."

"So we don't know who painted the inverted star on the Dunton girl's forehead, but we know who erased it," said Bernadette. "Then the eraser points us to Jordan Ashe to save the coven's butt and her own hind end."

"We take the bait and question Ashe in the Dunton girl's murder," said Garcia.

"Then word gets out around town that we paid Jordan a visit."

Garcia held up his hand to interrupt her narration. "How does word get out?"

"Jordan made a ton of phone calls before she was killed. Somebody told somebody who told somebody."

"Then what?"

"One of the real killers gets wind of our suspicions about Ashe and latches on to it as an opportunity to continue focusing attention on the witches," speculated Bernadette.

Garcia: "He murders Ashe. Paints a pentagram on her forehead."

Bernadette: "So the barn scene was either a weak effort to make it appear that Jordan had hanged herself—"

"Or the killer did a purposely sloppy job so that it was clearly a murder *staged* to look like suicide," said Garcia.

"Either way, the star on Ashe's forehead would place blame on the coven," said Bernadette.

"What about the pig fetus left on the altar?" he asked. "What was that about?"

"I imagine it was meant to be an exclamation point on the coven's involvement," she said. "Insurance that the witches were viewed as a group that practiced blood sacrifices."

"Then you surprised the killer in the woods."

"It probably didn't faze him," she said. "He figured the witches would be blamed. Again."

"Was he the same guy as the one who tampered with your motel door in Brule?"

She shook her head. "I don't know."

"What about Benjamin Rathers? If the witches didn't kill him, was the star you saw being drawn on his head yet another red herring?"

"Sure. It was insurance. If he's found, the witches are blamed again." She looked toward the trees, tall and uniformly black, even with the moon overhead. Dumped somewhere in their midst was the body of Dunton's chief of staff. Search teams were out looking for him.

"If the inverted pentagram was a ruse and the coven members are scratched as suspects—"

"We need a new short list," she said.

"According to the ME, we're still looking at a medical person with birthing background. Where do we go with that?"

"Remember what I saw with my sight: The killer—witch or not—was in the cabin where the senator and his wife are staying. The senator's chief of staff is dead. His daughter is dead after following blackmail letters to Brule and then Walker. It all leads back to the Duntons. That's where we go."

The sound of a helicopter vibrated the nighttime air, and they both looked up. The first of the television-news stations had arrived. Garcia pulled the truck keys out of his pocket. "I guess our guys and Wharten's folks have this mess under control."

She pulled open the truck door. "Let's go wake the senator and his wife."

# CHAPTER THIRTY-FIVE

The Duntons were already wide awake.

"Ben had a wife! He had young children!" said Michelle Dunton, hugging a robe around her narrow shoulders. "Where is he?"

"That's enough, Mickey," said Mag Dunton, his eyes locked on the gun aimed at his chest. The senator, dressed in flannel pajama bottoms and a white T-shirt, was next to his wife on the trophy-room couch. This time they were sharing the same cushion, because the home invader had ordered them to sit close together.

The maid was long gone. The two drivers had already left for the Twin Cities in one of the cars. The chief of staff was going to drive the Duntons himself in the morning. It became clear to the Duntons, however, that Rathers wasn't coming back.

"Where is he?" asked Michelle Dunton. "What did you do to him? Tell me what you did to him."

"Didn't do anything to him," said the intruder, who was dressed in a parka. "Didn't see him at all tonight."

"We sent him to your place," said Dunton.

"There's open water," the intruder said evenly. "He must have fallen in."

"Liar." She rocked slightly as she hugged herself. "You're a liar. You killed him."

"Quiet, Mickey," said Dunton.

"Be a good wife." The silver barrel moved so that it was pointing at the rocking woman. "Listen to your husband."

Michelle Dunton fell back against the cushion and twined her arms even tighter around her body, as if she could stop a bullet that way.

The gun traveled back to the primary target. "Where's the cash?"

"I already told you people, I can't put my hands on that large a sum all at once. It'll take time."

"Bullshit."

"You're asking for a ridiculous amount," said Dunton. "I don't have it on hand."

"Don't give me that. You've got more money than God."

"Why did you have to hurt her?" asked Dunton. "At least tell me that much. Why did you kill my little girl?"

"We didn't," said the intruder. "The witches—"

"Oh, please," said Dunton. "I'm not a fool."

"The hell you're not," snapped his wife. "You've been helping them. Telling them what you know about the FBI's moves. Covering up for them."

"I was protecting us," Dunton said.

"Protecting your office," continued his wife. "Be honest. For once in your life, be honest."

Dunton returned his attention to the person with the gun. "Answer my question: why did you kill Lydia?"

A grim smile stretched across the invader's face. "You want honesty? Let's get it all out in the open. *She* came to *us*."

"You lured her somehow," said Dunton. "You wanted to use her for leverage, for more money."

"She found us. I have to give her credit. She figured that much out. Got that much right. We accommodated her. Gave her a place to stay. Food to eat."

"Why did she go looking for you?" asked Dunton.

"Who cares?" asked Michelle Dunton. "It doesn't matter now."

"It matters to me," said her husband.

"She wanted to know more about her birth mother, and felt like she didn't have anyone else to ask," said the parka. "Pathetic, really. Thumbing rides all the way over to Brule because she thought we lived there. She read something about Brule in a letter."

"How did she find you?"

"Lydia told us she called home while she was in Brule. Someone at home set her straight. Told her we lived in Walker." The parka looked at Michelle Dunton. "Now who would have done that?"

Dunton shot his wife a look and continued asking questions. "Why did you kill her?"

"One night she overheard the two of us talking in the kitchen. She completely misunderstood what we were saying and—"

"What happened?" snapped Dunton.

"Little bitch threatened to go to the police."

"So you killed her," said Dunton, swallowing hard. "You killed my daughter and tossed her body in the woods for the animals to finish."

"It wasn't like that. She ran outside. Slipped and fell and hit her head. We had to take the baby or it would have died with her."

"Sounds familiar," Michelle Dunton said.

"What's that supposed to mean?" asked her husband.

"You think *I'm* a fool?" asked Michelle Dunton. "Lydia's mother, that whore, didn't die during childbirth."

"Shut up about her," said Dunton.

His wife's eyes narrowed, and she sat forward on the couch so that she could turn in her seat and glare at him. "This is all because of you, you and your wandering cock!"

"Mickey, this isn't helping," he growled.

"You got that tramp pregnant and hired two backroom butchers to kill her during the delivery."

"Hey, hey, hey," said the invader. "That's not what happened."

"Then you bring her daughter into our house, a girl destined to take after her mother. Another little slut!" Michelle Dunton turned and pleaded to the person with the gun, "Let me go. Please."

"Why should I?"

"Let me go and keep him. Make him pay you. He's got it."

The barrel was trained on the angry wife. "You've got it, too."

"But this has nothing to do with me," she said.

"It's always been about you, Mickey," said the senator. "If you hadn't been so frigid, I never would have looked around for someone else."

"I can't believe you have the nerve to—"

"Save it for the marriage counselor!" The barrel went from one Dunton to the other. "All I give a shit about is the money! Where in the fuck is the cash?"

Magnus Dunton looked up at their captor. "I am not paying you or your partner another dime."

"We'll go to the cops. It'll be the end of your career."

"I'm going to them first," he said.

The gun moved in closer to the senator's sweating forehead. "You wouldn't. You'd go to jail. We'd all go to jail."

"I don't care anymore," said Dunton, his eyes moving from the gun to the angry face hovering over him. Back to the gun. "I've had enough of this crap. I can't live like this, always afraid."

"What about your granddaughter?" asked his captor. "Don't you care about her?"

"Where is she?" asked Dunton. "I've never laid eyes on her. Show her to me. If she exists, let me see her."

Bernadette sees the granddaughter while using her sight in the truck, on the fly. Someone dressed in pink is cradling the child. The killer is having trouble holding the baby while feeding her and keeps readjusting the bundle as she rests in the crook of the large left arm. The infant is fussing, throwing up its tiny fists.

Bernadette blinks and she's in another place. The trophy room. There are two people seated on the couch in front of the second murderer, and Bernadette recognizes them by their hair. One has a short shock of auburn on his head and the other has a long ash-blond mane. Dunton and his wife. They're sitting with their thighs touching. They didn't suddenly become friendlier toward each other. Something is seriously wrong with this picture.

Back to the baby. The first killer is still struggling, trying to feed the infant. The nursemaid sets the bottle down on the kitchen table and stands up with the child. Readjusts the bundle. Why is this person so clumsy? It suddenly occurs to Bernadette.

The couple on the couch again. The senator rises from the couch. A glint of something silver comes into view. It is aimed directly at Magnus Dunton. Large hands extend the weapon. Bernadette thinks she recognizes something on the killer's left wrist but can't be completely sure. Dunton keeps coming. What is he doing? He reaches for the gun.

A bright light.

Bernadette gasped and opened her fist, dropping the knotted thread onto her lap. "Hurry!"

"What's wrong?" asked Garcia. "What did you see?"

Bernadette blinked twice, but all she saw was blackness. *Not now!* she thought. She raised her hands to her eyes and rubbed hard. Closed her lids tight and opened them again slowly. Nothing. Still blind.

"Cat," said Garcia. "Talk to me."

Struggling to keep a calm voice, she told Garcia, "The Duntons are in trouble."

"What's going on?"

She closed her eyes and hoped. Prayed. Turned her head toward the passenger window and continued talking as if nothing was wrong. "The senator's been shot."

"You sure?"

"Someone is holding him and his wife at gunpoint. He went for the gun. I saw a flash."

"Where?"

"His buddy's place."

"Call an ambulance. Tell the troops."

She took her phone out of her pocket and opened it. Felt around for the right keys. Dropped the cell on the floor. "Fuck," she breathed, and bent down. Fumbled around the floor.

"Christ!" said Garcia. "You're blind again!"

She sat up straight and stifled a groan. Her head was throbbing. "You'd better call."

After several seconds, she heard him on his cell. She and Garcia would be the first to arrive at the cabin on Walker Bay—and she was blind. Useless.

She closed her eyes tight and dropped her face in her hand. Offered a silent prayer: *"Lord, help me see. Please."* Then an angry addendum: *"What do you want from me?"*

Bernadette lifted her face out of her hand and opened her eyes. She saw a wall of wrought-iron bars in front of her and hollered, "The gate!"

"Fuck it," said Garcia, flooring it and smashing through the metal barrier. As the truck barreled through, he looked over at her with relief. "You can see now, I take it."

"I can see."

"Good," he said shortly.

As they pulled up in front of the house, she glanced down at the knotted string in her lap, the object that had taken her to the two killers. As she dropped the yarn back into the plastic bag, she suddenly realized what purpose the bracelet could have served. Who would have worn it, and why. It was the equivalent of a string tied around a finger. A rubber band slipped over a wrist.

*"Let me get you a catalog. Where did I put it? I can't remember anything, I swear. I have the worst memory."*

Garcia popped open his door. "Are you okay?"

She opened the passenger door. "I'm good. Let's do this."

With guns and flashlights in hand, they went around to the back. The drapes on all the patio doors were closed, but they could see that one of the windows was lit. It was the trophy room.

"There," she whispered, motioning with a tip of her head.

"I see," he said.

They went under the deck. The basement door had been kicked in, but no alarm was sounding. The Duntons either didn't know how to use the home's security system or they hadn't bothered to activate it.

The two agents went inside and shined their lights around. No one in the basement. They ran up the basement stairs. The main level was dark, except for a light shining down a hallway. The hallway that led to the trophy room.

That's where they found the Duntons. His T-shirt more red than white, the senator had been hit square in the chest at close range. He was on the floor, crumpled at his wife's bare feet. Michelle Dunton was sitting on the sofa, tipped to one side as if she'd fallen asleep while watching television. She'd taken a bullet to the gut.

Garcia put his fingers to her neck. "She's alive."

"Stay with her while I go through the rest of the house," Bernadette said.

"Watch yourself," he said after her.

Gun and flashlight still in hand, she went from room to room, checking out the main level and then the second floor. The rest of the place was dark and empty. By the time she got back to the main level, Wharten and Cahill were running up from the basement with guns drawn, a small army behind them. "The killer got away," she told them as she holstered her gun.

"Who're we looking for?" asked Wharten.

She spotted the medical crew bringing up the rear and pointed them to the room. "In there. Garcia's with them."

As he rushed past her in the hall, the lead ambulance guy asked, "What are we looking at?"

"They were shot," Bernadette told him. "Dunton's dead, but his wife is still breathing."

"Who?" asked Cahill. "Who did it?"

Instead of answering B.K., Bernadette ran out the back and went down to the lake to check out a hunch.

Shining her light around, she spotted a set of fresh tracks.

A line of squads followed Bernadette and Garcia to a different house on Walker Bay. After finding snowmobile tracks behind the massive log home where the Duntons had been staying, Bernadette deduced that the shooter had gotten to the couple by avoiding the front gate and entering through the back. Wharten confirmed that one of her suspects lived on the bay.

"He said she inherited it from her grandparents. Went there summers. I'll bet that's how she met Dunton. I have no idea what she had on him, but it goes back to that body found in the woods in Brule."

"And you think she's the one you saw because of the way she held the baby?"

"Lydia must have told her boyfriend that she felt like *The Fugitive,* not *a* fugitive."

"I still don't get it."

"*The Fugitive.* That old show. He was always looking for the one-armed guy."

"You said there were two of them."

"I spotted a rubber band on the second killer's wrist." She pulled the packaged string out of her pocket and held it up. "This was the same thing. A reminder tool. Something tied around a wrist to re-member something."

Garcia shook his head. "I hope you're right."

"I am," she said.

# CHAPTER THIRTY-SIX

Alerted by the roar of the snowmobiles as she hopped out of the truck, Bernadette started running down the hill toward the lake. The only illumination was coming from the snowmobiles' headlights and the full moon overhead, but it was enough for Bernadette to identify the two accomplices. "FBI! Sonia Graham! Stop!"

Garcia followed, yelling the other woman's name. "Rachel White! This is the FBI! Get off now!"

The midwife extracted something from her jacket.

"Gun!" Bernadette hollered, and she and Garcia fell on their bellies. Two shots rang out, slamming into the incline behind them. Both agents were dusted with the snow that scattered upon impact. Bernadette raised her head and saw White pull on her helmet and speed away. Graham's sled had killed, and she remained behind.

Garcia crawled down the hill next to Bernadette and rasped, "Take cover."

They scrambled to their feet and dove behind a pair of old evergreens, the lower quarter of the trunks bare of branches. She and

Garcia were across from each other, hunkered about fifteen yards apart. Bernadette looked down toward the shoreline, but she couldn't discern if Graham had the weapon in hand while she was fiddling with the snowmobile. The machine was sputtering and killing. The woman had probably flooded it. Bernadette and Garcia pulled out their Glocks and flashlights and trained both at the large figure.

Bernadette yelled, "Sonia Graham! Drop your gun and get off the sled! Now!"

A shot punched the ground between the pines, releasing another cloud of snow into the night air, and the agents ducked behind the trees.

Bernadette waited ten seconds and peeked out from around the trunk. Graham was again preoccupied with her sled. Bernadette looked at her boss and motioned with a tip of her head. Both moved forward, and closer to each other. The agents were behind pines planted less than five yards apart, and less than ten yards from the shoreline. They took aim at Graham with their guns and flashlights. "Sonia!" hollered Bernadette. "She ditched you! It's not worth it! Drop it and get off! Hands up in the air!"

Graham turned, the big gun between both her hands. Two cracks sounded, and one of them found its mark. The midwife flew off the seat of the snowmobile.

Bernadette ran over to the sled.

"Shit," muttered Garcia, holstering his gun.

Bernadette leaned over the sled and shined her flashlight on the body that had landed on the other side of the uncooperative machine. Graham was on her back, the revolver on the ground at her right and her helmet at her left. Her eyes were wide-open, and her hands were thrown up over her head in a kind of postmortem surrender. "Stupid," Bernadette said, holstering her Glock.

"The others just pulled down the driveway," said Garcia, coming up next to her while closing his cell. "I told them we'd go for the nurse while they look for the baby."

"I hope the bitches didn't kill her."

Garcia trained his light over the entry wound, a wet hole in the middle of Graham's parka. "Which one of us—"

"I don't know or care," said Bernadette.

Graham's left foot was still propped against the side of the sled. Bernadette kicked the big foot off and hopped on the seat. She hadn't ridden in a while, but she remembered the basics. Mounted on the right handlebar was the throttle, and all she had to do to put the sled in idle was take her thumb off the spring-loaded lever. The brakes were mounted on the left handlebar. She put her thumb over the throttle and slowly pressed down. As she pulled away from shore, she hardly noticed that Garcia had hopped on behind her. The big woman drove a big sled.

"White was headed north!" Bernadette yelled.

"Going for Leech!" Garcia hollered, referring to the massive main lake. "We'll never catch her!"

The headlights of their snowmobile shined two hundred feet in front of the sled, allowing them to follow White's tracks at night. Garcia was right. The nurse was heading for Leech. Bernadette wondered if White had an escape plan beyond fleeing across the lake. She suspected that the women had simply panicked after the shooting and decided to get the hell out of town in the quickest and stealthiest way possible.

Bernadette steered the sled north through the bay and hung a right onto the frozen narrows that led to the massive white expanse. At first, the tracks of the nurse's sled indicated that White was hugging the south shore. Then the tracks went between two clusters of fish houses, one group close to shore and the other farther out in the lake. Suddenly the trail was lost in a tangle of crisscrossing lines.

"Shit!" Bernadette said, and stopped the snowmobile.

Each took out a flashlight and shined it around the snow-covered ice. Two sleds had exited the fish-house neighborhood recently. One hooked left, toward the middle of the lake, and the other hung a right, going up onshore between two rustic log cabins.

"I think she stayed on the lake," Garcia said, training his beam over the tracks leading to the middle. "She'd get bogged down in the woods."

"But she'd be too easy to pick off in the open," said Bernadette. "Your call."

They pocketed their lights, and Bernadette steered the sled to the right. They bounced over a snowbank and onto shore, and cut between the cabins. Behind the log homes was a road and then a farmer's field. Bernadette crossed the road and stopped short of entering the field.

"What's wrong?" Garcia asked.

She took out her flashlight again and shined it around. "You don't want to drive into that," she said, her beam landing on a strand of barbed wire that was stretched in front of them.

Garcia took out his flashlight and shined it to their left, along the farmer's fence line. "Did we lose her?"

Bernadette worked her light to their right and spotted a gap in the fence twenty yards down. A set of tracks went through and then stopped. There were footprints, and then the tracks continued. "Bike's giving her trouble. I'll bet she had to get off and pull-start it," said Bernadette, referring to a cord that resembled that of a lawn mower.

She pocketed her light and steered the sled toward the right, taking the same path to enter the field. Bernadette was going more slowly. She knew that farmers' fields could be filled with land mines: Pieces of machinery. Wads of barbed wire. Piles of boulders and tree limbs. Cow and horse carcasses. In the winter, they would look like harmless humps covered by snow.

Bernadette and Garcia went up over a rise, and when they peaked they saw the lights of a sled ahead of them. It wasn't moving. It had to be White; no one else would be stalled in the middle of a farmer's field in the middle of the night. Bernadette wondered why the woman hadn't killed or smashed her lights to avoid being seen. Maybe she figured no one had followed her.

Bernadette gunned it, and the two agents went flying down the hill.

As they came up on White, she was just getting back on her sled. She looked over her shoulder at the agents and gave her snowmobile the gas. The sled jackrabbited forward, and the nurse shot up another rise. Bernadette and Garcia were close behind, the nurse's sled trapped in the far edges of their snowmobile's headlights.

White's sled became airborne at the top of the hill and dropped down on the other side, disappearing from sight. Bernadette's snowmobile got some air at the top, and both agents grunted upon landing but managed to stay on the sled.

As they hit a flat stretch of open field, White remained in their crosshairs, her snowmobile still caught in the headlights of their sled. Though one-handed, she was navigating the flying sled without a problem. Both machines were going better than sixty miles an hour, a dangerous speed at night. By the time they spotted an obstacle in the headlights, it would be too late to stop. Bernadette's face was frozen and her gloved hands were growing numb. Though her body served as a windbreak for Garcia, she suspected that he was getting dangerously cold as well.

Bernadette saw a dark silhouette in the distance and recognized the shape. It was an old barn, leaning to one side. As the two speeding sleds neared the building, White opened her throttle further. Bernadette hung back. Where there was a decrepit barn, there was farm trash.

"What's wrong?" Garcia hollered.

Both agents suddenly saw in White's headlights what the nurse spotted too late: a stretch of old fencing poking up through the snow, at neck height.

Bernadette stopped her sled and screamed, more a reaction than a warning. It was far too late to warn.


Bernadette remembered reading somewhere that after a guillotine comes down the executed individual remains conscious for thirteen seconds, long enough to blink once for yes and twice for no. The agents didn't make it to White's head soon enough to ask it any questions.

# CHAPTER THIRTY-SEVEN

A search team on snowmobiles discovered the body of Benjamin Rathers a week later.

Inside the ski jacket worn by Rathers was a map and directions—in Dunton's handwriting—leading to White's home. Found in the nurse's garage—apparently dropped there while the body was being loaded into a vehicle—was an envelope addressed to White, also in Dunton's handwriting. Next to that was a balled-up slip of paper with a message: *Don't come tonight. Don't call. FBI watching and listening. Funds are forthcoming.* Also found on White's property was a set of snowshoes and poles, as well as Rathers' boots and gloves.

Found inside the White house was Lydia's shoulder bag. While she'd turned her backpack over to the tatt-shop owner, she'd managed to keep the purse. Inside were more letters from White and Graham to the Duntons. They contained enough detail to lead the girl to Brule, the beginning of her quest to learn about her birth mother.

Of particular interest to Bernadette was White's living room. It was exactly as she'd seen it in her dream, down to the pile of broken *Peanuts* Christmas statues. Bernadette guessed that the two women had been fighting, and one had taken her anger out on the other's cherished statue collection.

Sitting unharmed on an end table was the little wizard statue stolen from Ashe's barn.

Michelle Dunton—who'd been airlifted to the Twin Cities— kept her lawyer by her hospital bed. She grudgingly answered some questions and the rest of the details were filled in by a paper trail.

The senator's home and offices were raided, as was the cabin where he and his entourage had stayed in Walker. Michelle Dunton's personal journal was seized, as were records showing cash withdrawals over the years. The bank transactions weren't large enough individually to attract attention. When they were added together, they came to a handsome sum and, with the other documents, painted an ugly story.

Dunton and White had met in the lobby of a real-estate office in Walker about seventeen years earlier. Dunton was in the early stages of a land deal that would eventually become the gated community on Walker Bay, and White was there to investigate putting her late grandparents' lake home up for sale. The two ambitious professionals hit it off, and Dunton persuaded White to hold off meeting with an agent until he could get a look at the cabin.

As the pair walked around the White property, the nurse confided that she hated selling the place but needed money to help her partner—a woman she'd met in Vermont—relocate her midwife practice to the Midwest. She also had to pay off a pile of loans. White had spent years in medical school and had her dreams dashed by an accident: she'd lost her left hand while using a chain saw at the cabin.

Dunton made his own confession: he had a mistress who needed to quietly and privately give birth outside the state. Outside a hospital, if possible.

Dunton and White came to an arrangement: for a lump sum, the nurse and her midwife partner would deliver the baby in the woods of northwestern Wisconsin. They'd hiked in Brule and knew of a cabin they could rent.

At the last minute, Dunton's mistress balked: she wanted to deliver in a hospital. In the process of trying to escape from White and Graham, she either fell or was struck in the head. While she was unconscious, they cut out the child. It was unclear how much Dunton had witnessed or participated in—Michelle Dunton repeatedly raised the question in her journal while refusing to discuss it from her hospital bed—but the end result was that the body of the mistress was dumped in the woods.

Dunton's payments to the two women never stopped. Whenever they needed funds, they wrote to him and he sent cash. They liked to gamble, and a lot of their money went to the area's casinos.

The infant survived, and was raised in the senator's home. False adoption papers were cooked up, and the story told to Dunton's intimates was that the couple never wanted Lydia to know that she wasn't their biological child.

Sixteen years later, Lydia's relationship with her parents—particularly with her mother—turned sour. The girl began misbehaving at home and at school. Became pregnant. In her journal, Michelle Dunton wrote about a huge fight shortly before she sent Lydia packing:

Wanted to tell her the truth about her mother, but Maggie begged me to keep my mouth shut. All these years, that's been my most important job: keeping my mouth shut. I hate it. Hate her. Whenever I look at her, I see that Everette woman.

A brief entry after Lydia was kicked out hinted that Michelle Dunton may have been complicit in the girl's death.

What a relief! Should have tossed her out years ago. Would have saved us so much expense and grief. This will be a happier Thanksgiving for me. For Maggie, too, if he'd only see the light on his spoiled brat. When Lydia calls for money—and she will—I'll send her straight to her mother's caregivers and let them deal with her. It's their fault we got stuck with her.

Michelle Dunton faced multiple surgeries to repair the damage done by the bullet, and her attorney was adept at playing the sympathy card. Political pressure—combined with sketchy evidence that the woman had had any direct involvement in any of the murders—stifled efforts to file state or federal charges against the senator's widow.

# *EPILOGUE*

Spring came surprisingly early to the north woods that year.

Garcia parked the truck outside the manicured patch of green and turned off the engine. "Gorgeous day," he murmured, looking through the windshield at the blue Wisconsin sky.

Bernadette addressed the backseat passenger while scratching his head. "We won't be long." Then to Garcia: "Roll the windows down more."

"Should have left him at home," Garcia grumbled. "We could have taken a smaller ride."

"He likes country drives." She threw open the front passenger door and inhaled deeply. "Smells like fresh-mowed grass."

They closed the truck doors gently, as if doing otherwise would wake the dead. Garcia pushed open the rickety wooden gate and held it for her while she stepped through. A hedge of lilacs sat on either side of the entrance and served as a fence of sorts, buffering the graves from the dusty road that ran in front of the cemetery. The sweet scent of the purple flowers was intoxicating.

The two agents walked side by side on the sidewalk, a band of tar that sliced down the middle of the square of grass. Standing at the far corner was Jerry Dupray, his hands folded in front of him as he looked down at the ground. He was dressed in a windbreaker and khakis.

Making their way to Dupray, the two agents wove carefully around the headstones. A few of the monuments were tilted and seemed on the verge of falling over. Most of the markers were very old, and their inscriptions had been worn away by the elements. Fading snippets of information remained, making the stones seem even more tragic.

*Beloved wife and mo . . .*

*Died at bir . . .*

*In memor . . .*

*Died Nov. 16, 18 . . .*

"Jerry," said Bernadette.

He looked up and grinned. "Bernadette," he said, and took her hand in both of his. "Nice to see you again."

"I'm Tony Garcia." The two men pumped hands.

"Those for me?" Dupray asked, looking at the bouquet in Garcia's free hand.

"Maybe next time," Garcia said, and handed the flowers to Bernadette.

She leaned down and placed the roses on the grave. Bernadette said a quick, silent prayer and made the sign of the cross. The trio stood for a minute, staring at the stone marker. It was nothing more than a flat rectangle of rose-colored marble buried in the ground. How many lawn mowers had glided around it? How many shoes had stepped over or on it?

In the distance, barking. All three looked toward the truck. "Did you bring a furry friend?" asked Dupray.

"Baby," said Bernadette.

"Doesn't sound like a little dog."

"He's not," said Garcia. "He's a moose."

Bernadette explained that it was named Baby because it had been found guarding the baby at White's house.

"Sounds like a pretty smart pooch," said Dupray. "If you don't want him—"

"Saint Clare and I have joint custody," Garcia said with a grin.

Bernadette's attention returned to the gravestone. "We're happy we could come up with her identity, so you could change it."

*Jane Doe* was now *Samantha Everette.*

Dupray hunched over the grave, rearranging the roses a bit. "Too bad her parents still don't give a shit."

Bernadette and Garcia had traveled to the mother's home in Phoenix to deliver the news that her estranged daughter had died sixteen years earlier and had finally been identified. After hearing the sordid details of Samantha's murder, and examining a photo of her dead granddaughter and her living great-granddaughter, the woman had shrugged. "What do you expect me to do?"

Contacted by telephone in Alaska, Everette's father had given a similarly muted response. "Sam and me, we never had much to say to each other."

Dupray stood up. "How'd the little baby make out?"

Garcia: "We're not privy to—"

"Spare me," said Dupray. "You FBI guys know my mother's maiden name and what I had for breakfast last Tuesday."

"David Strandelunder gave her up for adoption," Bernadette said. "We heard a farm couple got her."

He nodded. "Good. That's good."

"I grew up on a farm," Bernadette added. "She'll work her hind end off, but she'll be safe and happy."

"Did they give her a name yet?"

"I have no idea," said Garcia.

"Do me a favor and find out," said Dupray, his eyes locked on the rose stone. "I could amend the marker again."

"What would you add?" asked Bernadette.

Dupray looked up. "Loving mother of Lydia and grandmother of . . ."